SUDDEN AWAKENINGS

A Pride and Prejudice Variation

The Other Paths Collection

By

AMANDA KAI

Copyright © 2024. Amanda Kai. Regal Swan Publishing.

All rights reserved. No part of this book may be used or reproduced, transmitted, downloaded, decompiled, reverse engineered, stored in or introduced into any information storage and retrieval system, in any form or by any means whether electronic or mechanical, without written permission from the authors and copyright owners, except in the case of brief quotation embodied in critical articles and reviews. Please purchase only authorized electronic editions and do not participate in or encourage electronic piracy of copyrighted materials. Your support of the author's rights is appreciated.

WARNING: The unauthorized reproduction or distribution of this copyrighted work is illegal. Criminal copyright infringement, including infringement without monetary gain, is investigated by the FBI and is punishable by up to 5 years in federal prison and a fine of $250,000. Anyone pirating ebooks will be prosecuted to the fullest extent of the law and may be liable for each download resulting therefrom. Your support of the author's rights is greatly appreciated.

NOTE: NO AI/NO BOT. The copyright holder does not consent to any Artificial Intelligence (AI), generative AI, large language model, machine learning, chatbot or other automated analysis, generative process, or replication program, to reproduce, mimic, remix, summarize, or otherwise replicate any part of this creative work, via any means. The copyright holder supports the right of humans to control their artistic works.

Dedication

To Jennifer Wilson, without whom this book would not exist, and her sweet family.

Editorial Reviews

Sudden Awakenings by Amanda Kai is an engaging *Pride & Prejudice* Regency variation that will entice and captivate readers with several deviations from Canon. This forced-marriage scenario features a dark twist or two before reaching its delightful ending!

Kelly Miller, author of *The Mysterious Disappearance of Mr. Darcy*

Chapter 1

It is a truth universally acknowledged that sleepwalking runs in families. If both parents are afflicted, the odds are two to one that their children will also suffer from some form of somnambulism or other troubled slumbers.

It was a great misfortune then that Mr. and Mrs. Bennet, of Longbourn in Hertfordshire, both suffered such a disorder at some time in their lives.

Mr. Bennet outgrew the condition in his youth, and therefore never thought to mention it to his wife during their courtship.

Mrs. Bennet's sleepwalking proclivities were well known to her family at the time of her marriage, but her persistent denial of it and her family's reluctance to speak of it, lest it frighten away her eligible suitor, enabled her condition to be kept secret.

This carefully crafted silence remained unbroken until one fateful night, not long after her marriage, when Mrs. Bennet, lost in her throes of slumber, ambled down to the larder, ate up all the jellies that were prepared for an upcoming dinner party, and returned to bed.

Naturally, she denied having done so, insisting there was a thief among the servants. Mr. Bennet could not have believed it himself, but the hall boy, who had fallen asleep by the fire in the kitchen, reported he had awakened to see her gobbling up the freshly made jellies, which, in turn, caused Mr. Bennet to recall he had woken slightly when Mrs. Bennet returned to bed, and that she had peculiarly smelled of strawberries.

Their children, except for the eldest, also inherited their parents' somnambulism. Though the three youngest daughters all outgrew their nocturnal perambulations before their tenth birthdays, Miss Elizabeth Bennet remained afflicted.

Even at the mature age of twenty, she would, from time to time, rise from her slumber during the night and wander the house, performing various tasks, all the while remaining completely unconscious of her actions.

Preventative measures had been taken to ensure her safety. They kept the kitchen knives locked away, the doors and windows secured, and a bell attached to each door to alert them if someone tried to leave the house during the night. Despite these measures, there were occasionally incidents which caused a stir at Longbourn. The occasional misplaced object or a peculiar nighttime disturbance were often a source of amusement, and at times exasperation, for members of the Bennet family.

On one such occasion, shortly before Michaelmas, the household had not been asleep for more than a few hours when one of the bells rang, alerting Mr. Bennet that somebody had managed to open a door. He glanced next to him to ensure his wife still remained abed, her gentle snores undisturbed by this alarm. Concluding it must be his daughter, he rose from his bed and went down the stairs. His other daughters, also awakened by the sounds, followed him.

"Is it Lizzy?" Lydia asked, her soft slippers padding on the polished floorboards. "Has she gone out of doors?"

"It would appear so," Mr. Bennet answered. "Fetch your shoes, girls, in case you are needed."

They obeyed their father. It was not the first time they had needed to go in search of their sister.

By this time, Mr. Hill had also arisen and made his appearance in the hall. Helping his master into a dressing gown and boots, he offered him a lantern and the pair set out in search of Elizabeth.

"She cannot have gone far, sir," the old butler said. "I will check the gardens if you will search the barns."

Mr. Bennet nodded, and they separated. Pulling his dressing gown tighter to ward off the cool night air, he tramped through the dewy grass towards the side yards where the barns lay. A faint luminescence gleamed from the doorway of the barn where the livestock were kept. Inside the barn, Elizabeth stood beside the pigpen, feeding an apple to a large pig. Her eyes were glazed over in a trance, and she did not appear to notice the happy snuffles of the animal nibbling from her hand.

Mr. Bennet moved towards her slowly so as not to alarm her. A pungent aroma assailed his nostrils. The foul odors of the pigpen ought to be enough to wake anyone, he mused. Yet Elizabeth did not stir.

Lydia and Kitty, ever the impetuous ones, rushed in, still in their nightdresses, each with a dressing gown hastily thrown over it.

"Lizzy! What are you doing?" Kitty cried, grabbing her sister's arm away from the pig and causing the remainder of the apple to drop to the ground outside the pen. The pig grunted, trying to reach it with his nose through the slats in his pen.

Lydia jumped back with a shriek, narrowly avoiding stepping in a pile of refuse.

"Hush! Do not wake her," Mr. Bennet cautioned. "She may become frightened if she awakens here. She is in no immediate danger. Let us lead her back to her bed." He knew from experience that waking a sleepwalker often caused more harm than good, as the distress sometimes made them lash out in fear, potentially injuring themselves or others, before they could become aware of their surroundings.

Gently, he took his daughter's shoulders and began guiding her in the direction of the house. "It is time to go to bed, Lizzy," he whispered. Elizabeth nodded, her feet following the path she was led on, her eyes unblinking. They brought her safely into the confines of the house, sat her on her bed and watched as she instinctively laid down, her eyes slowly shutting.

Jane drew the covers over her and kissed her forehead. "I daresay she will not remember this in the morning," she murmured, before climbing back into bed next to Elizabeth.

"If my experience tells me anything, no, she will not," Mr. Bennet agreed.

✺

Just as predicted, Elizabeth woke the next morning with no recollection of her nighttime activities. She went about her day as usual, although the uncharacteristic dirt beneath her fingernails and mud on her slippers teased the question of some late-night escapade which her unconscious mind seemed determined to keep from her.

"You were sleepwalking again last night, Lizzy," Jane remarked casually as the two of them sat in the morning room. Elizabeth was sewing shirts for the parish poor, as she often did, while Jane occupied herself with retrimming a bonnet.

"Was I?" Elizabeth asked. "I had no idea of it. I hope I did not do anything too dreadful."

"Nothing more dreadful than attempting to fatten up George during the night," Jane said with a sly smile.

SUDDEN AWAKENINGS

"Oh dear!" Elizabeth laughed. "As he is already a contender for the top prize at this year's fair, I daresay he needs no further assistance in that!" Her needle flew across the fabric at an increased pace.

Jane astutely changed the subject. "I've had a letter from Mary. She writes that she is settling in well at Hunsford Parsonage. The house and parish are to her liking, and Lady Catherine de Bourgh is friendly and obliging. All in all, she appears content, even happy, in her new situation."

Elizabeth said nothing. She could not imagine anyone feeling happy as the wife of Mr. Collins and she felt it foolish that her sister, only two years younger than herself, had thrown herself away on a marriage of convenience.

The previous spring, Mr. Collins, their cousin who was the newly minted rector of Hunsford, had paid them a visit. He initially expressed an interest in Jane, but Mrs. Bennet, being certain that Jane was destined for a far superior match, steered him towards Elizabeth. Elizabeth found him pompous and tedious.

Mary, however, was not so scrupulous. As the middle child yearning for attention, she readily accepted Collins' proposal mere hours after Elizabeth's rejection, gaining the distinction of being the first sister to wed.

Mary's piousness and eagerness to please exactly suited his desire for a compliant wife. Her talents on the pianoforte, unappreciated by her friends and family, were highly acclaimed by Lady Catherine, who boasted to be a great lover of music. Out of all the Bennet sisters, Mary's temperament was the best suited for tending to a flock in the capacity of a minister's wife, and in her new life, she found a measure of contentment.

Elizabeth, however, failed to see this, and only imagined her sister's misery in such a situation. She herself would never marry except for love, she reasoned. Material charms and the distinction of being wed held no draw for her as it did for her sisters.

Despite her mother's insistence she would find herself an old maid if she did not make an effort to be agreeable to gentlemen of their acquaintance, Elizabeth felt content with her present situation and was in no hurry to marry. Until some worthy gentleman came along, there was no need to alter her way of life.

Therefore, she was unmoved that afternoon when her mother rushed home to tell them the news.

Mrs. Bennet, a woman whose primary focus in life was the advantageous establishment of her daughters, entered the drawing room all aflutter after her visit with Mrs. Long. The family were scattered about the room, each engaged in their own pursuits, and unperturbed by the matron's behavior. Mrs. Bennet did not even bother to remove her bonnet but immediately went to her husband, who was in his favorite chair, attempting to find solace in his newspaper.

"My dear, Mr. Bennet," she began, in a voice so eager it made her husband sigh. "Have you heard? Netherfield Park is let, *at last!*"

The park had been unoccupied ever since the owners had been forced to retrench.

Mr. Bennet ignored her and continued reading his paper.

"Do you not want to know who has taken it?" Mrs. Bennet rapped her fingers impatiently on the back of his chair.

Mr. Bennet finally graced her with a glance. "As you wish to tell me, my dear, by all means, let us hear it," he said dryly.

His invitation led her to communicate that a man from the north by the name of Mr. Bingley, whose income was estimated at four or five thousand a year and who was reportedly single, was to be their new neighbor.

Elizabeth listened with some amusement as her father, who found great enjoyment in vexing her mother, insisted he would not go to visit Mr. Bingley to establish the acquaintance. None of Mrs. Bennet's cries and pleas for the sake of their daughters could stir him to agree otherwise, though his wink towards Elizabeth told her he fully meant to do so.

"Your father is so stubborn, Lizzy!" Mrs. Bennet complained to her. "He will not take us to town so you may meet interesting and eligible gentlemen, whom you might marry, and here is a wealthy young gentleman who comes into our very neighborhood, and all your father has to do is cross three miles to meet him, but still, he will not stir! How am I ever to find husbands for you all, with such a father as yours?"

"I do not know, Mamma. Perhaps we shall all have to join a convent," Elizabeth quipped.

Her remark did not satisfy her mother, who soon left the house to complain about the situation to her sister, Mrs. Phillips, who resided in nearby Meryton.

<hr />

It would be interesting, Elizabeth supposed, to make a new acquaintance. Their circle of acquaintances, circumscribed by geography and limited means, comprised only four and twenty families with whom they had any degree of familiarity, and fewer still with whom they enjoyed the intimacy of regular calls and shared dinners.

A newcomer promised to be a delightful novelty for conversation, and by paying a visit to her particular friend Charlotte Lucas the following day, Elizabeth was able to learn more about their new neighbor.

"My father has already lost no time in calling on Mr. Bingley," Charlotte told her, with levity, "and he reported him to be a handsome and agreeable fellow. *I* have not seen him myself," she clarified, "but I have never known my father to exaggerate. Mr. Bingley has two sisters, one married, who are to join him at the end of the month. I hope they shall be as agreeable as their brother."

"Their amiability is of no consequence to us, surely," said Elizabeth. "For we are not dependent on their company, after all. If their brother is as agreeable as has been told, then I daresay he will bring sufficient life to our dull gatherings."

Charlotte heartily agreed.

Chapter 2

Having determined Netherfield Park to be satisfactory and affixing his signature to the lease, Mr. Bingley embarked on a brief journey to London. He aimed to tend to some business matters and, more importantly, to collect his sisters, who were to grace his residence for the duration of the shooting season. He hoped he might persuade his dearest friend Mr. Darcy to accompany them also.

"Do join us in Hertfordshire," Bingley urged him. "The weather promises to be fair, and the local birdlife plentiful. I have already had the pleasure of meeting some of the neighbors, and they all struck me as congenial. I daresay you will find it agreeable, Darcy."

Mr. Darcy gave a reluctant sigh. "I will not disagree with you. However, it is not in my power to join you yet. I must see Georgiana settled with her new governess and there are some other matters which I must tend to."

"But you will come soon, won't you?" Bingley persisted, a hopeful gleam in his eye. "There is to be an assembly in the middle of next month. All the locals will be in attendance. Some of their daughters are reportedly great beauties."

A grimace crossed Mr. Darcy's face. "You know how much I detest dancing with those whom I am unacquainted with ."

Caroline Bingley, her voice laced with a hint of playful entitlement, spoke up. "Then you shall have to spend your evening dancing with me, my dear man. For what am I to do for a partner if you are not there? Heaven only knows how few gentlemen there may be in that neighborhood, and I cannot for the life of me think there will be many good dancers in such a rural place. Charles," she glanced wryly at her brother, "will be monopolized by the women; he always is, wherever he goes."

Mr. Bingley chuckled, a hint of self-satisfaction displayed on his countenance. "I cannot help it if I enjoy a certain popularity among the fairer sex, nor that I find so many of them to be agreeable."

"Do not let yourself be snared, Charles," she reprimanded him. "Were you not in possession of a fortune, I daresay less than half of these women would be so agreeable. If there is one thing every woman desires, it is to marry well."

"The same is no less true for men," Mr. Darcy said. "*You* can afford to have your pick among women, Bingley, so long as she comes from a good family and is in possession of the social graces needed to function as your wife. A less fortunate man must be more discerning in his choice."

"As if you suffer from such a problem yourself!" Bingley's eyes twinkled. "I believe your income is twice mine, perhaps more. If anyone can marry where he wishes, it is you, Darcy."

Darcy pressed his lips together, shifting his position in his chair to better face Bingley. "When it comes to money, certainly, the lady's dowry holds no significance for me. However, given the weight upon my shoulders, I feel even more keenly the importance of making a suitable connection to someone whose family will not dishonor the Darcy reputation; someone equipped to serve as the mistress of a large estate and who will assist me in securing it for the next generation."

"By this you mean heirs, I suppose," Miss Bingley said, crossing the drawing room and resting her hand on the back of his chair possessively. "I am sure any woman would be honored to bear the next Darcy heir."

"Heirs are important," Darcy continued, ignoring the nearness of Miss Bingley. "but equally so is having a wife who can partner with me in the running of the estate. I am not so foolish as to believe myself wise enough to undertake the endeavor alone. Even with the assistance of my steward, I feel inadequate in my knowledge of the best ways to develop the land so that it flourishes or how to invest the wealth I have been given so that my children and grandchildren may see its dividends."

"These are heavy thoughts, indeed!" Bingley exclaimed, shaking his head. "I suppose I myself have not given much care to such things. I have been preoccupied with running my business these last two years, to be sure, but as I have yet to purchase an estate, I have given little thought to how I shall pass my legacy on to my children."

"I am sure, Mr. Darcy, you shall have no difficulty in finding a partner and wife to assist you in all the ways you seek," Miss Bingley simpered. "Why, I know at least one lady who would be happy with the job."

If she meant herself, Mr. Darcy did not see it. "I suppose that is the trouble," he said. "The greater one's wealth, the greater the number of those who would seek to lay their hands on it. I must be careful, not only in finding a wife who is willing, but in finding one who does not seek me solely for my fortune. She must still be a gentleman's daughter, however."

Miss Bingley sniffed, turning towards the window lest her expression betray her feelings on the matter.

Mr. Bingley's lips curled in thought. "I would not wish to be married to a fortune hunter, but neither am I as particular as you are, Darcy. If a pretty lady should come along, whose tastes and personality suit my own, I would not care if she should take me for my five thousand a year, so long as her love for me is also genuine."

"You know by saying so you quite contradict yourself," Miss Bingley scoffed. "Either her love for you is genuine, or her love for you is dependent on your money."

"She is right, it cannot be both," Mr. Darcy agreed. "The love for one will always outweigh the love for the other."

"Very well, I concede," Bingley nodded. "But so long as her love for me outweighs that of my money, I shall be content. I cannot think my fortune will have no bearing on her decision. No father would give away his daughter to a pauper if he had any say in it, nor would a gentleman's daughter be happy to live without the material comforts she is used to. It is right and proper that some attention to money be given when considering the benefits of a marriage."

"Well said," his sister clapped. "But I think Mr. Darcy is also right when he insists there are other, more important, considerations, and that the woman must be exactly suited for the job and come from a respectable family. Promise me, Charles, you will not let your head be turned by the next pretty girl who comes along who has her eye on your fortune, unless she is of good stock and her family not an embarrassment."

Mr. Bingley returned to Netherfield Park the following week, accompanied by Miss Bingley, along with his elder sister and her husband, the Hursts. During his absence, the servants set up the house for him. The rooms were cleaned and readied, the larder stocked, and Bingley's own possessions unpacked. He had little in the way of furniture or decorations, having lived the life of a bachelor for some time now, so it was fortunate the owners had left the house furnished and in good condition.

The quality was not up to Miss Bingley's standards, however. "When you purchase a house, Charles, I hope you shall let me decorate it. This house is positively ancient, and these furnishings are at least ten years out of date. I suppose it is to be expected in this rustic neighborhood."

"I find no fault with the furnishings, Caroline," he retorted, plopping himself onto the sofa and stretching himself out comfortably. He was the sort of man who could be comfortable in any environment, whereas Caroline loved to criticize at every turn. In her eyes, their abode, no matter whether in London or the countryside, always appeared to be too poor, too shabby, too outdated. The exception was when they were guests at the home of someone far wealthier than them. There, no room could go without praise or exclamation from her; she must comment on its size and proportion, the colors of the decor, the comfort and style of the furnishings, and the excellent taste of the art.

"I positively dread giving a dinner here," Miss Bingley continued. "Did you see how small the dining table is? We can hardly fit six couples. Such a large dining room could easily accommodate a table twice that size. What a pity the owners did not think to purchase a larger one before they vacated the house."

"Perhaps they could not afford to," Mr. Bingley suggested.

Mrs. Hurst quipped, "As you have no acquaintances in the neighborhood yet, I do not think you must worry about having too little room at your table to accommodate them. Your worry lies in filling the seats you already possess."

Miss Bingley glared at her sister over this remark, prompting a chuckle from their brother.

Mr. Bennet's call on Mr. Bingley was paid, despite all his assurances (and Mrs. Bennet's fears) that it would not, and the connection formed. Mr. Bingley, having heard of Mr. Bennet's beautiful daughters from Sir William Lucas, and finding Mr. Bennet to be an agreeable man, was keen to return the visit at the earliest convenient time.

Miss Bingley and Mrs. Hurst accompanied him to visit the Bennet family. Though themselves not anxious to develop acquaintances in that region, they wished to form an opinion of the people with whom they would be forced to mingle during their stay. Mr. Hurst, who cared for nothing that did not relate to his victuals, his sleep, or his recreation, saw no advantage to paying calls and chose to remain behind for an afternoon nap.

Mr. Bingley thought all of the Bennet sisters to be beautiful, but he was especially taken with the eldest. Miss Bennet's fair features and sweet disposition would have been enough to make him declare her an angel, but when coupled with her pert lips and her perfectly-proportioned figure, accentuated by the empire waist of her crisp, white, morning gown, he found himself completely entranced.

Mrs. Bennet noticed his immediate attraction towards her daughter and insisted that Jane exchange seats with her to be nearer to their guests. From then on, she took pains to promote Jane's finer qualities at every opportunity.

Mrs. Bennet's forward inquiries about Mr. Bingley's business, his prospects, and his intention to remain in the neighborhood were not lost on his sisters. It became equally apparent to them that the family's connections were nothing; no ties to the nobility, not even a baronet. Mrs. Bennet had a brother in trade and a sister whose husband was a country solicitor. Such a decidedly low situation was compounded by the estate being entailed on a cousin, the husband of one daughter. While *she* might expect a good life as the mistress of Longbourn, the others could have precious little in the way of a dowry.

The fact of the matter was, the remaining sisters must depend on making good matches, and it was plain by Mrs. Bennet's vulgar attention to Mr. Bingley's fortune that she saw him as an advantageous prospect.

Mr. Bingley, however, was all too ready to be taken advantage of. Having beheld his ideal woman, he was eager to further his acquaintance with her.

"Will you be at the assembly this month, Miss Bennet?" he asked, his eyes dilating at the prospect of seeing her in an evening gown.

Jane nodded, an alluring smile forming on her lips. "Indeed, I shall. My sisters and I always attend, for we dearly love to dance."

"Excellent! Then I shall look forward to the pleasure of dancing with you– with all of you, that is," he added, nodding at her sisters in turn.

"Does your brother-in-law dance too, Mr. Bingley?" Miss Elizabeth asked him eagerly. "For gentlemen are scarce in these parts, and we are often short on partners."

Mr. Bingley shook his head. "Mr. Hurst does not dance, I am afraid. Now that he is married, he spends all his time in the card room at such gatherings. But do not despair; I have it on good authority that my dear friend, Mr. Fitzwilliam Darcy, will be coming down in time for the assembly. He has accepted my invitation to stay at Netherfield this season, and was only delayed in coming by some pressing business."

"How delightful!" Mrs. Bennet exclaimed. "Where does your friend hail from?"

"Mr. Darcy's home is in Derbyshire, ma'am. At Pemberley."

Mrs. Bennet leaned closer in eager attention. "I confess, I have not heard of it. Is it a very large place?"

"To be sure!" Mr. Bingley nodded. "One of the finest estates in all of Derbyshire. And Mr. Darcy is an excellent fellow. I have known him long. I am certain he will make a welcome addition to all our parties."

"Oh, no doubt about it!" Mrs. Bennet said. "We shall be pleased to meet him."

The notion of having yet another eligible man added to their gatherings was a most delightful one, and before the guests had departed, Mrs. Bennet was already envisioning two of her daughters happily settled; one at Netherfield, and one at this Pemberley place. With her limited knowledge of geography, she knew not how far Derbyshire might be from Hertfordshire, but the distance could be of no consequence if the man were as rich as he seemed. She formed a mental note to begin making inquiries about him.

That Jane should be one of the two brides was a given; but which of her other daughters might also be chosen would depend on the gentlemen's preferences, she supposed.

Chapter 3

It was necessary, after Mr. Bingley's visit, for Elizabeth to call upon Charlotte to discuss it. By this time, Charlotte's family had also received a return call from Mr. Bingley, and so the two ladies were able to compare their visits. They concurred that Mr. Bingley was, indeed, as handsome and agreeable as their fathers had reported, and his addition to their society would greatly benefit them. Of his sisters, they were less certain. Elizabeth remarked that they were fine, elegant ladies, but proud.

"They did not appear to approve of our low connections," she said, shaking her head. "I could have sworn I heard Miss Bingley sniff when my mother mentioned that her sister's husband is a solicitor, and Mrs. Hurst practically sneered when I told her of my uncle's business in Cheapside."

"After all their brother's efforts to rise above his situation, I suppose they must be eager to distance themselves from anyone connected to trade," Charlotte surmised.

"How ironic, considering their own dowries came from trade!" Elizabeth pointed out.

Still, they agreed the Netherfield party's addition to the neighborhood would provide some interest.

"When one has dined with the same four-and-twenty families their entire life, even a haughty pair of sisters is enough to offer a diversion!" Elizabeth said with mirth.

AMANDA KAI

〜

It was raining when she departed from Lucas Lodge, yet Elizabeth declined the offer of the carriage from Lady Lucas. She clung to the lane on her return home, but even with an umbrella, the hem of her gown became embarrassingly heavy with water. A misstep plunged her boot into a muddy puddle, adding to her woes. The wind, a mischievous sprite, tormented her hair, threatening to free her bonnet from her head.

She paused for a moment to tuck a few stray whisps back underneath the bonnet, wrestling with the umbrella against the wind's buffeting. A sudden clatter of hooves startled her. Looking up, she adjusted the umbrella to see a lone rider slowly approaching, map clutched in his hand, brow furrowed in concentration..

"You appear to be lost, sir," Elizabeth called as he drew near.

"Indeed, I fear I have made a wrong turn," he replied. "By my calculations, I ought to have reached the town of Meryton by now."

"Then you hail from London? Did you travel by the Old North Road, and then veer northeastward, onto Meryton Road?" she inquired, stepping confidently beside his horse and peering up at him from beneath her umbrella. Even through the wind and rain, her view partially obscured by the edge of the umbrella, she discerned he was a tall, handsome man, his looks no worse for wear from the rain drenching his coat. She glimpsed dark hair beneath his beaver hat. He bore a noble countenance, and he rode with the posture of an experienced rider.

"Yes, that was precisely my route," he answered.

"Ah, then a turn to the left instead of to the right at crossroads was your misstep, sir. The right fork becomes Market Street and leads directly into the heart of Meryton, but the other path, Longbourn Road, leads to the village of that name."

"Then it is well I have encountered you, to guide me, miss. My gratitude for your assistance."

"The pleasure is mine. You are bound for Meryton, then, sir?"

"Netherfield Park, in fact," he answered.

Elizabeth's face brightened. "Ah, then you must be Mr. Darcy, Mr. Bingley's guest, whom we are told he is expecting."

"The very same," he confirmed. "Forgive me, miss, but you have me at a disadvantage. You know my name, but I remain ignorant of yours."

"And so you shall remain for the present. While I am not averse to offering assistance to a traveler, propriety dictates introductions be made by a gentleman. Another day, perhaps."

With a cheerful, "Good day to you, sir," she skipped off, turning down a side lane which branched from the road on which they were on, and was soon out of sight.

Safe within her home, Elizabeth began the process of drying her mud-caked boots. A pang of regret pricked her conscience. *Mr. Darcy might think me unfriendly. I could have at least given him my name.*

The truth, a secret smile playing on her lips, was the unexpected encounter with such a handsome stranger had flustered her, making her yearn for the comfort of her own home rather than prolonging their conversation. Unlike her younger sisters with their flights of fancy, Elizabeth prided herself on her composure. Yet, even the most sensible young lady could be affected by a pleasing countenance.

Mr. Bingley mentioned his friend would be at the assembly. Then I shall have the opportunity to meet him properly.

Mr. Darcy found the encounter with the young lady decidedly perplexing. Her initial boldness in addressing him was overshadowed by her curious refusal to offer her name. An enigma, indeed, especially since she bore prior knowledge of him! Her disheveled appearance he allowed due to the mud and wind. Yet what business could a young lady have, venturing out alone in such disagreeable weather? Certainly, his sister Georgiana would never be permitted such liberties.

The young lady must live nearby, he concluded, for the path she turned down appeared to lead to an estate.

At least her directions proved trustworthy.

Following her guidance, he soon reached the town of Meryton. From there, had no difficulty in locating Netherfield Park.

Mr. Bingley's warm greeting was only eclipsed by the effusive welcome he received from Miss Bingley.

"Mr. Darcy!" she exclaimed, descending the marble staircase to meet him in the hall. "We have missed your presence greatly. Our evening gatherings have been rather lackluster as of late. A pity you could not grace us with your presence sooner."

Mr. Darcy acknowledged her sentiment with a curt bow. "As promised, I am here in time for the assembly."

"I do not know how splendid an assembly it shall be. Likely no more than a few families gathered together at the town hall, with naught but a bit of watered down punch for refreshments," she speculated. "It shall certainly be nothing next to the assemblies we have attended together in Mayfair. I hope, at least, I may have the consolation of being promised to you for a dance, Mr. Darcy."

He tacitly gave his agreement to her suggestion, which pleased her. He would gladly have retired to his room, but Miss Bingley seemed disinclined to let the conversation lapse. As soon as Mrs. Hurst joined them, she proceeded to give a tour of the premises.

While they walked, Miss Bingley regaled Mr. Darcy with tales about the local gentry they had met, namely the Bennet family. "You would not believe the deficiencies one encounters in these rustic parts. A distinct lack of manners pervades all of the company we have encountered, but the Bennet family are the worst!" she exclaimed.

"Indeed," Mrs. Hurst agreed, nodding. "One cannot help but be bewildered by their aspirations. Lacking in any connections of consequence, they appear to possess an inflated sense of their own worth. We had not been to call more than five minutes before Mrs. Bennet began pushing her eldest daughter towards Charles."

Miss Bingley's disdainful sniff spoke volumes about her opinion of the Bennet family. "These uneducated people are utterly devoid of any connections, and yet they think Miss Bennet to be worthy of our Charles! As I predicted, there is a scarcity of gentlemen in these parts, and the women will instantly pounce upon any wealthy man who comes into their neighborhood. You had best be on your guard, Mr. Darcy," she warned him.

Mr. Darcy's lips curled sardonically. "If pecuniary gain is their intention, my fortune shall be out of their reach." He lifted his chin a fraction. "Besides," he added with a hint of disdain, "their lack of physical beauty hardly strengthens their case, does it?"

"On the contrary," Mr. Bingley exclaimed. He appeared discomfited by these uncouth remarks about their neighbors. "I found the Bennet sisters all to be uniformly charming, especially the eldest one, Jane. She possesses a beauty that is rare and captivating. One could argue that she deserves my money, if she would have me."

"Such pronouncements are premature," Mrs. Hurst dissented, believing herself to be the voice of reason. "The Bennets, from what I have observed, are nothing but greedy, scheming graspers. I am surprised you could not discern it as easily as I did."

Caroline nodded her agreement. "Such pretentious people with no connections at all can hardly be worth your notice. They have not one member of the peerage in their whole entire family, or so I am told by Miss Elizabeth. One uncle is a solicitor in Meryton and the other uncle is a tradesman residing in Cheapside! The audacity! To think that we must stoop to associating with such people when we could be fostering connections to members of the peerage instead is beyond the pale."

Mr. Bingley's eyes danced with amusement. "But Caroline, we have no such connections ourselves, and lest you forget, our family's fortune also originated in trade. If anyone are pretentious upstarts, it is us," he reminded her.

Caroline's withered expression communicated her disdain for her brother's opinion. "Mr. Darcy, " she drawled, directing her attention back to him, "you would do well to abstain from any connection with these Bennet people. Let your stay at Netherfield be brief, I pray. A hasty return to London, or better yet, Pemberley, is highly advisable."

Bingley, ever the peacemaker, interjected with a lighthearted scolding. His sisters' pronouncements were dismissed with a wave of his hand and a jovial laugh. But their sentiments left an impression on Darcy. The prospect of meeting this Bennet family soon grew in his mind from an inconvenience to a decidedly disagreeable event.

Anticipation for the Meryton Assembly grew leading up to the day itself. The Bennet sisters donned their finest gowns and new dancing slippers, and styled their hair becomingly. Their mother's excitement could not be contained as she bustled about, her anticipation brimming over until all her daughters, even Elizabeth, shared in her enthusiasm.

SUDDEN AWAKENINGS

Mr. Bingley and his party were already at the assembly room when the Bennet family arrived. Mrs. Bennet hurried over to him, her family rushing to keep up with her.

Mr. Bingley greeted them all with a courteous bow. "I hope you are well this evening, Miss Bennet," he addressed Jane. His face glowed with admiration as he surveyed her appearance.

She looked especially beautiful this evening. She followed her mother's advice and wore her beige silk gown with the surplice neckline which showed off her figure to advantage.

"Thank you, Mr. Bingley," Jane replied, curtsying low, her pearl teardrop necklace dangling midair near her *décolletage*. "I am quite well, thanks to your presence."

Introductions were made. Mr. Darcy, with an air of reserved courtesy, bowed and kissed Mrs. Bennet's hand before acknowledging each of her daughters.

Elizabeth, unable to suppress a flicker of curiosity, stole a glance at Mr. Darcy. His fine features, dominated by a prominent brow, and his impressive stature were undeniable. Clad in formal wear, he appeared even more handsome than during their unexpected encounter on the muddy lane.

A fervent hope formed in her heart that he might ask her to dance. He spoke little, his gaze lingering on her for a moment, a flicker of recognition passing between them, before moving on. Had he, perhaps, taken offense at her refusal of a formal introduction the other day?

With a shrug, she determined this would mark the beginning of their proper acquaintance.

The music swelled, and the room erupted in a flurry of movement as the first set commenced. Mr. Bingley, with a flourish, claimed Jane's hand for their promised dance. Elizabeth, her pulse quickening with a mix of anticipation and nervousness, cast a hopeful glance towards Mr. Darcy.

He, however, remained rooted to the spot, a stoic observer amidst the whirling couples. A flicker of disappointment washed over Elizabeth, quickly masked by a determined composure. Her younger sisters, Kitty and Lydia, flitted off like butterflies, eager partners secured in the Lucas brothers, leaving her behind. Mr. Bingley's sisters, too, were claimed by other gentlemen. Elizabeth hoped that, separated from the rest of his party, Mr. Darcy might decide to approach her. As the set progressed, she watched him from across the room, her heart fluttering at the thought of performing a country dance with him. He caught her eye, making her feel sure he would approach her with an invitation to join the set. Instead, he retreated further to the edge of the room, clearly intent on watching the dancing. A wave of disappointment crashed over her.

Charlotte spotted her and made her way through the throngs to greet her. "You are looking well this evening, Eliza," she remarked. "Have you yet had the pleasure of meeting Mr. Darcy?"

"Yes, we were introduced earlier." Elizabeth replied.

"All the ladies are talking of him. His popularity has surpassed even that of Mr. Bingley. He is quite a handsome fellow, is he not?"

"Undoubtedly, but he seemed so reserved by comparison to his friend." The tint of color on her cheeks betrayed her admiration.

"Perhaps he only wants for encouragement," Charlotte suggested. "A man who is naturally shy can only feel more so in the presence of so many beautiful ladies."

"That is true enough." Elizabeth's laughter mingled with the noise of the crowds around them.

"I suspect, my dear Eliza, if you sit in closer proximity, he might pluck up enough courage to ask you to dance," Charlotte encouraged.

"I suppose it could not hurt," Elizabeth shrugged. Taking her friend's advice, she crossed the room and took a seat near Mr. Darcy. Mr. Darcy kept his back to her.

Mrs. Long, who was seated beside Elizabeth, inquired whether she was enjoying herself.

"I confess I do not find much pleasure this evening," Elizabeth answered. "For as you can see, I have no partner." She was aware she was within Mr. Darcy's earshot.

"Oh, I am sure there will be partners aplenty for you tonight, Miss Elizabeth," Mrs. Long consoled her. "After all, you are so pretty. Why, that man over there might even be willing to dance with you," she said, gesturing to Mr. Darcy. "He appears to be unengaged."

"Perhaps," said Elizabeth, a little louder, "And if he should ask me, I would be grateful for his notice."

This hint alone did not seem enough. Jane, seeing her sister sitting down without a partner, left the dance for a moment to ask her why she had not found one. Elizabeth hinted in a low whisper that she wondered if perhaps Mr. Darcy might be inclined to ask her if his friend were to encourage him. Jane nodded and soon summoned Mr. Bingley, who came directly over.

"Darcy, my good fellow," he exclaimed, slapping him on the back. "I hate to see you standing about in this stupid manner. Come, we must find you a partner."

Mr. Darcy looked around the room with disdain. "There is not a woman in this room without whom it would be a punishment to stand up with," he remarked contemptuously.

Mr. Bingley laughed. "Upon my word, I would not be so fastidious. There are several girls in this room who are remarkably beautiful. In fact, I have never seen so many beautiful women in one room in all my life!"

"You are dancing with the only woman worth looking at." Mr. Darcy scoffed. "You had better return to your partner and enjoy her smiles. You are wasting your time with me."

"Come, come, Darcy," he said. "Miss Bennet is indeed beautiful, but yet here is her sister's equal in beauty, sitting just behind you."

Elizabeth's hope rose once more. She pretended not to be listening to their every word.

Mr. Darcy cast a glance directly at Elizabeth, then looked back to his friend. "She is tolerable enough, I suppose, but not handsome enough to tempt me."

Elizabeth was stunned. To receive such an insult from one whom she had barely been introduced! She blinked back tears, determined not to let anyone in the room see her cry.

Mr. Darcy soon moved away from her, and Charlotte, seeing the distressed look upon her friend's face, hurried over.

"Did Mr. Darcy not ask you to dance, Eliza?" she asked.

"No, he did not," Elizabeth answered, sticking her chin out. "In fact, he went so far as to call me 'tolerable but not handsome enough to tempt him,' and within my hearing, too!"

"Goodness, how shocking!" Charlotte exclaimed, sitting down to console her. "What a proud, disagreeable man Mr. Darcy turned out to be!"

"I quite agree with you, Charlotte," said Elizabeth. "And I do not think I shall like Mr. Darcy after all."

"Well, be thankful then that he did not like you, Eliza, for then you should have to dance with him," Charlotte quipped.

"Indeed," Elizabeth laughed, her mirth doing away with much of her disappointment. Though her pride was wounded, she would not allow Mr. Darcy's insult to ruin her evening. After all, what was he to her?

She repeated the story with great spirit to her other friends, and before the evening was over, half the room was in agreement that Mr. Darcy was the proudest, most disagreeable man they had met.

When Mr. Bingley's engagement with Jane concluded, he sought out Elizabeth and with a polite bow, requested the next set.

This turn of events gave Elizabeth the satisfaction of seeing Mr. Darcy's face as he witnessed her dance with his friend. The subtle shift in his expression made her feel smug as she determined to show him what he had missed by not dancing with her. Later that evening, she observed him dancing with Miss Bingley. His movements, however, lacked their usual grace, and a frown occasionally furrowed his brow. Elizabeth could not help but wonder if Miss Bingley's conversation proved as tedious as she herself sometimes found it, or if Mr. Darcy simply hated dancing altogether.

Despite Mr. Darcy's earlier slight, Elizabeth found herself enjoying the assembly immensely. Following her set with Mr. Bingley, she danced with Mr. William Goulding and Mr. Robinson, and the lively music and company kept her spirits high.

As the evening drew to a close, Mr. Bingley singled Jane out for a second set, a distinction not bestowed upon any other lady. This favoritism sent a thrill through Mrs. Bennet, who reveled in her daughter's success.

"Jane, my dearest!" she exclaimed upon their return home. "It is clear Mr. Bingley is already captivated by you! You must continue to cultivate his interest when you next meet. In fact, I gleaned from Mrs. Hurst that the Bingleys plan to attend the Gouldings' soiree next week. I have already hinted to Mrs. Goulding about securing invitations for us, and subtly suggested you be seated next to Mr. Bingley."

Jane readily agreed to her mother's plan. Together, they began strategizing about her attire and conversational topics for the upcoming event. By the time she retired for the night, every detail was meticulously planned.

When she entered the bedchamber, the light was still lit. Elizabeth sat at her writing desk, diligently chronicling the events of the assembly in a letter.

"Still awake, Lizzy?" Jane inquired, surprise tinging her voice. "I assumed you would be fast asleep by now."

"Merely documenting the evening's entertainment, for Aunt Gardiner's amusement," Elizabeth replied with a smile.

"I cannot help but be shocked by what Mr. Darcy said about you," Jane confessed. "The way he looked directly at you before speaking leaves no doubt he intended for you to hear it."

Elizabeth shrugged. "Perhaps I fell short of his standards in some way. He did not grace any other lady with his presence on the dance floor, except for Miss Bingley, of course."

"Perhaps an understanding exists between them," Jane mused. "Perhaps he deliberately avoided others to spare Miss Bingley's feelings."

"If there is some understanding between them, then they are perfectly suited! My only concern lies for you, Jane. If Mr. Bingley becomes your husband, and Mr. Darcy weds Miss Bingley, frequent encounters with them as in-laws would be inevitable," she said with mirth.

Jane smiled in response. "Miss Bingley is not without her merits. She and her sister possess undeniable elegance and grace."

"You would say that, Jane. But then, you never think ill of anybody. And that is why you are so well-suited to Mr. Bingley. You and he are of exactly the same disposition. And if Mamma's predictions are accurate, he will call on you to propose any day now," Elizabeth said with delight.

Jane's eyes carried a hopeful gleam. "Oh Lizzy, do you truly believe he harbors feelings for me? Is he the man fate has chosen for me?"

"Dearest Jane," she said, taking her hands and patting them adoringly. "Whatever Mamma's hopes for you, Mr. Bingley's admiration for you is evident. And should he win your affections, he would be a most lucky man."

Jane blushed. "I like him very much, and I hope the feeling is mutual."

Chapter 4

Mr. Darcy remained silent and contemplative throughout the return journey to Netherfield Park. Miss Bingley and Mrs. Hurst, however, displayed a starkly contrasting demeanor. Their tongues, loosened by the evening's entertainment, launched into a relentless critique of the assembly in the most abusive language. They had no compunctions about speaking ill of Sir William Lucas, recently knighted, whom they deemed insufferably pompous for abandoning his trade after receiving the honor. Nor were the Gouldings spared their scorn, derided for classing themselves amongst the gentry while still actively managing their bank.

But their favorite subject was the Bennet family. Towards them, their insults held no bounds, to the point that even their brother's good nature was tried by the time they reached Netherfield.

"Supposedly, they are a long-standing gentry family, but the way they carry themselves, one would suppose they were peasant farmers!" Mrs. Hurst scoffed.

They urged Mr. Bingley to avoid the Bennets at all costs, but he was already too smitten with Miss Bennet, and paid his sisters' warnings no heed.

Though he did not voice his thoughts aloud, Mr. Darcy agreed with much of what the sisters were saying. The entire Bennet family appeared to embody the very qualities Miss Bingley and Mrs. Hurst had ascribed to them. The younger sisters flitted about the room, securing dance partners with an alarming degree of success, while Miss Bennet herself wasted no time in securing Mr. Bingley's attention, readily accepting a second set and even prevailing upon him to dance with her sisters. Mrs. Bennet's role in this elaborate scheme was undeniable. Her persistent efforts to keep her daughters in close proximity to him and Mr. Bingley throughout the evening spoke volumes.

Mr. Darcy's attention drifted from the conversation as his thoughts became preoccupied with a particular Bennet daughter, the one he had encountered on the muddy lane and who had later graced him with her proximity during the assembly.

Miss Elizabeth Bennet.

Now that he knew her name, he could not remove her from his mind. Her audacity in positioning herself near him with the expectation of an invitation to dance was presumptuous, to say the least. The subsequent maneuverings, orchestrated through her sister's request to Mr. Bingley, were clearly a calculated attempt at securing his attentions.

Such blatant social climbing deserved a swift and decisive rebuff.

Feeling satisfied that he had put her in her place, he leaned back against the seat of the chaise and crossed his arms. Beside him, Mr. Hurst snored loudly, effectively drowning out the ladies' gossip and allowing Mr. Darcy to sink deeper into his thoughts about Miss Elizabeth. Although he deemed his reproaches of conduct entirely warranted, he found himself unable to overlook the lively gleam within her dark eyes. Indeed, her impertinence was undeniable, yet there lingered a vivacity about her that set her apart from other young ladies.

Elizabeth deliberately pushed the assembly from her thoughts, so it was not until the day of the Gouldings' dinner that Mr. Darcy intruded on her consciousness again, when her mother's pronouncement brought him sharply to mind.

Mrs. Bennet, having just bestowed upon Jane a well-considered list of conversation topics for Mr. Bingley, turned her attention to Elizabeth. "Now, Lizzy," she declared, "there's no need to fret about conversing with Mr. Darcy. After his egregious snub at the assembly last week, he deserves to be treated with disdain! I quite understand if you choose not to speak to him the whole evening. In fact, I have already asked Mrs. Goulding to seat him at the other end of the table, quite apart from you."

"Mamma, such measures are entirely unnecessary!" Lizzy complained. "I'm perfectly capable of handling Mr. Darcy's company myself. Surely, Mrs. Goulding will think I mean to give him the cut direct!"

"No, no, my dear," Mrs. Bennet soothed. "A touch of reserve on your part is certainly warranted. Some gentlemen find excessive eagerness in a lady rather off-putting. Perhaps I failed to prepare you adequately for the assembly, leaving you to appear overly forward. A display of indifference, Lizzy, is sure to captivate Mr. Darcy's interest and make him regret his hasty pronouncements."

Elizabeth's voice rose in defiance. "I have no desire to captivate Mr. Darcy! Nor will I stoop to childish games. If he does deign to speak to me, I shall treat him with civility, but neither will I exert myself to converse with him."

SUDDEN AWAKENINGS

The dinner at Haye Park proved to be a pleasant one. Though she'd protested her mother's interference over the seating arrangement, Elizabeth secretly rejoiced at the distance from Mr. Darcy. His aloof demeanor towards his fellow diners offered little incentive for conversation, and an evening spent in close proximity to him held little appeal.

Her dinner companions were Maria Lucas and William Goulding, a pleasant young man who had recently returned from his studies at Cambridge. It was no secret that he admired Maria. A lively discussion erupted over whether the rising cost of goods in Meryton was likely to affect the young ladies' clothing expenditures, which amused Elizabeth greatly. She maintained that she would simply rework her old gowns, rather than purchase fabric at such high prices.

After dinner, card tables were brought out. Elizabeth strategically sat on the other side of the room from Mr. Darcy. In this way, she managed to avoid him until close to the end of the evening. Her mother was engaged in an animated discussion with Mr. Bingley, with Jane close at hand. Elizabeth, knowing her mother's tendency to overshare, drew near to them, prepared to intervene should Mrs. Bennet begin divulging some details best kept to herself.

They were discussing the party Lady Lucas had thrown for Maria's coming out when Mrs. Bennet's tendencies took over.

"It was an excellent party, and it did Lady Lucas credit as a hostess, though I am not certain it bolstered Miss Maria's chances any. It is a pity the Lucas girls are not more handsome."

"Mamma!" Elizabeth gasped, grabbing her mother's arm, knowing Lady Lucas was within earshot, conversing with Mrs. Long mere feet away. But Mrs. Bennet paid her no heed.

"Not that I think Charlotte and Maria are so *very* plain, but then, they are our particular friends," she added.

"They seem to be especially pleasant ladies," Bingley offered congenially.

"Oh my, yes! But you must own that they are plain. Lady Lucas has often envied me for my girls' beauty, especially that of my Jane. She is renowned throughout the county as the most beautiful girl in Hertfordshire, or so many people have told me."

Elizabeth's cheeks reddened over her mother's impolite remarks, wishing she could put a stop to the conversation before it went any further. To make matters worse, Mr. Darcy chose this time to insert himself into their gathering and listen.

Her mother continued, heedless of her errors. "Did you know that when Jane was only fifteen, there was a gentleman at my brother Gardiner's in town who was so taken with her, we were certain he would make her an offer. However, nothing ever came of it. I suppose he thought her too young. He did, however, write her some very pretty verses."

"Which put a swift death to his love for her!" Elizabeth hurriedly interjected. "I wonder who first discovered the efficacy of poetry in driving away love." A nervous laugh escaped her lips.

Her comment must have surprised Mr. Darcy, for he said, "I have been used to consider poetry as the food of love. Would not affection grow and increase while feasting on a lover's ballad?"

Eager to defend her statement, she said, "Of a fine, stout, healthy love, it may, for everything nourishes what is strong already. But if it is only a vague inclination of affection, I am convinced that one poor sonnet would starve it away entirely!"

Mr. Darcy raised his eyebrows. "You have a low opinion of poetry then, Miss Elizabeth?"

"Not at all. I am as much an admirer of poetry as anyone. But I cannot recommend it as the surest way to win a lady's heart."

"What would you suggest, then, to encourage affection?"

"Dancing," Elizabeth replied, with a mischievous grin, remembering his earlier slight. "For as it is said, 'to be fond of dancing is a certain step towards falling in love.'"

Darcy's lip quirked. "I have never heard such a saying. Whom are you quoting?"

"I do not know where the saying originated, but it is general knowledge– at least, if you were to ask my sisters." She glanced in the direction of Lydia and Kitty, who had persuaded William Lucas and William Goulding into dancing with them. Maria Lucas sat at the piano like a disgruntled queen, plunking out a tune, her envious gaze drifting towards William Goulding and Kitty.

Elizabeth became aware that she and Mr. Darcy had overtaken the conversation at hand, and suddenly wished she could shrink away into the wallpaper. Her mother stared at her with a wide open mouth, no doubt astonished after her daughter's earlier insistence that she would not go out of her way to converse with Mr. Darcy.

He is the one who provoked me into debating him! Her barbs on the subject of dancing were intended to remind him of his slight to her and make him ashamed of it. *If I have succeeded in bringing him a little remorse, then I suppose my break in silence towards him was not in vain.*

Mr. Bingley, uncomfortable with the sparks flying between his friend and Miss Elizabeth, sought to bail from the conversation at hand. "Well, if dancing is the first step to falling in love, then I am quite ready to begin! Miss Bennet, if you would care to join me?" He held his arm out to Jane, who readily accepted it and joined the small fray of dancers in the middle of the drawing room.

Mrs. Bennet cleared her throat. "If you will excuse me, I have just remembered I wanted to ask Mrs. Goulding her receipt for the baked custard we ate," she said, before leaving Elizabeth alone with Mr. Darcy. Now, more than ever, Elizabeth wished she had an excuse to disappear as well.

"It must be a blessing, I suppose, for those who are fond of dancing, for they are sure to find love quickly in this manner," Mr.

Darcy said, continuing their conversation. "But it is a trial for those who lack the skill and grace to navigate a ballroom."

"Do you speak of yourself, Mr. Darcy?" Elizabeth asked, unable to resist provoking him further. "I can scarcely believe *you* to be the sort lacking the grace necessary for dancing. Aren't your sort taught to dance as soon as they're out of leading strings?"

He tilted his head slightly. "When it comes to technical performance, yes, I have been taught all the necessary steps. However, I do not possess the social graces to converse easily with those whom I am unacquainted."

"What about those whom you have met before on the roadside? I have noticed you did not lack the skills to converse with me then. I think your claim to shyness is a mask, to disguise your disdain for those whom you deem unworthy of your notice." Her eyes flashed.

Mr. Darcy's brow furrowed in response. Feeling suddenly that she might say something she would come to regret, she withdrew, curtsying to him, before hurrying off to find Charlotte.

"What were you speaking to Mr. Darcy about?" her friend asked.

"Nothing of any significance," Elizabeth dismissed.

"I am sorry you had to speak to such a proud, insolent man, after what he said about you before."

"I suppose I could more easily forgive his pride had he not mortified mine," Elizabeth grumbled.

"I feel for you, Eliza, I do!" Charlotte said, controlling her smile. "But I suppose some allowances must be made for a man in his situation. He must have been brought up to think meanly of others outside his own social strata."

"I agree with you, Charlotte. He claims a lack of social graces in the presence of unfamiliar company. But one must ask why a gentleman, brought up in the first circles, would not be taught all the social niceties one requires. I think it far more likely that he thinks himself above us. Observe now, how he sneers at us from the other side of the room, while engaged with Miss Bingley." She gestured with her chin across the room, where Miss Bingley had taken Elizabeth's spot beside Mr. Darcy and clung to his arm.

"I'll wager they are laughing amongst themselves over our little country gathering," Charlotte said, leaning in towards Elizabeth. The two shared a laugh of their own over this notion.

Charlotte and Elizabeth were both correct and incorrect in their assessment. Mr. Darcy was indeed staring, but out of wonder rather than disdain. Miss Elizabeth's quick wit had impressed him. Had she not fled his presence, he would have been sorely tempted to ask her to dance, if only to show her that he was not so afraid of dancing, if it might induce her to dislike him less.

Miss Bingley, however, was all too ready to lambast their present company.

"It is insupportable, spending so many evenings in this manner, among these country folk. How I long for the rich society that only London can provide! Meryton offers nothing in the way of cultural diversions. A night at the opera would set me up, or perhaps a visit to a concert. Such insipidity– such self importance among these people! I am sure you agree with me, Mr. Darcy, there is nothing here worth admiring."

"On the contrary, Miss Bingley, I have been meditating on the great pleasure that a pair of fine eyes on a pretty face can bestow."

Taking his compliment towards herself, Miss Bingley fluttered her lashes, her composure momentarily startled. "A-and what woman's eyes, pray tell, have you so utterly captivated?"

"Miss Elizabeth Bennet," he replied without blinking.

"Miss Elizabeth Bennet!" Miss Bingley repeated with incredulity, a frown forming on her lips before she corrected it. "The insolent chit you did not deign to dance with at Saturday's assembly? You told me how she behaved that evening. What a laugh, that you should fancy her, of all people!"

"I did not say I fancied her, merely that I find her eyes to be beautiful. She is, by all accounts, as you say, insolent."

Miss Bingley tittered. "And here I was, prepared to ask you when I was to wish you joy!" she teased. "I am glad to see you haven't been taken in by her 'fine eyes.' One may admire as much as they wish, but to allow it to go further would put a stain on your reputation and standing."

"You are correct, Miss Bingley," Darcy said, recalling the conversation he'd witnessed earlier. The Bennet family may have the necessary qualifications as members of the gentry, but Mrs. Bennet's vulgarity spoiled any chance they had of deserving his society. His parents certainly never would have countenanced such people; therefore, he would do well to follow in their example and dissociate himself with anyone undeserving of belonging to the circle of a gentleman's society.

"I only wish I could persuade Charles to avoid these people," Miss Bingley lamented. "He claims he likes them, declaring them to be good people, but it is clear he is besotted with Miss Bennet. He insists on staying through the shooting season, but I hope once he has killed as many birds as he likes, we may persuade him to return to Town."

Darcy, who was beginning to feel his own heart to be in as much danger as his friend's, "I agree with you, Miss Bingley. A few weeks is already too long a stay for such a place as this. The sooner we remove from here, the better."

Chapter 5

Despite his assurances to Miss Bingley that he did not fancy Miss Elizabeth, there was more than merely her 'fine eyes' which captivated Darcy's thoughts. He began to wonder if her insolence was not, perhaps, deserved. He *had* behaved rudely to her at the ball, after all. What was it she had remarked about his shyness? That it was a mask, to disguise his disdain for those whom he deemed unworthy? Perhaps so. But he was justified–when one considered the society around him!

In town, he regularly mingled with the nobility; his uncle was an earl, and his fortune allowed him to move freely among the *ton*. He could have his choice from any number of ladies who were daughters of viscounts, earls, and marquesses. Even a younger daughter of a duke might not seem too far out of reach!

But truth be told, none of those ladies could hold his interest. They were all bland, insipid, each one a reproduction of the last. Even their names were sometimes too similar! At the last ball he attended in Grosvenor, he insulted one lady by forgetting her name, calling her Miss Cottrell, when in fact her name was Miss Cockrell. Both ladies were almost indistinguishable– thin, blonde, delicate-featured, with high wispy voices and cloying manners, like a dozen or so women he'd met before them.

He could readily comprehend why Bingley liked Miss Bennet; she blended in perfectly with this stereotype, with precious little to distinguish her from Bingley's last "angel".

But Miss Elizabeth was different. Her lively temper would not be tolerated amongst the gatherings of the *ton*, her playful spirit too gauche to fit in, and her appearance too different from other girls. Where their eyes were languid and dull, hers sparkled with light and determination, her spirit full of wit and mirth. No one, not even his sister, had dared to make sport of him at a gathering, or to call him out so bluntly for his disdain.

Her family were unsuitable, to be sure, but might Miss Elizabeth be different from them? Were her motives as mercenary as her mother's and sister's appeared to be? His curiosity demanded that he learn.

Darcy seized his opportunity the next time he saw her at a gathering at Lucas Lodge the following week. Seeing her engaged in a lively conversation with Miss Lucas he decided to listen to their exchange. They were discussing the recent marriage of a local heiress, Miss King, to a member of the militia who were quartered in Meryton.

"I do think her fortune must have some bearing on their union, for it was not more than a month after Miss King inherited her uncle's fortune that Captain Carter proposed to her," Miss Lucas asserted.

"Perhaps coming into her inheritance merely enabled them to wed sooner," Miss Elizabeth argued. "For as I recall, the captain did dance with her at the Midsummer Ball prior to her uncle's demise, and he called on her from time to time. Miss King is a lovely, well-mannered girl, and we can readily suppose his prior attraction to her."

"His attraction to her must surely have increased when he learned she had come into ten-thousand pounds!" Miss Lucas quipped.

"You speak only of the advantages to Captain Carter. We must remember, too, that Miss King has inherited an estate in Shropshire. With no brothers to assist her in managing it, she must have wished for a companion to assist her. What more logical reason to marry the man she admires, than when it is most convenient?"

"Oh, I agree, it is most convenient," Miss Lucas replied, her eyes teasing. "And as it is the sort of match that everyone in society expected her to make– him with a brilliant smile, and her with a brilliant fortune– I will allow it to be a most splendid match, even if perhaps more favorable on his side than hers." Seeing Mr. Darcy hovering nearby, she took a step outward to admit him to their group.

He bowed deeply. "Good evening, ladies. I could not help but overhear your conversation. The topic seems most intriguing."

"Mr. Darcy," Miss Elizabeth acknowledged, "we were discussing the complexities of marriage and societal expectations. What are your thoughts on the matter?"

"My view is that marriage should be built on genuine connection and shared values rather than financial calculations," he said. Elizabeth's response to his sentiments might inform him of whether she shared her mother's transactional views of marriage. Having heard her remarks about Miss King, he hoped her views aligned more with his own.

She smiled. "Ah, so you are a proponent of true compatibility over material gains. How refreshing, Mr. Darcy! Tell me, what do you think of Miss King's match?"

"As I am unacquainted with the gentleman or lady in question, I cannot say whether their union was formed out of love or desire for financial stability," he answered.

"Miss Lucas seems convinced it is the latter."

Miss Lucas defended herself. "I merely observed the suddenness with which Captain Carter secured her to himself, following her inheritance, where before, their attachment seemed only a vague inclination."

Catching Miss Elizabeth's eye, he could not help but tease. "He must have abstained from writing her any poetry then, for surely doing so would have killed any affection she might have harbored for him."

Miss Lucas, who had not borne witness to their previous conversation, sensed some private jest must be at play. Finding herself superfluous to the conversation, she made her excuses, leaving Darcy alone with Miss Elizabeth in the corner of the room.

Miss Elizabeth's eyes twinkled. "I cannot say whether he wrote her any poetry, but you must have heard me mention that they danced together, and as we have already established, dancing is a sure way to win a girl's heart."

"The first step towards falling in love, as I recall you saying."

"Indeed!"

Feeling in the mood to provoke her, he said, "Then a gentleman needs only to dance with a young lady, and he can be sure of her accepting his suit. Is that how it stands?"

"Not entirely. For as I mentioned, it is only the first step. The gentleman must prove himself in other regards too."

"Such as?"

"His character. He must prove himself to be kind, generous, not above his company, and considerate of the feelings of others."

"And supposing all this, then allowances may be made for any disparity of fortune between them."

"Well, yes!" She said, slightly taken aback. "After all, there are few matches of equal fortune which take place. More often than not, one party possesses the greater share. But you seem to be concerned over this."

Feeling he had made a small headway with her, he allowed a hint of arrogance to creep into his tone. "Yes. All too often, the singular goal of marriage is to elevate one's own status or increase one's fortune. It is disheartening to witness such instances where individuals prioritize wealth and social standing over matters of the heart, as if love had no place in the equation."

His sentiments brought to mind Miss Bennet, who was at that moment hanging on every word of Mr. Bingley's in another part of the room, and on Mrs. Bennet, who, during dinner, had spoken altogether too loudly on the subject of her hopes and expectations for Jane.

"If only love were the sole deciding factor in a match!" Miss Elizabeth exclaimed. "It does seem as though too much weight is given to the size of one's dowry or estate. But then, there are not many who can afford to marry without *some* attention to wealth, I suppose," she said reluctantly. "My sisters and I, for example, have only a thousand pounds apiece. Our future depends on our marrying someone of means. As my mother loves to remind me, even our house will belong to my cousin as soon as my father is dead."

Her remark did nothing to assuage his fears that she, like so many others before her, was solely interested in making a financially prudent match.

Darcy, maintaining his air of superiority, remarked, "Miss Elizabeth, your perspective is admirable. However, the wealthy are often preyed upon by those without. I am of the opinion that marrying within one's social sphere is the safest way to ensure genuine intentions and eliminate the need for such material considerations. Where too great a disparity exists between two individuals, how can they hope for a happy marriage?" He hoped to spur her into revealing her true thoughts.

His words seemed to perturb her. She rapped her fan against her knuckles mindlessly. "Mr. Darcy, true love knows no bounds. I believe that love can transcend all social and financial barriers. Why should a rich man scorn to marry a poor woman, if they should both love each other? Or a rich woman decline an offer from a poor man, if her fortune can sustain them both?"

"Ah, but you see, such cases can only succeed where true love abides. If the marriage is founded solely on the material or societal gains to be had, then when the initial attraction fades, all that remains is the gulf that divides them. Nine times out of ten, it is better to restrict one's search for a partner to such suitable candidates as can be found in their social circle who share a similar background and are on equal footing financially."

"I concede your point as it relates to true love as a marker of success in marriage, Mr. Darcy, but to restrict oneself to such a small circle eliminates the possibility of finding love outside one's own class," she scoffed.

Darcy, a touch of irritation evident in his expression, conceded, "We may not see eye-to-eye on this matter, Miss Elizabeth. I am merely advocating for a pragmatic approach to safeguard against those who might exploit one's vulnerability."

Whether that vulnerability extended more to Bingley or to himself, he could not say. His heart was already on the verge of being lost to this entrancing young lady before him.

Miss Elizabeth, with a firm resolve, concluded, "Pragmatism, Mr. Darcy, should not eclipse the capacity for love. I believe in the power of genuine affection to bridge any divide. Our views on marriage may remain at odds, but I shall continue to champion the resilience of love."

"A worthy opinion, and one I shall not argue against," Darcy conceded. In his mind, he had successfully engaged with Miss Elizabeth in a debate and, despite their divergent views, had proved that they were more alike than not in their views about marriage and the importance of love. He felt confident that Elizabeth, unlike her family, would not sacrifice her own happiness for the sake of material gain, and in his heart, began planning for the next opportunity when they might meet. Writing her poetry was out of the question, but dancing, yes, perhaps he could summon the courage to ask her to dance.

As usually followed in these gatherings, the younger Bennet daughters clamored for music and dancing. This time Charlotte Lucas obliged them with a reel. Maria Lucas had the satisfaction of dancing with William Goulding, while her brothers danced with her friends.

Hearing the music playing, Darcy held out his hand to Miss Elizabeth with a slight bow. "I wondered, perhaps if you might join me for a reel? I recall your fondness for dancing."

"And I recall your disdain for it!" She exclaimed with a laugh. "I have no compunctions about dancing, in general, but at present, I can see that the room is too small to admit another couple. Do not think me ungrateful, therefore, when I spare you the discomfort of standing up with me in such tight quarters. Besides, I know perfectly well that a half hour's conversation with me would cause you to tire of my company and tax your good graces, and nobody would wish to bear witness to that." Giving him a slight curtsy, she skipped off to the piano to help turn the pages for her friend, and soon succeeded her at the instrument with a lighthearted country dance.

Chapter 6

Elizabeth, oblivious to Mr. Darcy's growing feelings for her, felt that his elitist views on marriage only furthered her dislike of him. *How pretentious of him, to claim that happiness in marriage could only exist between two equal parties!*

She repeated her conversation to her friend the next day when Charlotte called again at Longbourn, expressing her strong dislike for Mr. Darcy. "He is the most arrogant man I've ever had the displeasure of meeting. You were a beast to leave me with him, Charlotte!"

"I give you leave to dislike him, Eliza," Charlotte said. "But perhaps you misunderstand his motives in debating you."

"What motive could he have had, except to communicate that he does not think my family and I are of the same class as him? It is clear he does not think us suitable for his friend Mr. Bingley. His remarks on disparity of fortune can only be referring to the gulf between his friend's fortune and ours. But no matter; I do not think we shall ever get on well."

"But will you not be forced into his company frequently if your sister marries Mr. Bingley? They are great friends, after all."

"That is true enough, I suppose," Elizabeth conceded. "But I could endure it for her sake. It would be my dearest wish to see her happily married to him in due course."

"Yes, I am sure that is your mother's dearest wish also," Charlotte replied, her eyebrows raised in amusement.

"Indeed! But there would be no one more deserving of him than Jane. Such a good creature she is! I believe her to be much in love with him already."

"Is she?" Charlotte asked. "Only I have not seen it. There is a coolness in her interactions with him that belies the warmth of affection you describe."

"That is because Jane is modest. She does not wish to make a fool of herself in public like my sisters do. She is slow and cautious to reveal her innermost feelings."

Charlotte, however, remained unconvinced. "That he admires *her* is certain, but whether he can discern her feelings for him is another matter altogether. A man may feel many things but might not act on them without the proper encouragement. Jane ought to do all she can to promote herself and to make her feelings known to him. Once she is secure of him, there will be time enough to fall in love whenever she chooses."

"If nothing was in question but the desire of being well married, then your plan would be a good one. But I am sure Jane does not wish to rush into marriage after such a short acquaintance. They have only seen each other four times."

"Yes, four times is not long," Charlotte said. "But remember that they have not only been in each other's company four times but also dined together two evenings, and two evenings may do a great deal. Proposals have been made and accepted on a shorter acquaintance, you know!"

Elizabeth laughed heartily over this statement. "Two evenings may tell them whether they prefer *Vingt-un* over Commerce, but I am sure Jane would wish to know more about the man than his card preferences, before accepting an offer of marriage!"

"Would she? In my opinion, it is better to know as little as possible about the deficiencies of one's partner prior to marriage."

"Nonsense, Charlotte! What foolishness! You know that you would never act this way. You are too sensible."

"On the contrary, it is my being sensible that makes it all the more likely that I would accept a marriage of convenience. Happiness in marriage is entirely a matter of chance. If a man of Mr. Bingley's station, with four or five thousand a year, were to offer for me on a whim, I would accept him without a second thought."

"What if he were known to be a rake, or a drunkard? Suppose he is abusive?"

"If I were aware of such significant defects before marriage, then certainly, I would decline, but I am convinced that a twelvemonth of courtship could pass without a person learning the real character of the other, and such propensities are not likely to arise during the courtship period, now are they? Besides, there are plenty of people who have married after a brief courtship into a marriage of convenience, and are perfectly content with it. Consider your sister Mary, for example."

Elizabeth fell silent. Her views on Mary's marriage were known, yet none could dispute that Mary appeared content with her choice.

Mrs. Bennet entered, apologizing profusely that there was nothing to be had for tea, "For somebody has eaten up all the cakes and muffins in the larder," she complained, "and I do not know who it was, but my suspicions lie with little Timmy."

She hurried off to tell Mrs. Hill to quickly bake up a batch of biscuits.

Charlotte turned to Elizabeth with a smile.

"It was she who ate the sweets, was it not?"

SUDDEN AWAKENINGS

"I am afraid it is likely so," Elizabeth said. "Whenever things go missing in the larder, nine times out of ten, it is Mamma's fault. But she will never admit it was her!"

"No, how could she? It might make her subconscious appear to be a glutton. Far easier to blame the hall boy!"

Elizabeth joined Charlotte's laughter. Her own troubles with sleepwalking were far more concerning to her.

Two nights prior, she had arisen during the night and in her sleep attempted to light a candle from the dying embers of the fireplace. Were it not for Kitty, who grabbed her by the shoulders and shook her awake, the whole house might have caught on fire. Elizabeth worried that her sleepwalking episodes were growing more frequent and her activity more dangerous. Who knew what else she might do whilst in such a state?

⁂

Mrs. Bennet shared Charlotte's concerns about Jane's subdued demeanor, and took a quiet moment to address it with her daughter one afternoon, while the others were occupied with other pursuits.

"Jane, my dear," she said with maternal concern, "I sometimes fear your modesty might obscure your feelings from Mr. Bingley. If he cannot perceive your regard for him, how will he know to act? You must be a bit more forthright, my dear, so that he might understand and return your affections."

Jane said, "I have observed the way my younger sisters carry on when they are in company, and their flirtations have earned them scorn from our neighbors. I have also deduced that Mr. Bingley is not the sort of man who likes a coquette, but prefers a shy, demure woman; therefore that is the role I am playing. If I appear too eager, then that gentleman will be put off by my behavior. Instead, by making myself difficult to obtain, I increase his love by this manner of suspense."

"Ah, my dear, you are wiser than I thought!" Mrs. Bennet said, thoroughly pleased. "Still, you must be careful to temper it, lest you appear too distant, and he concludes you do not like him. Show a *little* more affection. A word here, a wink there, a toss of your hair– so he may feel confident that you do, indeed, wish for him to pursue you."

"Yes, Mamma," Jane answered obediently.

"Having heard your proposition, I am concocting a plan that may assist you in all of this," Mrs. Bennet said, the wheels of her mind turning as she spoke.

Only that morning, Jane had received an invitation to dine at Netherfield Park with Caroline Bingley and Mrs. Hurst. The gentlemen were to dine out with the officers and would not be there. But this did not dissuade Mrs. Bennet in the slightest, and she readily communicated her plan to Jane.

The skies that day were gray, foreboding. Rain was surely imminent. But still, the horses were needed on the farm and could not be spared to draw the carriage. Such exactly suited Mrs. Bennet's purpose. She sent Jane off towards Netherfield, riding atop Nellie, a mare too old and weak to be used on the farm anymore and kept solely to convey any of the Bennet daughters wherever they wished. By the time Jane arrived at Netherfield Park, the skies had already opened, and the clouds began to drizzle. Mrs. Bennet clapped her hands when she saw the rain.

"Now she will have to stay the night," she exclaimed with glee.

The following morning, a note arrived from Netherfield informing them Jane had contracted a cold and been sent to bed. The apothecary had seen her and pronounced that she could not possibly be moved until she had recovered, and her kind friends would not hear of her leaving, either.

"This is what comes of sending your daughter on horseback," Mr. Bennet chided Mrs. Bennet when he heard the news.

"On the contrary, this is providential," Mrs. Bennet replied. "For now she must stay until she is recovered, and Mr. Bingley will surely fall in love with her!"

"Well, Mamma," said Elizabeth with spirit, "if Jane should die, I suppose it will be a comfort to know it was in pursuit of Mr. Bingley."

"People do not die of trifling little colds," Mrs. Bennet scoffed, "All will be well."

But Elizabeth's concern for her sister made her determined to see her for herself. As the carriage was still unavailable to her, she set off on foot, taking a shortcut through the muddy fields rather than keeping to the lane, until she reached Netherfield Park. The rain had slowed to a gentle mist, but by keeping in motion, Elizabeth remained warm enough not to feel cold by it.

The residents of Netherfield were alarmed upon seeing Miss Elizabeth and inquired why she came by foot in such weather. She explained the situation and asked to see her sister at once. Caroline Bingley obliged and ordered a servant to take her upstairs directly.

Miss Elizabeth had barely left the room, when Miss Bingley turned to her sister and exclaimed, "How wild Miss Elizabeth looked this morning. Did you see her hair? So windswept, one might almost think she had worn no bonnet!"

Mrs. Hurst nodded. "I quite agree with you. She looked positively medieval. Her hem was nigh on six inches deep in mud. Did she pass through a pigsty on her way here?"

"*Your* sister would certainly never make such an exhibition, Mr. Darcy," Caroline said.

"Certainly not," Mr. Darcy agreed. But then, his sister had always been a timid girl who did as she was told, unlike Miss Elizabeth, who reminded him at times of an unbroken mare.

"I have never before seen such a creature as Elizabeth Bennet. Imagine coming three miles on foot in this weather!" Caroline added.

Their comments were intended to dissuade Mr. Darcy, but in fact, they did the opposite. Elizabeth's unkempt appearance touched his heart and reminded him of their first meeting on the lane. Those dark, lustrous eyes, which he first noticed at the assembly, seemed all the more brightened by the exercise, and her flushed cheeks looked thoroughly becoming.

Her loving concern for her sister, too, aroused his sentiments; her urgency in coming directly without a care for her appearance was the mark of a woman who would do anything for those she loved.

Elizabeth was not out of earshot when Miss Bingley and Mrs. Hurst began their criticism of her. Hearing their remarks only confirmed her suspicion of their low opinions of her. Mr. Darcy must concur, she supposed, for him to countenance such gossip behind her back. Well, no matter, she need not care what *he* might think of her! Her only concern was for Jane.

She found Jane reclining on the bed in an upstairs room.

"How are you, my dear?" Elizabeth asked as she entered the room.

"Oh, Lizzy, I feel simply terrible! I have had a headache since last night, and a fever too; though it is gone for the present." A series of coughs prevented Jane from saying more.

"Goodness! You *are* ill! But, as you are in no great danger of dying, let us ask our hosts if they might lend us their carriage to convey you home. You will rest better in your own bed."

Jane's eyes widened. "No! I mean, Mr. Jones insisted I am not to be moved. He feared I would be in danger of growing worse in this cold weather, if I were to move."

"Much as I respect our good apothecary's opinion, there are times when I feel his judgment is lacking. At home you shall have Mamma and your sisters to care for you. I do not think Miss Bingley and Mrs. Hurst shall be so attentive."

"Then you must stay with me, Lizzy, for I fear I cannot return home yet. I am far too ill." A sneeze came, followed by another string of coughs, causing Elizabeth to wonder if perhaps she had underestimated the extent of her sister's illness.

Elizabeth called for Miss Bingley and Mrs. Hurst to come.

"It pains me to impose on your good graces, but I am afraid my sister is unable to return home with me as I had hoped," she said.

"We wouldn't think of her returning home until she has recovered!" Mrs. Hurst replied graciously.

"I know it is much to ask, but I wondered if I might further impose on you to allow me to remain with Jane while she recovers. I am convinced she would benefit from my care."

"Certainly!" Miss Bingley said, though there was a hint of vexation in her voice. "You must not think of leaving."

Elizabeth said, "I hope you are not too put out by my presence."

"Not at all." Miss Bingley forced a smile. "Shall I send someone to Longbourn to inform your family and request your belongings?"

"Yes, thank you, that would be most helpful," Elizabeth answered.

Elizabeth recalled her recent sleepwalking episode and the danger she could have posed to herself and her family. She dreaded the notion that a similar incident could occur while she was a guest at Netherfield. But concern for her sister outweighed her fears to the extent that, at last, Elizabeth resigned herself to the idea of staying there. She trusted she would be able to lock her door at night and hopefully prevent herself from any dangerous or embarrassing episodes during her stay.

Chapter 7

Elizabeth spent the chief part of the day in Jane's room, sometimes accompanied by one of Mr. Bingley's sisters.

When Jane had fallen asleep, Elizabeth returned downstairs to find a book to read. She had begun reading Samuel Richardson's *Pamela* while at home, and was pleased to find a copy in Netherfield's library so she could continue where she left off.

Mr. Darcy was employed in writing a letter. The others were engaged in a card game.

"We would ask you to join us, but unfortunately, our game will not admit a fifth," Mrs. Hurst said, without glancing up from her cards.

"No matter." Elizabeth smiled, settling onto the sofa nearby. "I am content with the book I have chosen."

"Do you prefer reading to cards, then? How singular!" Miss Bingley remarked, a laugh escaping her lips.

Elizabeth saw Mr. Darcy steal a glance at her from his writing desk. She tried to focus her attention on the tale of poor Pamela's mistreatment at the hands of her employer, but Miss Bingley would not allow her a moment's peace.

"How much sooner one tires of anything than of a book!" she exclaimed. "When I have a home of my own, it must have an excellent library. Do you read often, when you are at home, Miss Elizabeth? Do you have a good library at Longbourn?"

"Yes, my father has a decent library. My sisters and I enjoy free access to any of the books we wish, and we supplement with regular visits to the circulating library in Meryton." Elizabeth barely looked back to her book before Caroline continued.

"I was never fond of circular libraries, myself. I find them too common." Turning her head towards Mr. Darcy, she said, "You have a spectacular library at Pemberley, do you not, Mr. Darcy?"

"I do," he said curtly, not raising his eyes from his letter.

"It is perhaps one of the largest and finest libraries in the country, is it not?" Caroline pressed, oblivious to her target's desire to be left alone.

"I would not go so far as to say that," said he, "but it is substantial. It has been the work of many generations."

"With such a blessing as that, I hope you take full advantage of it," Elizabeth remarked to him.

"I do, as often as my business allows. I confess, I am not at Pemberley as often as I would wish to be."

Caroline droned on. "There is no finer house in the country than Pemberley! How at home I feel there! When we visited last summer, I could quite picture myself living in such a place. Charles," she said, turning her head to her brother, "when you purchase a home, I hope you will take Pemberley for a model."

"I would purchase Pemberley itself, if I could!" Bingley laughed.

Caroline clicked her tongue. "I am speaking of possibilities! We all know Mr. Darcy would never sell."

"No, I would not," he asserted.

With such conversation happening in the room, Elizabeth soon gave up on her book and went to the pianoforte by the window. She began leafing through the selection of music on the stand, looking for something familiar.

"Oh, do you play, Miss Elizabeth?" Caroline asked.

"A little, though very poorly."

"Well, you must take advantage of this fine instrument to practice, while you are here. Do you have an instrument at home, then?"

"We do, but I seldom find the time to play on it. When my sister Mary lived at home, it was she who practiced regularly."

"Do play something for us, Miss Elizabeth," Mr. Bingley encouraged. "Some music would do us good to cheer us up. It is too dull around here, with the rain and mud keeping us from our hunt."

"Very well, then, if it pleases you, though I do not profess any great talent. You might well regret having asked me to play by the time I am done!" Elizabeth smiled.

She chose a Scottish air, one with a simple melody, and sang along with her playing. Her music stirred Mr. Darcy from his seat, who drew nearer to the piano so that he might listen more fully.

"That was lovely, Miss Elizabeth," he commended when she finished. "A most enchanting performance."

"Thank you," she said, suddenly feeling bashful.

"High praise, from one such as you, Mr. Darcy!" Miss Bingley remarked. "You would know good music when you hear it, living with a virtuoso!" Turning to Elizabeth, she said, "Miss Darcy is the most accomplished young musician I have ever heard. She plays the piano–and the harp–with far more superiority than other young ladies her age. She is quite devoted to her studies, is that not so, Mr. Darcy?"

He allowed that his sister was considered by many to be an exceptional talent, and she possessed an abiding passion for her music.

"Goodness, I had no idea I was to be judged by such a high standard!" Elizabeth exclaimed. "But you need not conflate my worth to make me feel better in the face of such competition; I know I do not practice with such diligence as your sister must."

"Your technical performance does not equal hers, it is true," Mr. Darcy admitted, "But there was nothing wanting in your voice.

You sang with an unaffectedness that was altogether quite pleasing to listen to."

His words warmed Elizabeth's heart.

Miss Bingley then insisted on showcasing her own talents next, and chose a demanding Italian piece. While her technical capacity far exceeded Elizabeth's, Miss Bingley's screeching voice was by no means pleasant to listen to, and though she received as much praise and commendation from the others as Elizabeth had, Mr. Darcy's remarks were not so warm and sincere, though he proclaimed it to be a "difficult piece" that "required much accomplishment."

***

Darcy would not admit it to anyone, but he was falling in love with Elizabeth Bennet faster than he ever believed possible. Her impertinence, which he had scorned the night of the assembly, was now the distinguishing feature which set her apart and made him admire her. When coupled with her tenderness of heart and her lively spirit, he found himself utterly captivated by her. *Her appearance is not wanting, either*, he thought to himself, recalling the way her eyes sparkled during their animated discussion during dinner.

If only he could reconcile himself to the inferiority of her family, and their greedy, grasping ways, he might bring himself to consider her as a marital prospect.

***

After dinner, the sisters and Elizabeth visited Jane again. She was awake now, but still appeared as ill and miserable as before. Her nose was red from blowing it, and her cough persisted.

"You poor dear!" Miss Bingley cooed. "I have asked Mrs. Nicholls to send up her special chicken soup, which she claims is guaranteed to improve your symptoms."

"Would you like me to read to you for a while?" Elizabeth offered.

Jane coughed before answering. "If it is not too much trouble, I would like it if Mr. Bingley were to read to me. I find his deep voice soothing, and he possesses a talent for voices." He had read aloud from *The Coquette* the first evening Jane arrived, before she fell ill.

Elizabeth found it strange that Jane would prefer Mr. Bingley's voice over hers; ordinarily, it was she who read aloud with great spirit and performed all the voices of the characters. Suspecting Jane's request came from her attachment to him, she conceded, though Bingley's sisters looked displeased by it.

Miss Bingley balked at the unusual request, claiming she was unsure it was entirely proper, but Elizabeth assured her she would remain in the room and suggested that the sisters could do the same.

Only Elizabeth remained to chaperone, however; Mrs. Hurst had no interest in listening to a book, while Miss Bingley saw her chance to monopolize Mr. Darcy's attention in the drawing room without Miss Elizabeth's fine eyes to distract him.

While Mr. Bingley continued reading *The Coquette* to Jane, Elizabeth was finally able to complete the rest of *Pamela*.

Pamela's story was both sad and intriguing. Pamela found herself in the uncomfortable position of serving her new master, her late lady's son, who repeatedly made untoward advances towards her. Her persistent virtue in refusing him drove him to resort to trickery and deceit. It was a riveting tale, but Elizabeth felt angry at the injustice of Pamela's plight as her many efforts to escape her wicked master failed. In a strange turn of events, once Pamela was finally free of her master's grip, she realized she was in love with him and returned to marry him.

Such a thing ought never to happen in real life! I cannot fathom that Pamela should fall in love with the very man she hated.

At least Pamela's sorrows ended in joy, however. In the story that Bingley read to Jane, the heroine Eliza sought happiness with the man that she loved, but came to grief when he betrayed her by marrying another. Her tale ended in disgrace and death, both for her and the child she bore out of wedlock.

Why must women's happiness be tied to the men in their lives and how they are treated by them? She mused. She hoped neither she nor any of her sisters would be so misused.

With the approach of night, Elizabeth's fears about her sleepwalking arose once more. Her mind returned again to the near-accident with the fireplace, and she regretted being a guest. She wished she could share a room with her sister, as she did at home. But with Jane being ill, she could not do so, nor did she wish to explain to her hosts her reasons for not sleeping in a room of her own.

Why did I consent to stay the night in a strange house? She wondered. *Anything might happen here.*

Despite her worries, the night passed without incident.

After checking on Jane, Elizabeth went downstairs to the breakfast parlor.

"Good morning, Miss Elizabeth, I trust you slept well," Miss Bingley greeted her, absently buttering her toast.

"Thank you, I did," Elizabeth replied, taking the empty seat beside Mr. Bingley as Mrs. Hurst vacated it. Mr. Hurst remained, eagerly stuffing his face on pastries and jam. Mr. Darcy must not be down yet, or perhaps he had already breakfasted and left, Elizabeth concluded.

"Has Miss Bennet improved?" Mr. Bingley eagerly asked.

"She seemed so, when I visited her," Elizabeth answered. She picked up a scone from the tray in the center of the table and began spreading cream and jam on it.

"What a relief, for I do not think she slept well last night," Miss Bingley said.

"What do you mean?" Elizabeth asked.

"I was awakened by her stirring last night, and she complained of insomnia. I assisted her by summoning a servant to procure a warm glass of milk."

"She did not mention any sleeplessness to me. I am grateful to you for assisting her."

Mr. Bingley requested more details about Jane's health. Elizabeth maintained that Jane looked well compared to the previous day, but that they must wait for the apothecary's opinion before making any conclusions.

Shortly after breakfast, Mr. Jones returned to check on his patient. Elizabeth thought Jane seemed improved before, but now, Jane displayed a fit of coughing every few minutes.

"I am afraid I still cannot advise her being moved," the apothecary told them. "She is in no danger while she lies here, but if she were to go out of doors, the chill in the air…" He shuddered, the posture of a man who had seen too many premature deaths due to preventable measures.

"Yes, I quite understand you." Elizabeth nodded.

"How many days longer do you estimate she will require?" Miss Bingley asked. Her voice was sweet and concerned, but the look on her face told Elizabeth she was eager to be rid of her houseguests.

"Not that we are in any hurry to have her leave!" Mrs. Hurst added, in an attempt to temper her sister's rudeness.

"I cannot say with any certainty," Mr. Jones replied. "If her cough improves, perhaps she may be well enough tomorrow; if it does not, then it may be days, perhaps even until the week's end, before she can safely depart without fear for her lungs."

Mr. Bingley did not seem at all displeased by the news when they told him. "Miss Bennet must stay as long as necessary! I would not risk her contracting consumption for the world! My only regret is that she is so unwell that we cannot enjoy more of her company while she is here."

"I do hate that my presence here is troublesome," Jane murmured.

"Nonsense!" Bingley said, gazing down at her adoringly. "It is no trouble at all."

"I do not wish to pass my illness to anyone, but I confess, I grow tired of this bed and these four walls. Would it be a great inconvenience if I were to join you all in the drawing room for a time?" she asked. "I would, of course, sit apart from you, so as not to spread my disease."

Bingley's face brightened. "It would be no inconvenience to us, I am sure. But are you certain you are well enough?"

Jane's cough, which had been so violent while the apothecary was present, had seemingly vanished for the moment. She had not coughed once in the five minutes since Mr. Bingley entered the room.

"Your presence fortifies me, Mr. Bingley. I feel I shall recover much quicker if I am among friends."

"Then let me carry you to the drawing room," he offered.

Jane protested that she could walk, but upon attempting to rise from the bed, her strength appeared to fail her, and Mr. Bingley caught her before she could fall.

"I'll brook no more stubbornness from you, Miss Bennet," Mr. Bingley chided her playfully. "Put your arm across my shoulders, if you please."

Jane obeyed, and he swiftly lifted her into his arms, causing a slight giggle from her.

"If Miss Bennet is so weak, perhaps she ought to remain in bed," Miss Bingley suggested, but to no avail. Elizabeth and Bingley's sisters followed him as he carried Jane down the staircase and deposited her into a large armchair.

"Thank you, Mr. Bingley," Jane said.

Mr. Bingley bowed. "I am your humble servant. Now tell me what else you require, and I shall fetch it at once."

"A blanket, perhaps, and a glass of water."

Bingley ordered the water and brought over an elegant quilted throw blanket with crocheted lace, presumably designed by one of his sisters, and draped it over her lap.

"There now. What else? Some entertainment, perhaps?"

"I am satisfied for now."

"Are you certain? I could read you a bit of poetry, or tell some jokes. Or perhaps one of my sisters could be imposed upon to play us some music. You wouldn't mind, would you, Caroline, to play us something?"

"I would be glad to," Miss Bingley said, her eyes glancing towards Mr. Darcy, as he entered the room.

"Yes, I would love to hear you, Miss Bingley. Elizabeth spoke of your playing yesterday, and I was sorry to have missed it," Jane said.

"And afterwards, we shall continue our reading of *The Coquette*," Bingley proclaimed. "Should you like that?"

"Very much!" Jane exclaimed, a smile of contentment on her lips.

Elizabeth observed her sister's condition over the course of the day. She certainly seemed well, despite her earlier fits. It was only whenever someone mentioned her illness that she began coughing or blowing her nose again. Yet it was not in Jane's nature to feign an illness.

Perhaps it is only my imagination that perceives such things, Elizabeth concluded. *I should like her to be well enough that we can return home.*

Elizabeth did not wish to remain at Netherfield a minute longer than necessary.

Mr. Darcy's presence irritated her, even more than Miss Bingley and Mrs. Hurst's idle gossip and disingenuous fawning over Jane. He seemed to look for opportunities to provoke her. That morning, they had argued over whether parliamentary reform ought to include universal suffrage. Later, he had questioned her love of dramatic novels, contending that books on philosophy provided more insights into the human condition than did fictional anecdotes of wonder and woe. At dinner, he had aggravated her further by insisting that modern industrialization was more valuable than traditional craftsmanship.

Why does this man always seek to be on opposite sides of an argument with me? Does he always consider his own opinion to be superior to mine?

The warmth inspired by his praise of her musical performance was fleeting; since then, she had found nothing good in his attitude towards her that would alter her opinion of him. Everything about him spoke of a pride beyond reckoning, from his bearing, to the condescending tone of his manners.

The only thing she found agreeable was his appearance. *Would that he were a congenial, friendly man, like Mr. Bingley, that would be something! It is a pity that such a fine-looking man must be of such a disagreeable nature as to render his looks unable to compensate for it.*

Chapter 8

Having passed the first night at Netherfield Park without incident, Elizabeth's false sense of security rose, supposing she might avoid any embarrassing sleepwalking episodes while Jane recovered. However, the second night proved to be a different matter.

Sometime in the early hours of the morning, Elizabeth rose from her bed, lost in a dreamless trance. She stumbled towards her bedroom door, having forgotten to lock it after Miss Bingley's maid left from helping her change. As a result, she was unfettered from wandering into the hall.

Her footsteps carried her by habit down the path which, in her own home, would have led to Mary's former bedchamber, where she sometimes wandered, and where Jane occasionally slept when she was ill. Had Elizabeth climbed into bed with her sister, all would have been well. However, the layout of Netherfield was quite different from that of Longbourn. Jane's room here was located in the opposite direction. The door which Elizabeth unconsciously opened, therefore, belonged to none other than Mr. Darcy.

Darcy was dislodged from his slumber by the muffled clatter of objects toppling over. He sat up in the bed, still in half-asleep confusion. In the darkness, he could make out the shape of a person, rummaging around his papers and belongings left out on the writing desk in his room.

"Who's there?" he called, but there was no answer. The candle had long gone out and he could not find a tinderbox handy, but the curtains were opened wide enough that in the moonlight, he caught a glimpse of his intruder's face. *Elizabeth!*

He stifled a shout. What was she doing here, in his room? Before he could make sense of the situation, she climbed into his bed, noisily threw herself onto the pillow and pulled the covers up.

He whispered, "Miss Elizabeth, you must get up. You cannot be here." He fought against his every instinct to let her remain.

He knew if Elizabeth were to be found in his bedchamber, she would surely be compromised. She appeared to be in a deep slumber, completely unaware of her actions. He contemplated what he ought to do.

There was nothing for it. Though he knew it could be dangerous to rouse someone from a sleepwalking state, he also knew it would be far more dangerous for her to be caught here. He must wake her.

He began to shake her, repeating hoarsely, "Elizabeth, Miss Elizabeth." But still, she did not wake. Turning over in her sleep, she found his body and snuggled up next to him. Though he had the strength to push away by force, he was momentarily enthralled by the beautiful woman nestled against his chest, wondering if this was perhaps some hallucination brought on by too many late evening drinks with Bingley and Hurst. His senses came to him when he heard the rattle of the doorknob, precipitating its opening.

AMANDA KAI

The sound of a door creaking on its hinge followed by footsteps outside her bedroom caused Caroline Bingley's eyes to snap open. Roused fully from her sleep by this disturbance, she rose from her bed and poked her head into the hall. *If Jane Bennet is out wandering the corridor again, I shall have words with her!*

But it was Elizabeth whose silhouette she saw outlined by the dim light from the window at the end of the corridor. She softly crept after her, her eyes widening as she observed Elizabeth slip into Mr. Darcy's room.

That little hoyden! If she thinks she can sink her claws into Mr. Darcy through such arts, she is mistaken. I will expose her for what she is. She contemplated a minute to be certain what course of action she should take. Then she knocked on her brother's door and woke him.

"I've heard noises in the corridor that sounded like footsteps, outside my door," she told him. "I fear perhaps there is an intruder! When I looked into the corridor, I am certain I saw someone enter Mr. Darcy's room."

Mr. Bingley repeatedly pulled the bell for his butler to come. Flying down the hall, he burst into Darcy's bedroom. Caroline was quickly on his heels. The rest of the household heard the commotion and awoke and came into the corridor, with the butler and the hall boy, bearing lanterns, just behind the family.

They were shocked to see Elizabeth Bennet in bed beside Mr. Darcy.

Mr. Darcy pushed Elizabeth from him with such force that she woke up.

A screech erupted from her when she realized who was next to her in the bed. "Mr. Darcy, what are you doing in my bedchamber?" She scrambled away from him so hastily, she fell off the bed.

"Your chamber!" he exclaimed, sitting up. "Begging your pardon, madam, but this is *my* chamber."

"Elizabeth Bennet is nothing but a wanton strumpet!" Caroline exclaimed, charging forward. "How dare she accost Mr. Darcy during the nighttime. Charles, I insist you have her thrown out at once. Do not even send her in the carriage back to Longbourn." Surely now, Mr. Darcy would see how grasping Miss Elizabeth was and be thoroughly disgusted by her.

"I–I could never," Mr. Bingley stammered.

Jane pushed between the Bingley siblings and rushed to her sister's side. "It is Elizabeth who has been compromised here," she cried. "Mr. Darcy has attempted to take advantage of her."

Mr. Darcy tried his best to explain. "I can assure you this was not my fault, nor Miss Elizabeth's. I do not know how she came to be in this room, but I declare there was nothing planned between either of us. I believe she must have been sleepwalking."

Elizabeth nodded her head vigorously, tears coming forth from her eyes.

"Nonetheless," Jane went on, "my sister's honor has been compromised, and if you have any honor in you, Mr. Darcy, you will marry her. At once!" Her uncharacteristic anger caused looks of shock all around the room.

The servants, all of whom had been roused by this point, now gathered outside the doorway, each trying to gain a peek at what was going on. A sharp word from Mr. Bingley sent them scattering, but they had seen enough to surmise the situation.

"Come now, Miss Bennet," Mr. Bingley pleaded. "We must be reasonable here. We cannot expect Mr. Darcy to marry Miss Elizabeth over so small a matter. Surely this is all just a misunderstanding."

"Regardless," Jane said, "tongues will wag when word of this gets out. How are my sisters and I to marry, now that our family honor has been ruined?"

"I do feel for you, Miss Bennet," Miss Bingley said, in feigned compassion. "I have often found your sisters to be wanting in propriety. It is a pity such conduct will reflect badly on you, an upstanding young lady. But it cannot be helped. Mr. Darcy must not be made to marry Miss Elizabeth." Her plan to see Elizabeth Bennet thrown out in disgrace had produced the opposite effect.

"I will speak for myself," Mr. Darcy said sternly to Miss Bingley, causing her to clamp her mouth shut and back away from him. "It is true, what happened here tonight was an unfortunate misunderstanding. However, that does not change the fact that Miss Elizabeth's honor has been compromised." He turned to Elizabeth. "I will do the honorable thing, Miss Elizabeth, and marry you."

Caroline's face paled. She had underestimated Mr. Darcy's sense of honor. Her miscalculation might cost her any chance she had of securing him to herself.

Elizabeth quickly spoke up. "There will be no need, I am sure, Mr. Darcy. Once you speak to my father and explain the situation to him, I am certain he will not force you to marry me. He is not the sort to resort to violence. He will not challenge you to a duel for my honor," she hurried to reassure him.

"Perhaps not," said Mr. Darcy, "But I shall speak to him in the morning nonetheless."

"Now, if you please," he said, turning to the rest of them, "let us all get some sleep. We shall have more clarity about this matter in the morning."

"Oh, Jane," Elizabeth cried into Jane's shoulder. She had retreated to Jane's bedroom, not trusting herself to return to her own room and stay there. With Jane's help, they had barred the door with a chair, lest Elizabeth manage to turn the lock in her sleep.

"What is to become of me?" Elizabeth wailed. "I could not abide being married to Mr. Darcy. You know how I detest him."

"Hush, Lizzy," Jane cooed. "All will be well. There are far worse things in the world than marrying Mr. Darcy. After all, he is rich, well connected, has noble relations, and a large house, or so I am told."

She shook her head. "Jane, Jane. None of these things matter to me. I cannot marry if not for love. And Mr. Darcy is the last man in the world whom I would ever be prevailed upon to marry."

"I am sure it will all be sorted in the morning. Lizzy, you need not worry. Now, come, let us sleep."

"You appear to be much better, Jane," Elizabeth remarked. "Has your cold gone away now?"

Jane coughed. "Oh, perhaps a little," she said. "I suppose if need be, I might be able to remove to Longbourn in the morning."

Darcy did not sleep the remainder of the night. His mind was too troubled. Had his engagement to Elizabeth come under any other circumstances than these, he might have welcomed it, even despite his objections to her family.

However, he could plainly see that Elizabeth had no wish to be forced into a marriage with him. Indeed, after his treatment of her at the Meryton Assembly, he could not blame her for her dislike of him. And yet his honor demanded he must do what he could for her.

Had it only been one or two of the servants who had witnessed what took place, perhaps he could have trusted they could be bribed to keep silent. But since so many of Bingley's household had awoken, there was no telling who might say anything to whom.

News among servants traveled quickly. All it would take would be one servant's account of the tale to servant in a different household, and the tale would spread like wildfire throughout their community. And before anyone could say, "Jack Robinson," the entire Bennet family would be ruined. No, as much as he disliked them, Darcy could not see that happen. Not for Elizabeth's sake. She must be protected, he decided.

But Darcy found his resolution challenged. The next morning, over breakfast, Miss Bingley tried to persuade him to give up the notion.

"I know what an honorable man you are, Mr. Darcy, but you cannot let yourself be entrapped into a marriage against your wishes. I am certain Charles will be able to keep the servants from talking. And you know that Louisa and I will be the soul of discretion. Hurst, too. You need not fear for your reputation."

"It is not my reputation I am concerned about, I am afraid I cannot let the matter drop," Darcy told her. Society always made the woman out to be a pariah in such matters, as if women were solely responsible for seducing men. Men, on the other hand, were praised for their sexual prowess–provided their paramours were not nobles or gentlewomen. But Darcy held enough standing in society he was confident he could weather any scandal, whereas Elizabeth and her sisters would be utterly ruined and unable to marry, if he did not take responsibility for what happened.

<hr>

Elizabeth stood outside the breakfast room, her hand hovering on the doorknob, when she heard her own name spoken.

"What is Miss Elizabeth to you, that you should owe her so much?" Caroline Bingley's voice was raised. "I cannot fathom why you would allow yourself to be ensnared by such a conniving family! Surely you must see that Miss Elizabeth and her kin are nothing but fortune hunters who would stoop to any lengths to catch a wealthy husband."

Elizabeth's fists clenched in anger, her feet rooted on the spot. Tears welled in her eyes at the injustice of Miss Bingley's words.

She heard Mr. Darcy's voice in response. "Her family appears to be everything that you have represented, but I cannot say the same about Miss Elizabeth. I do not believe her actions last night to have been intentional."

Elizabeth appreciated his defense of her, but she felt equally wounded to hear him agree with Miss Bingley's opinion of her family.

Miss Bingley went on, unaware that Elizabeth was listening at the door. "Then you have been taken in by the charlatan, for this whole situation is certainly by her design, and I believe it was only my own vigilance that prevented Charles from suffering a similar fate."

Elizabeth could not believe the words she was overhearing. How dare Miss Bingley suggest that she or Jane would conceive of anything so sordid!

"You may not know this, but the night before last, I also heard someone stirring in the dead of night. I opened my door and found Miss Bennet in the corridor. When I queried her, she claimed that she was thirsty, and was in search of a glass of warm milk. I assisted her and returned her safely to her bed, but I was quite certain that her destination had not been the kitchens. I found her near the entrance to Charles' bedchambers."

"If what you say is true, then that is a serious business. But as of yet, you have no proof of anything," Mr. Darcy said.

"See how ill Miss Bennet appears to be, and let that form your judgment."

"Are you alleging that Miss Bennet feigned her illness in order to remain at Netherfield?" Mr. Darcy asked.

"I am," she said.

"Miss Bennet has already sufficiently recovered. Whether or not her illness was genuine, none can determine, save perhaps Mr. Jones, and his professional estimation I cannot vouch for, as I do not know the man. As for Miss Elizabeth, without any proof of your accusations, I will proceed as my honor demands me to."

"Mark my words, Mr. Darcy, you are making a mistake!"

Elizabeth could listen no further. She stepped away from the door and returned to her room where she could nurse her tears in private. She had no appetite for breakfast anyhow.

Chapter 9

It was a somber company that journeyed to Longbourn that morning. Mr. Darcy sat opposite Elizabeth in the carriage, with Jane beside her, Mr. Bingley joined them as a chaperone. Caroline would dearly have loved to come on this visit as well, to be able to repeat the gossip to her sister later, but her brother forbade her. As it was, the carriage was already full.

The residents of Longbourn were in an uproar when they were informed of what had transpired at Netherfield.

"Why, of course, you must marry her, Mr. Darcy," was Mrs. Bennet's indignant response upon hearing of the incident between Mr. Darcy and Elizabeth. "Her honor could not possibly be restored otherwise."

Elizabeth angrily rose from her seat to intervene. "I have no wish to–"

"Calm yourself, Elizabeth," said Mr. Bennet, entering the room. "Mr. Darcy, if you would kindly wait here in the small drawing room."

Mr. Darcy nodded in response.

"Elizabeth, come with me, if you please," Mr. Bennet said.

Elizabeth silently followed her father to his study. In a tearful voice, Elizabeth told him of her sleepwalking trouble and how she had mistakenly ended up in Mr. Darcy's room.

"I do not know what came over me. I did not know how I came to be in *that* room and not any other room of the house. Oh, of all the wretched, wretched rooms to be caught in!" Her cheeks pinked at the memory of waking up, finding herself in bed with Mr. Darcy. "I cannot account for my behavior. I swear I was not even aware of what I was doing, Papa. Truly, honestly!"

"I know, child," Mr. Bennet said, shaking his head. "But it has taken place, and we must accept the consequences of it."

"I cannot marry him. You know what he is like–how arrogant he is! How disdainfully he scorns our family. How can I be married to such a man?"

She repeated part of the conversation she had overheard that morning outside the breakfast room.

"Miss Bingley would have him believe I did this deliberately, in order to entrap him. But I tell you the truth, he is the last man in the world I would wish to marry! Please, Papa, do not force me to marry Mr. Darcy."

"My child," he said, "it would never be my wish for you to marry against your will, but you find yourself in a precarious position. A lady's reputation is everything. Even if we can count on Mr. Bingley's guests to remain silent, all it would take is one servant's wagging tongue to ruin you forever. Gossip is like fresh kindling for the fire. It soon spreads throughout the whole community. Would you have your remaining sisters be shamed and disgraced, unable to wed, while you live out your days as a pariah?"

"No, Papa," said Elizabeth, barely above a whisper. "I could not do that to poor Jane, nor to Kitty or Lydia. Even Mary must surely feel the sting of having such a sister, though at least she has already secured a reputable husband."

"This is most unfortunate."

Elizabeth wept.

Mr. Bennet could not see his favorite child in tears without being moved. "If you truly cannot abide having Mr. Darcy for your husband, then I will not force the matter."

Elizabeth looked up, her eyes wide with wonder.

"But," Mr. Bennet continued, "I shall need Mr. Bingley's assurances that his servants will remain silent. If word of this gets out into our community, I will have no choice but to require you to wed, for the sake of your reputation and that of your sisters."

"Thank you, Papa!" Elizabeth threw her arms around him.

After a brief word with Bingley, Mr. Bennet called Darcy to his study.

"Mr. Bennet," Darcy began gravely, "I never intended to compromise your daughter. You must know that I–"

Mr. Bennet put up a hand to silence him. "I am well aware of the facts, Mr. Darcy. I readily believe my daughter's account that you are not to blame, and neither is she. And yet, this incident was witnessed by Mr. Bingley's household, his guests, and his servants. It cannot be ignored."

"Yes, sir," Mr. Darcy nodded. "I am prepared to do my duty towards your daughter. We will marry," he said solemnly.

"I thank you for being an honorable man, Mr. Darcy," said Mr. Bennet. "Lizzy, however, has expressed that she does not wish to marry you. She regards your disdain for our family as an impediment which cannot be overcome, even under such circumstances as these."

"Sir, I–" Darcy began, but Mr. Bennet silenced him.

"I would not have you marry under the misapprehension that you have been entrapped by a scheming fortune hunter. I am prepared to let the matter rest, but I will require your absolute assurances that not a breath of this incident shall ever leave your lips."

Darcy bowed his head. "You have my solemn promise, sir."

"Good. I will not have my Lizzy's reputation stained, nor her sisters by extension. Mr. Bingley has already given me his assurances that none of his household or his guests will repeat the tale. I have told Lizzy that she is absolved from marrying you so long as it remains an absolute secret she was ever near your chamber. But, should word of this get out by some means, and her reputation be threatened, I will not hesitate to make good on your promise to marry her."

"Yes, sir." Darcy said, feeling strangely disappointed.

<hr />

"This will not do at all," Mrs. Bennet complained to Jane in private.

As soon as the gentlemen had left, Elizabeth had gone out for a walk through the pasture to be alone with her thoughts. Kitty and Lydia went to Meryton to call on their Aunt Phillips, and Mr. Bennet remained in his study to meditate on the day's events.

"Lizzy not marry Mr. Darcy! How can she throw such an opportunity away? It is unaccountable!" Mrs. Bennet shook her head. "And here, I thought it would be you who would come away from Netherfield engaged!" She stroked her eldest daughter's cheek lovingly.

"I tried my best, Mother," Jane insisted. "I did everything exactly as you asked. It was difficult to fool my hosts, not to mention Mr. Jones, into believing my illness. In fact, I do not think Miss Bingley believed it at all. The first evening, I pretended so convincingly that I actually fell asleep! Then, the following day, Lizzy came and I was so worried she would insist on conveying me home."

"It was excellent thinking, on your part, to suggest she stay with you," her mother commended.

"Yes, but it made it all the more difficult. I told her she need not remain in the room with me while Mr. Bingley read to me, but she would stay. Such a good little chaperone!"

Mrs. Bennet shrugged. "She always did have rather too much of a sense of what was proper. But I suppose Bingley's sisters would not have let him remain alone with you regardless, so no matter."

"Quite true. And then, I attempted to enact our plan that night, but Miss Bingley caught me in the corridor! I was forced to make the assertion that I was thirsty and in need of a glass of warm milk before returning to bed. I did not dare make another attempt that night. I never expected Lizzy would be the one to rise the next night, though."

"That was truly surprising! But she did not do it deliberately?"

"No, it was that foolish sleepwalking of hers. I thought she might have taken a leaf from your book, at last, but she seemed so upset about the notion of marrying him! Perhaps *I* ought to have been pursuing Mr. Darcy instead of Mr. Bingley," Jane mused.

"Your fortune certainly would be greater if you had! But Mr. Darcy lives so far off, while Mr. Bingley is likely to remain here at Netherfield, especially if he were to marry. He might even decide to purchase it! And I could not bear to have you so far away from me."

Jane smiled. "And Mr. Bingley is so congenial, while Mr. Darcy is so cold and foreboding. Yet I think he would make a good match for Lizzy, if we can persuade her not to throw him away."

"We cannot let it happen, Jane. We must do something to ensure Mr. Darcy makes good on his promise to marry her," Mrs. Bennet insisted.

"You will never guess what has happened, Aunt Phillips!" Lydia exclaimed as she and Kitty rushed into her house. Mrs. Phillips was at home, alone, as she usually was while her husband was at his office. She had little better to do than to fill her days with gossip, especially when it came from her sister or her nieces.

"Tell me quickly, my loves!" Mrs. Phillips urged them.

Kitty and Lydia apprised her of what had taken place between their sister and Mr. Darcy the night before.

"But you must not breathe a word of it to anyone!" Kitty said. "Or Papa says Lizzy will have to marry Mr. Darcy and she hates him!"

Lydia nodded. "She told Papa that Mr. Darcy thinks we are all a mercenary bunch and that Jane is trying to trap Mr. Bingley into a marriage."

"Was Lizzy really found in Mr. Darcy's own bed?" Mrs. Phillips asked with eager eyes.

Kitty nodded. "Oh yes! I heard it myself when she confessed it to Mamma and Papa. They were found together in their nightclothes!"

"My goodness!" Mrs. Phillips exclaimed.

"Papa made us promise we would not tell anyone about all this so you mustn't say a thing!" Kitty said.

"My lips are sewn shut!" Mrs. Phillips promised. "You know I am the soul of discretion, and wouldn't do a thing to harm you girls."

Despite all Mrs. Phillips' promises, as soon as her nieces had left, Mrs. Phillips, who could not keep a secret to save her own life, hurried straight away to her husband's office to tell him the news. He chided her for sharing it, especially when they were not at home. He felt safe, at least, that they were alone, forgetting that his assistant had come into the office an hour earlier than usual, and was in the back room, able to hear the whole thing.

Mrs. Phillips, too, had forgotten about her maid, who, ever eager for the latest morsels of gossip and sensing that this was a particularly good one, had been listening behind the kitchen door when Kitty and Lydia had called and heard all that they had said. She repeated the tale to her mother, the baker's wife, and to her sister, who was a maid in the Goulding household.

✧

Meanwhile, Mrs. Bennet was more direct in her violation of Mr. Bennet's orders. She called on her good friend, Lady Lucas, where she made her promise not to repeat a word of what was said.

"I dare not think how this came about! My poor Lizzy, being taken advantage of by Mr. Darcy. And him not to marry her!" she wailed.

Lady Lucas was appropriately horrified. "It is utterly dreadful, Mrs. Bennet! If I were your husband, I would have called Mr. Darcy out with pistols at dawn."

"Oh, that Mr. Bennet would defend his daughter's honor so admirably! But I would be dreadfully frightened for his life. He is no marksman, you know. I believe he must have been thinking about his poor girls, and unwilling to give over his life, knowing that Mr. Collins and Mary might turn their sisters out of the house as soon as he is cold in his grave. But I have your assurances, Lady Lucas, that you will not say a thing to anyone?"

"Oh, certainly!" Lady Lucas swore. "It would be absolutely dreadful if news of this were to get out."

As soon as Mrs. Bennet had left, Lady Lucas told the whole of it to Charlotte and Maria, also begging them to keep it a secret. Charlotte could be counted on, but Maria shared her mother's propensity for gossip, and immediately told her friends Harriet and Penelope Harrington, as well as William Goulding, whom she met with in secret. In this way, the news of Elizabeth's disgrace quickly spread throughout their acquaintances.

Jane, however, had a far more cunning plan. She soon had a contribution to submit anonymously to the Meryton Gazette's gossip column, which she was sure would make a splash.

Elizabeth had scarcely begun to think herself safe from marrying Mr. Darcy, when her father summoned them all to the drawing room.

Mr. Bennet attempted to remain calm as he addressed his wife and daughters. "I would like to know how, despite my strict orders, your sister's disgrace has become known."

"We did not tell anyone we know," Lydia began.

"Except for Aunt Phillips," Kitty put in. "But she promised us she would not say a word! But we didn't tell anyone else, Papa. Honest!"

Mr. Bennet was angry. "You expressly defied my order! Are there any other confessions to be made? Jane? Mrs. Bennet?"

He looked at the two. Jane looked sheepish, while Mrs. Bennet protested, "I told no one, save for my particular friend Lady Lucas. But Mr. Bennet, you must own that I require someone with whom I can share my troubles! And Lady Lucas positively assured me that she would not repeat it to anyone, on her life!"

"Jane, what have you to say for yourself?"

"I told no one!" Jane insisted. "Do you honestly believe I would hurt Lizzy's chances of finding a suitable match, as well as my own?"

"Then how do you explain this?" He presented her with the morning's paper, folded over to the gossip section.

"We have received reports of a most peculiar occurrence at the grand estate of Netherfield Park. A young lady from a neighboring village, known for her spirited nature but lacking in social graces, has been accused of invading the privacy of a distinguished guest.

It seems that the gentleman, from a renowned Derbyshire family, was disturbed in his slumber by the uninvited visitor. Her motive, it is speculated, was to gain his favor and secure a match of convenience.

Such an audacious act is unheard of in polite society. A lady of refinement would never dream of behaving in such a manner. It is a scandal which threatens to tarnish the reputation of both the young woman and her family, which includes three unwed sisters.

We can only hope that the gentleman will act honorably towards the lady and her family by securing her to himself in holy matrimony."

Elizabeth snatched the paper from her father and looked at it in horror. "When did this appear?"

"In this morning's issue of the Gazette. I daresay everyone in town saw it. If they did not know of your disgrace before, they surely do now!"

"Who would do such a cruel thing?" Elizabeth cried.

Jane pulled her into her embrace. "Dearest Lizzy, it is positively dreadful! Someone who learned of your misfortune sought to make light of it so maliciously!"

"I'll bet it was Lady Lucas!" Mrs. Bennet raged. "For she has always been eager to see my daughters displaced so that hers might stand a better chance in society. And after I trusted her so implicitly!"

"It could have been anyone," Jane suggested. "Perhaps even one of the Harrington sisters, for they are good friends of Maria's. But we do not know that anyone will take this article seriously. After all, no names are mentioned."

"On the contrary," Mr. Bennet said. "It would explain the stares I received when I went into Meryton to purchase a new hinge for the pigpen gate, as well as the nasty comment I received from the ironmonger, who suggested my money would be better spent on new locks for my doors, to keep my daughter from wandering about."

"How awful!" Jane exclaimed, while Elizabeth muttered something about Mr. Ferris losing their custom, as they could be better served by the ironmonger in the next town.

Mr. Bennet shook his head. "Well, Lizzy, it pains me to say it, but now that this whole debacle has come to light, I am afraid I must insist on your marrying Mr. Darcy after all. There is no way around it."

Elizabeth's face fell.

Chapter 10

Darcy had seen the gossip column in the paper and knew it depicted him and Elizabeth. Somehow or other, word had gotten out. At Bingley's insistence, they had remained home the past few days, even refraining from attending Sunday service, but apparently it was not enough to prevent some one or other wagging their tongues. He was unsurprised, therefore, when a messenger arrived the next day, summoning him to Longbourn.

"You can be at no loss over why you are here, Mr. Darcy," Mr. Bennet began, pacing the floor of his study.

Darcy stood still, his hands clasped behind his back respectfully. "I have seen the gossip column, Mr. Bennet. It seems the secret is out. I am prepared to do my duty towards your daughter, as we agreed."

"It is not my wish to do this, you understand. Were my family's reputation not endangered, I would not force the issue."

Darcy gave a silent nod in response.

Mr. Bennet stopped pacing and settled into the chair beside his desk. "Lizzy, among all my daughters, is my particular favorite. I have never attempted to deny it. Her sleepwalking habit is unfortunate. She and her sisters, save for Jane, all suffered from nighttime perambulation as children, a trait they unfortunately inherited from their mother and me. The younger girls outgrew it, as I had. But Mrs.

Bennet and Elizabeth retained this condition even into adulthood. It has been no small task to keep them safe and to prevent others from learning of it.

"I had always intended I should communicate this news to whichever of Lizzy's suitors seemed most likely to marry her. However, I did not expect this circumstance would take place so soon. I wish with all my heart that I could absolve you from doing your duty towards her, but alas, I must think of my family and my remaining daughters, as well as Elizabeth."

"I understand," murmured Mr. Darcy. "It is a cross I am willing to bear. I will also do my utmost to protect her from further harm."

Mr. Bennet looked at Mr. Darcy with a curious expression "Mr. Darcy, do you have feelings for my Lizzy?"

Darcy felt his face redden. "I confess, sir, I allowed my prejudice to cloud my early impressions of her. I have since come to admire your daughter's wit and sense. It is unfortunate that I insulted her early on in our acquaintance, and she has yet to forgive me for it. But I will treat her with the care and respect she deserves as my wife and endeavor to love her as best as I can. I hope that in time she might come to think of me with something like regard."

"Such is more than many people can say upon entering the marital state." Mr. Bennet nodded. "And though I cannot say I give my 'blessing' upon this marriage, I will certainly not stand in the way of it."

Elizabeth had scarcely begun to think herself safe from marrying Mr. Darcy, and now this! The past few days had been relatively calm, with nothing to trouble them except the pig escaping from his pen. *I ought to have known that my fortune could not last.*

She could not bear to look at Mr. Darcy when he called. How could she? Knowing her father was to insist she marry this man could only confirm any suspicions Mr. Darcy harbored of their mercenary motives and give him every reason to hold them in contempt. If he did not despise her before, he surely would now. The thought of marrying him sickened her.

After giving Mr. Darcy a perfunctory greeting, she escaped to the barn, where she poured out her troubles to George while feeding him a few fallen apples she collected from the orchard on her way.

"I understand why you tried to escape, George," she told the pig. "I would too, in your position. We none of us like the feeling of being trapped." She patted the coarse hair atop his head. George grunted happily as he continued to munch his favorite treat.

"At least your life is simpler than mine," she continued. "You need only content yourself with rolling in mud and eating to your heart's content. But your day of reckoning will come, almost as surely as mine will." She imagined herself being led like a pig to its slaughter, a gruesome but fitting image of her future, she thought.

Her thoughts were disturbed by footsteps approaching, precipitating the appearance of Mr. Darcy.

"Your father told me I might find you here." He came beside her and leaned his arms against the rails of the pen, mimicking her stance. "Things are settled between us. We are to wed."

Elizabeth wrestled with the knot forming in her stomach, torn between cold silence and hot anger. Finally, she settled on a lukewarm declaration, willing herself to remain calm. "I will not pretend to feel grateful for what you are doing, Mr. Darcy."

"Given the circumstances, I would not expect you to. I am well aware I am not your choice of a husband." His tone was grave.

"If I were given the opportunity, I would release you from your obligation. I would carry the stain of what has transpired and move to some far-off county where no one knew me. But alas! I have my sisters and their well-being to consider. It is for their sake, and that of my father and mother, that I consent to this union."

"I comprehend you," he said in a strained tone.

She fed the last of the apple in her hand to the pig, wiping her hands on the front of her apron

Mr. Darcy looked at her quizzically. "Do you often tend to the animals on your estate?"

"No, only this one," she answered. "George has become something of a friend to me."

"George?" Mr. Darcy's eyebrows raised in amusement.

"Named after our dear Prince Regent. Do you not see the resemblance, Mr. Darcy?" Having concluded his snack, George was now relishing in a mud bath near the center of the pigpen.

"Oh yes, a perfect likeness!" Her comment brought laughter to them both, lightening the somber mood. "I can see that His Royal Highness lives to excess as much as his namesake." Turning to Elizabeth, he said, "You have no idea how much diversion his name brings to me, for I am well-acquainted with individuals by that name."

"Do tell."

"My late father, for one, bore that name, as did his godson, who grew up on our estate. The latter now resides at Kympton, as my rector there."

"Goodness, I had no idea my pig shared the name of such important people! Here, I thought he only shared it with our good king and his slovenly son!"

"Our good king, and his slovenly son. Yes, that is it exactly," Mr. Darcy chuckled.

"I confess, this George has become rather dear to me. I shall be rather sad when it is his turn to go to market. But such is the way of things. I ought to know better than to grow attached to something that I know I will one day part with."

Mr. Darcy reached out and put his hand on her shoulder, but she recoiled.

"I do not require your comfort over the loss of my pet, Mr. Darcy. He will face his fate one day, just as I must." The mirth from her face was gone, replaced by a tight frown.

Perhaps sensing he had overstayed his welcome, Mr. Darcy bowed to her and departed, leaving Elizabeth to watch him disappear from view.

<hr />

Charlotte called on Elizabeth, not long after Mr. Darcy departed. Elizabeth took her into the garden, where they might speak without Elizabeth's mother or sisters hovering. The air had grown cool and crisp, signifying the coming of winter, but it was not so cold yet as to make a garden visit unpleasant.

Charlotte was the first to speak. "I saw the article in the Gazette. How are you bearing up, Eliza?"

"Not well, I am afraid," Elizabeth said sadly. "I could not sleep last night, knowing what is to come. Mr. Darcy has been here and spoken to Papa. My fate is sealed. I am to marry Mr. Darcy."

"I am frightfully sorry, Eliza! I do not know how news of your scandal got out. It was not from my quarter, I assure you."

"Oh, Charlotte!" Elizabeth hugged her friend. "I know you are not to blame, but this is simply dreadful!"

"I know you are suffering, but is it truly as awful as it seems? My mother seems to think it a fortuitous thing, regardless of how it came about."

"Then your mother must have borrowed her sentiments from mine, for my own mother boasts every five minutes over my auspicious marriage, to my utmost discontent," Elizabeth said.

"I feel for you, I do!" Charlotte insisted. "I know you detest Mr. Darcy. But at least you may take consolation in the number of fine carriages and gowns you shall have."

"Now you sound like my mother! Pray, do not spend your days employed in schemes to see your daughters advantageously wed, or I shall have to disown you as a friend!" Elizabeth jested.

"Do not fear, Eliza. Before I can even begin to consider my daughter's futures, I must first secure my own. Does Mr. Darcy happen to have a brother?"

Her comment made Elizabeth laugh. "If he did, you would not want him, for surely he would be just as pompous, but lacking any of the material advantages!"

"I suppose I shall simply have to wait until another gentleman of several thousand per year decides to grace our neighborhood, then!" Charlotte's eyes twinkled.

"Dearest Charlotte!" Elizabeth pulled her into a quick hug. "Who shall make me laugh when I am apart from you?"

"I do not know. Perhaps you can find room for me in your trunk, when you depart!" she winked.

"I would throw out my entire wedding trousseau to make room for you, if I could!" Elizabeth laughed again.

Chapter 11

Mrs. Bennet crowed her satisfaction to anyone who would listen, oblivious to her daughter's misery and the dark looks she received from their neighbors.

She immediately wrote a letter to Mary, urging her and Mr. Collins to come for the wedding if they could, and bragging in the most unscrupulous terms about the advantageous marriage that Elizabeth was to gain with Mr. Darcy.

Kitty's style of communication was altogether different. In her letter to Mary, she relayed all she had overheard about Elizabeth's situation and the scandalous way in which her engagement took place.

Mary took these letters to heart. After conveying her displeasure to her husband, he immediately went to his patroness, Lady Catherine, and told her everything concerning her nephew's hasty engagement.

Mr. Collins and Mary traveled to Longbourn as soon as possible, accompanied by none other than Lady Catherine de Bourgh herself.

Mrs. Bennet was surprised by the visit of this esteemed person of whom she had heard so much, and took it as a great honor that this lady should condescend to grace them with her presence.

"I suppose you are here for the wedding of your nephew, then, Your Ladyship," she said after introductions had been made.

Lady Catherine did not dignify her with a response but turned to Elizabeth instead. "Miss Elizabeth, you have a small wilderness near your home. Will you show it to me?"

Without a word, Elizabeth nodded, rising, and Lady Catherine followed her to the path leading through the orchard. The harvest was now past, leaving the trees bare and forlorn against the gray skies. A northerly blast had blown in during the night, giving the air a bitter chill. Elizabeth pulled her shawl tighter around herself to stay warm.

"Miss Bennet, I am sure you can be at no loss to understand why I am here," Lady Catherine began, her feet crunching on the leaves beneath them.

Elizabeth blinked. "Indeed, I cannot account for this honor at all."

"Well, then I shall come right to the point. I have been told by your sister and Mr. Collins of your engagement to my nephew."

"Such a fact is public knowledge by now," Elizabeth stated, still bewildered at the reason for this lady's visit.

"Have you any idea of the degradation of this?" Lady Catherine's expression was cross.

"Degradation? I beg your pardon," said Elizabeth, her own face scrunching in anger.

"You may think, Miss Bennet, that you have a right to insist upon my nephew marrying you. I have heard the circumstances surrounding this whole debacle, and I must say, I am shocked! Such wanton behavior as yours ought not to be dignified by a marriage. My nephew must be under no obligation to marry you after the way you wormed yourself into his bedchamber."

Elizabeth turned her head sharply towards Lady Catherine. "If you think for one moment that I desired this match or sought it out—"

"Did you not? Was it not deliberately orchestrated by yourself?"

SUDDEN AWAKENINGS

"Not at all!" Elizabeth argued. "I have no wish for a union with your nephew."

"Good," Lady Catherine interrupted. "Then we understand each other. This match is not to take place. You will break off your engagement with my nephew at once and cease this whole talk of marrying him."

Elizabeth was thoroughly incensed. "Unfortunately, Lady Catherine, that is something I cannot do."

Lady Catherine ceased walking and whirled to face her. "Cannot do! But you yourself said you do not wish this."

"That may be," said Elizabeth, "but I have no choice in the matter. I will not see my family's honor destroyed. There is nothing for it but for Mr. Darcy and I to be married. My father insists upon it. Mr. Darcy has agreed to it, and so have I."

"This is not to be borne." Clouds of breath came from Lady Catherine's nostrils as she snorted. "Heaven and earth, are the shades of Pemberley to be thus polluted? No, I will not stand for it. Notwithstanding the gross impropriety of it all, Mr. Darcy is not free to marry you. He is engaged to my daughter. Now, what do you have to say to that?"

"Only this," said Elizabeth, coolly, "That if your nephew truly is engaged, you have no reason to suppose he would make an offer to me, under any circumstances. I know by now that his honor runs too deep to do otherwise."

"Are you calling me a liar?" The lady spat in indignation.

"No, Your Ladyship. But neither is Mr. Darcy a prevaricator. I cannot for one minute believe that he would conceal a prior engagement from his friends, if he had already trothed his affections."

Lady Catherine drew in her breath, her patience wearing thin. "The understanding between Mr. Darcy and Miss de Bourgh is of a peculiar nature. It was planned from their infancy. It was the particular wish of Mr. Darcy's mother and myself that one day our children would be wed. Would you really go against these deep maternal desires and see the hope of that union be destroyed?"

Elizabeth crossed her arms in defiance. "As I have previously stated, Your Ladyship, I have no choice in the matter. I must marry Mr. Darcy, or else my entire family will be ruined."

"So you would drag down the Darcy name along with yours instead." Lady Catherine snorted again.

"I hope I shall do no such thing," replied Elizabeth. "Although the start of our marriage may be unconventional, I am confident that my status as a gentleman's daughter will enable me to bring honor to the Darcy family."

"Honor? Honor indeed!" exclaimed Lady Catherine striding back down the path they came. "I can see nothing honorable about this. Mark my words, Pemberley shall suffer with you as its mistress, and the Darcy name shall be forever disgraced by you. If you had any sense–any sense at all, Miss Bennet, you would not proceed with this union. You have not heard the last from me. I take no leave of you. I send no compliments to your mother. You deserve no such attention."

They reached Lady Catherine's carriage, awaiting her in the front drive. Lady Catherine, without another word, climbed in and rapped on the roof to signal her driver to depart. Elizabeth did not wait for her to disappear from sight before returning to the house.

Mrs. Bennet hurried to Elizabeth as soon as she returned from her ramble in the orchard.

"Would Her Ladyship like to stay for tea?" she asked, looking around for Lady Catherine. "Where is she?"

"Her Ladyship has left, Mamma," Elizabeth told her. "She would not stay."

"Oh, how disappointing. I was so sure she would stay for tea, at the least."

"She will return again, though, I am sure of it. Is she staying at the Kings's Arms until the wedding?" Mrs. Bennet followed Elizabeth into the drawing room, where Mary and Mr. Collins were still waiting.

"I do not believe so, Mamma," Elizabeth said, busying herself with stitching a shirt from her workbasket. "I do not think Her Ladyship intends to come to the wedding at all. If I had to wager, she is currently bound for the London Road, and we will not see her darken our doors again."

"Perhaps she has returned to Rosings," suggested Mary.

"Her Ladyship has many things to tend to, I am certain," said Mr. Collins, equally surprised his ride had left him. "We will, of course, be staying here for the wedding, Mrs. Bennet," he told her. He supposed he and Mary would have to return home by post after the wedding was over. Turning towards Elizabeth, he said, "Mary and I wondered if we might speak with you for a few moments alone."

Not much in the mood for further discussion, but knowing her cousin would not let it rest if there was something he intended to say, she gave her assent.

Her mother muttered something about needing to see about dinner and rushed off to find Hill. Mary moved closer to her husband and took his hand. Elizabeth laid her work aside and gave them her full attention.

"What is it you desire to speak with me about, Cousin?" she said.

"It is in regard to your engagement to Mr. Darcy," he began.

"It seems everyone has concerns on that account," said Elizabeth, with no small bitterness.

Mr. Collins cleared his throat. "Yes, well, Her Ladyship was right to be concerned about such things. I know Mrs. Bennet is jubilant about your impending marriage. Ordinarily, I too would rejoice at such a union. Notwithstanding the fact that Mr. Darcy has long been engaged to Her Ladyship's own dear daughter, Miss de Bourgh. The Jewel of Rosings Park, as I often call her." He smiled as he said this. Mary poked him sharply in the ribs. "But I digress," he quickly added.

Mary looked at Elizabeth. "I shall be more to the point, sister. Do you not know that it is a sin to climb into bed with a man whom you are not wed to, let alone engaged to?"

Elizabeth's cheeks turned bright red. "It was not intentional, I assure you, Mary. You are no stranger to my sleepwalking."

"Intentional or not, you ought to have been on your guard. 'For this ye know, that no whoremonger, nor unclean person, nor covetous man, who is an idolater, hath any inheritance in the kingdom of Christ and of God.'" Mary warned, quoted from the Holy Scriptures.

"I am no whoremonger, Mary!" Elizabeth said, rising to her feet.

Mr. Collins sought to reassure her with a gentle, "Now, now Cousin," which was enough for Elizabeth to recollect herself and resume her seat, doing her best to rein in her temper. "We all know nothing of that sort is taking place," Mr. Collins went on, "but it is the appearance of it which matters. Your conduct has exposed this family to ridicule. Mr. Bingley, his sisters, his servants–they all saw what appeared to be an indiscretion between you and Mr. Darcy. And whether or not it is true, people are apt to talk."

"This is nothing new to me," Elizabeth reminded them. "After all, I have only agreed to this engagement in the first place because of such reasons as you have named. Need I remind everyone that this whole scheme was not my idea? I have no wish to marry Mr. Darcy at all!"

Mary continued to adjure her. "You must endeavor to lead a moral life if you are to restore any honor to our family, to Lady Catherine, to her nephew, Mr. Darcy. You must not be cavorting about climbing into bed with men to whom you are not married, whether you are sleepwalking or whether you are fully aware of your actions."

"As I am now to be married, I do not think that shall be an issue any longer," Elizabeth retorted. "Should I wander into my husband's bedroom, I think nobody would think worse of me."

"But suppose you were to walk into another man's bedroom," Mary suggested, "a servant, or perhaps a guest of Mr. Darcy's, what then? Will the Darcy name and ours be further still disgraced, and Mr. Darcy cast you out and divorce you?"

"I will take precautions to ensure such a thing never happens," Elizabeth said, her anger still brimming the surface. "You can rest assured this mistake will never again occur."

Chapter 12

Lady Catherine's fury would not rest until she had seen her nephew. The residents of Netherfield Park were as alarmed and honored at her arrival as those of Longbourn had been, but seeing that this was no ordinary social call, they left Darcy alone in the drawing room with his aunt.

Lady Catherine immediately launched her tirade, screaming, "Darcy, what is the meaning of uniting yourself to such an obstinate, headstrong, foolish girl?"

Darcy replied calmly and without any change in the inflection of his voice, "I assume you are speaking of my impending marriage to Miss Elizabeth Bennet."

"The outrage of it, Darcy," Lady Catherine went on, stamping the floor with her cane. "This wanton little strumpet has entrapped you! How could you let such a thing happen–letting a woman sneak into your bedchamber?"

"I assure you, it was not my intention, and as to entrapment, it was neither Miss Bennet's plan nor her design to find herself in my bedroom. She suffers from a sleepwalking disorder, and as such, mistakenly wandered into the wrong room during her sleep."

"If it was truly a mistake, then why did you agree to marry her? This is no doubt a machination of hers, or at the least of her sister or her mother. All of them are greedy, grasping sort of folk, as I have learned from my rector, Mr. Collins."

"Mr. Collins? What has he to do with any of this?" Mr. Darcy furrowed his brow in surprise.

Lady Catherine huffed and threw back her shoulders. "You may recall last spring when I mentioned to you that my rector had gone to his cousins in Hertfordshire and had taken a wife from among them there."

Darcy blinked. "I recall something of the sort, but I do not recollect the name of his wife."

"Her name was Miss Mary Bennet, now Mrs. Collins. And he intimated to me how Mrs. Bennet imposed on him to choose one of her daughters to be his wife and how she had purposely steered him, first towards the eldest of them, and then the second Miss Elizabeth. How when she rejected him, he felt compelled to marry the next eldest, Miss Mary Bennet."

"That was not the story as you told it last April. When I heard it then, you spoke of nothing but his good fortune in having secured a sensible, respectable wife."

"Well, that was before I knew what the Bennet family were really like. The whole thing was a ploy to be able to keep Longbourn in their family," she said, angrily. "As you know, Mr. Collins is the heir to Longbourn estate, thanks to the entail placed upon it, for Mr. Bennet has no other sons or living male relatives besides Mr. Collins. And Mrs. Bennet, devious as she is, could not stand to see her place usurped by another, unless it be her own daughter. So she contrived to invite Mr. Collins to her home last spring and would not let him leave until he was settled amicably with one of her daughters.

"And now she has done the same thing to you, Darcy. You have walked right into her snare. This Miss Elizabeth may have been an unwitting accomplice, but mark my words: this was all part of a plan to get their hands on the Darcy fortune! I dare say they would entrap your friend Mr. Bingley, too, if they could. As Mrs. Collins has told me, Mrs. Bennet and Miss Jane Bennet have spoken of nothing but their eagerness to develop the friendship with Mr. Bingley since his arrival here, and at every turn have positioned themselves to advantage. Do you deny it? Can you not say you have seen it yourself since your arrival?"

Mr. Darcy's lips tightened. He had seen altogether too much in that regard. But he would not speak out against his new bride's family. Not yet, at least.

"My recommendation to you, Darcy," Lady Catherine went on, "is that you disentangle yourself from this whole affair before it is too late. You have not yet pledged your troth. You may yet escape from this net."

"I have no wish to do so, Lady Catherine," Mr. Darcy said. "I have every intention of making good on my promise to marry Miss Elizabeth Bennet. Regardless of what they may have conspired to do. Because my honor demands it. And because–" He stopped, unwilling to say more. But Lady Catherine could discern what was left unsaid. Her eyes narrowed as she took a step towards him.

"Are you in love with this girl–this Elizabeth?"

Darcy shifted uncomfortably.

"You are!" she cried. "I knew it. You are a fool then, Darcy, and a bigger one than I ever took you for. I suppose the feelings of your cousin matter nothing to you then!"

"My cousin will be perfectly happy for me, I am certain." Darcy's lips tightened.

"You think so little of Anne that you believe she would not care the least if you were to wed another? Do you actually imagine she would be wishing you joy? Well, perhaps she would, for Anne is the best creature that ever lived. She may wish you joy, Darcy, but in her heart, she would be crying over its brokenness! You must know how long she has desired to marry you– how much in love with you she is."

"In love with me!" Darcy exclaimed. "That I have not seen. In fact, quite the opposite. She and I have long agreed that, though we love each other as cousins, there would never be more between us."

"So you intend to shirk your duty to her, to disregard my wishes and that of your own dear late mother! All so you can uphold some silly notion of honor towards this ungrateful *chit* who does not even desire to marry you herself! She told me so herself, Darcy; she does not wish to marry you. And yet she is being forced to by her family. All because they fear their honor will be destroyed by this, this *situation* that *they themselves* have put her in. I will not stand for it, Darcy! I will write to the bishop myself and tell him to cancel whatever license he has procured for you. I have connections in the church, you know."

"A license, once issued, cannot be revoked, Your Ladyship. Even you know that. I am afraid you have no power. I will go through with the wedding as planned, and there is nothing you nor anyone else can do to stop me," Darcy said with an air of finality.

"Well! Since you cannot be reasoned with, I will take my appeals elsewhere," Lady Catherine said, her anger building by the moment. "I have never been treated thusly in my entire life!"

Without another word, she stormed out the front door, slamming it behind her. The house shook in her wake.

Lady Catherine's threats were indeed idle, and it was only a week before the license was procured and the date set with the minister. Mr. Darcy, having now been a resident at Netherfield for four full weeks, found no difficulty in obtaining the license so they could marry expediently without waiting for the banns to be read.

Mrs. Bennet began making lists of items they would need for the wedding, and decided on the dress which Elizabeth was to wear.

"I am aware there is no time to have anything new made up," she told Elizabeth. "But we must do something for your best gown to make it more presentable."

"My gown will be perfectly adequate as it is, Mamma," Elizabeth protested.

"Nonsense, child, you must look your best on your wedding day, since you are to become Mrs. Darcy. Oh, how glad I am that the wedding is to take place so soon! And yet, at the same time, I wish there was only a little more time to prepare a wedding as grand as you deserve to have."

"Given the circumstances, Mamma, I think it for the best that the ceremony be as small and simple as possible, and as quick as can be," Elizabeth pointed out.

"Yes, yes, but we must do our best all the same. Now, let me see what I have among my things that I might give to you. Come with me, child."

She took Elizabeth to her room and rummaged through her jewelry box. "Oh my, yes, these will do nicely for you, my dear." Mrs. Bennet pulled out a string of pearls with a small jeweled cross attached to the center. "I wore these on my own wedding day. How happy I was then! Our engagement was rather a quick one too, you see. But still, I had these as a gift from my own mother. They've been in the family for several generations now. Mary wished to wear them at her wedding, but I would not give them to her. Instead, she received an amber pendant that had been your Grandmother Bennet's."

Elizabeth's cheeks pinked. "I am honored, then, Mamma, that you should choose to give these to me."

"Oh, but of course, my dear! Your marriage will be ever so much more grand than Mary's. Not that I mind, of course. As it turns out, Mr. Collins is well-suited for her. And they will have Longbourn someday. But you, my dear, to be mistress of Pemberley—why, that is really something! You deserve to have the family jewels as a reward."

Elizabeth's expression turned sour. "I do not wish for these if they are a reward for capturing a rich man, Mamma."

"Oh, do not be silly. I did not mean it that way. You always take my words too literally. I only mean that you will look so fine in these, like a medieval queen. Please, my darling, wear them with your gown."

With a heart less glad than before, Elizabeth nodded and accepted the necklace.

Chapter 13

Meanwhile, Darcy was busy with preparations of his own. His sister had written back to him, expressing her delight over the news that she was to gain a sister and wishing him well, although she could not fathom his insistence that she not be present for the wedding itself. She was to join them at Pemberley after the wedding, along with her governess, Mrs. Younge.

Now that his stay had been extended, Darcy sent for his valet to come, bringing Darcy's coach and additional luggage he would need for the journey to Pemberley. Perkins also safeguarded the ring Darcy planned to give Elizabeth, having retrieved it from the family's London residence.

Darcy hoped to find a moment to give it to her that evening. The Bennet family were to join them for dinner at Netherfield.

Darcy and Bingley were the first ones dressed and down. While they waited for the others in the library, Bingley surprised him with a novel idea for the wedding celebration. "I am thinking of throwing a ball, Darcy," he said out of the blue.

Mr. Darcy's eyes shot up. "A ball?"

Bingley nodded as he poured glasses of brandy for them. "Yes. In honor of your wedding to Miss Elizabeth."

SUDDEN AWAKENINGS

"I should think a ball would be the last thing on your mind, Bingley," Darcy said, taking a glass from him. "After all, are we not trying to draw as little attention to the situation as possible?"

"Well, I had thought the same, initially," Bingley said. "But it occurred to me that since the neighbors are already aware of the situation, it would be best to have some kind of celebration to legitimize the marriage in their eyes before you take Miss Elizabeth away to Pemberley."

"I see your point," Darcy nodded, "but do you think it will be enough time for your sisters to help you plan it? I do not wish to put them out."

"Oh, you need not worry about that! Caroline will complain about it, surely, but there is nothing she likes better than to show off her skills as a hostess. She has been harping on me since our arrival to host a ball. I will simply tell her this is the only opportunity she may have. If Louisa and I help, it will be no trouble. I have already asked Mrs. Nicholls to begin making the white soup."

"In that case, how could I possibly refuse! I am exceedingly grateful to you."

"Anything for my friend." Bingley smiled. "You know, you could stay here longer if you wish, Darcy. I plan to stay through the rest of the shooting season. You and your new bride need not hurry off to Derbyshire immediately."

"Actually, I think it is for the best if we do," Darcy said. "Already, there has been too much scandal surrounding this marriage. Your ball will go a long way to legitimize it, as you said, and help convince everyone it was a whirlwind love match. But when all is said and done, it will be much better if I take Elizabeth away from here. At least until the gossip has quieted down."

"So you are calling her by her Christian name, now," Bingley smirked, one eyebrow going up.

Darcy blushed. "Well, she is my betrothed, after all." He would not admit it had been a slip of the tongue; thus far, he had only thought of her by her first name in his own mind.

Bingley finished off his drink. He leaned in closer, dropping his voice. "Was it truly an accident she ended up in your room that night?"

"You know it was," Darcy retorted. "There may be many men who would invite a lady to their bedchambers without the bonds of matrimony, but you of all people should know I am not that sort. And neither is Miss Elizabeth," he said, reverting back to her proper title.

"Of course, Darcy, I meant nothing by it. Only I have seen the looks you've given her. Are you sure there are no feelings, even on your part?"

Darcy swallowed. "What would it matter? It is clear she dislikes me. She is only marrying me because she has no choice."

"But you are marrying her for more than that," Bingley said softly.

Darcy looked at his friend, but said nothing more, as they were joined that instant by the ladies and Mr. Hurst.

As the Bennets' coach drew to a stop in front of Netherfield's grand entrance, Elizabeth realized it was the first time she had been there since her fateful stay. They were shown into the library first. The door to the adjoining dining room was shut, making the room feel smaller and more cramped than when they had gathered here during her stay. Elizabeth avoided Darcy's gaze, keeping her head down when she curtsied her greeting. She hovered nearby as he discussed the wedding business with her parents. He informed them the minister had agreed to move the wedding date up to that Wednesday.

Elizabeth's heart sank when she learned it was to be so soon. She had counted on at least three more weeks while waiting for the banns to be read before she was to be ripped from her home and taken to some faraway place she had never before seen, all with a man whom she disliked.

"Three days is not a long time to plan a wedding," Mrs. Bennet said, with a hint of irritation in her voice. "Could we not wait a little longer? I shall hardly have time to invite our neighbors."

"I'm sure you can be at no loss to understand why our wedding must take place as soon as possible," Mr. Darcy said. "In fact, I would undertake this sooner if the Reverend Carmichael was available before then," Mr. Darcy told her.

"Do not worry, Mrs. Bennet," Mr. Bingley intervened. "There will be no need for you to plan anything. I have undertaken the task of throwing a ball in Mr. Darcy and Miss Elizabeth's honor. It will take place the night before the wedding."

"The night before? That won't do at all. I had counted on giving them a lavish wedding breakfast following the ceremony," she protested.

"I'm afraid that won't be possible." Mr. Darcy said. "You see, I intend to take Elizabeth to her new home in Derbyshire directly after the wedding. My sister is to join us there, and it is my wish that they should meet." He did not tell her of his desires to expediently remove Elizabeth from the neighborhood for the sake of gossip.

"Mrs. Bennet, allow me to do this for my friend, since it was under my roof that his engagement was formed in this manner," Bingley urged her, "and do not concern yourself with any of the wedding details. I will take it upon myself to invite all the neighbors for the ball. The wedding the following day ought to be reserved for family and the couple's closest friends."

"Well, if you wish it, then let it be so," said Mrs. Bennet softly. "At least I shall have the pleasure of showing off my Elizabeth at your ball."

Mr. Bingley smiled. "And a radiant jewel she shall be, I am certain, as will all your daughters." His eyes were drawn to Jane, whose brilliant smile towards him would have dazzled even a blind man. Jane wore a blue gown with a neckline even more daring than usual, which served to keep Mr. Bingley's attention on her while they enjoyed their glasses of madeira. She spoke sweetly to Mr. Bingley, giving him smiles that, as only Jane could do, combined the angelic and the coquettish all in one. Mr. Bingley was entirely under her spell.

Mr. Collins, who up till this point had remained in the background, now made himself known. "Mr. Darcy," he said, coming forward. "What a great honor it is to meet you at last, the nephew of my esteemed patroness, Lady Catherine de Bourgh." He bowed low before Mr. Darcy and then forced his handshake on him with great vigor, causing Darcy's head to bob up and down. "Forgive me, but I do not think we have been introduced," said Darcy.

"Begging your pardon, estimable sir," said Mr. Collins. "I am the Reverend William Collins, rector of Hunsford, which abuts Lady Catherine de Bourgh's great estate, Rosings Park. You might not have yet met my wife, your *fiancée's* dear younger sister, next to her in age and beauty, I might say. This is Mrs. Collins, formerly Miss Mary Bennet." Mary dutifully performed a curtsy for Mr. Darcy. She was dressed in a plain gray gown that did not show off any features. Her hair was tied back tightly in a bun, and with the glasses perched on her nose, she looked more like a schoolmistress than a married lady attending a dinner.

The Collinses were introduced to their hosts, who had witnessed the exchange with no small amusement, especially from Miss Bingley and her sister.

They were summoned to dinner, and Mr. Collins dominated the conversation during the meal, pandering the most to Mr. Darcy, but also to Mr. and Miss Bingley, peppering his speech with compliments on the fine furnishings and the courses which they were served, several times comparing them to the delights he had enjoyed at Rosings Park. Mary spoke less, but when she did, it was to recite an ill-timed proverb or remark upon something she had heard her husband mention in a sermon. Kitty and Lydia amused themselves by warming spoons with their breath and then hanging them from their noses in a childish display, while Mrs. Bennet spent the meal praising her daughters or commenting how wonderful it was that Netherfield Park was so excellently situated.

Elizabeth felt all the more ashamed for having such relatives. In a moment of mirth, she mused, *Well, if Mr. Darcy is frightened away after all this and decides to call off the wedding, I suppose my family will have served a useful purpose!*

Perhaps Jane believed her sister's marriage might improve her chances with Mr. Bingley. Darcy observed she seemed a more ready conversation partner than before, less reserved, more relatable. She chatted amiably about Bingley's favorite sports and whether he had shot as many birds as he had hoped during his stay.

Elizabeth, by contrast, was colder than ever. She did not speak to him or anyone else at the table, except by necessity, kept her gaze on her meal, and was so displeased to be among company at all that hardly anybody attempted a conversation with her, except for Darcy, who repeatedly tried to engage her, but without success.

When they repaired to the drawing room after dinner, Elizabeth stole onto the terrace. Darcy followed her. Hearing his approach, she glanced at him, but did not speak.

Darcy stood beside her at the railing overlooking the garden. The grounds were bare and lifeless with the approach of winter, almost as frigid as the woman beside him.

Taking a breath, he addressed her. "Miss Elizabeth, you have hardly spoken a word to me all evening. Are we to be strangers to one another then?"

"I would hardly call us strangers, sir," she replied disdainfully, "given how intimately we are now connected. But I saw no reason for idle chit chat."

Darcy's color changed "Is this how it is to be in our marriage then, with you barely speaking to me as we go about our lives?"

His comment caused her lips to tighten further. "I did not choose your company willingly, as you know," she said.

"Yet, by necessity, it will be yours," he stated. "I am not the sort of man who would live apart from his wife for the entirety of their marriage. I intend you should reside with me wherever I am at any given time during the year. I would not have society remark upon our absence from each other."

"If that is your wish, then let it be so," she answered, rather flippantly.

"Therefore, since we are to be housemates," Darcy went on, "do you not think it is time you laid down your arms? After all, we shall have to be in each other's company much when we are married, and we shall have to play the part of the happy couple when we entertain and are seen in society. Otherwise, people may remark that you have a lover elsewhere. I will not be seen as a cuckold when I have done nothing to deserve it."

"We could not have that," Elizabeth replied sarcastically. She turned to go back inside, but he caught her arm.

"I would love to know what exactly I have done to earn your disapproval."

"Too much to discuss in polite society." Her eyebrow quirked. "But most recently, it is because you moved forward the date of our wedding without even consulting me."

"I did that out of concern for your reputation," he said, his eyes flashing in indignation. "The sooner we are married, the sooner your neighbors will forget about the scandal of your wandering into my bedchambers during the night."

"My reputation was secured as soon as you signed the marriage settlement with my father. A long engagement would have been preferable to me, so I might delay the appointed hour when I shall lose my freedom and become the property of a man."

"Is that how you suppose I shall treat you? Like chattel, with no liberties of your own?" He was growing quite angry now.

"Is that not how most husbands treat their wives?"

"Some, perhaps, but not all. And certainly, that is not how I intend for my wife to live. As the mistress of Pemberley, you shall have all the freedoms accorded to you that you like, provided you conduct yourself with propriety."

"You mean, do not wander into other men's bedchambers," she scoffed. "I understand you perfectly, Mr. Darcy."

"You willfully misunderstand me," he argued. "Can you not see that I have no wish to control you? My only desire is for your happiness."

"My happiness was lost to me the moment I mistakenly entered your room in my slumber."

"If you cannot accept that I wish for your happiness, then at least know that I desire your comfort, your security, and that I wish to provide you with a respectable marriage and a home for the remainder of your life. Whether or not you choose to be happy in such a situation, only you have the power to determine."

Her voice softened. "Forgive me. It is not my intention to stir up contention between us. I know you are doing what you believe is the honorable thing. But you must excuse me if I cannot yet rejoice in my present situation."

With that, she left the terrace to return inside, and this time, he did not hinder her. Sighing, Darcy put his hands into his pockets. His left hand bumped against a square-shaped box, bringing to his realization that he had yet to present her with his mother's ring.

SUDDEN AWAKENINGS

Chapter 14

Elizabeth tossed fitfully that night. Some hours before the rooster crowed, she rose and went downstairs for a cup of coffee. She sat by the dying embers of the fire in the drawing room, sipping the warm concoction, her mind too full to find any rest. Her head turned at a soft noise of muffled footsteps. Jane shuffled over in her slippers and dressing gown.

"You are fully awake, not sleepwalking?" she confirmed.

"Yes, Jane, I am awake. I could not sleep." Elizabeth scooted over on the sofa to make room for Jane to join her.

"You are upset about your impending marriage," Jane surmised, wrapping her shawl around her sister's shoulders.

Elizabeth took another sip of her coffee. "It is not as though I were unaware that this would be taking place. But I had not expected it to be so soon," she admitted.

Jane stroked Elizabeth's hair gently. "All will be well, dearest," she sought to reassure her. "Mr. Darcy is a good man. You will see. He will take care of you. In fact, though this situation distresses you, it could prove a good thing for our family. For surely, your marriage to Mr. Darcy will connect you with many other wealthy families and might put your unmarried sisters in the path of eligible men, whom they might otherwise not have the opportunity to meet."

"Now you sound like Mamma," Elizabeth snorted. "But you know that Kitty and Lydia would not wish to marry for money, any more than you or I do. I hope, dear Jane, that you will find love in time. And Kitty and Lydia also. And you will all be extremely happy, unlike myself."

"Oh, my dear, sweet Lizzy!" Jane pulled her into a tight embrace. "I am sorry this is not as you wished it to be."

The following day was spent packing Elizabeth's things. "It distresses me to no end that you are not to have new wedding clothes!" complained Mrs. Bennet. "Had I the time, I would buy gowns both for the wedding and for your new life. However, I suppose Mr. Darcy shall tend to all of that, so I need not be too concerned," she said, brushing it off just as quickly as the concern in her voice had made it seem like a dire circumstance a moment before. "Still, you will need all your things, at least the ones that fit you presently," she said.

Elizabeth was made to try on every one of her gowns to determine which were still suitable and which had grown a little too short in the hem and could no longer be let out.

One change of plans was made regarding Elizabeth's wedding attire. Instead of wearing her best gown and the jewels from her mother to the wedding itself, Mrs. Bennet desired her to wear them to the ball the night before.

"For that will be your real celebration, my dear," Mrs. Bennet said. "The ceremony will be over so quickly, and then you will be setting off directly for your new home."

Elizabeth's throat tightened. She found she could not get any words out. She went to her mother and put her arms around her, holding back a sob.

"Sweet Lizzy," her mother crooned. "We shall miss you. It is true. You must tell me when we are to visit at Pemberley. We will come whenever you like. And I think perhaps not long after we may see Jane settled at Netherfield too."

Elizabeth lifted her head towards her in question.

"Yes, Lizzy, I am almost certain of it! Have you not seen the looks that Mr. Bingley has given Jane all this time? He must be in love with her. I know it in my bones. It is only your upcoming wedding which has prevented him from speaking up. I dare say as soon as you and Mr. Darcy are gone, he will come to your father and ask his blessing."

Elizabeth was not certain whether her mother was correct, but she hoped for Jane's sake that Mr. Bingley did love her and would marry her soon. It would bring her some consolation to know that her beloved sister had found love, even if she herself had not.

"I am increasingly concerned about the Bennet family," Caroline confided to Darcy the morning of the ball. "They are like bloodthirsty leeches, these people."

Despite having only a few days' notice, she had done everything required to show off Netherfield Park at its finest to the entirety of the neighborhood. Her brother had also thrown himself into the preparations, declaring everything must be made perfect for the celebration of his friends.

"You need not be concerned for me, Miss Bingley," Darcy replied. "I have made my choice and I am entering it with eyes wide open."

Caroline folded her arms. "You might be," she pointed out, with one eyebrow raised. "But what of Charles? It's evident he is being taken in. Did you not see the way Miss Bennet flirted with him at dinner the other night?"

"Bingley knows his own mind well enough," Darcy shrugged. "You need not fear for his sake."

"On the contrary," Caroline argued. "There is every reason to fear. Charles has never been one to behave logically. He thinks too much with his heart, among other things. This is not the first time his head has been turned by a pretty face or an alluring figure. Recall last winter with Miss Green. What a near disaster that almost turned out to be!"

"Yes," Darcy agreed. "But fortunately, it was prevented."

"Here he is about to make the same mistake yet again," Caroline pointed out. "He is falling right into Miss Bennet's trap. We must do something to pull him from her clutches before it is too late."

"You are overreacting," Darcy dismissed.

"Observe her tonight at the ball, and you'll see. The whole lot of them are after Charles's fortune. You may have sealed your fate, Darcy, but do not let your friend do the same."

Chapter 15

Elizabeth had never seen Netherfield Park look so beautiful as it did that evening. Every candle in the entire place was lit, casting the hallways and the ballroom aglow with light and warmth. Beautiful ribbons adorned the candelabras, the banister, and across every mantle. The tables were bedecked with crisp white linens, making the shining silverware and crystal atop them gleam. Musicians played from the gallery above the ballroom, where their music could be heard throughout the entire house.

Elizabeth, as the guest of honor, was the first to arrive with her family. She handed her velvet-lined cape to a footman before stepping into the ballroom. The sight there took her breath away, and it was not merely the candles and decorations, but the person who stood there before her.

Mr. Darcy leaned his arm against the mantle, his coat of black superfine wool cut trimly to the advantage of his figure. He wore white dress breeches that fit his legs nicely, and a perfectly tied cravat peeked out above his fine silver waistcoat. His black, curly hair, always immaculate, had been combed differently tonight, and Elizabeth could not help thinking how becoming it looked, with only a few tendrils of curls dangling across his forehead.

Her movement caught the corner of his eye, and he turned with a smile to her, causing a sudden warmth to rush to her heart. "You look well this evening, Miss Elizabeth," he greeted her with a bow.

"As do you, Mr. Darcy." She curtsied, trying hard not to let the flush of her cheeks betray her thoughts. In less than a day, they would be united as husband and wife, and she would be sharing a home with him—a fact she tried hard not to think about at that moment.

Then another thought occurred to her. *Will he expect me to share a bed with him?* A shiver ran up her spine. She would not be the first person to marry out of convenience or out of necessity, and surely Mr. Darcy would want an heir. She gulped as he drew near her.

She could not decide whether to be delighted or disgusted by the thought of bearing children for him. He was the most unpleasant man she had ever known, and she had no wish to be married to him, but when she considered his appearance–as fine a specimen of a human male as one could hope for– the notion was less unpalatable than before.

She quickly banished such thoughts as the heat in her face continued to travel down to her neck. "It is warm this evening," she remarked, opening her fan and fluttering it quickly to cool herself. "Mr. Bingley has all the fireplaces lit and so many candles."

"Yes," Darcy chuckled. "It is a wonder the whole place does not burn down."

"I suppose he wishes to make a good impression on his neighbors, given everything that has transpired since his arrival," she said.

"Bingley has never failed to impress others when he desires to. Though it is a mark of his character that he has gone to such trouble on our account."

Their host soon appeared, and Elizabeth was able to express her gratitude to him for his generosity. His sisters also appeared along with Mr. Hurst. Caroline was dressed in an ostentatious and revealing gown, the shade of a tangerine, with a turban of many plumed feathers perched on her head. Mrs. Hurst was dressed similarly in an elaborately-detailed russet gown. Mr. Hurst merely gave his perfunctory greetings, attending himself to the punch bowl and the trays of hors d'oeuvres that were beginning to circulate in the hands of the footmen.

"What a pleasure to be able to celebrate your wedding this evening, Miss Elizabeth," simpered Caroline.

"I thank you, Miss Bingley, for playing hostess," Elizabeth curtsied to her.

"Of course, the honor is all mine," she replied. "It is the least we could do, all things considered. Charles quite insisted upon it, in fact." The hint of irritation in her voice did not escape Elizabeth's detection, but it did her mother's.

Mrs. Bennet's head bobbed. "We are vastly obliged to you, Mr. Bingley and Miss Bingley. I originally had in mind to throw a wedding breakfast, but this plan is much better, and I am quite happy that Mr. Bingley made the offer. After all, Longbourn is so small to host all of our neighbors. And since we do not know when we are to see our Lizzy again, it will be so good for her to have all her friends come to bid her farewell before her departure."

Mr. Bingley could only smile and nod before Mrs. Bennet went on, "My, how impressive, the number of candles you have here at Netherfield Park! It must have cost you a fortune to light all these. And you have such expensive linens covering the tables." She went on and on in this manner, complimenting everything in the room, while the others turned to greet the rest of the guests who were now arriving.

The Lucas family were among these next set.

"Dearest Eliza," said Charlotte Lucas, drawing near and kissing her cheeks. "My heartfelt wishes to you."

"Thank you, Charlotte," Elizabeth said, with as much warmth as she could muster. Elizabeth knew it was the first of many wishes she would receive that day and the next, which she would have to accept graciously, no matter her real feelings on the matter.

"You have done well for yourself, my dear," Charlotte whispered under her breath. "Look how well he looks this evening." Her eyes glanced in the direction of Mr. Darcy, presently receiving a hearty handshake from Sir William. "And here I thought Jane would be the first one to catch her husband," she added.

Elizabeth's cheeks pinked. "It is not as you surmise, I assure you," she hissed, but Charlotte paid her no heed as she moved on to greeting her hosts before making her way to the refreshment table.

Elizabeth, seeing Mr. Darcy's eyes upon her, blushed and hurried after her friend.

Hearing the musicians tuning their instruments, Darcy knew it was nearly time for the ball to begin. But he could not locate Elizabeth among the throngs gathered in the hall, nor in the ballroom, which was growing more crowded as guests continued to filter in.

Finally, in the drawing room, Darcy found Elizabeth standing in one corner, chatting with her friend Miss Lucas.

"Miss Elizabeth," he bowed. "It is time for us to open the ball." She hesitated. "After all," he went on quickly, "we are to be married tomorrow. As the guests of honor, it will be expected of us."

"Yes, yes, of course," she said, taking his hand. Her friend grinned widely as they parted.

Darcy led Elizabeth to the ballroom, where the couples were lining up.

"It occurs to me that though we are to be married tomorrow, I know very little of you," he said as the strains of violin above them in the gallery began playing a minuet. "Aside from sleepwalking, what are your interests?"

She blushed, and he could not help but admire the beautiful rosy color it brought to her cheeks.

"Reading," she supplied. "All sorts of books, really. Anything I can lay my hands on. My father has always been an avid reader, and I confess I have followed in his footsteps. But I also love to be outdoors."

"Do you ride?"

"Oh, no," she said a little too quickly. "No. I mean, we do have an old mare designated for our use. My sisters sometimes ride her. But I have always had a fear of horses, you see."

"Have you never tried to learn, then?"

"I did try once when I was about seven or eight. We had a different horse then, a stubborn old unruly thing. He never threw my father or Jane, you see. But as for me, well, when I tried to ride him, something spooked him and he reared up suddenly and threw me off. And despite all my father's protests that one must simply climb back on the horse if one is to learn to ride, I found that I simply could not. I was too terrified any time I went near him."

"That is a pity, for Pemberley has many wonderful horses in its stables. I, myself, confess to a great love for riding. My sister, Georgiana, also loves to ride. I hope that you will enjoy meeting her."

"I am sure that I shall." Elizabeth smiled sweetly.

Darcy's heart warmed to hear her say that. "Good. I believe I told you, I am expecting her to join us at Pemberley, not long after we are settled there. Her governess, Mrs. Younge, will bring her."

"Does she not attend school then? I mean, I thought people of your class often did. Bingley's sisters seemed to think very highly of their school in London."

"I did, initially, on Miss Bingley's recommendation, send Georgiana to the same seminary in London where she and Mrs. Hurst attended. However, Georgiana quickly found it was not to her liking. The other girls there were petty and jealous. They teased and bullied her to the point that she became quite miserable and begged me to let her leave there and study under a governess, as she had before. I made inquiries and at last someone came to me by recommendation of my rector. As she had all the necessary qualifications and excellent references, I hired her to take charge of Georgiana's education. Georgiana has, for the past two months, been living at Darcy House with Mrs. Younge. But I hope she might stay at Pemberley with us, at least until we go down for the Season."

"Of course, nothing would please me more. Do you spend much time in London during the Season then?" Elizabeth said, changing the subject.

Darcy nodded. "I own a house in Mayfair, and spend a good part of the Season there each year. My uncle, Lord Matlock, also has a house in town nearby, as does my aunt, Lady Catherine de Bourgh, whom you have met."

"Yes, she had quite a lot of things to say to me," Elizabeth admitted.

"So I was told. She came to me straight from her visit to you, and I received quite the set down."

His comment made Elizabeth laugh. "Not enough to make you turn aside from your pledge to marry me, and marry your cousin, as you were ordered," she noted, unable not to tease.

"I told her my solemn duty to you lay above my duty to my family," he replied, in all seriousness. "Nothing could persuade me to withdraw my promise. I am, and always will remain committed to you."

Such a solemn vow stirred Elizabeth's heart and made her regret how coldly she had treated Mr. Darcy in the past. Here was a man who wore his honor like a badge on his breast. For better or worse, in less than a day, they would be husband and wife. She determined she would not regard him as her adversary, but allow them to come into an amicable friendship. They were, after all, to be companions for the remainder of their days.

Very well, Mr. Darcy, if an armistice is what you seek, then I shall accept your olive branch.

Their dance ended, and he surprised her by asking if she might take a stroll with him on the terrace again. This time, she readily consented. The moon had risen, and the garden looked less bleak than before. Torches had been placed along the terrace, illuminating their path and generating enough heat to stave off the cold as they walked.

Mr. Darcy cleared his throat. "There is something I wished to give you the other night, which I did not have the opportunity to do." Reaching into his pocket, he pulled out the box containing the ring.

Kneeling before her, he opened it. Flickers of light danced off the gleaming gems, a circular diamond surrounded by four smaller oval diamonds, laid at each point like a cross. Elizabeth froze.

"It was my mother's ring," he told her, taking one of her hands gently and putting the ring on it.. "Though we are already engaged, I wished to formally propose to you and ask you, whether you would consent to be my wife. After tomorrow, there will be no turning back. If you wish now, to renounce everything, I will ensure you and your sisters, along with your mother, are cared for, all the remainder of your days."

It was too much! Such generosity from a man who, until recently, she considered her enemy! Taking a step back from him, she removed her hand from his, then pulled the ring from her finger.

"I-I cannot accept this," she stammered, handing it back to him, her heart awash with feeling.

He sighed. "Am I to take this as a sign you wish to dissolve our betrothal?"

"The ring–it belonged to your mother. It is too precious a thing for me to wear."

"It was her wish that I give it to my bride, whomever she may be. But I shall return it to its chest to await the finger of the next lady, if such is your desire."

"You are too good, Mr. Darcy! To promise to care for me and my sisters, even if I should not wed you." She willed the tears that welled up, threatening to spill over, to maintain their bounds. "But I cannot allow you to do that. Even if we are financially provided for, the stain on our family would be irreparable. I could not send my father to an early grave, knowing I had the power to restore honor to my family. We will proceed tomorrow as planned."

"In that case, then this ring belongs on your finger." He moved to put it back on her, but she shook her head.

"Tomorrow, at the church. You may place it on my finger then. I do not trust myself with such a valuable keepsake."

He nodded, returning the ring to the box, and then to his pocket.

"Let us return to the party," she said, "before we are missed." She turned and walked from him quickly before her emotions overcame her.

Chapter 16

Darcy found it increasingly difficult to hide his admiration for Elizabeth. She looked absolutely radiant in a pure white gown that highlighted the creaminess of her skin and the beauty of her dark eyes and hair. She moved with ease and grace among the guests at the ball, welcoming friends and neighbors and accepting their congratulations with thanks.

Darcy marveled, knowing how much she must detest having to receive their well-wishes. A lump in his throat formed. Would she always despise him? Would there ever be a time when she could possibly care for him?

Her family, meanwhile, were becoming harder and harder to ignore. Such mortification could scarcely be endured, knowing these were to be his in-laws and in less than a day.

The youngest sisters were presently making a display of themselves, throwing themselves flirtatiously at the Lucas brothers, William Goulding, and even Mr. Robinson, the young fellow who worked as a clerk for their Uncle Phillips. It was clear they had already imbibed from the punch bowl too many times.

Mrs. Collins, meanwhile, installed herself at the pianoforte and displayed her accomplishments–or lack thereof–for a good forty minutes or so before her father came over, slammed the pianoforte shut, and exclaimed loudly that she had delighted them all long enough; the single ladies were now to present their accomplishments.

Mr. Collins was no more conscientious. He proceeded around the room introducing himself as the rector of the Great Lady Catherine de Bourgh. He prattled on about her many virtues, asking guests whether they knew of her, and dropped so many remarks about the grand estate Rosings in each conversation that Darcy was sure the other parties of those conversations could not be more eager to get away.

But the worst behavior of all came from Mrs. Bennet and Jane. Darcy was standing nearby when he overheard Mrs. Bennet speaking to Mrs. Long about her daughter's good fortunes.

"Oh yes, as you can see, my Lizzy is making a most advantageous match," she crooned. "I am told Mr. Darcy's income exceeds ten thousand per annum, and his estate, Pemberley, is surely the grandest in all of Derbyshire, perhaps even in all the realm!"

Mrs. Long, who had two unmarried nieces of her own, replied dryly, "Yes, you are fortunate. If only all young ladies were as favored as yours."

Mrs. Bennet bobbed her head. "And just think! My Lizzy's marriage must put her sisters in the way of other rich men. See how Mr. Bingley dotes on Jane. One can tell he is practically in love with her! I am quite certain he will be making her an offer imminently. He was so generous, after all, in offering Netherfield to us for this ball, which he claims is all for the sake of his friend. But I know it to be on Jane's account, that he might hope to impress her. There could be no other explanation for it. His income, though not so bountiful as Mr. Darcy's, is estimated to be somewhere around four or five-thousand per year; quite enough for my Jane, who is used to the country comforts of home. Yes, to see her established at Netherfield would be a fine thing in my opinion. It is my fervent hope that Bingley will purchase it when his lease expires."

"You must be pleased then," said Mrs. Long, still unimpressed.

SUDDEN AWAKENINGS

Mrs. Bennet giggled. "Oh, indeed, I cannot think of anything better for my dear girls."

Darcy suspected her of having had too much wine already that evening. She seemed oblivious, not only to her words, but to his proximity to her.

"Of course, I've told my Jane to do all she can to capture Mr. Bingley," Mrs. Bennet went on, to Darcy's utter shock. "It was my idea, of course, to have her come and stay at Netherfield when she was invited. I ensured she went on horseback, though it was a rainy day. Of course, I cannot take credit for having made her ill, the poor dear! But she did recover so quickly, sometimes I wonder if the sly thing had been pretending all along."

Darcy scarcely believed what he was hearing.

Mrs. Bennet leaned closer to Mrs. Long, as if it would do anything to muffle her loud voice. "I commended her for her efforts, though she denied it all. I encouraged her not to be overly demure, but to put herself forward as best she could. And the next time she saw Mr. Bingley, she did just that; she even wore a daring neckline I had recommended to her that morning."

It was too much for Darcy, to hear all of Caroline Bingley's fears confirmed right before his very eyes. He needed to be alone to think. The public rooms were all in use, but the door to the study was closed. He could regain his composure, possibly with the assistance of a quality bottle of brandy he knew Bingley kept there. He put his hand on the knob, but before he entered, he heard voices inside. Guests, stolen away for a *tête-à-tête*, or perhaps a romantic interlude, he conjectured.

He was prepared to walk away when he caught the name "Mr. Bingley" uttered by a female voice from within. He had just seen Miss Bingley dancing, and Mrs. Hurst attending the punch bowl. It could not be one of them. His first inclination was to not interfere. Bingley was a grown man and might have a perfectly valid reason to be alone in a closed room with a lady. Then again, Bingley was also hopelessly naive. If anyone else found him there, the lady might be compromised, and Bingley's fate sealed as surely as his own was. With this consideration in mind, Darcy entered the study, shutting the door behind him. He discovered Jane Bennet crawling on the floor with Bingley standing over her. Darcy blushed at the indecorous position he had found them in, especially Miss Bennet. Upon seeing him, she sat up suddenly, brushing back the tendrils of hair that had fallen from her coiffure.

"Mr. Bingley was helping me to look for my necklace. I am certain I lost it here the last time we visited, or perhaps during my stay while I was ill."

Darcy could not recall a time that Miss Bennet had ever been in the study, either during their dinner or her stay, but that mattered little.

"Miss Bennet, surely you could have asked one of the maids to assist you," Darcy said, unable to disguise the displeasure in his voice.

"The door to the study was locked, and only Mr. Bingley had the key," she explained.

"Yes, Darcy, it is entirely my fault. When I heard Miss Bennet had lost her pendant, I offered to help her look for it. I suppose, in hindsight, I could have asked a servant." Bingley's cheeks were reddened, indicating he at least had some realization of the impropriety of the situation.

"Perhaps when the evening is over, you might ask the servants to search the house for it while they are in the business of cleaning up," Darcy recommended. "I doubt if you will have much success finding it now."

"Yes, of course, you are correct, as usual, Darcy." Bingley's head nodded quickly. "We should return to the party."

Darcy opened the door, ushering Miss Bennet out. "After you, madam." But before Bingley could follow her, Darcy shut the door again.

"Bingley, I hope you realize the gross error of your behavior."

"Yes, Darcy. It was foolish of me to put myself in a situation which might have been misinterpreted. But it was entirely innocent, I assure you! We did nothing aside from searching beneath the cushions and the desk."

"I hope the view was worth your trouble," Darcy chided. "But you must exercise more caution in the future, lest you find yourself bound to the lady in a manner not unlike myself."

Shock fell over Bingley's face. "I had not considered that."

"If you love the lady," Darcy continued, "then by all means, propose to her. But let it be a proposal of your own choosing, to avoid the possibility of resentment on either side."

A nervous chuckle came from Bingley's lips. "You speak quite seriously, Darcy."

"The situation is more grave than you realize, Bingley. Miss Bennet is…to put it bluntly, after your fortune."

"Preposterous!"

"Can you honestly say tonight's incident was not an attempt orchestrated on her part to entrap you into marriage?"

"Without a doubt! Miss Bennet would never stoop to such lengths."

"Not even under orders from her mamma?" He related what he had heard Mrs. Bennet tell Mrs. Long. Bingley listened soberly.

"Mrs. Bennet, I will concede, is everything you have represented her to be," he admitted. "But I contest that Jane– er, Miss Bennet– does not share her mother's values."

"Does she not? How can you be certain? Bingley, you are on unstable ground, you know. Miss Bennet is not the first young lady to grasp at your fortune, nor will she be the last, unless she succeeds in doing it. I urge you to consider whether Miss Bennet is worth losing your head over, if she does not love you in return."

Bingley blinked. "You do not believe she loves me?"

"I cannot be certain of anything. Do you love her, Bingley? Do you love Miss Bennet enough to marry her?"

"Love! All this talk of love, and yet, we barely know each other still. I am *in love* with her, that much is certain. Whether I love her enough to marry her is another matter. We have known each other for only five weeks. How can anyone determine their future in such a short span?"

"If you are as of yet unsure, then you ought to consider the duration of your stay here at Netherfield. As this evening has proved, you are a hair's breadth shy of finding yourself compromised. If you do not wish a repeat of tonight– one which might prove more fatal to your happiness, then perhaps it would be better if you were to remove yourself from Miss Bennet's presence for a time. Go to London, until you can sort out your head and your heart. If your feelings for her have not abated after a month or two, then return and propose to her. But if your affection is as fleeting as it was for your last lady-loves, then you would do better to give up your lease and take up residence in another county altogether."

"You must have been speaking to my sisters," Bingley said, with a touch of bitterness, "for your words echo their own."

"I will admit, Miss Bingley did urge me to speak with you. But I did not do so until I had formed a judgment of my own."

"Well! Since you have all conspired to tell me the same advice, I suppose I would be a fool not to take it. Very well, Darcy, my mind is made up. The day after your wedding, my sisters and I shall quit Netherfield Park."

Chapter 17

The morning of the wedding came at last. Elizabeth, dressed in an elegant traveling ensemble with a dark blue pelisse and a matching bonnet, felt jittery. Every bone in her body seemed to quiver. A part of her wanted to scream and run away, to jump on a horse, and flee the country. However, it was not only her fear of riding horses which prevented her from doing so. She could not help but think of the stain on her family if she were to call off the wedding.

It is too late now. Your fate is sealed.

As if another angel were on her shoulder whispering contrary thoughts, a second voice battled within her mind. *It is not too late. You can still cry off. Your family could weather the shame. Do it now before it will be too late.*

But the first voice in her head then battled with the second. *No, I am nothing if not a woman of my word. I have given Mr. Darcy my promise that I will marry him, and to my family, so our name will not be tarnished. It is my own fault, and no one else's, that I found myself in Mr. Darcy's bedroom that night at Netherfield. And it is for that crime I must pay. I ought never to have stayed the night, or if I had, I ought to have barred the door to keep myself from wandering around a strange house where I had no business being.*

Besides, she mused with a hint of amusement, her punishment was not as severe as it originally seemed to be. Her mind drifted to the image of Mr. Darcy the night before, how well he looked in his breeches and superfine coat, and the memory of his hands upon hers as they danced. Heat rose to her cheeks over such thoughts. Her thoughts again drifted towards their wedding night. Would Mr. Darcy attempt to claim his husbandly rights? Her mother's voice interrupted before she could carry her thoughts too far.

"Come, Lizzy, the carriage is ready. You cannot be late for your own wedding."

Elizabeth dutifully followed her. There were no decorations at the church, and the party assembled was small. The Bennets, Mr. Darcy, Mr. Bingley with his sisters and brother, Charlotte Lucas, and the Collinses.

Mr. Collins, irritated that he had not been allowed to perform the ceremony, as he considered should have been his right, grumbled in his seat. The Reverend Carmichael, dressed in white ecclesiastical garb, emerged from his cloister.

Mr. Darcy looked no less fine on this day than he had the night before, dressed in a blue coat with dark trousers for traveling. Elizabeth thought he looked quite handsome, indeed. Nevertheless, her legs felt wooden as her father led her down the aisle. Mr. Bennet placed her hand in Mr. Darcy's, and helped her ascend the steps of the altar to face the minister.

The reverend offered perfunctory greetings to the small congregation and recited from the Book of Common Prayer. Elizabeth heard herself repeat her vows to Mr. Darcy, but it felt as though she were not the one saying them. She did not look at Mr. Darcy for fear she would lose her composure and not finish. He placed his mother's beautiful diamond ring onto her finger, a symbol of her role as the new Mrs. Darcy. Finally, when the minister pronounced them husband and wife, she at last looked up into his eyes and saw a strange look there, warm and altogether different from the haughty look she had seen on his face the night of the Meryton Assembly. Before she had time to interpret its meaning, the minister made his pronouncement and presented them to the congregation. They were married.

※

Their friends and family all wished them well, even Miss Bingley and Mrs. Hurst. Her sisters and Charlotte embraced her again and again, her mother cried hysterically, and even her father shed a little tear and gave her a firm squeeze. And then, before she knew it, they were headed to the church door, and then their guests were bidding them farewell as they entered Darcy's well-sprung traveling coach.

"Are you warm enough, Elizabeth?" Darcy asked her as they settled in for the drive.

"I am, thank you."

"We shall cover a little more than fifty miles today before we stop in Northampton for the night," he told her. "I hope it will not tax your energy too greatly. It is a good one-hundred-fifty miles from here to Pemberley, and I plan to cover it in three days' time unless we encounter bad weather on the road."

Elizabeth nodded. "I can assure you, I will be equal to it." But she was not thinking of the weather or the distance to her new home at all. Her mind was more occupied with the stop they would be making in Northampton, and what that night might entail for her.

※

Darcy tugged at his collar, feeling uncomfortably hot inside the coach despite the cooling weather outside as the afternoon grew. Darcy's valet Perkins sat beside him while Elizabeth occupied the seat opposite them. Having the valet travel with them did not make things any less awkward for Darcy, who was keenly aware of his new bride's presence so near to him. The notion they would soon be sharing a room together, perhaps even a bed, weighed on his mind.

If there is only one bed, I will sleep on a chair, Darcy told himself. *I have no intention of claiming my husbandly rights, nor expect her to share a bed with me.* He had already made peace with the idea that he would never have an heir as long as he was married to Elizabeth, and that he would one day pass Pemberley to Georgiana and her children, whoever they may be.

For most of the day, Elizabeth read a book, while Darcy looked out at the barren countryside, grateful there was no snow to delay their travels. Occasionally, he spoke softly with his valet. Elizabeth seemed to have no wish to converse with him.

Elizabeth eventually drifted to sleep, as did Perkins.

Darcy pretended to sleep as well, but every so often, his eyelid would peek open to look at his wife as she slept. Her long, dark lashes lay beautifully against her cheek, making him ache to stroke that cheek. Her bosom heaved with her gentle breathing, and her lush lips parted gently. Looking at her was both a delight and a torment. He willed himself to keep his eyes shut until sleep finally claimed him. He did not stir when they changed horses, but when they finally arrived in Northampton, where they were to stay the night, Elizabeth woke him by gently putting a hand on his shoulder.

Startled, he opened his eyes to see her beautiful face staring down at him. It took every ounce of willpower not to reach up and steal a kiss from her right then.

SUDDEN AWAKENINGS

The inn was crowded; only two rooms were left. The innkeeper assigned a room to Darcy's valet, footman, and coachman, who would share. Another one was given to Darcy and Elizabeth. Elizabeth gulped when she saw the single bed their room had to offer.

"I will sleep on the settee," Darcy hurried to reassure her. Elizabeth looked at the tiny settee next to the fireplace. It was covered in stains, the middle sagged, and it looked barely big enough for a child to stretch out on, let alone a fully grown man.

"No, let me take the settee," she insisted. "I do not think you will find a restful sleep there, with your long legs. I am smaller. Besides, we know well enough what a deep sleeper I am." A small grin escaped her lips.

"Precisely. Someone needs to be on guard in case you should rise in your slumber. Suppose you should wander into a total stranger's room this time?"

Her cheeks pinked at his suggestion. "The door is equipped with a lock. And you will surely hear me if I am moving about."

"But I will hear you better if you are in this creaky old bed, should you try to rise," Mr. Darcy argued. He pressed his hand on the bed, which squeaked and groaned, proving his point.

"Then let us strike a compromise," Elizabeth suggested. "We shall share the bed. We are married, after all." She wondered if his cheeks felt as flaming hot as hers did at that moment. If they did, he did not show it. He accepted her suggestion without further protest. He flopped down on top of the coverlet, perhaps testing out the bed to ensure its stability and cleanliness. The reality of her proposal sank in, and suddenly, the room felt too small, his presence too near.

"I require privacy," she declared suddenly. Then, seeing his surprise, awkwardly added, "I wish to change into my night shift."

Darcy nodded. "Of course. I will change in another room."

He left while a maid helped her into her nightclothes, and was in his own nightshirt and banyan when he returned. Elizabeth presumed he must have gone to his valet's room to change. How odd that must have seemed to his servant, she mused.

Despite it being the second time they had seen each other in their nightclothes, Elizabeth felt bashful. Her thin muslin shift seemed bare and too transparent. She pulled her wrapper tighter to cover herself, then climbed into bed, shifting as far as she could towards the edge. Mr. Darcy walked around to the other side and entered, pulling the covers over himself and rolling away from her, giving her as much space as the small bed allowed. Within minutes, she heard his heavy breathing and tried to shut her eyes. She was sure she would not fall asleep all night, so keenly aware of the male presence beside her. Nevertheless, she too drifted off to sleep.

Darcy awoke to find the warm soft body of another person nestled beside him. With a jolt, he realized Elizabeth had shifted during the night and cuddled up to him. Her nearness, coupled with the memory of seeing her standing in her night clothes, which clung to her curves and left little to the imagination, caused his body to flood with heat as blood rushed through his veins.

Unable to resist, he gently brushed her hair from her face, watching her slow breathing as her chest gently rose up and down. She was, without a doubt, the most beautiful woman he had ever seen.

He drew in a breath, his heart aching over the knowledge that she despised him. She stirred in her sleep, and he quickly withdrew his hand, looking away towards the window.

"Oh, you are awake," she murmured. He heard her movement as she sat up, then rose from the bed. She shuffled around the room, and when he turned to look at her, she had tied her wrapper securely around her nightgown, hiding her form from view.

"Shall I order breakfast?" He asked, his own stomach growling.

"I suppose so, although if we are to depart soon, we might eat downstairs."

Darcy shook his head. "This inn does not offer breakfast in the main dining room. If we wish for a morning repast, we must eat it here. I shall leave so you may dress," he told her.

She nodded in response.

Perkins was ready for him when he knocked on his door. The coachman and footman had already gone down to the mews to ready the carriage.

"I trust you slept well, sir?" Perkins asked, his eyes light, though not impertinent.

"As well as one can expect at an inn," Darcy replied.

"Naturally, sir. Only one more night on the road, and then we shall be home at Pemberley."

"Yes."

Home. Pemberley was the dearest place on earth to him. He wondered if Elizabeth would come to regard it as her home too, or if she would always view Longbourn as her true home. Of course, he had other properties too, including a townhouse in London and a home by the coast, but it was Pemberley where he had spent the happiest days of his childhood. *Before tragedy came to our family.*

His mother's death, followed by his father's, had forced him to grow up more quickly than he had liked. He had gone from a carefree schoolboy and scholar to a master of a vast estate, upon which hundreds of people depended for their livelihood. Added to this his father's investments in various joint-stock ventures, which often took him to London, and Darcy shouldered far more responsibility than many young men his age were called to do.

Will Elizabeth be one to share these burdens with me? Or will she be as Miss Bingley is– content to order the meals and redecorate the drawing rooms, but not take any concern over the matters of the estate?

He supposed their situations were different. After all, Miss Bingley was only keeping house for her brother until he married, and the home in which they lived was leased, not theirs to keep. Also, Miss Bingley had grown up as a tradesman's daughter, living in a townhouse in Liverpool, while Elizabeth was raised on an estate. Perhaps she had a better understanding of the burden of caring for those who worked the land or were in the household employ.

Elizabeth was dressed and waiting when Mr. Darcy returned to their room. A moment later, a servant knocked on the door, bringing a tray of hot rolls and coffee, followed by eggs and bacon. Elizabeth ate quickly and quietly, hardly daring to look at Mr. Darcy. She felt surprised, waking up beside him, despite knowing they had gone to sleep in the same bed.

Will he expect us to share a bed at Pemberley, or will we sleep in separate quarters?

Darcy was the first to break the silence. "Our journey tomorrow takes us near the famous petrifying wells in Matlock. Would you like to pay one of them a visit? It would only take us a short distance out of our way."

The well sounded interesting to Elizabeth. "Yes, let us make the detour." Anything to delay the inevitable arrival at a strange new home with a husband whom she could barely tolerate. Her cheeks flushed at the memory of him in his nightshirt, with the barest hint of chest hair peeping from beneath the collar. His masculine appearance prompted a strong reaction from her; strange yearnings which an unmarried woman ought not to have.

But a married one might, if she wished...

She looked away before he might discern her innermost thoughts. She chided herself for allowing her imagination to wander so. Did the Good Book not warn about the dangers of such carnal lust? And yet, theirs was an unusual situation.

The second day's journey passed much like the first, although this time, Elizabeth occupied the time by conversing with Darcy's valet. Perkins was a pleasant man, older, with graying hair, who had served Darcy's father before him. In passing her time in this way, Elizabeth kept her thoughts preoccupied so she did not think too much about the gentleman she had shared a bed with.

The inn that evening was not as crowded as the last one had been, so she and Mr. Darcy slept in separate rooms. What the servants might think about it, Elizabeth neither knew nor cared. *If anyone questions me about it, I shall tell them I cannot abide Mr. Darcy's snoring, ha!*

Chapter 18

Darcy felt he must have done something wrong, for Elizabeth hardly spoke to him the entire day. She seemed to have made a friend in Perkins, however.

"I will hire you a ladies' maid after we reach Pemberley," he promised her. "Then you shall have someone of your own sex to converse with when we travel without my sister. It was an oversight on my part not to provide you with someone for our journey."

"It is of no matter," she assured him. "I grew up sharing a maid with my sisters, and as Sarah could not help all of us at once, we often assisted one another to dress as well."

The following day marked the final stage of their journey. With less than forty miles left to cover, they had plenty of time to visit Matlock Bath and still reach Pemberley by nightfall.

Shortly after midday, they reached their destination. Matlock Bath's wells were famous for the mineral waters dripping from the roof of a cavern or ledge, which covered items left there with deposits of minerals, eventually giving them the appearance of having turned to stone. Such "petrified" objects were popular souvenirs, to be retrieved by their owners at a later time when the petrification was complete. In addition to this, many people broke off small petrified spars from the rock formations and took them as souvenirs. The town boasted several wells, but there was a particular one Darcy felt might interest Elizabeth.

SUDDEN AWAKENINGS

It was a short walk along the river to the ledge which formed the petrifying well. The air near the ledge was cool, and there was a constant dripping sound coming from the water flowing off the ledge into the pool below.

Elizabeth found the well fascinating. "To think that all of this was formed by water!" she exclaimed, examining the rock formations and various hats, wigs, gloves, ribbons, rings, coins, and other trinkets left behind by their owners which were gradually becoming covered in minerals themselves.

"Indeed! It is one of nature's marvels. Do you know why I chose this particular well to visit?" he asked.

She shook her head.

"This is the well of Saint Elizabeth, your patron saint, and the mother of John the Baptist."

"How interesting!" she exclaimed. "I am a little familiar with the story from the Holy Scriptures, but what is she known for?"

"She is the patron saint of expectant mothers, which is why many women come here to pray for a child, just as Elizabeth was blessed with a child in her old age.

According to legend, Saint Elizabeth herself visited this very well and blessed it with her holy water. It is believed that leaving an offering at the well is a way to honor Saint Elizabeth's spirit and to receive her blessings in return. The well is said to possess the power to transform ordinary objects into symbols of hope, love, and perseverance. Many have claimed their wishes have been granted after leaving personal items at the well's edge. Some say the well has healing properties, both for the body and the soul. Others believe the well can offer guidance and clarity in times of doubt."

"I had no idea you were bringing me to such an auspicious place, nor did I know these legends about the very saint for whom I am named! I would like to leave an object as an offering for Saint Elizabeth, but I do not know what."

"I do." Mr. Darcy removed his left glove. "We shall leave this here and retrieve it at a later time, as a souvenir, and under the hope that Saint Elizabeth will bless it in our absence." He winked.

"Suppose we do not return?"

"I shall take it as your promise then, that we will return, Miss Elizabeth–er, Mrs. Darcy," he corrected himself.

He saw Elizabeth's cheeks redden. He supposed it would take some time for her to grow accustomed to being called "Mrs. Darcy." He wished he were bold enough to simply address her as "Elizabeth" as he did in his own mind.

"All the rest of your gloves are packed in the trunk. If you leave your glove here, you shall be half-gloved," she pointed out.

Darcy shrugged. "Only until we reach Pemberley tonight. I think I can suffer a little with only one glove if we are in a closed carriage." A teasing smile formed on his lips.

"In that case, I shall leave one of my gloves too," Elizabeth declared, her mirth matching his. "So you will not have to suffer alone. That way, when we return, we shall each have a souvenir to claim." She took off her right glove and laid it on one of the rocks, before skipping off gaily in the direction of their carriage.

Darcy looked at the two gloves, so far apart, and decided it did not suit. Casting a glance to ensure Elizabeth was not looking, he took her glove and intertwined it with his own, so it resembled a pair of clasped hands, then laid the gloves beneath the dripping waters once more.

They were on the road again, passing through the town itself of Matlock Bath, when another carriage, coming the other direction, hailed them to stop.

SUDDEN AWAKENINGS

As Mr. Darcy signaled his coachman to oblige, Elizabeth wondered who the other carriage might belong to.

A tall gentleman, older than Darcy, stepped out of the barouche, followed by an elegant lady in a feathered hat.

Mr. Darcy's footman opened the door for them, and she and Mr. Darcy stepped out to greet the couple.

"Darcy, what a surprise to see you here!" The gentleman said. "I recognized your crest on the side of your coach and asked my driver to signal you."

Mr. Darcy introduced the man and woman to Elizabeth as his uncle and aunt, Lord and Lady Matlock. They were taken aback when he introduced Elizabeth to them as his wife.

"Your wife!" Lord Matlock exclaimed. "Lady Catherine mentioned something about a girl who threatened to ruin her schemes for Anne, but I had dismissed it as drivel. But here I find it to be true–incredible!"

"We did not know you had gotten married, Darcy," Lady Matlock said. "Our congratulations to you." She surveyed her nephew's new wife, making Elizabeth feel bashful as the object of her scrutiny.

"It was all rather sudden," Darcy explained. "I intended to write to you both once we reached Pemberley."

"A love match?" Lord Matlock asked. "Or something else?"

His wife quickly intervened. "Here is not the place to discuss such things. Return with us to Matlock Manor. We will dine together this evening, and I hope you will consent to stay the night with us."

Darcy, without a glance to Elizabeth, replied, "It would be our pleasure."

As Darcy handed Elizabeth back into their coach, Lady Matlock remarked with amusement, "Why, but you have but one glove each!"

"Yes, Your Ladyship," Elizabeth supplied. "We have paid a visit to Saint Elizabeth's Well and left our offerings there."

"Oh yes, Saint Elizabeth's Well, I am familiar with it," Lady Matlock nodded. "I prayed to God there, that he might give me a son, when we thought I could not have any. I like to think Saint Elizabeth heard me and interceded on my behalf, for I was soon blessed with a son, and another one to follow. If you have left an offering there, I pray you will be as blessed as I was."

Elizabeth, unsure what to think, merely smiled and nodded as the carriage door shut.

"You did not tell me your aunt and uncle lived near Matlock Bath," Elizabeth grumbled as their coach followed the Matlock barouche along a winding lane leading up to a stately manor.

"As you recall, our courtship was a hasty one. There is much I could have told you regarding my family, had we been given the proper time," Darcy replied icily. "I did not wish to inconvenience you by paying a visit to Matlock Manor on our way to Pemberley, but now that my aunt and uncle have seen us, it would be a great affront to them if we did not stay the night."

"I see," Elizabeth replied curtly.

"I hope you do not mind adding a day to our journey."

"I am at your disposal."

Matlock Manor was an imposing, Tudor-style house. When Elizabeth remarked on the architecture, Lady Matlock informed her it had been the family's seat since the reign of Henry the Eighth.

Elizabeth conjectured Lord Matlock must be the brother of Lady Catherine de Bourgh; they had the same nose and proud bearing.

SUDDEN AWAKENINGS

She thought she could detect a trace of resemblance between Lord Matlock and Mr. Darcy as well.

At dinner, Lord Matlock quizzed Elizabeth about her family, her education, and her father's estate. He seemed to be sorting out how a country girl with no connections or fortune managed to land a wealthy husband such as his nephew.

Lady Matlock was congenial, but carried an air of superiority. Her own inquiries were less intrusive than her husband's, but still Elizabeth felt as though she were under examination the whole time.

When bedtime came, Elizabeth was grateful she and Mr. Darcy were given a suite of rooms, with separate beds. They would not have to share a bed. She made sure to bolt the door, lest she wander during the night, and asked him to do the same.

"I hope you do not think my aunt and uncle were too severe on you," he said to her, as they were readying for sleep. When she did not answer him, he went on. "The Fitzwilliams have always been a proud lot, as you can imagine; even more so since the Matlock earldom was created for my grandfather. You are already aware that my Aunt Catherine expected me to marry her daughter. Lord and Lady Matlock knew I did not plan to follow through with her wishes, but they still expected I would marry someone from the first circles. My decision to marry someone not from that sphere has come as a shock to them."

"I am well aware I am not what your family expected," Elizabeth said bitterly. "You could not be expected to rejoice over the inferiority of my connections."

"Your connections are nothing to be ashamed of. If I were unwilling to associate with those outside the *ton*, I would not have become friends with Bingley. As far as you are concerned, you are a gentleman's daughter, and my equal."

Elizabeth's spirits momentarily lifted. But before his words could warm her heart too much, though, he went on. "My objection has always lay, not in your family's connections or lack of fortune, but in their conduct. Their efforts to snare wealthy husbands, at any cost. Yourself excepted, of course."

"Let us not speak of this further," Elizabeth replied, walking over to close the adjoining door between them. "I am tired from our journey and wish to go to bed. Good night, Mr. Darcy." Without waiting for his reply, she shut the door firmly. Tears threatened to burst forth from their dam. Burying herself under her covers and putting the pillow over her head, she allowed her tears to come out.

<hr />

"Do come and visit us again soon," Lady Matlock bid them before seeing them off the next morning. "Pemberley is only nine miles away, and you are welcome here anytime."

"Thank you, Your Ladyship," Elizabeth replied with a curtsy.

She remained silent for the remainder of their journey.

The road followed the River Derwent northward, but towards the end of their drive, they crossed the river via a bridge and through a large set of gates. The road led them through a woodland, and soon a grand, sweeping mansion came into view. Perched on a hill, it overlooked a large lake fed by the river.

"Welcome to Pemberley," Mr. Darcy said. His chest puffed slightly, as if he could not be more pleased to show off his domain.

The coach came to a stop at a large, circular drive. The house looked even more grandiose up close.

Elizabeth was introduced to the housekeeper, Mrs. Reynolds, along with the butler and the cook.

"We have been awaiting your arrival, Madam," Mrs. Reynolds said. "Your rooms are ready for you, if you wish to rest."

"Thank you, but I am not tired,' she said.

"Perhaps you might like a tour then," Mr. Darcy offered.

She agreed. While the servants removed their things from the carriage, Mr. Darcy led her through the principal rooms of the house. Every room oozed with elegance and finery, and yet, there was a comfortable, inviting air to the house. Natural light seeped in from the large windows, each which offered a prospect greater than the last. The library boasted a view of the pastures and woodlands, while the drawing room overlooked the rose gardens and the reflecting pool. The dining room had a view of the lake, across which Elizabeth glimpsed a Greek folly.

"I hope you will be pleased to live here," Mr. Darcy told her.

Elizabeth was unable to say she would not. Despite having come here against her wishes, she found this was exactly the sort of home that suited her tastes. Had she chosen this home for herself, she could not have found it to be more perfect.

Had I imagined I might be the mistress of all this, perhaps I would not have been so reluctant to marry! she mused with an inward laugh.

"This is your home now, so you may go anywhere you wish. Allow me to give you a tour of the gardens and the stables next," he said, with a smile.

Although she had permission to enter any part of the house, there was one place Elizabeth knew she did not care to enter: the master bedchambers where Mr. Darcy slept.

Having already endured one night in the same bed with him on the road, she knew her willpower to resist his masculine charms would weaken if they were to share a bed again. She was grateful he had assigned her to a suite of rooms separate from his. There would be no danger of her wandering into his bedchambers during the night. The rooms were spacious and comfortable; she was told they belonged to Darcy's mother, Lady Anne Darcy, during her lifetime.

Darcy felt a distinct sense of pride as he showed off his beloved home to Elizabeth. He genuinely wished for her comfort and happiness, and ensured her every material comfort would be tended to.

"Tomorrow, I shall place an advertisement for a lady's maid for you," he told her when they returned from touring the stables and the grounds. "In the meantime, Mrs. Reynolds or my sister's maid shall tend to your attire. Georgiana is to arrive tomorrow, along with her governess, Mrs. Younge. If there is anything you require– anything at all– simply ask Mrs. Reynolds or one of the other servants. I've asked Mrs. Reynolds to order the meals for the week, but once you are settled in, you may meet with her to discuss the weekly menus. Oh, and I shall take you into Kympton tomorrow to order new clothing. I am afraid the modiste is not as good as those in Town, but you may order additional ensembles in the latest styles when we go down for the Season."

It was much for Elizabeth to absorb. Not knowing exactly what to do to occupy herself, she wandered to the library. Miss Bingley had not been exaggerating when she called it 'spectacular'. The library was vast, containing many books Elizabeth had never seen before. All were meticulously arranged by topic, then alphabetically by author. A whole shelf was dedicated to the works of Mrs. Radcliffe. Elizabeth found a copy of *The Romance of the Forest* and was soon so immersed in it, she failed to hear the library door open.

A hand on her shoulder startled her and she looked up. "Mr. Darcy!" She exclaimed.

"My apologies for alarming you."

Elizabeth shut the book quickly and put it back on the shelf.

"There is no need," he said. "You may keep out any books you wish. If you are in the middle of one, you may leave it on the table, or even bring it to your bedroom or another room of the house to finish. As I said before, the house is open to you. Now, as for my errand, I have come to tell you, Cook has dinner ready for us."

There were hundreds of servants on the estate, yet aside from them, she and Darcy were essentially alone in this huge house. The long dinner table seemed empty with only the two of them, seated at opposite ends of it. She would be glad to have his sister's company to displace the awkward strain she felt.

As soon as the meal was finished, Elizabeth declared herself to be tired and retreated to her chambers.

"I hope you sleep well, Mrs. Darcy," he bid her.

"And you as well," she replied.

She walked the corridor alone. Mr. Darcy disappeared into his study, leaving Elizabeth to her thoughts. *Perhaps I can grow accustomed to such a home as this. Besides, Mr. Darcy is not as terrible as he once seemed.* She had once imagined him to be like the beast in a French fairy tale she had read, and pictured herself as his prisoner, trapped in a vast castle. But quite the opposite was true. She had as much freedom as she desired, perhaps even more than some women could claim upon entering the marital state, and her husband was anything but a beast.

Chapter 19

The next day, Mr. Darcy took her to the nearby village of Kympton, where she spent the morning with the modiste, choosing all manner of new gowns, petticoats, chemises, and other items for her wedding clothes. Elizabeth protested the extravagance of it all, but Mr. Darcy insisted no expense was to be spared and continued to request more items.

When attempting to decide on a material for a new day dress, Elizabeth asked the modiste which one was less costly, but Mr. Darcy interrupted.

"Never mind that. Which do you prefer?" he asked, eager to please.

"I prefer whichever one is less," she answered, a bit defiantly.

"The cost is nothing to me. You needn't worry that the funds will be taken from your pin money. This will be in addition to it. So, which do you prefer?" he repeated.

"I do care for needless waste. Either one will do for me. So, tell me," she addressed the modiste, "which material costs the least?" She found herself growing irritated that she was not being allowed to purchase according to her wishes.

"Er," the modiste began, unsure whether she should answer her.

"Buy them both!" Mr. Darcy insisted. He ordered the modiste to make up two dresses, one in each fabric.

"Why did you do that?" Elizabeth asked crossly, as they left the shop.

"I wanted you to have whatever your heart desired, without consideration for the cost," he said.

She folded her arms. "But as I had already expressed, my heart's desire was for whichever material was less expensive. Why did you insist on buying both?"

"Because it is shameful to be discussing the cost of the material with the shopkeeper in this fashion!" he retorted. "The Darcy family has no need to consider whether this material or that might save a few pennies per yard on a new gown!"

"So you consider it to be embarrassing, for a wife to be financially prudent with the money she has been given? If that is the case, you might have done well to marry my mother, for she has always been given to excessive extravagance without consideration for any sort of economy, and it drove our family nearly to ruin!"

"Keep your voice lower, if you please, madam. We are still in public," he said, glancing sideways to ensure no passerby were standing too near.

"Oh, no, I would not want to embarrass the great Fitzwilliam Darcy," she spat. Elizabeth began walking away from him, but Darcy stopped her.

"Let us not argue about such things, please." He implored, his tone gentler. "Look, there is an inn nearby. Let us stop by for a drink and a bite to eat before returning home."

※

Elizabeth agreed and allowed him to purchase her a cup of tea and a savory meat pie, while he ordered a coffee and a bowl of potato soup.

"About earlier," he began. "I apologize for my outburst."

"It was not your outburst which offended me, but your overbearing manner, and your snobbishness in regards to my efforts to economize."

"I recognize that, and I ask for your forgiveness. I was not acting out of any unkindness towards you."

Elizabeth could not disguise her bitterness. "No, only your embarrassment at having such an uncouth wife who would ask for the cheaper fabric over the more costly one."

A wry laugh escaped from his lips. "I admit, my pride was wounded by the insinuation that such measures would even be needed. But the truth is, I wanted to spoil you a bit, and I felt you were not allowing me to do so, so I behaved petulantly."

"You wanted to spoil me?" Elizabeth's eyes widened. "By buying me clothes?"

"Yes," Darcy admitted. "I regret that I took you away from your family so suddenly, you had no time to prepare a proper trousseau, as is fitting for a new bride. My heart's desire is for you to have everything you should wish; anything that money can buy and is in my power to give to you. I would have ordered twice as many clothes and gowns if I thought you would have accepted it. The entirety of your wardrobe is a mere trifle to me, in terms of cost.

"At home, you may have had to economize your wardrobe thanks to your mother's spendthrift ways when you were younger, but you need not worry about putting me in financial ruin. Not unless your extravagance extends to purchasing multiple carriages, houses, or ships!"

His unexpected quip made her laugh, breaking the tension between them.

"I promise I shall limit my purchases to only one new carriage, house, and ship each!"

"You would be welcome to!" He chuckled. "Whatever your heart desires, I wish for you to have it. And I beg you not to consider it wasteful; rather, it is our duty to patronize the local shops, who depend upon our custom for their livelihood."

It was a notion Elizabeth had never before considered. She had only ever seen the wastefulness and extravagance of her mother's spending, and not realized the importance of the local gentry in upholding the village trades.

She thanked Darcy for enlightening her, and for the new items he had ordered.

"It will be my pleasure to see you wear them," he said with a smile.

After finishing their repast, they stepped outside, and were prepared to board their carriage once more, when a passerby recognized Darcy and waved, coming over to greet them.

"Mr. Darcy, how pleasant to see you! This must be your new bride the congregation has been talking about." The man was young, clean-shaven, with a pleasing countenance.

"Word travels quickly, I see," Darcy replied. He introduced the man to Elizabeth as Mr. George Wickham, the Kympton rector.

"A pleasure to meet you, Mr. Wickham," Elizabeth greeted him. "I hope you will join us at our table sometime. Is there a Mrs. Wickham as well?"

"Not yet, ma'am. The Lord has not yet sought fit to bring her into my life," he bowed his head.

"Ah, well, you are welcome nonetheless," she repeated congenially. "Mr. Darcy's sister is to join us this afternoon, so perhaps you might come tomorrow evening, if you are available."

Mr. Wickham's face brightened even further. "It would be a delight! I have not seen Miss Darcy since last year."

"I am glad to hear you are acquainted with her. I have yet to meet her, myself," Elizabeth said.

"Oh yes, ma'am. I grew up on the Darcy estate. As Mr. Darcy will tell you, he and Miss Darcy are like siblings to me." Mr. Wickham looked to Mr. Darcy, who regarded him coolly, without speaking further.

Mr. Darcy tipped his hat to Mr. Wickham before extending his hand to Elizabeth to help her into the carriage.

Elizabeth bid Mr. Wickham farewell.

"Why did you invite Mr. Wickham to join us?" Darcy calmly asked her, once they were on the road again.

"I was merely being friendly with your rector. Was I wrong to do so?" Elizabeth's eyes widened.

"No. You have perfect freedom to invite whomever you will to our table. I only wondered at your sudden desire to invite our neighbor over."

"I suppose I felt I ought to become acquainted with those in our vicinity, and as Mr. Wickham is a member of the church, and a longtime friend of your family–practically family himself, in his words– there could be no harm in including him in our party from time to time."

Mr. Darcy was silent, so Elizabeth asked him again whether she had committed some error.

"It is true, Mr. Wickham grew up on the estate with us. His father was the estate's steward up until his untimely death. My father paid for Mr. Wickham's education and recommended in his will that he be given the preferment of the Kympton living."

Elizabeth sensed hesitation in Darcy's voice. "But?" she pressed.

Darcy sighed. "George was a few years behind me at university. While he was there, he got into a few scrapes over some gaming debts, which I helped him to settle. He was not particularly studious, either. He graduated by the skin of his teeth, and received his ordination. When the living became available last year, he requested it be given to him, as per my father's wishes. I reluctantly did so, partly out of hopes that being a member of the church might straighten him out a bit."

"Did it?"

"All outward appearances have suggested it. But I confess, I have never felt too easy whenever he is near Georgiana. There is something about his manner towards her which unsettles me."

"Goodness! I wish I had asked your opinion before inviting the man."

"It is not your fault. And I daresay my being ill at ease likely stems from being an overprotective brother. I have no reason to suspect he would do anything untoward against Georgiana. After all, they often played together as children. Georgiana positively adores him."

"Is there a possibility your dislike of him stems from jealousy?" There was a hint of a smile as she said this.

"Perhaps," he admitted, a little ashamedly. "It is no secret that my father doted on him. I confess, my resentment over their relationship likely clouds my feelings towards him. Still, I cannot help but worry. Georgiana is to inherit a substantial fortune, and George has always possessed a propensity for spending large sums."

"Should I recant the invitation? I could always invent some excuse."

"No, no. Keep the engagement. After all, I have no foundation for my fears other than the love of money in the one and the possession of it in the other. I shall have to grow reaccustomed to George's presence if we are to spend most of the year at Pemberley."

"Are there any other neighbors we might invite as well, to make the party less awkward for you?" she asked.

Darcy thought for a moment. "Perhaps we might invite the Wilsons to join us, and Mr. Kirby, Mr. Wickham's curate."

"Excellent. I shall send out the invitations and discuss the menu with Mrs. Reynolds."

Georgiana arrived that afternoon, along with her governess and a maid. Georgiana was tall, nearly the same height as Elizabeth, with the same noble features and nose that her brother bore. She was a little shy, but eager to meet Elizabeth.

"I am so pleased to finally have someone I can call my sister!" she exclaimed, turning to face Elizabeth after receiving her brother's embrace.

Elizabeth laughed. "You may find that sisters are more trouble than you would like. I ought to know– I have four of them myself!"

Georgiana's blue eyes widened. "Four sisters! How marvelous it must have been, growing up with four sisters. I should have liked that very much. Not that I mind having grown up with a brother!" she added.

"I am certain you would have traded me in for a sister in a heartbeat, had you been given the offer!" he teased.

She leaned closer to Elizabeth. "It would have been nice to have someone with whom to play with dolls and braid hair; Fitzwilliam isn't any good at those!"

"Yes, I was too preoccupied playing with my toy soldiers," he retorted.

"Fitzwilliam loved to torment me by making his soldiers stage a massacre against my poor dolls!" she exclaimed.

"Goodness, how violent!" Elizabeth laughed.

Darcy shrugged. "Such is how the mind of a boy ten years his sister's senior thinks! At least, until I went away to school."

"Then, when he returned home, all he wanted to do was moon over girls!" Georgiana quipped.

"Enough of that!" He chided playfully.

※

Elizabeth observed that Georgiana's governess suited her moniker; Mrs. Younge was indeed young, perhaps only a few years older than Elizabeth.

Over dinner, after Mrs. Younge remarked about her late husband, Elizabeth made a polite inquiry about how long she had been married.

"Three years, ma'am," Mrs. Younge answered. "The fever took him two years ago, in the spring of the year nine."

"My condolences for your loss," Elizabeth said.

"Thank you, ma'am. Our time together was altogether too short. Afterwards, I was left to shift for myself. Fortunately, my husband's schoolmate, Mr. Wickham, recommended me to Mr. Darcy when he heard he was seeking to fill the position of governess to Miss Darcy."

"I met Mr. Wickham only this morning!" Elizabeth exclaimed. "I did not know you were acquainted with him as well, Mrs. Younge. Mr. Wickham is to join us for dinner tomorrow evening, along with a few others."

Georgiana's face brightened. "Oh, how lovely! I have been longing to see Mr. Wickham again for some time."

Elizabeth saw Mr. Darcy's expression change at her mention of this, but she did not remark upon it.

Chapter 20

Elizabeth felt nervous about hosting her first dinner at Pemberley. She had seen her mother host many dinners at Longbourn, but she wondered whether she would be equal to the task. As per Darcy's suggestion, they had invited their nearest neighbors, the Wilson family, along with the curate, Mr. Kirby. The clergymen were the first ones to arrive.

"It has been an age since I last saw you, Mr. Wickham!" Georgiana greeted him. "How have you been?"

"Well enough, Miss Darcy, thank you for asking." He inquired about her time in London and her schooling there, and expressed his gratitude at her return to Pemberley, claiming the neighborhood had been sorely deprived of her.

Elizabeth found Mr. Wickham's manners to be utterly charming. His wit and sense of humor were equal to her own, and his appearance altogether pleasant. She found nothing wanting in his behavior or address. Perhaps Mr. Darcy's hope had been fulfilled, that the pastoral life of a clergyman had helped Mr. Wickham to settle down from whatever previous troubles the young man had been in and to accept his lot in life.

Mrs. Younge was chatty with Mr. Wickham; it was plain the two were old friends from the time that Mr. Younge had been alive.

Elizabeth nurtured a private thought that perhaps Mrs. Younge might find a comfortable life as the wife of a clergyman, if she could find it in her heart to open herself up to the possibility.

Mr. Kirby was a pleasant fellow, whose thin, scruffy beard did not manage to hide his pimples and youthful appearance. Elizabeth learned he had only recently been ordained and taken up residence in the spare room at the parsonage. He hailed from a small town in Kent, not far from Rosings Park. Lady Catherine had been the one to recommend him. It seemed Lady Catherine loved to be of use to eager young clergymen. *At least this one appears to be worthy of the position*, Elizabeth mused.

Mr. Kirby spoke fondly of his ten brothers and sisters, and of a mother who encouraged them to be charitable, despite their limited means. He mentioned his plans to form a school, a project he hoped Mr. Wickham would assist him with, and of his visits to the local poor and a convalescent home for soldiers.

Mr. and Mrs. Wilson were also pleasant; they had two young boys, and lived a mere six miles away, not far from the village of Lambton. They had known the Darcy family since settling in that part of the country. Mr. Wilson had made his fortune through his innovations in iron mining methods, which enabled him to purchase his estate and marry the bride of his choosing about ten years prior.

"We always wondered who would ever be good enough for Mr. Darcy," Mrs. Wilson remarked. "It seemed nobody I ever put forth as a contender could spark his interest, nor could any of the ladies of the *ton*. But I see now he was holding out for a more excellent creature." She grinned.

"I thank you for your compliment," Elizabeth said with a blush.

"How did you meet your lovely bride?" Mr. Wilson inquired.

"At my friend's residence in Hertfordshire, where I was staying as a guest," Mr. Darcy replied. "Mrs. Darcy's family lives in that vicinity, so our parties were often thrown together in company."

"And that is how you fell in love with her," Mrs. Wilson surmised with a smile.

"It is," Mr. Darcy said.

A rush of warmth filled Elizabeth's heart when he said this. It was the first time, in her recollection, that he had admitted any feelings for her. *Such an honest admission could not be merely a pretense, could it?* Then again, he could hardly admit they were forced into a marriage due to being compromised!

All in all, the evening was a success. The guests remained after dinner to play cards, and then they all took a stroll along the lake's edge at sunset.

"You are fortunate, Mrs. Darcy," Mrs. Wilson told her as they walked along behind the menfolk. "Mr. Darcy is the kindest, gentlest man I have ever had occasion to meet, except my own Mr. W, of course." Seeing Elizabeth's curious look, she continued. "Of course, I need not tell *you* all this. I am certain you have observed it, being in his company. He is known throughout these parts as a generous man, and a good master, like his father before him. Whenever there is some family in need, he can always be counted on to do whatever he can to assist them, and no tenant of his has ever had cause to complain of unjust treatment."

Elizabeth soaked in Mrs. Wilson's words. Her account of Mr. Darcy varied so greatly from her perception of him in Hertfordshire.

"How did you meet your husband, Mrs. Wilson?" she asked.

A mischievous grin formed on the lady's lips. "You will think me forward, but it was through a classified advertisement."

"No! Truly?" A laugh escaped Elizabeth.

Mrs. Wilson nodded. "Placed in *The London Chronicle*: A Lady, of good upbringing from County Cornwall, with a dowry of two-thousand pounds, seeks a respectable gentleman willing to pursue courtship, provided he be between the ages of twenty-four and forty, having property or employment in some profession above a thousand pounds per annum, and in possession of all his teeth and limbs. Applicants may apply to Mrs. Blake in Lincoln Street."

"My goodness!" Elizabeth exclaimed.

"Indeed! Needless to say, my chaperone was surprised when we began receiving callers by the dozen the next day. However, only Mr. Wilson stood out. I was taken with him at once, and he invited me to partake of refreshments with him at a tea shop in Mayfair– under supervision, of course. But Mrs. Blake was all too happy to sit at a respectable distance from us," she winked.

"She had grown tired– as I had– of my rejecting potential suitors, and wished for me to settle down amicably before my time in London expired. The trouble was that none of the usual gentlemen held any appeal for me. They were all gamesters, or excessively proud, or dull, or lacking any ambition.

"Mr. Wilson intrigued me, for he was unlike any of the others. He was driven to excel in his business, and did not depend on my fortune for his success. He was learned, for a tradesman, and well-read, like myself. His business interests have often allowed us to pursue our dreams of traveling– although the Tyrant has sadly put the Continent off limits for the time being," she quipped.

"It sounds like an excellent match!" Elizabeth said.

"The very best," Mrs. Wilson smiled. "I knew at once that we would be happy together, that our situations and temperaments were exactly suited for a felicitous union."

Elizabeth asked, "Do you think that is often the case then– that when one finds one's life partner, they are keenly aware of it from the start?"

"Not always. Sometimes it takes time before one can recognize the treasure standing before them, and some never find their ideal match and are forced to settle. I consider myself particularly blessed to have found my match, before circumstances persuaded me to accept a mediocre situation. Women with modest dowries have less opportunity than those with dazzling fortunes, you know."

"Yes, that does seem to be the case," Elizabeth agreed.

"There were precious few opportunities in Cornwall, and my mother was desperate to see me wed– hence she sent me to London to stay with her former schoolmate. I came from a family of all daughters, the same as you, Mrs. Darcy. My mother bore no sons, as did her mother, and her mother's mother– the horror of it all, as she liked to say!"

Elizabeth giggled. "Your mother does sound quite like my own, in that regard."

They were nearing the house again. Elizabeth said, "You know, I think I shall quite enjoy having you as my neighbor, and I have a feeling we are going to become great friends."

"I am counting on it, Mrs. Darcy!" Mrs. Wilson replied, with a gentle elbowing. "You must call on me at Kenshire soon. I shall be expecting you!"

"And I shall look forward to it with pleasure," Elizabeth beamed.

Chapter 21

Darcy could not help but feel a sense of pride over his new wife's seamless transition into being the mistress of the estate. After her exceptional skill hosting her first dinner, she was soon navigating every aspect of her new role, from planning the meals, to visiting tenants.

But Darcy was not used to sharing his responsibilities, and sometimes their views clashed. She initially resented his choice of a lady's maid for her, claiming it should have been her responsibility to hire such a role, and upon further reflection, Darcy realized she was correct in her estimation.

But Parker's easygoing manner and Yorkshire accent soon had Elizabeth charmed, and her skills as a hairdresser and seamstress were so adept that Elizabeth was forced to admit he had made an excellent choice in her.

The hiring of staff was not the only household responsibility Darcy found hard to relinquish.

"The house seems so dark," He remarked one evening when they were together in the drawing room. "I could have sworn there were more candles in this room yesterday."

He was attempting to read a book, while Elizabeth played cards with Mrs. Younge and Georgiana practiced on the pianoforte.

"There were more," Elizabeth said. "I asked Mrs. Reynolds to put away a third of the candlesticks. We do not need so much light in this room in the evenings."

"I disagree. I can hardly see the words on the page," he complained. "I shall go blind at this rate."

"Then move closer to the fire," she suggested. "Or do something else besides reading, if you cannot see well enough."

"Why would you ask her to remove the candlesticks?" he asked.

"When I went over the accounts this morning, I noticed nearly a fourth of the household budget is spent on lighting this house. By not using as many candles in each room, we can reduce our expenses in that area by at least twenty percent," she explained.

Darcy felt his ire rise. He bit his lip to hide his irritation. "I see. And what other economies have you made?"

"I instructed Mrs. Reynolds to have the maids light the fires thirty minutes later in the morning, which will reduce our fuel consumption, and to keep the drapes closed in any unused rooms, so the rooms will remain insulated. Oh, and I asked her to reduce our weekly grocery order by ten percent whenever we are not entertaining. We do not need so much food for just the four of us."

"Madam," he said through gritted teeth, "I beg you would discuss such things with me first, before making changes."

Mrs. Younge, sensing the master and mistress required a private discussion, quietly ushered Georgiana to another room.

"Why are you angry?" Elizabeth asked, folding her arms across her chest. "The household accounts are the purview of the lady of the house, are they not? I am simply taking necessary steps to reduce waste and run the household more efficiently. It has been long, has it not, since there has been a lady of the house to do so?"

Darcy laid aside his book and stood to face her. "The economies you take are, for one thing, unnecessary, and for another, unwise! Did I not tell you, firstly, that there is no need to scrimp and save? This house could easily boast twice as many candles lit in the evening, and we would suffer no losses! We could have the fires lit all day, every day, even in summer, and would only be worse for wear by the sweltering heat it would cause!"

"The rich do not stay rich by wasting their fortunes on needless extravagance!" Elizabeth argued. "A little economy goes a long way in ensuring your fortune endures for the next generation."

Darcy forced himself to count to four, taking a deep breath before replying. "I know you meant well, Mrs. Darcy, but I do not think you considered all the ramifications before acting. The cutting of the food budget, for instance. Did you not consider where all the excess food went? What we do not use is distributed to the servants and the poor, of which there are many. No food is ever thrown out in this house. I have ordered that anything we do not eat off our table be taken to the beggars on the streets of the village, and anything in our larder which might go to spoil is distributed among the widows and orphans.

"By reducing our consumption, you alter the ratio of uneaten food which remains to be distributed to those without means. They may be poor, but they often will not accept charity. However, if they believe they are doing us a service by taking that which would otherwise spoil, they are happy to accept our gifts."

"I did not realize," Elizabeth said, feeling ashamed. "I only wanted to help."

"I know you did. I shall speak to Mrs. Reynolds in the morning regarding the food orders. As for the other economies you have made, it would be best not to deprive the chandler of his usual order; he depends upon the large number of candles purchased to keep Pemberley lit. Please ask the maids to return the candelabras to this room and have them lit, so I might see to read my book," he ordered grumpily.

SUDDEN AWAKENINGS

Elizabeth felt frustrated with Mr. Darcy. Lacking any other occupation, she had thrown herself into the role she had been given as mistress of the house, had done everything she could to learn the ropes from Mrs. Reynolds, and taken initiatives to manage the household funds more economically. But did Mr. Darcy appreciate any of it? No! Instead, he scolded her and made complaints about the reduction to his comforts.

She supposed a gentleman such as him, having grown up with every comfort in life, was ill-used to suffering the loss of those physical comforts, even by a small measure. But it aggravated her to find her efforts so underappreciated. To what better use could she employ herself, if not these pursuits? Was she expected to spend her days visiting neighbors and entertaining, or engaging in idle needlework, as other ladies of fashion did?

She expressed her dissatisfaction to Mrs. Wilson, when she paid her promised call at Kenshire.

"I am certain Mr. Darcy will come to appreciate your efforts to economize when your neighbors have all retrenched and moved to smaller quarters in Bath or Manchester," Mrs. Wilson reassured her. "Of course, *we* will still be here— my mother always taught me to live within my means, and Mr. Wilson abides by the same principles. But many families have come to ruin for paying no heed to the bills running up, failing to examine their spending until it is too late."

Elizabeth nodded. She had seen that very thing happen to Netherfield Park's owners, whose wasteful spending drove them to lease their home and remove to smaller quarters in Sidmouth, where they could give off the appearance of being fashionable people among the set of seaside resort tourists.

At home, Elizabeth had assisted Mrs. Hill with the household accounts once she turned eighteen. Her father saw she had a head for numbers and a knack for finding ways around her mother's spendthrift habits– cutting down the grocery bills, using less firewood and candles, and reworking gowns and bonnets when her mother would have preferred to buy new ones.

Of course, she could not curb her mother entirely; all too often, Mrs. Bennet and her younger daughters would return from Meryton, their arms laden with new hats and gloves and gowns cut in the latest fashion of expensive material. Mrs. Bennet insisted it was necessary for them to dress in the manner of the upper classes, in order to attract wealthy husbands.

But her careless spending often negated the savings Elizabeth had gleaned in other areas, frustrating her and making her wish her father would take his wife to task for it. However, Mr. Bennet, who had never been much good with numbers, was all too ready to relinquish his responsibility over the bookkeeping to his daughter, and to attend only to his books and overseeing the farms. She hoped the estate would not fall into ruin, now that she was no longer living at Longbourn.

Her thoughts were interrupted by a small boy, no bigger than three years of age, crawling on the floor by her feet. He wore a patch over one eye and had tied a scarf around his head. In one hand, he carried a wooden sword.

"Shh!" He whispered, putting a finger to his lips. "I'm hunting for pirate treasure."

"I see," Elizabeth said to him in a hushed voice. "I wish you success on your expedition, sir."

He resumed his crawl, searching beneath the netted cover of the side table beside them.

"Edward," his mother said, in a gentle voice, "what did I tell you about remaining in the nursery with Nanny when I have guests?"

"But Henry says we gotta find the treasure!" The small boy protested, sticking his head back out from beneath the table cover.

Just then, a loud yelling erupted, preceding another boy, just slightly older than the other, who tore into the room at breakneck speed, brandishing his toy sword. He leapt onto the empty settee across from them, bouncing up and down. "Avast, ye villain! Get away from me buried treasure or I'll make ye walk the plank!"

Elizabeth put her arms above her head in surrender. "I swear, upon my honor, I have not laid a finger upon your treasure." She feigned fear and trembling, but a grin and a wink in Mrs. Wilson's direction indicated she was enjoying this little pretend play.

"Then what be that there, wench?" The older boy pointed, jumping off the settee and running up to Elizabeth. He reached behind the small cushion next to Elizabeth's arm and pulled out a tiny wooden box, fashioned to look like a pirate's chest. He opened it to display a small hoard of pennies and a few farthings. "Proof ye tried to steal me treasure! Get up, wench, and walk the plank!"

"Henry," his mother reprimanded. "Speak to Mrs. Darcy with respect, I beg you, or I shall put you in the corner."

Henry sobered. "Begging your pardon, Mrs. Darcy. It was all a bit of fun."

"No harm done, Master Henry. Pray, let us continue our game," Elizabeth said jovially. Affecting a humble expression, she threw herself to her knees. "Have mercy, Captain, and grant a poor soul clemency! I did not know the treasure here belonged to you, nor that it was buried so near. I beg you, do not make me walk the plank, for I cannot swim!"

The younger boy reemerged from his hiding place beneath the table. "Arr, make er walk the plank, Cap'n!"

"Methinks I've a better idea. Ready the cannons, bo'ssun. We'll send 'er down to ol' Davy Jones' locker– unless the sharks get to 'er first."

"Not the cannons!" Elizabeth exclaimed.

Edward looked quizzically at his brother. "What cannons? We haven't got any."

"Get the little ones from the toy soldier box," Henry hissed.

"They're not big enough for her." He pointed a finger at Elizabeth.

"Get 'em anyway!"

Edward began running in the direction of the nursery, but was blocked by the entrance of his nurse.

"There you both are!" Nanny said sternly, putting her hands on her hips. "My apologies, mistress, I do not know how they got away from me. I've been searching the whole house for them. Come along, Master Henry, Master Edward, it is time for your snack. Who would like to have some milk and biscuits?"

The youngsters cheered and followed their nurse happily to the kitchen for their treats, leaving Elizabeth and Mrs. Wilson in peace once more.

Mrs. Wilson gave a hearty laugh. "Pirates are their favorite game recently. We have been reading Robinson Crusoe at bedtime. I appreciate your forbearance, Mrs. Darcy."

"It was my pleasure. I do not know when I was last so diverted. Your boys are darling."

"They are rambunctious, to be sure, but I love them with all my heart. You will make a good mother one day, you know."

"Thank you, Mrs. Wilson. I hope I shall have the opportunity," Elizabeth said softly.

"If the Lord wills it. Until then, you are welcome to entertain yourself at playtime anytime you wish. Goodness knows Nanny and I could both use a rest!" she chuckled. "Now, about your problem. You said you require an occupation. Have you considered charitable endeavors?"

SUDDEN AWAKENINGS

Mrs. Wilson's suggestion held merit. While living at Longbourn, Elizabeth had often made clothing to give to the poor. When she considered such endeavors as part of her responsibility as a pillar of the community, she realized she had been remiss not to undertake some venture sooner. Making shirts would be an easy but meaningful task that would help to occupy her time.

Georgiana was happy to join her in this task, though she warned Elizabeth her skills with a needle were not so adept. Mrs. Younge declined altogether, saying she could be of no help to them, and employed herself with clipping fashions from a ladies' magazine instead.

Mr. Darcy returned sometime later, having ridden out to visit one of his tenants. He smiled when he saw them diligently cutting and stitching together material, their projects spread out across a table in the drawing room.

"What are we making today, ladies? This looks to be an odd shape for a table cover," he teased, pointing at the various pieces of fabric Georgiana had laid out before her.

"Shirts, brother." Georgiana told him.

"Shirts! I see now," he said, picking up a completed garment from the pile. "Yes, an excellent shirt. I will look very well in this one, do you not agree, Mrs. Darcy?"

He held the white shirt over his chest to demonstrate.

"Yes, very well, indeed!" Elizabeth said, with an air of levity.

"They are not for you, brother! They are for the poor," Georgiana said, failing to recognize they were jesting.

"Oh no, these are far too fine to give to the poor!" Mr. Darcy said. "You had better give them all to me. I will make good use of them."

"No, sir!" Georgiana exclaimed indignantly. "For you have far too many fine shirts as it is."

"Well, then I suppose it is just as well you have designated these for the poor, otherwise Perkins would not know what to do with them all, and I should have to buy a new chest of drawers. Excellent work, ladies. Carry on!" He returned the garment to Georgiana before heading to his study.

Elizabeth smiled. It pleased her that her efforts had not gone unrewarded.

Chapter 22

Elizabeth looked at the pile of letters for her on the breakfast table. She had received little communication since her arrival at Pemberley, only a brief note from her mother, and now– three!

Letters from her mother were always a trial, so she saved that one for last, and opened Charlotte's letter first. It contained little other tittle-tattle besides a shocking piece of news: Mr. Bingley had quit Netherfield Park the morning after the wedding, along with his sisters, and gone to Town.

She communicated this piece of news to Mr. Darcy, sitting across from her at the table, and asked him, "Did you know Mr. Bingley planned to leave Hertfordshire?"

"He mentioned his intention to, before the wedding," he replied nonchalantly.

"Mamma will surely be upset over this."

The next letter, from Jane, proved even more surprising. "Jane has gone to London as well!" Elizabeth exclaimed. "My mother's cousin, Mrs. Jennings, has invited her to stay with her at her residence on Berkeley Street. She is to remain there the whole winter and through the Season."

Mr. Darcy's eyebrow quirked, but Elizabeth could not discern the thoughts behind it. "How fortuitous for your sister," he said.

"Yes," she answered. "Though I cannot account for why she might choose to stay with Mrs. Jennings, instead of our Aunt and Uncle Gardiner."

"Perhaps she felt the Mayfair district would be better suited for mixing with the upper classes," he suggested.

"A fair postulation. My aunt and uncle do not keep company with many from the *ton*. And on Berkeley Street she might have more opportunity to call upon Mr. Bingley's sisters. They reside on Grosvenor Street, do they not?"

He affirmed that they did, though he did not seem pleased by the notion. Elizabeth felt a touch of irritation. "You must still be thinking that Jane means to capture Mr. Bingley," she ventured, "but I can assure you Jane isn't at all like my mother; her heart is too good and genuine to marry a man solely for his fortune."

Mr. Darcy managed a smile. "You know your sister better than I, so your judgment can be relied upon. I do wonder how you managed to escape your mother's influence."

"Would it surprise you to learn I spent two years living with my aunt and uncle in London?" she said.

His eyes shot up in response.

"Yes," she went on. "From the age of sixteen, my aunt and uncle undertook my upbringing before I entered into society. My aunt was an excellent instructor on ladylike comportment, and she taught me how to manage a household as well."

"So it is she who I must thank– or blame– for not being able to see my food at dinner," he quipped.

"Mrs. Gardiner is an industrious woman, much like my uncle, and frugal. When they first married, my uncle had just begun his cabinetry business and they had little money to live on. She made do with what they had and creatively sought measures to reduce their expenditures as much as possible. They are well-off now, thanks to my uncle's success, but she continues to manage her household efficiently with little extravagance. I employed some of her methods into the care of Longbourn when I returned home. I like to think my efforts might have spared us from entering financial debt, but I do not know that they did little more than countermand my mother's excessive spending."

"Perhaps it made a greater difference than you think," he offered generously. "I shall be more appreciative of your efforts to manage our household funds in the future." He smiled warmly, causing a ripple of emotions to course through her belly.

The third piece of communication, from Mrs. Bennet, expressed her wishes for the residents of Longbourn to join them at Pemberley for Christmas.

"I have no objection to their coming," Darcy answered her, though inwardly he resented it. "Your family is always welcome here."

If he had his choice, Mrs. Bennet and her kin would never darken his doorstep, but he could not refuse his wife the comfort of having her family near to her on such a holiday; not when he had been the means of removing her from them.

"She writes that, if it would not trouble us to have them for such a time, they mean to arrive on the twentieth and stay through Twelfth Night," Elizabeth conveyed.

Nearly three weeks with my wife's family! Lord, help me to endure it, he silently prayed, doing his best to disguise his inward groaning at the thought.

"Goodness!" Elizabeth continued, still reading further down the page. "She adds that Mr. Collins and Mary would be pleased to join the party as well, and she mentions something about their patroness attending them. Are we expecting your aunt?"

"Perhaps I had better open Lady Catherine's letter," he said, borrowing Elizabeth's letter opener rather than fetching his own. His intention had been to wait until after breakfast to read it in his study. He expected it to contain further insults towards his bride and a repetition of her admonitions that he break off his marriage by way of annulment– a foolhardy notion, if there ever was one. Instead, her letter contained a declaration that she, along with Anne, planned to join him at Pemberley for Christmas.

"It seems we shall have a full house this Christmas– my aunt and cousin are to join us as well," he said.

It is too much, is it not?" She looked up from the page. "Shall I write and tell my mother and father not to come?"

"No. The more the merrier," Darcy answered, feeling all the more pained. Large holiday gatherings were not his idea of a pleasant time.

He recalled the previous Christmas, in which he spent a quiet holiday with Georgiana and no one else. This Christmas would certainly be anything but quiet!

"My, but isn't this the most magnificent house!" Mrs. Bennet exclaimed as the Bennet family were shown into Pemberley's grand entrance hall. "Would you look at the painted ceiling? It's like a cathedral! And this staircase is truly wondrous– fit for a duke or duchess." She went on in this fashion, exclaiming in every room about the fine furnishings and decor.

Elizabeth heartily wished her mother would curb her tongue. She did not need any reminders of how great a triumph her mother thought it, that she had married into such wealth. Mr. Darcy seemed to be taking it all in stride. Soon, Lady Catherine and her daughter arrived, along with Mr. Collins and Mary. The Collinses joined in Mrs. Bennet's effusion of everything around them, supplemented with the occasional remark on how perfectly appropriate it was for the nephew of Lady Catherine de Bourgh to live in such splendor.

By contrast, the great lady made no compliments to the house or the persons within it, merely greeted her nephew perfunctorily and added, "I did not know you would be entertaining other guests during our stay."

"Had you asked, rather than declared, your intention to come, I might have informed you that you would be sharing the visit with Mrs. Darcy's family," Mr. Darcy told her. Elizabeth hid a smile at the way he smoothly managed his aunt. Lady Catherine merely huffed before retiring to her rooms to rest before dinner.

※

Dinner proved to be arduous. There seemed to be a competition happening between Mrs. Bennet and Lady Catherine as to who would dominate the conversation.

Mrs. Bennet, eager to showcase her eldest daughter, launched into a detailed account of Jane's triumphs in London. She described in vivid detail Jane's popularity, her elegant attire, and the admiration she garnered from the *ton*. Lady Catherine, her expression one of thinly veiled disdain, listened with a bored air, occasionally interjecting a curt remark.

"It must have been quite the ordeal, sending a daughter off to London," Lady Catherine finally remarked, her voice dripping with condescension. "I cannot imagine the stress involved."

"Oh, not at all, Your Ladyship," Mrs. Bennet replied, her voice rising in indignation. "Jane is staying with my cousin, who is managing the whole affair. Are you acquainted with Mrs. Jennings, on Berkeley Street?"

Lady Catherine replied dryly that she was not.

Mrs. Bennet continued on, without any regard for Her Ladyship's interest."Jane has made friends with the most charming people, the Ferrars family. Somehow or other they are distantly related to Mrs. Jennings, I can't quite recall how, but they are great friends of hers and her daughters. They positively adore Jane, I am told. Jane has friends in town of her own, too. You are surely acquainted with Mr. Bingley and the Hursts, given their close friendship with your nephew."

"I do not know everyone that my nephew associates with, especially those with such strong connections to trade," Lady Catherine muttered, her contempt showing strongly.

Even Mrs. Bennet was able to discern the insult. "Well, there is nothing so terrible about trade! Even Sir William Lucas, our mayor who has been received at St. James' Palace, began as a printer. My brother has been successful in his cabinetry enterprises, and my own father lived out his days as a respectable solicitor."

Elizabeth's cheeks grew pink. She wished she could say something to intervene. Her mother's blustering served only to lower Lady Catherine's opinion of her and their family.

Lady Catherine swirled the wine in her glass before sipping it delicately. "If I had come from such low origins, I would do everything in my power to obscure it. Fortunately, I come from an illustrious line of earls in the Fitzwilliam lineage, and married into an old and respectable family. My sister, too, married well, for the Darcy family is as ancient and formidable as the most distinguished of aristocratic families."

As the conversation progressed, the tension between the two women grew palpable. The underlying rivalry for social superiority became increasingly apparent.

Mr. Collins, in a vain attempt to cool the tension, advocated the merits of both connections to trade and the social mobility that noble ties offered, but his proclamations satisfied neither lady, nor did Mary's spouting scripture, stating that "the first shall be last, and the last shall be first," followed by a condemnation on those seeking a lofty earthly status.

Lady Catherine, in particular, took offense at this, and Mr. Collins spent the next five minutes placating her with his toadying remarks, assuring her that Mrs. Collins merely meant one must be content with whatever station the Lord had blessed upon them, and as He had already sought fit to bless her with an exalted status, she had nothing to fear.

This caused a ruffle from Mrs. Bennet, who took him to mean that her family must be grasping, and began scolding Mary for it. She calmed down only when Mr. Darcy reminded them all that Christmas was a time for Christian charity, and a time to celebrate with one's family.

Then, with a sudden shift in tone, Lady Catherine turned to Elizabeth. "Speaking of Christian charity, Mrs. Darcy," she began, her voice authoritative, "I understand tomorrow is St. Thomas' Day. Have you made adequate preparations for the mumpers who come to beg?"

It was common practice for the poor to visit the local gentry on St. Thomas' Day, where they could expect to receive some charitable handouts for their "mumping" or begging.

Elizabeth, caught off guard, hesitated. She had indeed made arrangements, but she knew Lady Catherine's standards were impossibly high.

"Yes, Your Ladyship. I have prepared baskets of food and warm clothing for every single person."

But her answer was not satisfactory for Lady Catherine, who demanded assurance of the adequate quantity and the quality of what was to be given. Elizabeth outlined for her the types of baked goods, preserves, and salted meats she had prepared, as well as the shirts that she and Georgiana had sewn.

"Shirts!" Lady Catherine exclaimed in astonishment. "Whoever heard of giving shirts for mumping day? Mrs. Darcy, you ought to have prepared woolen mittens, scarves, and other knitted items." A cold smile crept across Lady Catherine's face. "I do hope," she said, her voice dripping with sarcasm, "that your preparations are sufficient. I would hate to think the poor of this parish are neglected due to a lack of foresight."

Mrs. Bennet, ever protective of her daughters, bristled. "Does Your Ladyship knit items for her mumping baskets?" she asked in a challenging tone of voice.

"I confess, I have never learnt. A pity, for if I had, I should have been a great proficient," the lady replied, tilting her nose in the air slightly. "Fortunately, knitting is Anne's favorite pastime; and her craftsmanship is most excellent." She gestured to her daughter beside her, who had remained silent the entire meal. "Anne blesses all the local poor in Hunsford with her gifts, and every year, they are grateful for the warm garments she provides."

"Like yourself, I do not knit, Your Ladyship, therefore it would have been less practical for me to supply," Elizabeth explained. "Besides, Mrs. Reynolds informed me that the greater need was for everyday work shirts, and when I visited the families in our villages, I found it to be true. Most of the laborers' garments were threadbare, and many confessed to only having one shirt. I am sure Your Ladyship can imagine the smell," she said, lowering her voice slightly.

Lady Catherine wrinkled her nose in distaste.

Mr. Darcy attempted to lighten the mood. "I have seen the shirts Mrs. Darcy and Georgiana have been making and can attest to the quality. The families of Derbyshire will be well-blessed to receive such fine garments."

Elizabeth flushed with pride.

The conversation again shifted as Mary remarked on the chicken dish they were enjoying, prompting Lady Catherine to launch a lecture on various sauces and methods of preparation, supplied with directives to Mary and Elizabeth as to which particular breeds of chicken produced the tastiest meat. Her advice was supplemented with earnest praise of Her Ladyship's own chickens from Mr. Collins' quarter.

At length, the dessert course came, and then they repaired to the drawing room for cards, making Elizabeth grateful to have survived the whole ordeal. She hoped the remaining dinners would not prove so taxing. A holiday visit with both matrons under her roof was already proving to be quite disagreeable!

"I am sorry for my mother's behavior during dinner," Elizabeth said to Darcy afterwards, when the rest of their guests had retired for the night. She followed him to his study, where they could speak freely.

"You are not your mother's keeper," he reassured her, busying himself by tidying the papers on his desk.

"Still, I feel responsible for my inability to curb her tendencies."

"You mustn't feel sorry. I do not expect her nature to change through any efforts of your own. She remains the same person I have been acquainted with from the start."

"I worry, lest she offend your aunt."

"My aunt has, as ever, been prone to offense at the smallest thing. If she chooses to let her ire be raised, it shall not be the fault of your family."

"I am amazed at your forbearance! I expected your patience already to be tried."

"My patience is of no consequence to you. However difficult it may be tried, rest assured, I will not lose my temper before our guests, nor suffer you any embarrassment from my quarter. You receive enough of that from your family," he quipped. "Besides, I think my own family are equal to providing me with plenty of embarrassment in return, as you have witnessed."

Elizabeth could not help but smile. "I will retire now," she said, passing by him in the corridor. "Good night, Mr. Darcy."

"Before you go, there is something I wish to give you."

Elizabeth turned around again, a look of surprise on her face. Darcy opened his desk drawer and retrieved a box wrapped in brown paper and tied with a red ribbon.

"Your Christmas gift," he said, handing it to her.

"But it is not yet Christmas," she protested.

He shrugged. "That matters not. Besides, with the house this full, it may be the only moment we have alone."

A hint of pink crept on her countenance. She untied the ribbon and removed the outer paper to reveal a polished wooden box with a hinged lid. Inside the box, resting on a cushion of velvet, lay a gold tiara studded with pearls and attached to a comb.

Elizabeth gasped. "It's exquisite!"

"It belonged to my mother," he said.

Hearing this, Elizabeth snapped the lid shut and handed it back to him. "No, I couldn't take something so precious from you. I already possess your mother's ring. This ought to belong to Georgiana."

But Darcy shook his head. "Georgiana has her own share of jewels and family heirlooms. This piece is intended to be worn by the mistress of Pemberley. Which is you." Without waiting for her permission, he reopened the box and removed the tiara. Elizabeth instinctively bent her knees in a small curtsy as Darcy placed the tiara onto the crown of her head.

"It suits you," he said.

"I do not know what to say."

"Perhaps 'thank you,' would suffice." Darcy smiled.

"Thank you!" Elizabeth beamed, catching a glimpse of her reflection in the small mirror hanging on one wall of the study. After admiring her appearance for a few moments, she gently returned the tiara to its box. "Wait here, please. I have something for you also. I had intended to give it to you on Christmas Eve, but I feel now might be a better time."

She hurried to her room and soon returned with a lumpy parcel, hastily tied with a piece of twine. "I did not have time to wrap it better," she said sheepishly as she handed it to him.

Inside was a white shirt, similar to the ones Elizabeth and Georgiana had been making for the poor. Darcy immediately noticed this one bore more intricate details. Instead of a simple, straight neckline, a beautifully pleated white ruffle had been added, and on the points of the collar, she had embroidered the Darcy crest along with his initials. The buttons on the neck and the sleeves were made from mother of pearl, and on the cuffs, she had again added his initials.

As Darcy examined the workmanship of her tiny stitches in wonder, she mumbled, "I know you must have dozens of shirts already, and if you do not like it, please, do not feel obligated to wear it. I will not be offend–"

"I love it," he said softly, interrupting her. "Thank you. The amount of effort this must have taken you, and to undertake this in secret– I am impressed!"

He watched with delight as a blush spread across her cheeks.

"It was simple, really, to hide my project. With so many other shirts being worked on, I knew you would not notice this one if you happened to enter the room during one of our working days."

"It was hidden in plain sight."

"Precisely!" she laughed.

Stepping closer, Darcy took Elizabeth's hands in his. "Thank you, Elizabeth. Truly, I am touched." He felt her hands tremble. His gaze fell to her lips, full and pink. He felt himself being drawn inexplicably nearer. He bent his head towards hers, intending to kiss her, but she withdrew, removing her hands from his grasp.

"You are w-welcome...Mr. Darcy," she stammered. "The hour grows late. I shall retire now. Good night!" She picked up the wooden box containing her tiara and made a hasty retreat from him.

Darcy watched as she continued down the corridor to her room. A mixture of admiration and confusion swelled in his breast.

Elizabeth's heart pounded as she shut the door to her bedchamber and leaned against it. The memory of her name on his lips, and the way he had drawn near to her...she was almost certain he had meant to kiss her! His appreciation for her gift, coupled with the joy she had felt upon receiving the tiara from him, filled her heart with strange new sensations. *Should I have let him kiss me?*

She could scarcely fall asleep that night, thinking about their encounter, and when sleep finally claimed her, it filled her mind with images of Darcy's lips pressed against hers.

Chapter 23

Despite Lady Catherine's assertions that the Derbyshire poor would prefer woolen garments, Elizabeth's handmade shirts were popular with the locals who came mumping on St. Thomas' Day.

Elizabeth urged her mother not to provoke Lady Catherine, and to avoid her as much as possible, and in this way, the friction between them was reduced to bearable. The weather was good, allowing them to enjoy the grounds, which assisted in keeping the matrons out of each other's way and providing all the guests with some much-needed space, even in such a large house as Pemberley.

On Christmas Eve, the families exchanged their gifts. In addition to the embroidered handkerchiefs from her sisters and books from her father, Elizabeth was pleased to receive a carved wooden jewelry box from her Aunt and Uncle Gardiner.

"It is meant to be a belated wedding present, and also contains my Christmas present," Mrs. Bennet told her. Inside the box, Elizabeth found a sachet of lavender and herbs from Longbourn's gardens.

"Thank you, Mother, this is lovely," Elizabeth said.

"The Gardiners send their regards, since they are unable to travel at present," Mrs. Bennet said. Elizabeth nodded. In Aunt Gardiner's last letter, she mentioned their joyous expectations of an addition to the family, and that she would be entering her confinement soon.

Christmas Day arrived, and with it additional guests. A lavish party was planned, following morning service, which included the Wilsons, Mr. Wickham, and Mr. Kirby. Lord and Lady Matlock were also expected, along with their younger son, Colonel Fitzwilliam. His elder brother, the viscount, was visiting his wife's family, they were told.

Elizabeth could tell having such an overflowing house taxed Darcy's patience greatly, even more than it did hers, but he maintained his forbearance.

"I see you have a full house, Mrs. Darcy!" Mrs. Wilson came over to her. "How are you bearing up?"

"Tolerably well, all things considered," Elizabeth answered. "Though it has not been without its trials."

"I hope when all your guests have gone, you will pay us another visit at Kenshire," Mrs. Wilson said, with a welcoming air. "My boys continue to pester me, asking when you might play pirates with them again, if it is not too much to ask."

"It would be my pleasure!" Elizabeth replied cheerfully.

The guests maintained as much decorum as could be expected from such a large party. But aside from a few ill-timed laughs from Kitty and Lydia and a few awkward remarks from Mary and Mr. Collins, they managed to finish dinner without any incidents.

Mrs. Bennet, in awe of dining with an earl, was on her best behavior, perhaps stunned into silence for the most part. Lady Catherine, having her brother to converse with, did not bother trying to goad Mrs. Bennet into any arguments.

After the meal, Mrs. Younge pressed Georgiana to play something for them, which she did, albeit reluctantly.

She played a selection from Handel's *Messiah*, which earned her due applause from all their guests and a request for an encore. But Mrs. Bennet spoke out of turn, saying "Oh, that was pretty, Miss Darcy! It reminds me of my own Mary's playing. Perhaps I may entreat Mary to play for us next?"

Mary, who never missed an opportunity to showcase her abilities, affected false modesty, saying she would not supplant Miss Darcy's seat, which led Georgiana to say, "I have no objection to yielding to you, Mrs. Collins. Pray, do play something for us."

Mary sauntered to the piano, all too ready to exhibit. She played a showy piece, but rather poorly when compared to Georgiana. Elizabeth suspected her practice had been much neglected as of late, due to her responsibilities of parish and home. Despite there being no entreaties to follow it with another, Mary played two more pieces before Mr. Darcy intervened.

"I thank you, Mrs. Collins, for sharing your talents with us. I wondered now, if perhaps my lady might treat us to a display of her abilities next," he said.

Despite Elizabeth's protests and Mary's unwillingness to move from her seat, she soon found herself installed at the pianoforte.

"Well, what shall I play for you all?" Elizabeth asked cheerily.

"Something bright, befitting the season," Mr. Collins suggested.

She chose a selection of Christmas carols, and soon their guests were singing along with her. While she performed, she noted with pleasure the warm expression on Mr. Darcy's face as he watched her.

Their marriage had begun under less than ideal circumstances, but she had come to esteem him for his kindness, his generosity, and his excellent treatment of all those under his care. Her heart ached, knowing he could never esteem her family as they were. But she wondered about his regard for herself. Did she detect a growing admiration on his part?

She prayed her family's behavior during their stay would not destroy any respect he may have gained for them, nor ruin the glimmer of hope that there might be a chance for an amicable marriage between her and Mr. Darcy.

※

When the musical performances had concluded, Lady Catherine felt it necessary to express her opinions.

"Mrs. Darcy plays admirably, though her performance cannot compare with Miss Darcy's."

"Your Ladyship is generous," Elizabeth said, closing the lid to the pianoforte and stepping away from it.

Lady Catherine did not reply directly to Elizabeth. Turning to Mr. Darcy instead, she said, "Mrs. Darcy would not play at all amiss if she practiced more. I have often told Georgiana that no accomplishment can be made without constant practice."

Mrs. Bennet spoke up. "Mrs. Darcy has never been one so diligent with her music. But Mrs. Collins practices with such regularity, one cannot deny that her talents are equal to Miss Darcy's."

"Mrs. Collins plays well enough, one supposes, for the wife of a country parson. And I have often let her come to Rosings, to practice on the pianoforte there. But I will not allow her talents to be equal to Georgiana's, no matter how much I enjoy her performances," Lady Catherine said with an air of condescension.

Mary, quite offended at hearing this, said, "No, I do not suppose I could ever surpass Miss Darcy in excellence. She has had the benefit of studying under the masters, whereas I have only my own study and a little progress made under the tutelage of our church organist as a child. But I suspect Miss Darcy and I are alike in our love of music, and hope it shall bring us to a greater appreciation of each other, now that our families are united."

"Well said, Mrs. Collins!" her husband praised.

Mr. Wickham gallantly added, "I could not find anything wanting in any of the lovely ladies' performances. Here I find before me, three exceedingly talented musicians. Could I listen to all three interminably for days on end, I should never tire of hearing them."

It did not take long for Kitty and Lydia, who adored the idea of a regimental officer, to discover that Colonel Fitzwilliam was presently unattached, nor for Mrs. Bennet to encourage them in his direction.

"His father is an earl, after all! And though he is a second son, and therefore his portion must be less, it cannot be so pitiful as to render him ineligible," Mrs. Bennet told them.

Lydia was the first to approach him and to make inquiries about his regiment, where he was presently stationed, and whether or not he thought he might be called upon to fight on the Continent.

The colonel answered her with all due politeness, but one as young as she could not hold his interest for long, and he soon excused himself to speak to his cousin, Miss de Bourgh.

Kitty tried her hand next, using her arts of batting her eyes coyly and smiling, as she was wont to do in Hertfordshire. But her efforts to detach him from his cousin's company were equally unsuccessful.

Failing in her quest, she moved closer to the fire, where Mr. Kirby found her. "A pleasant party we are having this evening," he said.

"I suppose," Kitty murmured. "Though we are quite a number, when put together."

"Are you unused to such large gatherings as this, back at your home?"

"Not at all. We regularly dine with four and twenty families, and our assemblies often consist of such as to make a large gathering, indeed. Is there much in the way of society around these parts, Mr. Kirby?"

"There have been one or two assemblies in Kympton since my arrival this autumn, but I have not attended any of them," he admitted.

"Do you believe them unfit for a member of the clergy?"

"Not at all. In fact, Mr. Wickham is known to attend them with regularity. But I confess to a certain shyness which has thus far prevented me from attending."

"Do you not enjoy the society of your neighbors then? Are there none of your acquaintances whom you would wish to see at such gatherings?"

"There are many, I suspect, from my parish, whom I should know and be glad to see. I suppose, my shyness stems, not from lack of familiarity, but from an ineptitude at dancing."

"If such is the case, then it is easily remedied. Someone or other shall have to teach you to dance!"

"If you would be my instructor, Miss Bennet, I should be happy to learn." Mr. Kirby smiled. "But I think, now, that our party is breaking up. I see the others are making their way down, and I suspect the carriages have been ordered."

"It has been a pleasure making your acquaintance, Mr. Kirby." Kitty remarked, with sincerity. Although at first, she had given the curate no notice, thinking his beard made him look rather Jacobean, his smile rendered him boyishly handsome, and she found a certain appeal in his quiet manners, unlike the boorish toadying her cousin displayed or the excessive charm of the rector, Mr. Wickham. Mr. Kirby suited

Kitty's idea of how a minister ought to look and behave, and she found she rather liked him for it.

"Likewise, Miss Bennet. Shall I have the pleasure of seeing you again at church on Sunday?"

"Undoubtedly," she smiled sweetly.

*

After the guests had departed, Mrs. Bennet queried her daughter. "Who was that man you were speaking to for so long, Kitty?"

"That was Mr. Kirby, the curate."

"Only a curate? I thought I advised you to direct your interests towards Lord Matlock's son."

"I did try, Mamma, only he did not appear interested in conversing with me," she insisted. She would not admit she cared little for the colonel, who was more than ten years her senior.

"Well, you must try harder! Perhaps you might suggest to your sister that she invite Colonel Fitzwilliam to come stay at Pemberley for a few days while he is in this part of the country."

"Perhaps," she mused.

*

"I have been thinking," Darcy said to Elizabeth the next day, while they were taking a stroll through the gardens. "How would you like to have your two youngest sisters remain with us a while longer after your mother and father leave?"

"You wish for Kitty and Lydia to stay with us?" Elizabeth's eyes shot towards him in surprise.

Though the weather had been reasonably pleasant for December, there was a chill in the air, precipitating another northeasterly blast. Darcy's breath fogged in front of him as he spoke.

"I beg your leave for speaking frankly, but at home, they appear to be without much governance, and under the influence of a mother who encourages them to seek out marriage for all the wrong reasons." Seeing her bristle, he continued. "Under our care, we might hope to reform them, before they find themselves attached in an unequal union of lifelong unhappiness, purely out of financial consideration."

"May I ask what spurs you towards this particular act of generosity?" Her words were tempered, but the anger in her voice was thinly veiled.

"Last night at our party, I observed Mrs. Bennet in close conversation with them, precipitating what I could only term as their attempts to flirt with my poor cousin, Colonel Fitzwilliam."

"Did you witness their interactions with him directly?"

"I did. I happened to be standing near, in conversation with Lady Catherine, and the impropriety of it was not lost on us."

"Because my sisters are so far beneath your cousin?" Her voice rose.

"Not at all. It is because of their youth that I fear for them. The colonel is an excellent man of good character, but he is more than a decade their senior, and experienced in the ways of the world, with a heart tainted by battle. I could not see either of your sisters, as young and naive as they are, in a happy relationship with him. Not to mention, I suspect his heart already lies with another."

"If that is the case, then surely there can be no harm done. He is too much of a gentleman to do anything but rebuff their advances." Elizabeth quickened her pace, forcing Darcy to walk faster to keep up with her. The dry leaves and grass crunched noisily beneath their feet, and the wind whistled past their ears.

"As he has done," Darcy continued. "He neatly sidestepped their flirtation, but it did not go unnoticed, and I fear the remarks made about their forwardness outside our family circle, if this is the kind of behavior that may be expected from them towards gentlemen with whom they are so little acquainted."

Seeing Elizabeth's hardened expression, he spoke gently. "Do not mistake me, Mrs. Darcy. If I thought there was any chance of an equal union between one of them and my cousin, and his heart not otherwise engaged, I would have no objection to the match, were he to pursue it. But it is not seemly for them to throw themselves at him, nor any other man. They must be taught restraint, and to seek out the companionship of young men of similar age and disposition to their own. To that end, we might facilitate their upbringing, and bring them out into society at the proper time."

"Kitty and Lydia are already out in society," she stated, fixing her gaze ahead of her.

"*Out* being a relative term," Darcy said. "They have been permitted to dine in company and attend assemblies, but I do not think either of them are ready to settle down; they are both so very young. Consider my own sister, the same age as Lydia. She is permitted to dine with the family when we have company, but I would by no means allow her to attend a public assembly or to mingle with society at other's homes. Not for a year or more, at least."

Elizabeth's mouth wrinkled. "You are quite hard on your sister. Do you not think she deserves her share of amusement?"

"Amusement, yes. But these may come in other forms, until she is ready."

"If we were to do as you suggest, and invite my sisters to stay with us, do you not think your own sister would feel jealous, being excluded from participating in such gatherings, were we to dine out or attend the assembly, while my sisters are with us?"

Darcy coughed slightly. "My point is that your sisters ought to be removed from such events, for a time, while we undertake their reform. They would find plenty of amusement in Georgiana's company, and I daresay would feel no loss of society while they are here. And Mrs. Younge could supply their education, which I fear may be lacking."

"Now you think my sisters are uneducated and in need of tutelage!" Elizabeth snapped. "I have heard enough, Mr. Darcy. I shall return to the house." With that, she broke from him and made free to walk as quickly as she could from the gardens.

Chapter 24

Elizabeth had not suffered any sleepwalking episodes since her arrival at Pemberley. But fatigue, coupled with the anxiety of maintaining the peace between their family members and this latest argument with Mr. Darcy, took a toll on her. When Parker departed from her, Elizabeth forgot to lock the door to her chambers, as was her custom.

Her sleep that night, being of the deep, troubled kind, filled with strange dreams, led to her arising from her bed. In her stupor, her feet led her down the stairs and out the side door to the gardens.

Georgiana, whose room was closest to Elizabeth's, heard the door next to hers open. Wondering what could cause her sister to arise at such an hour, Georgiana sleepily opened her door a crack and peered into the corridor. Seeing Elizabeth making her way down the stairs, Georgiana stepped into the corridor and whispered to her. "Elizabeth, are you well?" Hearing no answer, Georgiana followed her.

She watched Elizabeth pass through the exterior door into the gardens, still barefoot and in her shift. Elizabeth passed through the gardens, and opened a side gate leading to the woods. Georgiana's alarm grew as she realized Elizabeth was unaware of her behavior, and still more alarmed that she would enter the woods, alone and unprotected, in the dead of night. Fearing Elizabeth might injure herself, or that she might wake from her stupor and be lost, Georgiana rushed to inform her brother what had happened.

Darcy knew at once that he must find Elizabeth before she wandered too far. He wasted no time in throwing a greatcoat and trousers over his nightshirt and pulling on a pair of Wellington boots. Discretion was necessary, but he awakened Perkins to assist him. Together, they set out with a pair of lanterns in the direction Georgiana had indicated.

Once Darcy was out of earshot from the house, he began calling for her.

"Elizabeth! Elizabeth, where are you?"

"Mrs. Darcy!" Perkins echoed.

Their cries rang through the darkness, disappearing into the depths of the woodlands.

A feeling of panic shot through Darcy's breast. Pemberley's woods were vast– several miles square in all, bordered by the river on one side and stretching far beyond the house and gardens on the other side.

She cannot have gone too far, he assured himself.

He shivered against the cold night air, wishing he had dressed warmer. *How cold must Elizabeth be, in only her nightshift, with no shoes even?*

A light rain began to fall as the temperature continued to drop. He was thankful there was no snow on the ground. Still, Elizabeth might freeze to death on a night like this, if she were exposed overly long. *Lord, let us find her soon,* he silently prayed.

***

Elizabeth awoke shivering and damp, her feet hurting. *Where am I?* She wondered. From the trees and underbrush surrounding her, it was plain she was somewhere in the woods, but she had no sense of bearing. She could not see the house, nor any familiar landmark. Even the moon was covered over by the clouds on this night. Something sharp was poking into her foot. She leaned her back against a tree and tried to determine the source of her pain.

"Ouch!" she exclaimed aloud, pricking her finger on a thorn embedded in her foot. In the dim light, she could not see to remove it from her sole. Her feet appeared to be covered in scratches.

I must locate the house, she determined. But without any idea of a heading, she worried she might inadvertently wander deeper into the woods and never be found.

I must have been sleepwalking. But how have I wandered so far?

Her teeth chattered as she crouched down in the leaves, trying to keep warm with the rain splattering down on her through the openings in the canopy above.

She contemplated whether she should seek out the river, and follow it northward until she reached the bridge, and by that means find her way back to the house. But when she strained her ears, she could not hear any sound of rushing water. She could be miles from the river, for all she knew.

Will anyone realize I am gone before morning? What if I expire here in these woods, and no one finds me until I am but a skeleton?

The thought was too horrifying. She wished she were safe in her bed at Pemberley, not here, alone, cold, miserable, and frightened.

In her despair, she thought she imagined a voice, calling her name. But the voice soon grew louder, and she realized she was not imagining it. The light from a lantern came into view, along with the sound of Mr. Darcy's voice, growing still nearer.

"Elizabeth!"

"I am here!" She cried. "Over here!" Though her foot still throbbed from the thorn in it, she forced herself to stand and wave her arms towards the light. "Here I am!" she repeated, until at last, Mr. Darcy saw her and rushed to her.

"Elizabeth! Are you hurt?" She could not see his face, but the concern was evident in his voice.

"My foot," she said. "I think there is a thorn in it, but I cannot see."

He held the lantern near her foot, trying to examine it. "It is too dark to tell. We must get you back to the house."

Perkins was not far behind. Handing Perkins his lantern, Mr. Darcy's arms were free to pick up Elizabeth and carry her to the house.

Elizabeth clung to Darcy's chest, her body still shaking from fear and cold. His arms felt strong; he carried her as if she were nothing, his feet sure and steady on wooded trails that were well familiar to him. She nestled her head against him, feeling the softness of a patch of exposed hair around the open neck of his nightshirt, his body warm despite the dampness of the rain falling on them.

❧

Elizabeth's maid Parker was awake and ready to assist when they reached the house, with Georgiana also hovering nearby.

"Oh, thank the Lord, you found her, sir!" Parker exclaimed. "If you would bring her upstairs, I have drawn a warm bath for her." He carried her upstairs to her bedroom before depositing her on the edge of her bed. It was only after he had released her that he began to feel the ache in his arms from carrying her such a distance.

"Her foot needs tending before the bath. She believes there is some thorn or other embedded in it," he told Parker.

He left to allow the women to tend to Elizabeth.

"Shall I draw a bath for you as well, sir?" Perkins asked him.

"No, that will not be necessary, thank you. You ought to return to bed, Perkins. I am grateful for your assistance."

"Of course. My services are always at your disposal, sir." Perkins bowed, bidding him goodnight.

Darcy went to his own quarters. His heart had finally returned to its resting pace, but his mind was still disturbed. *Suppose I hadn't found her when I did? Suppose she was still lost in the woods all night?* He tried to reassure himself, all was well, that they had, in fact, found her and she had come to no harm other than a chill and a thorn in her foot. He raised a prayer of thankfulness for her rescue.

Knowing he could not sleep until he was assured of her comfort, he changed from his damp clothing into a clean nightshirt, wrapping a banyan around himself and donning a pair of slippers. He waited outside Elizabeth's chambers until Parker appeared.

"Is she well?" he asked, his voice full of concern.

Parker nodded. "She is, sir, thanks to you. She appears no worse for the wear, despite being caught in the rain. The thorn in her foot was a tedious one to remove, but small."

"Is she sleeping?"

"She is resting, yes, but not yet asleep. Miss Darcy has chosen to remain with her. Would you like to see her, sir?"

He shook his head. "No, I'll not disturb her. Thank you, Parker."

Elizabeth awoke the next morning with a sore throat and a stuffy nose. Her family wondered at her lack of appearance at the breakfast table, but Mr. Darcy explained to them that she was unwell. None of their guests seemed to be aware of Elizabeth's nighttime peril, for which he was thankful. Mrs. Bennet seemed peeved that their morning plans had to be rearranged; she had counted on her daughter taking her to visit the shops in Kympton. Fortunately, she had two other daughters who were more than willing to accompany her, as well as Georgiana, who was fast becoming friends with Lydia and Kitty.

Georgiana came to check on Elizabeth after returning from Kympton, and was pleased to find she was little worse for wear after her nighttime wander.

"It is fortunate that Fitzwilliam and Perkins were able to locate you," she said.

"I feel foolish for not bolting my door, as I usually do," Elizabeth said. "If you would be so kind as to not mention to anyone what happened, I would be grateful. I should hate to think how Lady Catherine would react if she were to learn I had sleepwalked my way into the woods in only my nightgown!"

"Of course," Georgiana answered with a smile. "Your secret is safe with me."

"How was your shopping venture?"

"We had a wonderful time. Miss Lydia helped me select a new bonnet. She has the most excellent taste in hats, I discovered. And Miss Kitty suggested I might need new shoes, so we tried on dozens of pairs together, before I found the most darling boots in blue leather which match my dress."

"I am glad to see you are becoming friends," Elizabeth said. "I do miss my sisters at times."

"Why don't you invite them to stay here?" Georgiana suggested. "I am sure Fitzwilliam would not mind it."

Elizabeth's heart pricked over the reminder of Darcy's proposing the very same, and their subsequent argument. She quickly changed the subject. "Did you have many friends when you lived in London?"

Georgiana shook her head. "Not at all. At school, the other girls teased and bullied me. They dubbed me prudish for my refusal to join them in sneaking out of the school at night and said I was dull for always practicing my music."

"How cruel!"

"Julia Culpepper was my one friend; she stood by me when the other girls made fun of me, and was my confidant. How she cried when I left the school! That was when Fitzwilliam engaged Mrs. Younge to be my governess and I removed to Darcy House."

"Did you see each other afterwards?"

"Oh yes, the headmistress was kind enough to let her call on me once a week at Darcy House, at least until I came here, and we have written to each other since then. But I do miss her."

"Perhaps you can visit, or invite her to Pemberley."

"I hope so," Georgiana replied. "In the meantime, I am glad that your sisters are here. It does grow lonely at times, without anyone else my age to visit with– not that I do not love you and Fitzwilliam!" she quickly added.

Elizabeth laughed. "I do understand."

By the time the week was out, Elizabeth had recovered, and all were looking forward to the ball to be held at Matlock Manor.

"I shall wear my beige gauze," Lydia declared, "with the lovely gold turban I purchased at the milliner. What will you wear, Miss Darcy?"

Georgiana kept her eyes focused on her needlework. "I do not plan to attend the ball," she answered.

"Not attend!" Kitty exclaimed. "But it is your own uncle who is giving the ball. Surely you cannot be serious."

"But I am not out yet," Georgiana said. "I do not think my brother means for me to attend such a public affair."

"What a shame, to be kept at home on such an occasion. I am sure I would die of boredom!" Lydia declared.

"I do not like large gatherings," Georgiana told them, in a half-whisper. "In truth, I am glad I am not yet out; I feel unready to be forced into society."

"Lord, but all the fun is to be had in public! At home there is little more to do but sew and read," Lydia scoffed.

"Or play the pianoforte," Kitty added. "But then, Miss Darcy never seems bored when practicing her scales and arpeggios."

"Indeed, I find it invigorating. In fact, I am thinking I shall begin a new piece. I can spend the whole evening practicing it in peace," Georgiana determined. She went to the bookshelf beside her instrument and began looking through her music to find a new piece to master. When she was last in Town, she had purchased a large selection of new music, but had yet to even touch much of it.

Lydia shrugged. "To each their own, I suppose."

Matlock Manor glowed with the lights of hundreds of candles when the party from Pemberley arrived. Lord and Lady Matlock's Twelfth Night balls were the toast of the countryside, with families from all across Derbyshire and the neighboring counties traveling to attend. Such notable persons as the Earl of Chesterfield and the Duke of Rutland were known to attend, not to mention numerous baronets. Among these estimable guests, a small gentry family from Hertfordshire seemed out of place, and it was solely by their connection to Darcy that they merited an invitation.

Mrs. Bennet, eager to curry the favor of their hosts, lingered long in the receiving line, thanking Lady Matlock profusely for her invitation and remarking on the magnificence of her home.

Elizabeth deftly came alongside her mother and, taking her arm, said, "Mamma, you must come listen to the string quartet. They are playing your favorite piece." Despite Mrs. Bennet's protests that she did not have a favorite, she allowed her daughter to take her into the ballroom. Mr. Bennet followed behind silently.

As soon as the dancing was underway, Lord Matlock pulled Darcy aside. "Come, let us have a drink together. There is something I wish to say to you."

Darcy nodded, following his uncle through the side door adjacent to the hall. Lord Matlock poured two glasses of gin and handed one to Darcy. His brow furrowed and he appeared to be deep in thought.

"Lady Catherine has informed me of the circumstances surrounding your marriage, Darcy."

"I am surprised she did not apprise you sooner," Darcy replied coolly.

"How could you, Darcy!" Lord Matlock said angrily. "Involving your family in such a scandal!"

"The scandal would have been far greater had I abandoned Elizabeth. Rural gossip travels far, and Hertfordshire is not so far away from London as to make it impervious to spreading news, especially as it pertains to members of the *ton*."

"But what was she doing in your bedchamber in the first place? Had it been a scullery maid, no one would have blinked an eye, but you had to go and involve the daughter of a landed gentleman in an affair?"

Darcy's grip on his glass tightened. "There was no affair, I can assure you. Elizabeth found herself in my bedroom entirely by mischance, as a result of her sleepwalking."

"So she claims! But I think my sister is right in her presumption that the whole debacle was a scheme concocted by the Bennet family."

"I disagree with you, sir, but even if I did not, the matter is too late to be remedied. Elizabeth is my wife."

"Are you entirely certain the marriage is valid? You were officiated by a real minister? Were the banns read?"

"We were married by common license," Darcy answered. "And I am certain the marriage is valid."

Lord Matlock shook his head. "I wish you had consulted me first, Darcy, before entering into such a union. I could have told you to break it off. You could have claimed a prior engagement with Anne, and hastily married her instead. Lady Catherine would not have objected."

"I am sure she wouldn't, but your warnings were unnecessary. Lady Catherine delivered to me almost the exact same warnings, but I chose to ignore them."

"But why, Darcy? Why does this girl's honor matter to you? Why did you feel the need to go through with marrying her, instead of some other, better suited, young lady?"

"Elizabeth is my choice, uncle, and you shall have to accept it. Now, if you shall excuse me, I believe there is a party to attend." Darcy turned on his heels and left the room before Lord Matlock could stop him.

Elizabeth admired the score of elegantly dressed ladies and gentlemen dancing while listening to the strains of music coming from the musicians. She was grateful she had worn her new gown, a deep crimson satin, with a complicated folded pattern on the sleeves, and a split-skirt overlay trimmed in gold lace. A standing collar of the same lace showed off her neck, and she displayed the tiara Darcy had given her.

Her senses were assaulted by raucous laughter. She cringed as Kitty and Lydia passed by, arm in arm, uproarious over some joke they had shared.

"Your sisters are in good spirits tonight," a voice said. She turned to see Colonel Fitzwilliam beside her. He bowed. "Mrs. Darcy, good evening. I trust you are well."

"I am, thank you, Colonel Fitzwilliam. I trust you are the same?"

"Never better," he smiled. "If Darcy will not mind it, I wondered if I might claim you for a dance this evening."

"I am sure he will not," Elizabeth said, offering him a curtsy before accepting his hand. The first set was about to begin, so he led her to take their places on the floor.

The colonel displayed his skills well, and Elizabeth commended his lightness of foot. "You must have many occasions to dance, when you are stationed at home," she said.

"More than I care for," he admitted. "The London Season keeps me on my toes with eligible ladies vying for a dance. I have to say, I shall not be disappointed if this business with Napoleon keeps me away from the crush this year."

"But how mournful the young ladies shall be, without your presence to grace them!" Elizabeth teased.

The colonel's eyes twinkled. "I daresay I disappoint them already, by my failure to choose a bride."

"Has there been no one to catch your eye?"

"There are plenty of beauties, to be sure! But it will take a special lady to induce me to retire from bachelorhood." His lips twisted, and Elizabeth could almost believe he had cast a longing glance towards Miss de Bourgh, seated on the edges of the fray. The lady's long standing ill-health prevented her from dancing, or so her mother claimed.

"Well, whoever she is, your parents could hardly disapprove of your choice. Being the second son, you need not worry about providing heirs, and your good name must allow you to have your pick from the suitable families of the *ton*."

"My mother, I think, would be happy even if I married a milkmaid, so desperate she is to see me wed. But there are others in the family who have definite opinions on the subject." The colonel's expression was downcast.

Elizabeth let the matter rest and turned to other topics. They discussed some of the colonel's adventures on the Continent, both before Bonaparte's tyranny and after, and he returned the favor by inquiring about Elizabeth's childhood in Hertfordshire, which she was happy to supply a detailed description of.

"And how are you liking life at Pemberley?" he surprised her by asking.

Elizabeth said, "Pemberley is all I could have hoped for. A more beautiful place does not exist within England, I think."

"Well said," Colonel Fitzwilliam nodded. "But I meant not so much your opinion of the house and grounds, which undoubtedly have no equal. I am curious how you are getting on with its residents."

"Georgiana is the sweetest creature there is! I could not love her more if she were one of my own sisters. As for the other...I begin to know him better on further acquaintance."

"He certainly speaks highly of you. He bragged to me the other day of the improvements you have made since the time of your arrival."

"Has he? He once complained that my reduction of our candle usage would result in his blindness."

Colonel Fitzwilliam chuckled. "That does sound like him. He has always been used to a certain style of living and has never wanted for anything his entire life. But it has never spoiled him; despite the benefit of having every comfort, he never fails to think of those less fortunate, and his generosity is limitless towards those he feels are deserving of it."

Elizabeth nodded. The character sketch he provided aligned with the man she had come to know in the past month.

"Speaking of, here is the man himself," Colonel Fitzwilliam said. Their dance had ended, and he led her to where Darcy stood beside a marble column, his posture tall and elegant.

"Mrs. Darcy," he bowed, "would you care to dance?"

Wordlessly, she curtsied and accepted his hand. It was the first time they had danced since the Netherfield Ball, and their first time as a married couple.

The colonel gestured to them both before leaving to find another dance partner.

"You are looking well this evening, Mrs. Darcy," Darcy said as they took their places for the set.

"As are you, Mr. Darcy." A small smile formed on her lips. He did indeed look well. The cut of his suit against his athletic form made her breath hitch slightly, his soulful eyes seeming to pierce hers as if he could see right into her.

"I am glad to see you make use of the tiara."

"It seemed the perfect opportunity to wear it."

He glided her across the ballroom floor effortlessly, like a stream gently guiding a boat along its course.

"You disappeared earlier," she observed.

Darcy nodded. "Large crowds intimidate me."

"I have known you long enough to realize that nothing intimidates you. You may dislike large gatherings, but you are able to maneuver them as easily as you guide me across this floor."

"I was with my uncle, having drinks in his study."

She judged by the expression on his face that it had not been a pleasant encounter.

Out of the corner of her eye, Elizabeth saw Lydia dancing with Colonel Fitzwilliam, a silly grin on her face. Kitty had been asked to dance with an elderly gentleman, probably an earl or a baronet who had been kind enough to favor her, but she did not appear to be happy about it.

Next to Kitty and the gentleman, Mr. Collins and his wife bumbled along, neither of them a great dancer. At one point during the dance, Mr. Collins tripped over Mary's feet and landed on the hem of Lydia's skirt, earning him a screech and a rebuke from Lydia to kindly watch himself.

"It is good to see your sisters are all dancing tonight," Mr. Darcy said. "I recall Kitty's displeasure over sitting out one or two dances at the Netherfield Ball."

"Yes, it is a great misfortune for a young lady to find herself without a partner at a ball," Elizabeth said, sorely tempted to remind him of their first assembly in Meryton.

Perhaps her comment reminded him nonetheless, for he became silent and did not speak the remainder of the dance except to comment on the number of couples.

༄

Elizabeth's remark was teasing, but Darcy knew there was a hint of truth beneath her smiles. *She still holds my behavior at the assembly against me.* Inwardly, he vowed he would make it up to her somehow. Perhaps he could begin by ensuring she and her sisters were never without a partner that evening if they wished for one.

But it appeared they had no difficulty obtaining partners on their own. After the set with Lydia, Colonel Fitzwilliam danced next with Kitty, and lastly with Mary. Lord Matlock also honored each of them with a dance, and Lydia and Kitty were thankful to never be without a partner at any point in the evening. Mrs. Bennet worked tirelessly to ensure it.

The colonel seemed to be her primary object. She expressly insisted that Colonel Fitzwilliam dance a second time with Lydia during the supper set, knowing he would be obliged to sit by her during the meal as well. Colonel Fitzwilliam, too gracious to do otherwise, acquiesced. Such pronounced attention drew the remarks of several of the peers in the room.

One of them, standing close to Darcy, said, "Who is that young girl your cousin is dancing with? I declare I have never seen her before, but she looks to be about the same age as your sister. I marvel that he should dance a second time with such a child– he must be twice her age!"

The comment stuck with Darcy the remainder of the evening. His sentiments were echoed by his aunt, who approached him towards the close of the ball after they witnessed Lydia try, and fail, to solicit the colonel for a third dance.

"You must not allow your sister-in-law to be so obvious in her pursuits!" Lady Catherine said under her voice. "It is plain her mother has designs for her to attach herself to Colonel Fitzwilliam, but you and I both know such a thing is beyond the realm of possibilities. I urge you to do what you can to curtail this, so as not to cause the family any further embarrassment. We are still recovering from the shame of your own hasty union."

Darcy was in no mood to rebuke her. Besides, what good would it do?

With a huff, Lady Catherine left to find her daughter, who was sitting alone in the corner to observe the dances. No doubt, she wished to repeat all her thoughts and feelings to Anne while her ire was still raised.

◆

Elizabeth hadn't meant to overhear Lady Catherine's sharp words to Mr. Darcy, but having just returned from the retiring room, she could not help being mere feet away when Lady Catherine made her remarks about their sudden marriage. Her cheeks burned to hear Lady Catherine speak so openly of the shame their union brought. She knew her own father felt the shame of it as well, though her mother seemed to think it a wondrous thing for her daughter to have caught such a wealthy husband. *Does Mr. Darcy feel ashamed to be married to me as well?*

Though she had despised him initially, she had come to esteem him since their marriage. She had observed him to be a fair and generous master, a kind brother, and a gracious host. He was kind to her as well, respectful of the invisible boundary between them, and had yielded to her methods of running the household as its mistress. She recalled the tender moment between them when they had exchanged Christmas gifts, and Darcy's bravery in venturing out into the stormy night to rescue her after her last sleepwalking episode. Her heart beat at the memory of her relief at hearing his voice call out to her in the dark, and the feel of his strong arms as he carried her to safety.

But it stung her that he merely stood there calmly and listened to his aunt's berating, without even a word in her defense. Perhaps he still saw his marriage to her as nothing more than an obligation to be fulfilled, another measure of his generosity towards a poor unfortunate soul.

If I had not wandered into his room that night, I doubt whether he would have given a second thought to marrying me.

Nor would she have given any thought to marrying him. But still, they were married, and she was determined to bring no further shame to his family, either through her own conduct, or her family's.

Lady Catherine was right about one thing, though: something must be done to curb Kitty and Lydia's behavior, and to diminish their mother's influence, before they brought further ruin to the Bennet name. Perhaps Darcy had been right in his suggestion to invite Kitty and Lydia to remain with them at Pemberley for some months, where they might receive the governance they lacked at home.

The next day, she communicated her agreement of Darcy's plan to him, then shared it with her parents. She found Mrs. Bennet in the drawing room, idly reclining on the sofa, nursing a slight headache from the night before.

"Oh, Lizzy, there you are," Mrs. Bennet sat up straighter. "I wondered if I might speak with you. I have been thinking how good it would be, if Mr. Darcy were to invite his cousin, Colonel Fitzwilliam, to stay here at Pemberley for a few days before our departure. His noble manners would surely make a welcome addition to your party here."

"No, Mamma, I do not think Mr. Darcy would welcome any more company at this time, not even from his own family. The house is altogether too full as it is."

"Nonsense! This house must have dozens of bedrooms. It cannot be too full to admit one more."

"Be that as it may, I do not think I shall try my husband's patience for it. There is, however, another matter which Mr. Darcy and I spoke of, and I wondered your opinion on it."

"Certainly! I would be happy to give you my opinion on any matter you require."

"Mr. Darcy and I have been contemplating the need for more young ladies of Georgiana's age among her circle of companions. At the same time, we discussed how beneficial it might be for Lydia and Kitty to spend some months here with us, if you can spare them. They could study under Mrs. Younge's guidance, to further their education and refine their manners, which might improve their chances in society."

Mrs. Bennet clapped her hands in delight. "Oh, what an excellent plan! I knew I could count on you to think of your sisters, and how you might use your newfound influence to further their chances of making an excellent match. Perhaps Mr. Darcy might even see fit to invite some of his friends to stay with you for a time. The house will be less crowded, without all of us, so he would have room for additional guests. You might even suggest the colonel to him. He will surely wish to spend more time with his cousins before he departs for the continent. "

"I shall think on it. In the meantime, I must put this proposal forward to Papa."

"You know he shall have no objection to the loss of Lydia and Kitty. Daughters can always be spared!" Mrs. Bennet said.

"Yet it is proper I should ask him, now that I have confirmed your interest," Elizabeth said firmly.

Mrs. Bennet merely shrugged and returned to her resting posture.

Chapter 25

Mr. Bennet was quite amenable to the notion of leaving behind his youngest daughters at Pemberley. "My only regret is that I shall be home with only your mother for company," he winked to Elizabeth.

With the plan in motion, Mr. and Mrs. Bennet set forth for home a few days after without their girls. Mary and Mr. Collins accompanied Lady Catherine and Miss de Bourgh to Kent.

Kitty and Lydia's tutelage began. Mrs. Younge was by no means the most devoted of governesses. An hour a day was spent on lessons in history, mathematics, and Latin, which mainly consisted of her giving them a passage to read or a set of sums to work out, none of which she checked for accuracy. Another hour was given to music, for which neither Kitty nor Lydia showed any aptitude. Lydia's screeching almost made Elizabeth yearn for Miss Bingley's arias while Kitty lacked any sense of rhythm on the pianoforte.

The remainder of the day was spent in painting or drawing, needlework, parlor games, or cards. Georgiana devoted an additional three hours per day to the pianoforte and harp, but the rest of them were content to while away their hours in idle pursuits.

Elizabeth attempted to engage her sisters in her and Georgiana's regular pastime of shirtmaking and visiting the poor, but such charitable notions disgusted them. Furthermore, they resisted

Elizabeth's attempts to instruct them in comportment, something Mrs. Younge spent precious little time devoting her energies towards.

"I heard from Mr. Wickham, there is to be an assembly on Wednesday evening at the hall in Kympton," Lydia told Elizabeth one day. "Can we go?"

Since his visit on Christmas Day, Mr. Wickham was a regular caller at Pemberley, and had several times been invited to dine, usually accompanied by Mr. Kirby or Mr. and Mrs. Wilson.

"Mr. Darcy deems you are not old enough to attend such public gatherings," Elizabeth replied, not breaking a stitch on the shirt she was sewing.

"How unfair! In Hertfordshire, we were regular participants at all the assemblies." Lydia folded her arms across her chest, her lips pursed.

"I am aware of the liberties you are used to enjoying. However, you are not in Hertfordshire. Mr. Darcy wishes you to learn proper deportment before returning to society."

"Whoever heard of a girl being removed from society once she is out? It is unthinkable, unless she had some secret to conceal. Suppose people think such about me or Kitty?"

"No one with any sense would conceive such of either of you," Elizabeth argued. "And neither of you shall be away from society so long as to be possible for such a situation to occur, so you had best put that thought from your head at once," she assured them.

Nevertheless, Elizabeth wondered if too much seclusion from society might have a negative effect on the girls. It might be prudent to widen their social circle to some degree.

Mr. Darcy agreed with Elizabeth, to her surprise. "Perhaps you might consider taking the girls to accompany you on your visits to Mrs. Wilson. She is a respectable woman, who might have a positive influence on their developing minds. And being in her society would give some variety to your daily pursuits. Perhaps she might even be successful in persuading your sisters to join you in your charitable endeavors."

"It feels as though we have been cooped up in the house for ages!" Kitty said with a skip in her step as they entered the sitting room at Kenshire. A sudden heavy snowfall had kept them all housebound for the past twelve days. Even venturing forth to church had been impossible. The remaining thaw had turned to slush, necessitating they wear their thick boots and mind their skirts when descending the carriage, but at least they could venture from their home at last.

"I feel its effects as well," Mrs. Wilson nodded. "My boys have been frightfully rambunctious. It is all Nanny can do to keep them from tearing the house apart. They have been in desperate need of a romp out of doors. Nanny has taken them for a stroll in the garden, so we have a bit of peace and quiet for the moment."

The bell rang, announcing more visitors, and presently Mr. Wickham and Mr. Kirby were shown into the room.

"Such a gathering of beautiful ladies– we gentlemen are quite outnumbered!" Mr. Wickham said, bowing to greet them. His gallantry seemed most welcome, especially to Georgiana, whose countenance brightened at the sight of him. Mr. Kirby bowed as well before taking his seat.

"The ladies and I were just discussing the weather," Mrs. Wilson said. "Such damp conditions have prevented us from meeting anyone, and it has been rather dull."

"Yes," Lydia added. "One can only study Latin and paint pictures of flowers so much."

"There is always music to entertain you," Mr. Wickham suggested. "Especially when you have at your disposal such an able musician." He smiled in Georgiana's general direction.

"Our days are filled with her music," Kitty said in a droll voice. "Georgiana does little other than practice her pieces, with exacting repetition."

"Not that we mind it," Elizabeth interjected, before Georgiana could take offense at the slight. "I could listen to Georgina's playing endlessly."

"As could I," Mr. Wickham said. "I see here there is an instrument in the corner. Miss Darcy, would you play something for us?"

Georgiana looked to her hostess for approval, who readily admitted her pianoforte had long been wanting for someone to play upon it, although she was not certain how well in-tune it might be. Georgiana opened the instrument and began to play a piece she had committed to memory. The pianoforte was indeed a little out of tune, but it did not diminish her playing.

"This weather kept you all from church, I presume?" Mr. Kirby asked.

"Yes, it has been positively dreadful," Lydia said.

"I hope with the snow clearing, we might see you all this Sunday?"

Kitty nodded. "We shall certainly endeavor to be there. Will you be preaching, Mr. Kirby, or will Mr. Wickham be doing the honors?"

"I will be standing in for him. Mr. Wickham has plans to go to West Riding."

"Oh? Do you have family there, Mr. Wickham?" she asked, turning to him.

Mr. Wickham smiled. "No, but I have been invited to stay for a week or two with the Silverman family, in that part of the country. I was once their parish's curate, and formed a fast friendship with them. Perhaps I may even stay longer, if they allow it. Mr. Kirby is quite capable of managing in my absence."

"The loss of your presence will be keenly felt, Mr. Wickam," Elizabeth said.

Mrs. Wilson spoke up. "When you return to this part of the country, I have a mind to give a little dinner here at Kenshire. You would not object to being a part of it?"

"Not at all!" Wickham replied. "Nothing would give me greater satisfaction than dining at your table, Mrs. Wilson."

"You are all invited, of course," Mrs. Wilson said, turning to Elizabeth. "That is, if Mr. Darcy believes it a fitting outing for the young ladies. It would only be ourselves and these two gentlemen."

Elizabeth considered the prospect with eagerness. She too longed for a bit of society after their winter spell of confinement. "I do not think Mr. Darcy would have an objection to such a gathering. I shall bring it up to him later."

"Excellent! I shall write to you later to confirm the details."

Mr. Wickham rose and came over to the piano to listen to Georgiana's playing.

"A delightful piece of music!" he commended. "May I ask what it is called?"

Without missing a beat, Georgiana answered him, "This is one of Dussek's sonatas for piano."

"Sublime! You play with such passion, the heart of an artist. You boast a natural talent that ought to be displayed for the world to see. It is a pity that women of your station cannot appear on stage, or surely all the concert halls of Europe would beg for your condescension."

His remarks caused her color to change. "Music is my true love in life, but I cannot claim any greatness except what I derive through diligent practice."

Georgiana concluded the piece and was persuaded by them to play another, but before she could begin, their gathering was interrupted by Mrs. Wilson's boys who, heedless of their nurse's warnings, chose to enter the house by the sitting room doors connected to the garden. They were eager to show their mother the rocks and twigs they had collected from the garden. As soon as they saw Elizabeth, they rushed to her and begged for her to play with them.

"Now boys," their mother said, "Mrs. Darcy is not here to be your playmate."

"But we want to tell her all about our expedition!" Henry protested.

"An expedition, you say?" Mr. Wickham exclaimed, his eyes gleaming with amusement. "By all means, you must tell us of your adventures!"

"We have been to the tip of South Aff-er-ick-a," he said, drawing each syllable out.

"Africa," his nurse supplied.

"That's it! We saw penguins, and Eddie almost got ate by a killer whale!"

"Eaten," Nanny corrected him.

"What I said," Henry nodded.

Mr. Wickham crouched down on the boy's level. "It sounds dreadfully dangerous, but also exciting. How many penguins did you see?"

"Hundreds! And they walk real funny, did you know?"

"No, I did not. Can you show me how they walked, Master Henry?"

"Like this." He proceeded to waddle, to everyone's amusement. Little Edward began copying him.

Nanny laughed too. "Very well, Master Henry, Master Edward. Now, both of you, waddle off to your rooms to change your clothes, and mind you don't track your muddy boots on the rug."

Both boys slipped off their shoes and handed them to the nurse, who carried them while the boys continued their penguin imitation out the door.

"You have a generous disposition to allow your boys such freedom, Mrs. Wilson," Kitty remarked.

"I have found I must take their playful antics in stride, or else they would surely drive me mad," she chuckled.

Chapter 26

"Did you really mean it when you said we would be allowed to dine at Kenshire?" Lydia asked Elizabeth, her eyes wide with delight as they returned to the carriage.

Kitty could not withhold herself from skipping. "It will be the first time we have dined out anywhere since Twelfth Night! I wonder what sort of dinner Mrs. Wilson will give?"

"An excellent one, if I am any judge of her abilities," Elizabeth said.

Elizabeth noted Georgiana's withdrawn manners. She addressed her later when they were alone. "Are you nervous about dining at Kenshire?"

Georgiana's eyes were wide. "I have never been to anyone's home to dine before, except to Matlock Manor and Rosings, and those do not count as they are the homes of family members."

"Did you never dine out while you were living in London?" Elizabeth asked her.

"No, never. Your sisters have already been out in society for a year or more. I fear their social graces will surpass mine."

Elizabeth had to suppress her laughter. "If there is one thing you need not fear, it is their graces outstripping yours."

She told Mr. Darcy of Mrs. Wilson's plans for them.

"Yes, I will consent to the arrangement," he said. "If it is to be only the clergymen who are in attendance with us, then such a gathering will be a fair opportunity for our young charges to exhibit the decorum we have attempted to instill in them these past few weeks."

※

The following weeks passed slower than ever before, made worse still by another winter storm, dampening their spirits and making it impossible to travel further than the grounds of Pemberley. Everyone felt relieved when the snow melted again and word came that Mr. Wickham had returned to Kympton, followed presently by the promised invitation from Kenshire.

Lydia and Kitty were such a bundle of excitement on the day of the dinner, it was all Elizabeth could do to contain their energy.

"Lydia, please might I borrow your pearl hair comb?" Kitty pestered her as they readied themselves.

"Only if I might use your fan," Lydia answered.

"Why? You shall not need a fan on a cool night like this one, and I was planning to use it myself," Kydia protested.

"Because it makes me look elegant," Lydia explained. "And because I want something of yours in return if you are to take my comb."

Kitty reluctantly consented.

The pair were laughing and snorting over some joke when the carriage was called for them. Mr. Darcy shot them a look as if to remind them how to comport themselves. They immediately straightened up and fell silent, but as soon as they were handed into the carriage, they began giggling again.

Elizabeth and Georgiana sat opposite them in the coach. Mrs. Younge squeezed in beside them. Georgiana began twisting her handkerchief in her lap. Elizabeth placed one hand on top of Georgiana's.

"Do not fret. You already know what good sort of people Mr. and Mrs. Wilson are."

"It is not that, truly."

"Then what has you so worried?"

"I cannot say," Georigiana murmured.

They heard the coachman and Mr. Darcy climb up to the box, and then they were off.

"It must be because of who will be in attendance this evening," Lydia said with a teasing air.

Kitty let out another giggle and a snort.

"It is all Kitty and I have thought about, for certain," Lydia laughed.

"Girls, I expect you not to be silly over the men this evening. Remember my instructions to you," Elizabeth warned them.

"Yes, Lizzy," Kitty demurred.

"Do you think Mrs. Wilson will seat you beside Mr. Wickham, Georgiana?" Lydia's head bobbed as the carriage rolled over a dip in the road.

Georgiana stumbled to answer. "I...that is, it is at Mrs. Wilson's discretion where to seat me."

"I know, but where do you *hope* she will seat you?" Lydia pressed.

Georgiana's eyes lowered. "It is of no consequence."

Mrs. Younge spoke up. "Mr. Wickham is as fine a gentleman as any of these great men I ever saw. Had the circumstances of his birth been higher, I have no doubts he would have already made a great match. He is so fortunate to have had the patronage of the elder and younger Mr. Darcys, for his education and his present situation. I wonder now whether some lady might not catch his eye, now that he is settled at Kympton."

Elizabeth wondered again whether Mrs. Younge might not have hopes where the young rector was concerned. Her sister's insinuation of Georgiana's possible infatuation with Mr. Wickham was unsettling, however. Her age notwithstanding, the difference in their situations was so great, she could not fathom Mr. Darcy approving of a match between his sister and Mr. Wickham.

The conversation around the dinner table mainly revolved around the diversions of country life, interspersed with humorous anecdotes from Mr. Wickham.

"Shall I tell you about the time Mr. Darcy and I fell into the river and almost drowned?" Mr. Wickham asked.

"I think you must, Mr. Wickham," Mrs. Wilson urged.

"Well, the two of us had determined to go fishing on the lake, and we took out one of the rowboats. The lake had swelled from recent rains and was much higher than normal, spilling over the dam which flowed back into the Derwent. Despite being warned not to go near the dam, we rowed a little too close to it, and the current pushed us over it. The boat tipped, and we both fell out. Mr. Darcy, having no knowledge of how to swim, cried out in a panic, his arms flailing about wildly." Mr. Wickham waved his own arms to demonstrate. "Fortunately, I was able to grab ahold of him before he went under and we caught hold of a piece of floating wood– the boat was long lost– and then a local farmer saw us and rescued us."

"What a tale, Mr. Wickham!" Mrs. Wilson clapped. "To think you were both almost lost to us."

"You are positively a hero, Mr. Wickham!" Lydia echoed.

Georgiana said nothing, but her eyes were shining with admiration as she smiled at him.

Mr. Darcy drank his wine in silence.

Elizabeth noted his displeasure, but did not remark upon it.

Wickham's tale stretched the truth, to say the least. It had been Wickham who insisted on taking the boat out, despite warnings of the danger; Darcy had only gone along in a vain attempt to keep him out of trouble. Wickham, too, was responsible for going too near the dam, causing their boat to capsize. Without these reckless actions, there would have been no need for them to have been rescued by that farmer. Certainly, Wickham was far from the hero he portrayed himself as; according to Darcy's recollections, it was he who had pulled the sinking George Wickham from the river, not the other way around.

Still, Darcy did not correct him. He kept his concerns to himself during the visit, preferring to observe those around him and how they conducted themselves. Kitty and Lydia behaved only slightly better than they had at Christmas. Lydia talked altogether too loudly and laughed a great deal too much, while Kitty spoke to Mr. Kirby almost the entire time, to the point of her declining to join their card games after dinner, preferring to remain on the settee with him to continue their conversation. Such, in and of itself, was not a grievous offense, but Darcy worried if she repeated this behavior at other gatherings, it might draw remarks about her relationship with Mr. Kirby, and Darcy still deemed her far too young to think of matrimony.

But it was Georgiana's wordless awe of Mr. Wickham which worried him the most. She appeared enthralled by his presence, and though she spoke little unless spoken to, she blushed whenever he addressed her. After dinner, he had persuaded her to spend much of the evening at the pianoforte, where he remained by her side on the pretext of turning the pages for her.

He resolved to speak to Elizabeth about it. After the girls had retired for the night, he asked her to join him in his study.

"Goodness, am I in trouble, that you should summon me?" she asked, a quizzical expression on her brow.

"No, Mrs. Darcy," he replied, motioning for her to take a seat, "but I wondered your opinion on my sister's feelings towards Mr. Wickham. Has she indicated anything to you?"

"If she had, I might feel bound by sisterly confidence not to reveal it to you," Elizabeth began. "But as it stands, no, Georgiana has said nothing, although there has been some lighthearted teasing from Lydia and Kitty on the matter. I suspect if you wish to know more, you might need to query them, as they are perhaps in her confidence."

"There is no need," Darcy said. "I merely suspected some feelings on her part by her manner towards him that I have observed."

"I observed it also, and if some feeling does lie within her breast, I suspect it is nothing more than a girlish infatuation. Georgiana knows, I am sure, you would not countenance a match between her and Mr. Wickham."

"My fear is that he, seeking her fortune, might prey upon her vulnerable young heart," Darcy said.

"Yes, I am well aware of your feelings regarding fortune hunters," Elizabeth said tersely, "but not all poor gentlemen and ladies are predators towards the rich. I know Mr. Wickham has had some scuffles over debts in the past, but he appears to be on the straight and narrow now. As a respected clergyman, I do not think he would risk his position on an unhonorable attempt, nor would he venture his suit if he did not think you would approve of his candidacy."

"You are correct, I am certain, Mrs. Darcy," Darcy told her. "Thank you for your opinion."

Elizabeth curtsied before retiring to her chambers.

The distance spanning himself and Elizabeth seemed to have increased as of late. Ever since Twelfth Night, she had held herself back from conversing with him unless it was necessary. He wondered if there was something he had said or done to cause offense. Perhaps it was for the best, though. If theirs was to be a marriage in name only, it would be better to keep themselves at arm's length.

Chapter 27

With the weather growing warmer, there was hardly a day when a visit did not take place between the ladies of Kenshire and Pemberley. Mrs. Wilson and Elizabeth soon became fast friends. They discovered their mutual great love of reading, and Elizabeth opened to her friend the vast tomes of Pemberley's library.

Mrs. Wilson also became a valuable assistant in Elizabeth's undertaking for the poor. Mrs. Wilson was a regular volunteer at a nearby convalescent home for soldiers returning from France, and soon, the ladies' shirts were being sent not only to the poorest villagers in Lambton and Kympton, but to soldiers in need of fresh garments before returning home to their families.

At Mrs. Wilson's suggestion, Georgiana and Elizabeth began to sit with the soldiers and read to them one day a week. At first, neither Kitty nor Lydia wanted to participate. These soldiers, maimed by war and lacking their regimental finery, did not have quite the same charm as a parade of fresh young recruits.

But in time, curious to see the men after hearing some of the stories Elizabeth and Georgiana reported, they ventured forth as well. Lydia found she liked sitting with the soldiers, who were endlessly grateful for any diversion she could provide them, and listened with rapt attention to her tales and jokes.

Visits from the rectory were equally common. Mr. Wickham called on them at least twice per week, usually accompanied by Mr. Kirby. When the weather was not overly wet, the gentlemen would often walk out with the ladies through the gardens or take one of the shorter wooded paths.

"Would you believe it is already March?" Kitty said to Mr. Kirby one morning as they strolled through the rose gardens. "Lydia and I have been at Pemberley nearly three months complete."

"Only a few more weeks of your stay remains," he said. "Do you find your time is well-spent?" The Darcys planned to return Kitty and Lydia to Hertfordshire when they traveled to London after Easter.

"I think so. My lessons are progressing. I have learnt much more Latin than I ever cared to before, and though I do not play the pianoforte much better than I did when I arrived, my oratory skills have improved greatly, thanks to reading to the soldiers."

Elizabeth, having discerned Mrs. Younge was not the strictest of tutors, had begun to assist her sisters with their lessons, and seen much progression from both of them. Kitty, especially, had flourished and grown, beginning to resemble the young lady that Elizabeth and Darcy expected her to be. Lydia, less so, however, and for this reason, Darcy remained adamant they not be allowed to join them in London for the Season, much to Lydia (and Mrs. Bennet's) disappointment.

Kitty and Mr. Kirby had allowed themselves to lag quite a ways behind the others. Elizabeth and Lydia were at the forefront of their group, while Georgiana walked alongside Mrs. Younge and Mr. Wickham.

The weather that day was particularly fair, the air cool, but not damp. Dressed in their pelisses and wraps, none of the ladies felt overly cold, and they were grateful the ground was not muddy.

Lydia turned back to face them as they neared the garden gates. "The ground is so dry, we might take the longer path through the woods today. What say you all?"

Their party was amenable, but Elizabeth said, "I must return to the house to tend to some matters with the housekeeper, but you are all welcome to continue without me."

In her absence, their party reorganized. Lydia continued to keep the lead with Mrs. Younge, with Mr. Kirby and Kitty following behind at a reasonable distance. Georgiana and Mr. Wickham, however, fell further and further behind, until they could no longer be seen by the others along the wooded trail.

Lydia remarked upon it. "I think perhaps Mr. Wickham and Georgiana wished for privacy, for they have gone from us completely."

"Miss Darcy does seem quite taken by Mr. Wickham these days," Mrs. Younge added.

"But we must consider their longstanding friendship, having grown up together on the estate," Kitty pointed out. "Their friendship must, by nature, be more like brother and sister than anything else."

"Perhaps it may have begun as such," Lydia said, "but I do believe there might be something more. Georgiana does moon over him so!"

"Has she indicated her feelings for him?" Mr. Kirby asked.

"Not in so many words, no," Lydia admitted. "But I have seen the way she looks at him whenever he is near. It is the same way you look at Kitty!"

"Lydia!" Kitty exclaimed.

Mr. Kirby's cheeks reddened. "It is not proper to remark on the looks of others when they have not expressed their regard themselves. One might come to an incorrect conjecture, when they rely on such speculation."

"But you do hold Kitty in regard, do you not?"

Being put on the spot, Mr. Kirby stammered, "Naturally, I hold Miss Bennet in esteem, but our acquaintance is still short. I hope, in time, our friendship will continue to grow."

"'Friendship', la!" Lydia danced. "We are all friends, indeed! But if you should yearn for something more, you have my blessing. Though I am but the youngest sister, I know I speak for my mother who would wish our Kitty to be happily married!" She teasingly skipped over to them and put Kitty's hand into Mr. Kirby's. Kitty bashfully pulled her hand away from him and gripped her parasol tighter.

"That is quite enough now, Miss Lydia," Mrs. Younge reprimanded, though her tone did not have the commanding effect it should have. With a grin on her face, she said, "Let us not embarrass poor Mr. Kirby any further, and let nature take its course, lest we scare him away from us!"

Mr. Kirby, in an attempt to recover, said, "It is not for me to be driven away by embarrassment. A little lighthearted ribbing I can endure."

<hr>

Meanwhile, Georgiana walked in step with Mr. Wickham, enjoying the sounds of the birds and the woodland animals and the patterns of sunlight filtering through the oaks, ashes, and beeches which bordered Pemberley. Her heart palpitated slightly, finding herself alone in Mr. Wickham's presence. The affection she had known for him as a child had only increased now that she had grown. She longed for him to see her as a woman, but the struggle against her own feelings of inadequacy and childishness made her feel it less of a possibility.

"It is amazing how much these trees have grown up, since we walked these paths in our youth," Wickham said.

"I am sure the woods of Pemberley have been here long before you or I ever walked this earth," Georgiana replied.

"Certainly. But not all of them predate us. I am sure this tree here was but a sapling when we were younger." He pointed to a sturdy young ash tree near the bend that wound by the river.

"How can you be sure?"

"Long ago, I carved my initials into it. See, here." He pointed to a part of the tree trunk where the bark had been peeled away by a knife to reveal the letters GW.

"Poor tree! You have hurt its trunk, to carve it so."

"Sometimes pain is what strengthens us," Mr. Wickham said casually. "The tree has grown up tall and strong, no worse for wear, despite all its hardships, great and small. Just as you have, Georgiana."

Her heart beat even faster at the sound of her Christian name on his lips. He had not called her by that name since she was about ten years old.

"We both of us have suffered great losses in life, but we have not let these define us."

She knew he referred to the deaths of his parents and hers.

"We ought to carve your initials into the tree too," he suggested. Pulling a small knife from his pocket, he began to etch out the letters GD next to his own.

"There, now our names will stand together in perpetuity," he said when he had finished.

"Or at least so long as this tree shall remain," Georgiana added.

"Then may it endure forever!"

They continued walking.

"How long has it been since we last walked this path?" he asked.

"I am not certain. Not since before you went away to Cambridge, I am certain. You did not return to Pemberley so often in those days."

"Yes, my studies kept me quite occupied at that time. I had no opportunity to return to my old home. It is fortunate that your dear father left me the Kympton living in his will, or else I might have had to make my way in the world somewhere far from here, and never return."

Georgiana gulped. "That would have been a tragedy, indeed! We are so blessed to have you serving in our community, to have your return to this neighborhood after all these years. We– I– am grateful to see you again."

"As am I."

Mr. Wickham's handsome countenance as he smiled at her sent more thrills of nervous delight into Georgiana's heart. She no longer saw him merely as an older brother figure, but decidedly something more. She wondered if he viewed her differently now as well.

"Now that you have come into your living, I suppose you must be thinking of marrying soon," she ventured, summoning her boldness and at the same time, fearing for what the answer might be. If Mr. Wickham already had a sweetheart in mind, then all her hopes were lost.

"Marriage, yes, it is something all men desire at some point or other, I suppose. In my case, although I have been given a good living, I fear it is not enough to support a family on. I suppose I could marry some tradesman's daughter and we could live in comparative poverty on my income until such time as I am able to acquire additional livings.

"But if the lady in question had some money of her own to contribute to the marriage, we would be far better off. I am afraid growing up with a gentleman's education and lifestyle has made me spoilt; I have become used to certain little luxuries, and I would find it difficult to revert to a diminished standard of living."

"Your explanation makes perfect sense. Have you any suitable ladies in mind?" She waited with bated breath for his answer.

"Eh…not exactly," he said, exhaling slowly. "There was a lady, a daughter of my friends Mr. and Mrs. Silverman in West Riding. I traveled there recently hoping to persuade her of my regard for her.

However, I was too late. There was another fellow in question, whose prospects were better, and it seemed she preferred him over me."

"How sad for you!"

"Ah, no matter!" He laughed, as if the matter were merely a triviality. "I suspect it can only mean the Lord has someone better in mind for me, someone whose personality exactly suits my own, and whom I can share my life with in a style befitting us both. In fact, I think He may have already shown me who that lady is to be, but, ah– I am speaking too rapidly! Pay no mind to my prattling, dear Georgiana."

His use of the endearment, coupled with such a hint, made her heart beat even faster. But perhaps he felt it too soon to speak further. Or perhaps he felt her too young, still. She was not even out yet.

And then there was the matter of her brother. Fitzwilliam had formed a dislike of Mr. Wickham in recent years, but she could find no fault in Mr. Wickham's character to explain why. He was everything good, kind, and well-mannered, and had a good position– a man of the cloth even! Next to her brother, there was no better man in the world, she felt. The only objection she could postulate was that of his low birth, the son of their late steward.

But for her brother to be a snob over such things– when their own father had loved Mr. Wickham so dearly and paid for him to be brought up as a gentleman! She wished she had a mother to guide her in such things. She loved Elizabeth, but the relationship was still new; she did not know whether she felt ready to confide such feelings in her breast as those which she held for Mr. Wickham.

Chapter 28

Lydia, however, was determined to get out of Georgiana what she could about her feelings for a certain clergyman. Her appetite could not be sated until she had some fresh gossip, and as Kitty could neither confirm nor deny anything, she knew it could only come from the source. When the girls had retired to their bedrooms for the evening, Lydia knocked on Georgiana's door.

"It is me, Lydia. May I come in?"

"Certainly," Georgiana said, rising from her bed to open the door. Lydia bounded across the room and bounced onto Georgiana's bed.

"Kitty has already fallen asleep, and she snores. And as her room is right next to mine, I have to listen to it all night long. Positively dreadful! Do you mind if I stay here for a while? I am not tired in the least!"

Georgiana was quite fatigued from their long walk, but she graciously nodded and settled herself gently on the bed opposite Lydia.

"I noticed you were absent from us a long while during our walk today," Lydia observed.

Georgiana tried to hide the color rising to her cheeks. "Yes. I suppose I am not used to walking such long distances these days. City life has caused my limbs to atrophy. I used to take long rambles through those woods in my former days, however."

"What did you and Mr. Wickham talk about for so long? I can only assume you did not walk in silence the whole way." Lydia's eyes, like an eager puppy's, were hard to ignore.

"We spoke of many things. I cannot remember everything," Georgiana mumbled.

"Surely you remember some part!" Lydia pressed.

"Well, we spoke of how happy we are that he has settled near to us at Kympton, and...and whether he is thinking of taking a wife now that he has his income."

Lydia scooted nearer. "And? Is he thinking of taking a wife?"

Georgiana let out an embarrassed laugh. "He said he wishes to marry, but his income is such that he requires a woman of fortune, in order to raise a family without falling into poverty."

"A woman of fortune, eh? Did he mention any particular woman?"

"A Miss Silverman, but it seems she has chosen another."

"And nobody else?"

Georgiana blushed further. "I think there is the *hope* of someone, but he did not mention any other names." She could only wish it might be *her* he hoped for.

Lydia bounced on the bed slightly as she changed her position. "You know, Georgiana– I hope I am not being too free when I call you that– *you* happen to be a woman of fortune– quite a considerable one, I might add. Not that I am jealous or anything! Oh, no! Had I some money of my own, I am sure gentlemen would be lining up so quickly, I would have to fend them off with a stick! It would be quite troublesome. But it *would* have the advantage, I suppose, of granting some choice as to who one's partner would be. You, for example, need not worry about what the gentleman's income might be, for your own dividends must be good enough to support you both."

"That is true enough, yes," Georgiana said, her mind turning with possibilities. "Do you– do you suppose Mr. Wickham might have me in mind?"

"Seeing how attentive to you he has been all these weeks, I have no doubts about it! His regard for you is evident, and your long standing connection makes it all the more probable that he should see you as a prospect. He might only be prevented from applying to you out of fear for your brother. Mr. Darcy can be quite fearsome, you know!"

Georgiana laughed. "Yes, he can."

"So, do you like him?"

"Of course I like my brother."

Lydia playfully swatted Georgiana's arm. "Not him! Mr. Wickham, you goose!"

Georgiana's face was beet red now. "I—I…"

"Well, do you?"

"Y-yes, I do like him. Why wouldn't I?"

"Like him– as a friend and old acquaintance– or like him as something more?"

"More," Georgiana said, almost in a whisper. "Much more."

Lydia pressed. "Are you in love with him?"

Georgiana nodded slowly. "I think I am. I think I have been for a long time."

Lydia sighed dreamily. "I knew it! Just by looking at you, I could tell. I am always able to discern these things, you know."

"You will not say anything to him, will you?" Georgiana's eyes were wide with concern.

"No, of course not! My lips shall remain sealed. It is not for me to blab about other people's secrets. But you must keep me apprised of any developments."

But of course, Lydia's word could not be trusted as far as she could be thrown. It did not take long for her to pass a hint of what her friend had divulged to her. Some nights later, when Mr. Wickham and Mr. Kirby were again invited to dine at Pemberley, and they were all enraptured witnessing Georgiana's performance on her harp after dinner, Lydia whispered to Mr. Wickham, "I see you admire Miss Darcy very much."

"Who among her friends could not?" He whispered back.

"You must know, the feeling is mutual. Her regard for you is strong, though her shy disposition and sense of modesty prevents her from showing it freely."

Hearing whispering behind her, Elizabeth turned her head and motioned for them to be silent, which ended Lydia's discussion with Mr. Wickham. She felt satisfied, however, that her point had been carried, and determined she would leave it to the hands of fate as to what came next.

※

Mr. Wickham's frequent presence at Pemberley and Kenshire did not go unnoticed by Mr. Darcy.

"I do not like his calling here so often, Mrs. Darcy," he told Elizabeth one morning when they were together in the breakfast parlor before the others came down.

"I thought you held no objections to it, given he is a man of God and a longstanding acquaintance," she replied.

"I told you before of his troubles at Cambridge, and my need to rescue him from his creditors."

"Yes, but all that is in the past. You fulfilled your father's wishes and gave him a living, so he need never return to the life of a gamester. And it appears he has turned over a new leaf in the process."

"I do not think he is satisfied with his life as a clergyman. There are rumors he has begun gaming again, and I'm told he spends far too much at the tailor and the haberdasher."

"I did not think you were one given to unsubstantiated rumors, Mr. Darcy," Elizabeth casually defended, taking a sip of her tea. "As for his clothing expenditures, well, you cannot expect him to dress in cassocks all the time! A man must have some outfit besides his clerical vestments. Even Mr. Collins does not solely dress in them, though he wears them with frequency even outside of his parish duties."

"And there are his other spending habits," Darcy continued. "Did you know he recently bought a new curricle and horse?"

"Is it a sin, then, to buy a new curricle to replace one's old broken gig which has belonged to the rectory forever, and to invest in a high-stepping mare which can drive it without tipping it over? That old mare of his was ready to be put out to pasture. She was more used to pulling farm wagons than a gig or curricle. I find no fault in his wishing to purchase a new animal," Elizabeth argued.

"I can see you are eager to find no fault with him," Darcy said, unable to disguise the irritation in his voice.

Elizabeth raised her chin. "I am more than happy to recognize faults where they exist, but in this instance, you appear to be searching for something which is not there. Mr. Wickham might have dabbled with gaming in the past, but I give no credence to any rumors he has returned to that life without some proof of it."

"Well, what of his courtship of Miss Silverman? He spent nearly three weeks there," Darcy pointed out.

"What of it?"

"You must know, Miss Silverman holds a considerable fortune, over twenty-five thousand pounds, almost equal to Georgiana's dowry."

"And you think Mr. Wickham was courting her merely for the money?"

"It would provide an explanation for his sudden interest in her."

"To my knowledge, Mr. Wickham was there merely to visit with his friends. It is my understanding that he served as the curate there for a year, before coming into his present living. Surely the friendships he formed with that family were lasting and equal to his coming to visit, without suspicion of any designs towards Miss Silverman."

Darcy persisted. "Even if that were true, I cannot condone his having such a close relationship with Georgiana. The intimacy they shared as children cannot be allowed to continue into adulthood. Sooner or later, Georgiana shall have to marry, and when she does, it will not be to Mr. Wickham."

"My goodness, what a snob you are, Mr. Darcy!" Elizabeth exclaimed, in a tone so light, Darcy could not discern whether she were teasing him or seriously insulting him, or perhaps a bit of both. "I see no harm in their friendship. But your sister is in your charge. How shall you plan to diminish their ties? You cannot bar Mr. Wickham from calling here, nor hope to suspend their meeting each other at church or other places."

"True. I have been giving it some thought as of late. Georgiana has mentioned her desire to visit her schoolmate, Miss Culpepper in Gloucestershire. With your sisters' visit soon to conclude, I thought we might send Georgiana to her friends, if they are amenable, while you and I go to London for a month or two at the height of the Season."

Elizabeth mused. "It is a plan, I suppose, albeit a temporary one. What shall you do when Georgiana returns here, and everything resumes as normal?"

"I suppose it is a bridge I shall have to cross at that time, but my hope is by then, her infatuation with him will have diminished. Then after her next birthday, I plan to bring her out into society so we might introduce her to more suitable prospects."

"If that is your wish," Elizabeth said solemnly.

Chapter 29

After Elizabeth's nocturnal wander into the woods, Parker began sleeping in Elizabeth's dressing room to prevent her wandering again. The servants readily accepted the explanation that Mrs. Darcy suffered from night terrors and occasionally required attendance during the night, and knowing their master's views on gossip did not speculate further.

This arrangement had served them well the past few months, but Darcy worried what might happen when they removed to Darcy House, which was smaller, and had no adjoining dressing room to the chambers for the lady of the house. He brought up his concerns to Elizabeth.

"It may be dangerous for you to sleep alone, especially once we are in London. Suppose you wander out into the street and are kidnapped or set upon by robbers– or worse?"

"Your concerns are valid. I, too, have been thinking of what to do once our sisters are all gone from us. Perhaps Parker would consent to have a cot in my chamber?"

This solution satisfied Darcy for the present.

Following Easter, Georgiana departed for her friends' home, accompanied by Mrs. Younge. Many embraces were exchanged between Georgiana and Lydia and Kitty, and Georgiana promised to write faithfully. She had especially grown close to Lydia in the previous month thanks to their talks and giggles, which had become a nightly occurrence. Lydia and Kitty promised to write too, although Elizabeth, knowing Lydia's propensity to neglect her correspondence, guessed she might not be as diligent in returning Georgiana's letters.

Once Georgiana was off, the Darcys prepared to travel south. They would stop in Hertfordshire for a few days, to deliver Kitty and Lydia to their parents, before journeying on to St. James's Square.

The journey was easy, and they took their time over four days to reach Hertfordshire. Mr. Bennet, having suffered too long with only his wife for company, received his daughters with more gladness than usual.

"At last, I shall have some sensible conversation!" he said, greeting Elizabeth with a warm embrace.

"I do not know what he means by that," Mrs. Bennet complained. "My conversations with him are as sane as anybody else's."

Kitty and Lydia, he found improved, with far less silliness than before. In the company of their elder sister, they had formed the ability to carry an intelligent conversation and to discuss topics besides bonnets and balls.

Mrs. Bennet seemed dismayed that her daughters had returned to her without any change in their marital status. Once out of Elizabeth's hearing, she complained to them. "I thought your stay at Pemberley might put you in the way of other eligible men of Mr.

Darcy's status," she said. "Did Lizzy not take my suggestion to heart, to invite Mr. Darcy's cousin to stay with you all?"

"No, Mamma, she did not," Kitty told her. "We were a ways off in the countryside, with not much in the way of company, but we did further our acquaintance with the rector and his curate, whom you met, and another family nearby."

Mrs. Bennet was not impressed. "It does you no good to fraternize with young married couples and poor clergymen. Your sister Mary was permitted to marry one, but only because he is the heir to Longbourn and will one day have this house." She further railed because Lizzy and Darcy had refused to take Kitty and Lydia with them to London.

"I do not know why they should not– you are already out, and they have the means to introduce you to the first circles. It is entirely unfair."

Two nights at Longbourn was enough to try Darcy's patience. At Pemberley, he had plenty of rooms in which to escape, while Longbourn had few such places. He spent as much time out of doors as he could during their stay and when obliged to remain indoors due to the weather, he found refuge in Mr. Bennet's book room, where he could entertain himself with a book and sit in quiet solitude with the master of the house.

He was grateful when they set off for St. James's Square.

"I long to see Jane again," Elizabeth said, as they drew near to Darcy House. "I wonder whether we might even call on her before the day is over."

Jane's letters to her the past few months had been few and infrequent. Jane used to write long, detailed letters to her when

Elizabeth had lived with the Gardiners. But now her letters were short, almost in the hurried style of Lydia, and detailed little except the pleasure she took in various balls, card parties, dinners, and excursions to the theaters, the museums, and the parks. She had rekindled her friendship with the Bingleys and the Hursts, it seemed, and had also grown acquainted with Mrs. Jennings' daughter, who resided nearby. There was also mention of a Mr. Rushworth, a young man of fortune from Northamptonshire, who was often of their party.

"If it pleases you to do so, I shall order the carriage to take us to Berkeley Street," Darcy said.

An hour later, after a brief rest to change from their traveling clothes and eat a light meal, they set off. Jane was not at home when they arrived.

"I suppose I cannot complain, since she will not have been expecting me until tomorrow at least," Elizabeth said sadly. She left her card, however, with a brief note informing Jane of their arrival.

When they returned to Darcy house, several letters awaited them.

Darcy plucked the first one, written in his sister's hand, and read it quickly before sharing it with Elizabeth. "It is from Georgiana," he said. "She writes that she has arrived safely at Culpepper Manor, and sends her love."

"Excellent," Elizabeth said, scanning the short missive before handing it back to him. "I hope she has a marvelous time with her friends."

The next item bore the Matlock seal. "Lord and Lady Matlock have invited us to join them for dinner this evening at Fitzwilliam Place," Darcy told her after he opened it.

"How did they know we are in town when we have only just arrived?" Elizabeth asked.

"I mentioned in my last letter to my uncle our plan to come down at this time for the remainder of the Season. He and Lady Matlock arrived a week ago. They must have planned to invite us."

There was also a letter waiting from Mrs. Gardiner. Elizabeth took it and read it in her chambers.

Dear Lizzy,

How pleased I was to hear of your coming to town! I did not want to take the chance that my letter would not reach you at Pemberley or Longbourn before coming, so I directed it to Darcy House, knowing you would receive it upon your arrival. I have greatly missed you and look forward to spending time with you during your stay.

In addition to my eagerness to see you, there is a matter which I wish to speak to you of, concerning Jane. I will not put it to pen here, but I hope you will call on me as soon as it is convenient, so we may discuss it.

Yours sincerely,
M. Gardiner

Aunt Gardiner's remarks puzzled Elizabeth, and she longed to ask her what she meant. However, there was no time.

She dispatched a quick note to Gracechurch Street informing the Gardiners she planned to call on them the next day. Then she turned her attention to the upcoming dinner and what she ought to wear to Fitzwilliam House. With Parker's help, she selected a pale yellow gown which reminded her of a daffodil.

When dressing her for dinner, Parker coughed a few times, and again while styling Elizabeth's hair.

"Dear me, Parker, I hope you are not ill!" Elizabeth said.

"Just a little sore throat, ma'am," Parker answered.

"Do take care of yourself, please. I'm ordering you to go down to the kitchen and have Cook make you a cup of tea with honey, and some lemon, if any is to be had."

"Yes, ma'am," Parker smiled. "And thank you for your consideration."

"Certainly! We cannot have you becoming ill. I do not know what I would do without you."

<hr/>

Darcy frowned when he saw a familiar carriage ahead of theirs when they pulled up to the stately mansion on Grosvenor Street. "Lady Catherine is here," he told Elizabeth.

"Is that not to be expected, considering this is her brother's house?" she asked.

"I was unaware she was in town. She often does not come for the Season, due to Anne's health. The London air does not agree with my cousin. She must have gotten wind that we were to be coming and decided to make a spectacle of herself."

Elizabeth's brow furrowed. "What purpose could she have in doing so?"

"I believe she still intends to prove to the world that you are unfit to be my wife, as if it would somehow induce me to transfer my affections over to her daughter. Preposterous." With a brief huff, Darcy exited the carriage ahead of Elizabeth.

<hr/>

Elizabeth gulped. *Transfer of affections?* That implied an existence of affections. Had she somehow misheard his words?

Perhaps he only meant the sort of affections one has for a cousin or a friend. *Best not to read too deeply into it.* Besides, she had bigger issues to contend with, if it was true that Lady Catherine intended to prove Elizabeth as unfit to bear the title of Mrs. Darcy. She may not have asked for the title, but it was hers by right, and she could allow no person to shame her family–or Darcy– by trying to discredit her.

Standing up straighter, she took Darcy's arm as he helped her up the stairs to the house. In the drawing room, Lady Matlock greeted her warmly and welcomed her to their London abode. Lord Matlock was polite, but stiff, while Lady Catherine gave only a nod in acknowledgement of her presence. Lady Catherine greeted her nephew effusively with a smile and pat on the back, so uncharacteristic of her, that Elizabeth was sure she must be putting on a display for some purpose.

"I hope you will not mind," Lady Matlock said as they took their seats and accepted the glasses of cordial and sherry they were offered. "I have invited our neighbors, whom I believe you are friends with, Mr. and Mrs. Hurst, and their guests, Mr. and Miss Bingley."

Darcy's face brightened at the mention of his friends, and he remarked how good it would be to see them again.

"I met Mrs. Hurst and Miss Bingley while I was out for a walk in the square the other day," Lady Matlock explained. "After we had been introduced, they mentioned their connection to you, Darcy. I thought it only fitting to invite them, seeing how their residence is only a few doors from ours. They asked if they might bring their brother also, since you are acquainted with him."

Elizabeth had forgotten Mr. Hurst kept a house on Grosvenor Street, but was reminded now of one of her earliest conversations with Mrs. Hurst, when the lady had asked her how far her uncle's residence might be from Grosvenor. Mrs. Hurst had seemed rather dismayed when she learned Elizabeth's relatives resided in Cheapside.

The Hurst and the Bingleys arrived soon after. Miss Bingley and Mrs. Hurst were cool but polite towards Elizabeth, while Mr. Bingley was, as usual, cheerful and amiable to everyone. Mr. Hurst merely grunted his acknowlegements before moving towards the footman carrying the sherry.

Lady Catherine eyed the newcomers with suspicion, as if contemplating whether they were worthy to appear at Lady Matlock's table. During dinner, she asked them a series of questions, and learned Mr. Bingley's father had been in trade.

"My father was successful in his business endeavors. He purchased a cotton mill in Lancashire, which, I am pleased to say, is now mine," Mr. Bingley told her proudly.

"A cotton mill; how industrious!" Lady Catherine said dryly. She was even less impressed to hear that Mr. Bingley owned no estate, lived in rented quarters while in town, and was leasing a property in Hertfordshire.

"Yes, Lady Catherine. In fact, if it were not for my taking up residence at Netherfield Park, Mr. and Mrs. Darcy may not have met!" Mr. Bingley said brightly, failing to observe the sour expression forming on Lady Catherine's lips.

Elizabeth saw it, however, and changed the subject. "Mr. Bingley, I am told you have seen my sister often, as of late."

Mr. Bingley bobbed his head. "Oh yes, we continue to be great friends, as always. She often accompanies us to the parks or the theater. Why, only this afternoon, we all had a lovely carriage ride together!"

"Yes, Miss Bennet has become a regular fixture in our outings," Miss Bingley echoed. "She calls so often at Hurst Place, it sometimes feels as though she lives there." Elizabeth discerned the touch of bitterness in Miss Bingley's tone, but she was certain it escaped the others' notice.

Bingley was certainly oblivious. "I am exceedingly grateful to Mrs. Jennings for inviting Miss Bennet into her home, so our acquaintance could continue without interruption. I do not know when I shall return to the countryside; London is so diverting! At this rate, I may not return until the summer months, when the Season wanes," he said.

Lady Matlock overheard part of their conversation and decided to join in. "Your sister is in town, then, Mrs. Darcy? Had I known of it, I would have invited her to join us tonight as well. You must arrange an introduction at the next available opportunity."

"Certainly, Lady Matlock, I would be pleased to do so," Elizabeth replied.

Lady Matlock turned to her husband. "Do you not think we would have room to include Miss Bennet, along with the Darcys, in our boxes for the opera Saturday sennight?"

"For the production of *Don Giovanni?* No, I don't think so," Lord Matlock replied gruffly. "The Linningtons have already accepted our invitation for that night, as has my sister."

Lady Catherine nodded her agreement.

"Well, then put them in Jamie's box. It is right next to ours. I want Miss Bennet there," Lady Matlock argued.

Mr. Bingley cleared his throat. "I believe Miss Bennet is already engaged. I myself will be at the opera, as a guest of Mr. Rushworth, and I am told Miss Bennet and her chaperone are to be of our party as well. Mr. Rushworth has a box at Covent Garden also, although probably not as favorably situated as yours is."

"Then it's settled," Lady Matlock said. "The Darcys shall accompany us, along with the Linningtons. Lady Catherine may sit in Jamie's box, if she pleases, so we shall not be overcrowded."

Lord Matlock gave her a look of displeasure, but did not argue further.

Elizabeth was confused. "I apologize for not knowing, but who is Jamie?"

"My eldest son, James," Lady Matlock said.

"Though you may address him as the Viscount Fitzwilliam," Lord Matlock added.

"Ah, Colonel Fitzwilliam's brother!" Elizabeth exclaimed. "I will be pleased to meet another cousin of Mr. Darcy's."

Lady Catherine gave her a strange expression, as if she were astonished that Elizabeth would not know about all of Mr. Darcy's relations to the fourth generation ancestor by now. Nevertheless, Elizabeth survived the dinner without incident and even found herself looking forward to the opera the following week. She was determined to prove herself worthy to be on Mr. Darcy's arm at such a public place.

Elizabeth decided she would go shopping for a new gown before the opera. Mr. Darcy had been generous in his gift of pin money to her, insisting she deserved to be spoilt with new gowns and accouterments befitting her station. She would take him up on it.

She kept thinking about Mr. Darcy's remarks about his aunt looking to discredit her as his wife, and the slip of the tongue which suggested he might have some affection for her. *But what is that to me, anyhow? It is not as if I hold him in any affection. He is merely my husband in name only. I only have to appear in public as his wife and not embarrass him in any way.*

Chapter 30

Jane returned Elizabeth's call the following morning. "I am dreadfully sorry for having missed you yesterday," she said. "Mrs. Jennings and I had been invited by Mr. Bingley and Mr. Rushworth to join them for a ride through the Park, and as it was such nice weather, we could not refuse. Besides, though I knew you were arriving, I had thought you would be settling into your new quarters, and would not be making or receiving calls for at least a day."

"It is of no matter," Elizabeth reassured her. "It was only my eagerness to see you which led me to leave the house, otherwise I would have been doing exactly as you suggested. So, you saw Mr. Bingley *and* Mr. Rushworth, did you? You have seen much of them lately, have you not?"

Jane nodded. "Indeed. Mr. Bingley calls regularly, and we often see him at our social gatherings. And as for Mr. Rushworth, Mr. Bingley seems to have taken him under his wing. Poor Mr. Rushworth was taken in by a fortune hunter who left him for another man. Sad to say, she got nothing out of the dreadful affair, for the fellow in question, though he was also rich, abandoned her soon after.

She went on, "I cannot say I feel terribly sorry for her, however. Mr. Rushworth is a most deserving man, though society has treated him abominably, as if being cuckolded were somehow *his* fault. Mr.

Bingley and I are doing all we can to reintroduce him to society, in the hopes he might find a better wife in time."

Jane's use of "Mr. Bingley and I" was not lost on Elizabeth, but she allowed her sister to continue, uninterrupted. "Miss Bingley seems to like him. I think perhaps her sister hopes she may make a match; Mrs. Hurst hinted as much when last I saw them. It would be well for them, if she did, for the Hursts are still a young couple, and it must be tiresome for them, having an unmarried sister living with them."

Elizabeth shifted her position. "You speak much of your friends, but what of you? How are you, Jane?"

"Oh, I am quite well! London is such a merry place! I am never without some form of amusement. Mrs. Jennings is well-connected and takes me to all the best places. One day we are at the theater, the next at some assembly or concert, and the next at a dinner or card party. There is much more to see and do here than there ever was in Hertfordshire, despite the number of families living there. I am as happy as I could ever be. In fact, city life suits me so exactly, that when I am married, I think I shall persuade my husband to live in town all the year round if his situation allows for it."

"Have you thoughts of marriage then?" Her mind flew to the mysterious letter from Mrs. Gardiner, and she wondered if her aunt perhaps knew something that Jane herself was keeping a secret from Elizabeth.

"Certainly, I have thoughts– not that I have had any offers yet, mind you. But you, who knows me so well, cannot be blind to my desires. They are the same as they ever have been, since last autumn. Mr. Bingley has been the apple of my eye ever since I first laid eyes on him."

"Do you love him?" Elizabeth probed.

"Of course, I do!" Jane laughed. "What lady who has met Mr. Bingley, with all his good-nature and pleasing manners, could not love him in an instant?"

"But do you truly care for him? Will he make you happy, if he were to ask you to share his life with him?"

"I believe I have as much chance of happiness with him as with anyone else; perhaps more so, since I know his character and what a good man he is. A lady could do far worse than Mr. Bingley for a husband. Consider poor Mary, and what she must endure as the wife of Mr. Collins!"

Jane had a point, Elizabeth conceded. And Elizabeth was hardly an expert on love matches– she who had married a man she despised out of sheer desperation to save her own reputation. Who was she to judge the depth of love that Jane felt for Mr. Bingley?

Mr. Darcy entered the room and made his greetings to Jane, sparing Elizabeth from continuing the conversation, and after a few more minutes, Jane glanced at the clock and made her apologies that she had gotten carried away with the time, and must return home, for she and Mrs. Jennings were to attend a party at the home of Mrs. Robert Ferrars that evening, and as Mr. Bingley would likely be there too, she required extra time at her toilette to prepare.

As Jane rose to leave, Elizabeth made mention of the opera.

"Yes, of course, dear Mr. Rushworth has invited us to join him in his box," Jane said. "I quite look forward to it, and am glad to hear you will be there as well. We ought to go shopping beforehand, for I should love to have a new set of gloves, but, ah! I do not know if I shall have the time. We are quite engaged every day until then! Call on me in Berkeley Street, all the same, and if I am able to spare the time, I shall join you at the shops for a while," Jane said. "If not, *au revoir* until Saturday next!"

As soon as Jane had exited the house, Elizabeth excused herself to her chambers. The alterations to Jane's personality were so great, Elizabeth hardly recognized her sister.

She wondered if the changes were due to Jane's being in the company of Mrs. Jennings, her London friends, or some other influence.

~

Elizabeth had much on her mind as she traveled to Gracechurch Street that afternoon. Jane's call, coupled with her aunt's cryptic message, gave her an uneasy feeling which refused to settle.

Elizabeth's little cousins all rushed into the hall to see her when she entered the door, with one of them wrapping their arms around her legs and another one clamoring for sweets. Elizabeth pulled a few lemon drops from her reticule and distributed them. The children eagerly grabbed the sweets before running off to play.

Mrs. Gardiner moved closer to receive her with a tight embrace. "Ohhh, my Lizzy! It has been far too long since I have seen you!"

The Gardiners normally traveled to visit them at Longbourn for Christmas, but the past holiday, Mrs. Gardiner's expected confinement, coupled with the distance to Elizabeth's new home, made travel impossible.

"You are looking well, Aunt Gardiner!" Elizabeth exclaimed. "How is the new babe?"

"Sleeping through the night, at last! It has been difficult, the past few months, in such a small house as ours. The other children had grown used to not having a baby around, until this one came along. We have all been a little out of sorts, but, as they say, patience is a virtue. Come and meet him."

Mrs. Gardiner took her upstairs to a cradle in the corner of the children's nursery, where a small, round baby lay sleeping.

"He looks so peaceful. Quite cherubic, if I may say so." Elizabeth smiled down at the littlest Gardiner, inadvertently bumping the cradle with her hand, causing it to rock wildly. She tried to still it, but the motion caused the baby's face to shrivel up, precipitating a loud wail.

"Oh dear, it seems I have woken him."

Instead of swooping in to pick him up from his bed, Mrs. Gardiner made quiet shushing noises, rocking the cradle gently until her little boy calmed down and resumed his nap. Motioning for Elizabeth to be quiet, they exited the room and went downstairs.

"I find, sometimes, if I am not too hasty, he will return to his slumber for a while longer," she explained.

"Now, my dear, I am so glad you called!" Mrs. Gardiner said as they settled into their seats in the drawing room. The children were playing in the garden, and all was peaceful for the moment. "Not the least because it has been so terribly long since I last saw you– and you are married now! I feel I have not properly congratulated you on your marriage."

"I did receive the letter from you and Uncle Gardiner," Elizabeth said, "along with the beautiful jewelry box you entrusted my mother to deliver to me at Christmas. Thank you very much for that."

"I knew you might need something special to hold all those jewels you have as the new mistress of Pemberley," her aunt smiled. "One can never have too many jewelry boxes, I say. And your uncle was keen to make you something in his shop. Too often, his time is occupied with business affairs, all the comings and goings, dealing with merchants and cargo vessels, managing books and the like. He much prefers to work with his own two hands, making things for people. But most of the craftsmanship is performed by his workers nowadays."

Mr. Gardiner had made his mark on the world as a master cabinetmaker. His love for woodworking and carpentry, which began as a boy, led him to abandon his father's plan for him to become a solicitor and join him at the law offices in Meryton and instead strike out on his own in the world.

His success was so spectacular that he soon had his own warehouses and workshops, where craftsmen worked under his tutelage, and a shop where he sold furniture orders to customers who came from all over London to purchase his wares. It was nothing to scoff at, in Elizabeth's opinion, though many looked down on those whose fortune came from trade. Mr. Gardiner had enough money that he could have purchased an estate in the countryside, if he chose, but wanting to remain an active participant in his business affairs, he decided to remain in Gracechurch Street instead.

"I have seen Jane since my arrival in town," Elizabeth said, changing the subject.

"Yes, Jane," Mrs. Gardiner said, pressing her lips together. "How do you find Jane, since you departed from her last autumn?"

"Honestly, aunt, she is so altered, I do not know what to make of it," Elizabeth admitted. "Her call was brief, however, so I have had little time to observe her. You must have called on her often since her arrival. What is your opinion?"

"I confess, I have seen Jane very little. My confinement kept me too preoccupied to call on her when she first arrived. And though she promised to call on me, she did not do so until my little one was already a month old. Her attitude, by then, was already so different, I could scarcely believe her to be the same girl I always knew, but I attributed it to her finally emerging from her shell, as is wont to happen in such a place as this. I returned her call a few weeks later, but she was on her way out the door to some such place or other and had only time for a few words with me, and when she called here again at Gracechurch Street, her visit was also brief, and she declined to take any dinner with us, on the pretext of some other engagement."

"She may well have had an engagement," Elizabeth pointed out.

"True," Aunt Gardiner admitted. "But this does not excuse her refusal to accept an invitation for some other evening when her schedule permitted." She shook her head. "Being too busy to see her aunt and uncle with a new baby and a house full of children is one thing, but I confess I was completely taken by surprise last week, when I received a letter from her friend, Miss Caroline Bingley."

"Miss Bingley wrote to you?" Elizabeth exclaimed, in utter shock. "But you are not even acquainted!"

"Precisely. I am not even certain how she knew of us, except perhaps through mention by you or Jane."

"What could Miss Bingley have possibly wanted to say to you?" Elizabeth asked, still astonished.

"I have the letter here. If you like, you may read it." Mrs. Gardiner opened a drawer in her writing desk and retrieved a missive bearing Caroline Bingley's neat, narrow handwriting on the outside, directed to Mrs. E. Gardiner of Gracechurch Street. Elizabeth read it.

Dear Mrs. Gardiner,

I know not how to properly address you, seeing as how we are not yet acquainted. I am sure you shall think me very impertinent.

I write to you out of concern for our mutual friend, your niece, Miss Jane Bennet. I first became acquainted with her when my brother, Mr. Charles Bingley, leased an estate in Hertfordshire and invited me to join him there. In that neighborhood, we often spent time with the Bennet family, and it was there that I first became concerned about Miss Bennet's intentions towards my brother. Though not wishing to assume any mercenary designs on her part, I allowed the friendship between our families to continue, all the while observing the evident ardor forming on my brother's part towards Miss Bennet.

Had their affection been mutual, I would have been quite content to allow their relationship to progress naturally for, as you will undoubtedly learn if you speak to your niece, our family fortune comes from trade, much like your own, and a union between our families would prove to be mutually beneficial, with the comparative social standing to be gained more than enough to compensate for any lack of dowry on Miss Bennet's part, and my brother's fortune more than equal to sustain them both.

However, circumstances arose, along with numerous public remarks from your sister Mrs. Bennet, which made it evident that Miss Bennet's affections were unequal to my brother's; that her primary object was his fortune, and that she would stop at nothing to acquire it. It pains me to say such things, knowing the love you must feel for her, but I owe it to my conscience to be forthright in my observations.

Following Mr. and Mrs. Darcy's marriage, my sister and I took pains to remove our brother from Hertfordshire, in the hopes he would forget his infatuation with Miss Bennet. Nevertheless, Miss Bennet followed us to town and insinuated herself back into our brother's life and he, like a blind puppy, continued as he ever did in encouraging her flirtatious behavior and openly courting her, despite my sister and I urging him to dissuade from it.

I hesitate to write you all this, not only for the esteem I feel for your family, but not wishing to suppose Miss Bennet's motives to be so base, I gave her the benefit of the doubt, thinking perhaps, away from her mother's influence, a tenderness of heart towards my brother might manifest. All this I did heartily wish, and hoped it may be true these past four months, until recent comments Miss Bennet made in my presence led me to believe her as unfeeling and ungenerous towards my brother as I feared; that, though she esteems him greatly, her heart as yet remains untouched.

Even then, had my brother been sure of his own love for her, and willing to accept that her affection did not equal his own, I might have been able to overlook the situation. For we all know many couples in whom there is a disparate, or even complete lack of affection, and such does not necessarily undermine happiness in a marriage, especially where such mutual benefit as I have described exists between the two parties.

But, as several months have passed, and my brother appears to be no closer to proposing to Miss Bennet than in the early days of their meeting, I now begin to wonder whether, despite all his attention towards her, he means to marry her at all, or whether he is stringing her along like one of the many "angels" he admired in the past. Not that I think my brother capable of willfully misleading any young lady; no, rather, I think he is perhaps not yet ready to settle down, and in his naïveté, is unaware of how his actions may appear to the public. In short, he does not realize the expectations he is raising, by courting your niece.

Miss Bennet's behavior, in turn, has grown more provocative, to the point that I fear her reputation may be in danger should Mr. Bingley decide not to propose to her. And while I know my brother to be an honorable man, I would be sorry indeed if he were to suffer the fate of a marriage of honor, rather than one of his own choosing.

I contemplated many hours before deciding to write to you. Miss Bennet's parents, I did not trust to act in her best interests– whether due to the indolence of one, or the cupidity of the other, and it pains me to say, even her own sister is not above such suspicions, due to the nature of her recent

marriage. Though not wishing to insult you by saying such things, I appeal to your love for your niece, in the hopes you might act before irreparable damage has been done. Miss Bennet and Mrs. Darcy have often spoken of you with fondness, and if your affection for them is as great as theirs is for you, then I can trust you to respond accordingly to these concerns.
    Yours, etc,
    Caroline Bingley

Elizabeth needed to re-read the letter twice before she could find words to speak. At first, she was affronted, and communicated such to her aunt. But upon the third reading of the letter, felt more than ever the same genuine concern for Jane's welfare that she experienced after meeting with Jane.

"I too, felt outraged by the gall Miss Bingley displayed in writing to me," Mrs. Gardiners expressed. "She certainly does not hold our family in high regard, however much she might pretend to. I doubt the authenticity of her concern for Jane as well; I think it far more likely that it stems from a desire to protect her brother from her perceived threat of a fortune hunter."

"But Jane is no fortune hunter!" Elizabeth exclaimed.

"Naturally, I could not take Miss Bingley at her word in regards to Jane. I had to see for myself. I had spent so little time in Jane's company since her arrival, it was necessary for me to call on her, which I did about a week ago. I made no mention of Miss Bingley's letter, but I did question Jane on a number of subjects, and I brought up, as tactfully as I could, my concerns over her spending time too frequently with Mr. Bingley and company and displaying too warm a sentiment towards him until a proper engagement had been formed. Jane dismissed it all, saying she had done nothing which was deemed improper in the eyes of her chaperone, Mrs. Jennings, and therefore I had nothing to be concerned about. But her language suggested a familiarity towards him which I did not deem entirely proper."

Elizabeth was distressed. She rose from the settee and began pacing the room.

"You are acquainted with Miss Bingley," Mrs. Gardiner began. "Do you think it likely that her letter holds some truth?"

"It is entirely possible she speaks only out of jealousy and a desire to drive Jane from her brother's arms, as you suggested. But I must make my own observations, in order to garner the truth." Elizabeth mentioned the upcoming opera, and the opportunity it would no doubt afford her to witness Jane and Mr. Bingley in public. "If there is any truth to what Miss Bingley writes, then what are we to do about Jane?" she asked.

"I do not know. I could write to your father or mother. Unfortunately, I think Miss Bingley is correct in assuming that they will be reluctant to do anything."

"My father might," Elizabeth said, recalling how he stepped up when her own reputation was at stake. "If I write to him and urge him to act, and impress upon him the severity of the situation, perhaps he might insist that Jane return home, or at the very least impress upon her the need to remedy her behavior, if she will not listen to you or I."

"Make your observations first, before you write to anyone," Mrs. Gardiner advised. "It does not do to act upon speculation. I think it wise not to put too much stock into anything Miss Bingley says, until you have seen for yourself whether Jane conducts herself properly."

At that moment, one of the children came in from the garden, crying because her brother had pushed her into the dirt, causing her to scrape her knee. Mrs. Gardiner's attention was therefore diverted in assisting the child and reprimanding the other. Meanwhile, the baby awoke upstairs and his cries could be heard. Mrs. Gardiner dispatched her eldest child to console him until she could make her way upstairs to tend to him.

Elizabeth, seeing her aunt was now fully preoccupied, excused herself, promising to call again another day.

Chapter 31

That evening, Elizabeth rang for Parker but was surprised when another maid entered the room.

"Miss Parker asked me to apologize on her behalf, mistress. She is presently too unwell to attend to you," the maid informed her.

Elizabeth gasped. "Dear me! I hope it is nothing too serious."

"Merely a cold, I believe, ma'am, but she did not wish to pass her illness to you. Mrs. Hastings has sent her to bed." The maid helped Elizabeth dress for bed, then said, "I am told by Parker that my duties include staying the night to guard you, ma'am?"

Elizabeth flushed, embarrassed that Parker should have said such a thing. "That will not be necessary. I am capable of sleeping alone." She had not suffered any incidents since that night at Pemberley, and concluded she ought to be safe for a few nights until Parker recovered. She hated the thought of more servants becoming aware of her propensity for sleepwalking. Thus far, those with knowledge of her condition did not extend beyond Parker and Perkins.

"Thank heavens, ma'am! I were worried. Not that I have any objections, mind you, but I've been told my snoring could wake the dead. I would hate to disturb your sleep, mistress, for havin' to share a chamber with me."

"I appreciate your concern, Polly. Please pass on my regards to Parker, and accept my appreciation for your attending to me in her absence."

The maid curtsied and departed.

Elizabeth climbed into bed, but could not fall asleep. She kept thinking of her visit with Mrs. Gardiner, the letter from Caroline, and her own impressions after meeting Jane.

Eventually, her tossing and turning led her to drift off.

*

Darcy awoke sometime during the night by the sound of footsteps outside his door. Knowing the servants would all be abed, he rose and opened the door in time to catch a glimpse of Elizabeth heading downstairs. She did not appear to be conscious, moving slowly in the same sort of stupor he had found her in when she entered his room that fateful night in November. Fearing for her safety should she manage to wander into the London streets, he followed her. Elizabeth's footsteps carried her down the servant's stairs to the kitchen, where her arm knocked over a copper pan left out to dry. It clanged onto the stone floor with such a loud noise, that Elizabeth was startled awake. Darcy reached the kitchen just in time to witness the incident and hear his wife cry out in terror.

"Where am I?"

Instinctively, he pulled his arms around her. "Shhh, you are in the kitchen, Elizabeth. You have been sleepwalking again, but you are safe."

The noise awakened Parker, who came out of one of the servants' chambers on the lower floor.

"Parker, what is the meaning of this? Why was Mrs. Darcy left unattended?"

"I beg your pardon, master, it was not my intention–"

"Do not blame Parker," Elizabeth interrupted. "She has been ill this evening, and sent Polly to me in her stead, but I dismissed her. I did not want the other servants knowing of my condition."

"I do blame Parker. She ought to have consulted me before handing you over to the care of an inexperienced maid." Turning to the lady's maid, he reprimanded her further. "Do you not know what might have happened to Mrs. Darcy, had I not intercepted her? Suppose she went outside, and some vagabond or miscreant attacked her? Or suppose she injured herself on something in this kitchen?"

Parker was in tears now, and humbly asked for mercy.

Darcy relented. "We will discuss your fate tomorrow, Parker. For now, I must have a word with my wife."

Elizabeth followed him meekly to his study on the ground floor.

"If your maid was sick, you ought to have told me. Or at least accepted the substitute she offered."

"I told you, I could not bear it if my condition were widely known."

Darcy sighed. "Then I shall have to assume the duties myself."

Elizabeth's eyes widened. "What do you mean?"

"I mean that if you will accept no other, then I will assume Parker's responsibility until she is well. It would not be the first time that you and I have shared a chamber. If that is not acceptable to you, then I insist you allow Polly to remain with you instead."

Elizabeth gave a wry laugh. "I suppose you would be preferable as a companion. At least I know that you do not snore in your sleep!"

"You have only slept with me the one night. How do you know that I do not?" Darcy allowed a slight grin to cross his face.

"If you do, I shall kick you out!" Elizabeth returned with a smirk of her own.

Elizabeth slept the remainder of the night. When she awoke, Darcy was not in the bed with her, but laying on the small cot where Parker normally slept. He had not gone to sleep when she did, claiming he wished to read a book for a while, as being up had made him not tired.

Her rising stirred him from his sleep.

"Did you not wish to lay on the bed after I fell asleep?" she asked him.

"I did not wish to disturb your slumber," he mumbled.

"Hardly likely," she mused. "We both know how deep my slumber is. I do not think you would have awakened me."

"Be that as it may, I felt it better to remain on the cot." Darcy stood up, a groan escaping his lips as he stretched and sat up. He rubbed his lower back.

"Does your back ache?"

He nodded in response. "I will be well enough, though, after I move about."

But his behavior the remainder of the day indicated otherwise. He moved with a slight limp, and winced whenever he turned his upper body.

✦

Elizabeth, still upset by the contents of Miss Bingley's letter, determined to speak to Jane again the next day. She called at an early hour, expecting to find her alone. Elizabeth was surprised, therefore, to find Jane already had callers.

"This is my youngest daughter, Mrs. Palmer, and my cousins, Mrs. Robert Ferrars, and Miss Steele," Mrs. Jennings introduced, as Elizabeth took an empty seat near Jane. "Ladies, this is Mrs. Darcy, my cousin, and the sister of our Miss Bennet."

"A pleasure to meet you, Mrs. Darcy," Mrs. Palmer beamed, her cheerful disposition and rounded figure resembling her mother's. "It is so wonderful to meet another member of the family."

Elizabeth had met Mrs. Jennings once, some years ago, when that lady passed through Hertfordshire. Mrs. Jennings was a distant cousin of Mrs. Bennet's, but how exactly they were related, Elizabeth was not certain, and she had never troubled herself to study the family Bible enough to work it out.

Miss Steele exclaimed, "If you're Mrs. Jenning's cousin, then that must make us cousins as well, I suppose. La! Imagine, finding another set of cousins you knew nothing about!" A snort escaped her lips. She was thin and gangly, with a largish mouth and an even larger nose that looked disproportionate to her frame.

Mrs. Jennings laughed. "Not quite, my dear Miss Steele. Miss Bennet and Mrs. Darcy are cousins on my mother's side, while you and Mrs. Ferrars are cousins on my father's side."

Miss Steele appeared confused, apparently trying to puzzle out how both sets of sisters could be cousins of Mrs. Jennings but not of each other.

"It matters not how we are related," Mrs. Ferrars said. "Any cousin of Mrs. Jennings is a friend of ours." She was as thin as her sister, and the prettier of the two, but her face had a taut, shrewish look that Elizabeth disliked.

"It is good of you to call on us, Lizzy," Jane spoke up. "I did not expect to see you again so soon."

"I happened to be in the neighborhood," Elizabeth said. She wished the others were not in the room so she might discuss Miss Bingley's letter with Jane.

Their conversation centered on tittle-tattle about people whom Elizabeth did not know, interspersed with jokes from Mrs. Jennings, which were usually followed by snorts from Miss Steele or loud giggles from Mrs. Palmer. Elizabeth hoped the other guests might leave soon, but they lingered. The clock ticked past, first a quarter's hour, then a half, and still, none of the other ladies made any motion to leave. Mrs. Palmer might be forgiven, she supposed, given her relationship to Mrs. Jennings, but what motive could Mrs. Ferrars and Miss Steele have for remaining so long? Surely they must have other calls to make over the course of the morning!

Elizabeth wondered if she might entice Jane away from her company, as presently occupied as they were with Mrs. Jennings' gossip.

She turned to her sister. "It is such a lovely morning. I wondered if you might perhaps like to take a turn with me in the square."

Jane's face brightened. "An excellent idea, Lizzy!" She rose from her seat, looking around the room. "You do not mind, do you, Mrs. Jennings, if I stroll the square with my sister?"

"No, no, not at all!" Mrs. Jennings replied cheerfully.

"A stroll sounds excellent," Mrs. Palmer piped up. "I could use a turn out of doors myself."

"Let's all go!" Miss Steele exclaimed.

Elizabeth inwardly groaned. Would she never be rid of these people?

A few minutes later, their company set out. Mrs. Jennings' stately townhouse was within an easy distance of Berkeley Square. Elizabeth hoped the narrow pathways lining the square, which necessitated their walking in twos or threes, might afford her the opportunity to speak with Jane without the others hearing. However, Mrs. Jennings monopolized Jane's attention, drawing her into a conversation with Mrs. Palmer and Miss Steele about the architecture of the buildings on the square and their residents.

"Of course, I am sure there is one *particular resident* whom you are hoping to see," Mrs. Jennings said with a wink.

"Now Mrs. Jennings," Jane scolded. "You mustn't presume I walk in front of his house solely in the hopes he might notice me from his windows and come out to greet me."

"Ho, ho, but would it not be a fine thing now, if he did?" the older lady chuckled.

Nevertheless, Jane lingered before the fine, brick residence to the right of them, giving the appearance of using her reflection in its windows to adjust her bonnet.

A carriage waited in front of the house. Presently, the door of the house opened and a footman exited, followed by none other than Mr. Bingley and his sisters, along with Mr. Hurst.

When he spotted Jane, Mr. Bingley's face lit up. He crossed the street between the houses and the square and came to them. His sisters followed slower, their haughty sneers towards Jane displaying their distaste for their former friend.

Mr. Bingley greeted them warmly, expressing his surprise to find them all outside his house. His eyes fixed on Jane, his pleasure evident at her presence.

"We were merely taking a stroll through the square, to enjoy this nice weather," Elizabeth explained.

"Yes, the weather today is excellent! In fact, my sisters have just come to collect me. We are on our way to take tea and survey the amusements at White Conduit House," Mr. Bingley told them.

"Oh, how lovely!" Jane exclaimed. "I have long wished to see the gardens at White Conduit. I am told they have an excellent fish pond."

"If you were not already engaged with your present company, I would ask you to join us," he said.

"Oh, you needn't stand on ceremony on *our* account!" Miss Steele blurted.

"Indeed," Mrs. Ferrars added. "If you wish to go, then by all means, let us not be a hindrance to you. Mrs. Palmer can see us back to our carriages at her mother's house."

Miss Bingley stepped forward. "I hesitate to remind you, Charles, but our chaise is small and cannot accommodate six. Therefore, I must protest the alteration to our plans."

"No, I would not intrude upon your plans for the world," Jane said. She gave Mr. Bingley a becoming smile. "We shall meet again soon."

But Mr. Bingley, still desirous that Jane should accompany him, suggested they could attend Mrs. Jennings and her company back to her residence, to collect her carriage, so that they might join their party. He even extended the invitation to all her guests.

Mrs. Jennings proposed a simpler solution. "I cannot blame you for wishing such a pretty thing as Miss Bennet to join you on your outing. But I am happy to let her go without me, as presently occupied as I am. Oh yes, you may take her off my hands as soon as you please!" She winked.

"Mr. Bingley," Jane said. "Do you suppose your carriage could admit one more? I promise I am small and do not take up much room." She batted her eyes, taking an eager step towards him.

Mr. Bingley nodded excitedly. "Yes, I believe we can accommodate you. You are certain you do not mind, Mrs. Jennings?"

The lady assured him she had no need of Jane, and that nothing would please her more than to see Jane enjoy herself on this fine day. Before Miss Bingley had a chance to protest further, Mr. Bingley handed her into his carriage, then took the seat beside her. Mr. Hurst settled himself in the middle of the seat opposite, leaving Miss Bingley and Mrs. Hurst to choose whether they would squeeze next to him, or share a seat with Jane and their brother. In the end, they chose the former, and then they were off, leaving Mrs. Jennings and Mrs. Palmer to wave cheerfully in their wake.

Elizabeth's spirits sank. She had not had any opportunity to speak to Jane. Furthermore, Jane's behavior appeared brazen to her, from the way she had angled for an invitation, to her taking the seat beside Mr. Bingley rather than the one opposite him. Her going off without the company of Mrs. Jennings was also distressing, although Elizabeth supposed the Hursts and Miss Bingley would suffice as chaperones in her stead. It was clear that they did not wish for a match to take place between Jane and their brother. But she still needed to know whether Miss Bingley's allegations were true.

Chapter 32

Elizabeth did not see Jane again until the night of the opera. She called again at Berkeley Street a few days prior, in hopes Jane might accompany her to the modiste, but was told Jane was not at home. Jane did not return the call, but merely sent a note expressing her regret that she had missed Elizabeth.

Elizabeth's new gown was a vivid blue silk with a demi-train, adorned with lace, pearls, and sapphires. Elizabeth had never owned anything so fine in her life before, but Mr. Darcy insisted no expense should be spared, and Lady Matlock, who had accompanied her for the choosing of the gown, declared this was the latest fashion and was certain this style would soon be featured in *La Belle Assemblée,* though how she could know such things, Elizabeth was uncertain. Rather than a turban or feathers, Elizabeth chose to wear a sheer lace cap adorned with ruffles. Miss Walters, the modiste who crafted the gown, assured her it was exceedingly fashionable this season. When paired with a set of white kid gloves and a gold lace fan, Elizabeth did, indeed, feel *en vogue.*

Mr. Darcy's eyes widened as she descended the staircase to meet him in the hall. "Mrs. Darcy, you look exquisite," he said. "That color suits your complexion exceedingly."

Elizabeth blushed as she thanked him, taking his arm so he could lead her to the carriage. Darcy stopped before they reached the doors.

"Before I forget, there is something I wish to give you." He released her hand and went to a side table, where a beautifully wrapped little parcel lay. He handed it to Elizabeth who took the wrappings off. Inside was a small opera glass, elegantly shaped from ivory and carved wood, with a brass monocle on the end. Elizabeth found she could extend the lens, much like a spyglass used at sea.

"How elegant!" she exclaimed.

"For your first opera," he said, "so that you may better see the performers."

"You are too generous!"

"Nonsense! I wish for you to have the best experience, and this will surely assist you."

"Then, I thank you, sir." She smiled as she took his arm once more.

※

Covent Garden was a crush of people when they arrived, as if all the *beau monde* had turned out for the evening. Elizabeth felt less spectacular when she observed the multitude of painted peacocks in their shimmering gowns and feathered headdresses. But her appearance still turned their eyes. Self-consciously, she wished she had chosen to wear a turban or add a feathered bandeau.

"They are all looking at you," Mr. Darcy whispered, "and wondering who is this stunning woman that has become the new Mrs. Darcy."

Elizabeth felt a flush of pride at his words.

They located Lord and Lady Matlock in their box. In the next box, Lady Catherine de Bourgh sat, accompanied by a distinguished couple who were introduced to Elizabeth as Lord and Lady Linnington. Elizabeth made her greetings, then began scanning the other boxes with her new opera glass, until she at last spotted Jane beside Mr. Bingley in the box directly opposite theirs. A portly man in a pink coat, whom Elizabeth assumed must be Mr. Rushworth, sat on Jane's other side, next to Mrs. Jennings.

"If you'll excuse me, I see my sister across the way," Elizabeth curtsied to their party. "I shall greet her and return to you all before the performance begins."

"My legs could use a stretch as well, before the performance begins," Lady Matlock said, rising from her seat. "Shall we promenade together to find her, and you may introduce me?"

Elizabeth nodded. They reached the other side of the theater just as Jane emerged from the boxes into the gallery, followed by Mr. Bingley and the other two Elizabeth had seen.

"Lizzy!" Jane exclaimed. "I thought I spotted you across the way. How wonderful, that we are all here tonight! I am sorry I did not receive your message in time to accompany you to see Miss Walters about your gown. My, you look stunning, though!"

The portly gentleman behind her cleared his throat. Mr. Bingley quickly introduced him as Mr. Rushworth, as Elizabeth had suspected.

"And this is my daughter and her husband," Mrs. Jennings said, as another set emerged from the next box over. "Lady Matlock, may I present Mr. and Mrs. Palmer to you?"

"It is monstrous good of you to come all this way over here to meet us," Mrs. Palmer beamed.

Mr. Palmer, meanwhile, said nothing, but let out a barely stifled yawn.

Before Lady Matlock had time to recover from the shock of such introductions being thrust upon her without warning, their party was accosted by Mrs. Ferrars and Miss Steele. The two ladies rushed towards them, the ostentatious plumes of their headdresses bobbing vigorously as they caught their breath. Behind them, another gentleman walked at a slower pace.

"Oh, La! But we had such a terrible time locating you all!" Miss Steele exclaimed. "Franklin drove us to the wrong entrance. Can you imagine, thinking we should be sitting in the pits! So there we were, crushed on all sides by scores of ruffians, and unable to make our way up the stairs to reach our boxes, until finally, Mr. Ferrars was able to ask the people to make way for us so we could get through. And then, wouldn't you know it? We found we were on the opposite side from our box! La! What a joke!"

"Ho, ho, ho!" Mrs. Jennings chuckled. "Lord bless you, Nancy! But you're here now, so all's well that ends well."

Mrs. Ferrars cleared her throat, prompting Mrs. Jennings to make the introductions. They appeared to be in awe of Lady Matlock.

"A pleasure to make your acquaintance, Your Ladyship," Mrs. Ferrars gushed, curtsying deeply.

"La, I'm so starved, I declare I could eat a horse!" Miss Steele exclaimed. "We a'nt ate since morning, on account of the opera. Lucy said t'would be a shame if we couldn't fit in our gowns!"

Mrs. Ferrars promptly rapped her sister's knuckles with her fan to silence her. "My sister seems to be finding herself a wee bit peckish. We shall pay a visit to the refreshment room and rejoin you all soon."

"I shall accompany you, for I believe I am as hungry as you are." Mrs. Palmer piped up.

"Let's all go!" Mrs. Jennings suggested. "The performance will begin soon, and I should like to enjoy it on a full stomach. Will you not join us, Lady Matlock, Mrs. Darcy?"

"We must return to the rest of our party, but thank you for the invitation," Lady Matlock answered graciously.

Lady Matlock and Elizabeth returned to the other side of the theater. They found their party assembled in the antechamber adjoining their boxes. Elizabeth noticed a gentleman and lady had joined their party.

"Jamie, there you are!" his mother said, greeting him with a kiss on each cheek. "This is Mrs. Darcy, your cousin's wife."

"A pleasure to meet you." The gentleman bowed low. The lady beside him drew closer and wrapped her arm around his possessively.

"Likewise, my lord. My lady." Elizabeth said with a nod and a curtsy to each, presuming the lady to be his wife.

A murmur came from Lord and Lady Linington and Lady Catherine, who were within earshot.

The viscount's ears turned pink. "Ahem, may I present to you Signorina Valentino, the acclaimed opera singer. She will be performing tonight."

"Oh, I beg your pardon," Elizabeth said, realizing her mistake. "I shall look forward to your performance this evening, signorina. Which role will you be performing?"

"I will be appearing as Zerlina," the singer replied.

In her peripheral vision, Elizabeth noticed Darcy had approached.

"A favorite role of mine," Darcy said, addressing the performer with a bow. "I especially enjoy the aria *Vedrai, carino* in the second act."

Signorina Valentino and Viscount Fitzwilliam returned Darcy's courtesy with a nod, then excused themselves, promising to rejoin their party before the end of the act.

Lord and Lady Linington also declared their need for refreshments, and left with Lord and Lady Matlock.

Seeing Lady Catherine coming towards them, her expression livid, Elizabeth braced herself.

"Did you not realize that person was his mistress?" she leveled at Elizabeth. "How could you countenance speaking to such a person?"

Elizabeth blinked. "Your Ladyship! I realized I erred in my assumption of her being his wife. But the shame rather ought to belong to the viscount, if indeed he brought his mistress, instead of his wife."

"The viscount's marriage is understandably undergoing difficulty at present. But your assumption has drawn undue attention from the Linningtons. Now, there will surely be talk of this tomorrow. It might even make *The Tattler*!"

Darcy stepped in to defend her. "If the gossip rags should choose to report on the status of the viscount's marriage, it shall not be Elizabeth's fault, but Jamie's own. But I daresay that most in attendance will presume he merely wished to introduce us to our star performer, and will not speculate on the unholy relationship between the viscount and Signorina Valentino."

Lady Catherine huffed. With a swish of her skirt, she departed from them to locate her seat. Darcy began heading towards their own seats, but Elizabeth tugged on his sleeve.

"I did not realize she was his mistress. I feel ashamed for having assumed she was his wife, by the intimate way she clung to him."

"As I told my aunt, the shame is not yours to bear, but my cousin's. I should have acquainted you with the state of the viscount's marriage prior to our coming here. In December, his wife left him along with their children, on the pretext of visiting her parents in Dorsetshire. Family acquaintances were told that Jamie had gone with them; however, he spent some months at Fitzwilliam Castle in Scotland in an attempt to let the rumors die down… But now that the Season is in full swing, he has returned to his residence in Town, and has, apparently, resumed his affair with Signorina Valentino."

"How awful! No wonder your aunt wished to silence me on the matter. I am deeply sorry for having said anything to her at all. Had I known, I am sure I should have declined to speak a word to Signorina Valentino." Elizabeth shook her head soberly.

"That would have made matters worse. You did nothing wrong by speaking to her, and it will certainly not be your fault if my cousin features in *The Tattler* tomorrow," Darcy reassured her.

The Matlocks returned with the Linningtons, and they all took their seats for the performance. In the pit below, they could hear the orchestra tuning their instruments.

The opera began. Viscount Fitzwilliam did not return until well into the second scene. His clothing was rather more rumpled than before and his cravat was improperly tied, but no one dared to remark upon it. Signorina Valentino appeared in the third scene, as the bride of Masetto, whom Don Giovanni tries to seduce. Her singing was excellent, but Elizabeth found she could not enjoy the performance after what she had learned.

She fixed her gaze instead on Jane, making good use of the opera glass, but did not like what she saw. The flirtatious behavior she displayed was entirely unfit for a lady to exhibit in public. Jane laughed loud and hard over something Mr. Bingley said, bending forward so much that she gave the gentlemen beside her a good view of her *décolletage*. Then she leaned close to Mr. Rushworth's ear and whispered something to him, before bursting into laughter again. She teased alternately between the two men, giving each of them coy glances, but mostly to Mr. Bingley. Several times, she placed her hand upon his shoulder, his hands, and even, briefly, his leg. Elizabeth felt sickened and could watch no more. Mrs. Jennings did not appear to pay any mind to her charge, being too engrossed in talking with her daughters, who had come over from their own box to converse with their mother.

Jane's behavior drew remarks from Lady Matlock, who whispered to Elizabeth. "Your sister appears to be quite familiar with Mr. Bingley. Do they have an understanding?"

"I am unsure, Your Ladyship," Elizabeth replied, fighting back the tears swelling in her eyes. "If they have, it has not been communicated to me."

"I think if they have not, an engagement will surely be forthcoming," Lady Matlock said.

Lady Linnington, who had been listening near, and watching the audience with her opera glass, chose this moment to join their conversation. "They will need to form an engagement after tonight–such shocking behavior!" She used her closed fan to point across the theater.

Elizabeth turned her own glass back to Jane. To her horror, Jane had wrapped her arm around Mr. Bingley's waist and was leaning her head upon his shoulder. Then, to make matters worse, she lifted her head and planted a kiss on his cheek!

"Young couples ought to be more discreet in their affection," Lady Linnington continued. "If they wish to carry on in such a fashion, they ought to withdraw to the antechamber and draw the curtains, rather than expose us all to such vulgarity."

"I quite agree, Lady Linnington," Lady Catherine interjected, leaning her head around the partition from the second box to speak her mind. "Mrs. Darcy ought to reprimand her sister for such behavior."

Elizabeth could hear no more. She left her seat and hurried to the antechamber, where she found a sofa and promptly burst into tears upon it.

Chapter 33

Darcy saw everything as well as overheard the ladies' conversation. Knowing Elizabeth was in distress, he followed her to the antechamber and sat beside her on the sofa.

"You are right to be upset," he told her. "Your sister has behaved in a way that defies all she ought to know as proper."

"Oh, Mr. Darcy, this confirms all my fears!" Elizabeth said. She proceeded to tell him of the letters and visits pertaining to Jane's conduct.

"I could not believe it of Jane, until I had seen it for myself. I am afraid she has become entirely ungoverned, and whether it is due to her friends' influence or her chaperone's, I cannot say. She has never behaved thusly when at home."

Darcy's distress was nearly equal to Elizabeth's after hearing her report. "This is a serious business, indeed! You were right to confide in me, though." He stood up from the sofa.

"What do you plan to do?" Elizabeth asked.

"I will call on Bingley tomorrow morning, and urge him to propose to your sister. He must understand the precarious position he has put Jane in, to allow their courtship to carry on so publicly without declaring himself. A lady's reputation hangs by a single thread, and a situation such as this is nearly as grave as the one you and I found ourselves in."

Darcy observed the deep anguish written on Elizabeth's face. He put his hand on her shoulder reassuringly. "I will not rest until this is settled."

"Ought I write to my father?" she asked, remembering her conversation with Mrs. Gardiner.

"Hold off until after I speak to Bingley. If he can be brought to reason, as I believe he will, then there is no need to alarm your father."

Elizabeth nodded. "Thank you, Mr. Darcy."

Though the hour was late, Darcy knew Bingley's habits enough to know he would still be awake. He paid him a call at his quarters on Berkeley Square.

Bingley answered the door himself, still dressed in his opera clothes, although he had shed his outer coat and cravat. "Darcy, good fellow! I am surprised to see you at this hour. To what do I owe this visit?"

Darcy explained he had something of importance to communicate regarding his relationship with Miss Bennet.

"Goodness, this sounds serious!" Bingley exclaimed. "I had better pour us some drinks while you tell me about it." Heading to the room which doubled as a sitting room and study, he took out a decanter of brandy and two glasses.

Darcy took only a sip from his, before setting it down, situating himself on the sofa opposite his friend to begin. Without naming anyone in particular, Darcy told Bingley of the reports which had been circulating about their behavior in recent weeks. "Elizabeth is, rightfully, concerned for her sister's reputation."

"But, we have done nothing wrong!" Bingley insisted. "Trips to the theater, carriage rides in the park, dancing together at the assembly, or conversations at a dinner party– these are the sorts of innocent diversions we have partaken of. Nothing untoward in the slightest."

"Nothing untoward, really?" Darcy's eyebrows raised. "You seemed rather too close tonight at the opera. Your intimacy drew the remarks of others, even across the theater from you."

Bingley's cheeks pinked. "Well, it is not as though we have been discovered in the same bedroom in the middle of the night," he said, with a touch of bitterness.

Darcy ignored the slight and continued. "Be that as it may, the flirtation between the two of you has not gone unnoticed, and the length of your courtship is by now such that people have begun to speculate whether you mean to propose to Miss Bennet or merely string her along."

"People ought to concern themself with their own affairs and leave others to manage themselves!" Bingley complained. He downed the remainder of his glass and poured himself another.

"I could not agree more; however, you are aware, as well as I am, of the harm that comes from malicious gossip. Miss Bennet deserves better than the unkind remarks of the *ton* and deserves to be treated with respect from the gentlemen of her acquaintance."

Bingley cried, "I do respect Miss Bennet, entirely!"

"I have no doubt of it!" Darcy sighed. "I hate to ask you, but what are your feelings towards Miss Bennet?"

"I feel nothing but the warmest regard for her. She is, in every sense, an angel– her appearance, her manners, her disposition– all are exactly suited to my own. In short, she is perfection itself."

"Then you love her?"

"Love her!" Bingley laughed. "Yes, I suppose I do love her, as much as I have loved any woman; perhaps even a bit more."

"Bingley," Darcy said, his tone growing more serious, "I must insist, for Miss Bennet's sake as much as my wife's, that you not trifle with Miss Bennet. If you love her, and mean to marry her, then I ask that you not hesitate in making her an offer, for the sake of her reputation after the expectations which you have raised."

"Good gracious, Darcy!" Bingley exclaimed, setting his glass down on the side table. "Of course, I mean to marry her! I had always intended that I should, at some time, settle down with a woman of my choosing, and as I have said, there is no one who better suits my tastes and desires than Miss Bennet. I have been in no hurry to make an offer, perhaps out of my own selfish desire to continue enjoying the freedom that a bachelor's life affords me and having, at present, full command of the fortune left to me by my father.

"I suppose, if I am honest, I have been overly indulgent in enjoying such a life, without a care except for my own whims, and without considering the ramifications to the lady in question. But I have no wish to injure the lady– far from it! Nor would I suffer you, who is now her brother in law, to have any cause to challenge me for her honor."

"Nor would I ever wish to!" Darcy declared, a laugh escaping his lips, despite the seriousness. An image of himself and Bingley, facing off with pistols in Hyde Park, seemed ludicrous.

Bingley shifted his position on the sofa. "I thank you, Darcy, for bringing to light the graveness of this business, and with your blessing, procured in advance of that blessing which must surely follow from Miss Bennet's own father, I shall propose to Miss Bennet without delay."

"Excellent. The sooner it is accomplished, the sooner we may celebrate your impending marriage," Darcy said, picking up his glass from the side table and downing it.

Darcy returned home to a still-anxious Elizabeth, who was pacing the drawing room floor in anticipation of his return.

"How did it go? Was he able to be brought to reason?"

"Bingley has declared his intention to propose to your sister, and I trust he will do so imminently," he told her.

"Oh, thank goodness!" Elizabeth said, sinking onto a nearby chair in relief. "In truth, this is a far better outcome than I could have hoped for. I feared I would need to implore my father to act on Jane's behalf. Now, I am spared from the necessity of writing such a letter. I am grateful to you, Mr. Darcy, for what you have done."

"I have only done as a brother of my wife's sister ought to do," Darcy said. Nevertheless, there was a feeling of warmth in his breast, to be the recipient of her gratitude. The smile it brought to her face— one he had seen her display on many occasions, but which had rarely been bestowed on him particularly— sent a rush of emotions flooding through his brain. He fought against the sudden desire to take her into his arms and embrace her, and to kiss those sweet, luscious lips of hers.

The knowledge that she did not like him— that she had married him against her will— battled in his heart, waging against the hopes that perhaps he had earned some degree of estimation in her eyes, and the still deeper wish that he might one day make her love him.

His love for her was certain. He had known it from so early a time, even before their fateful night, when the first tender stirrings of his heart induced him, along with his sense of honor, to marry her. And now, so many months into their marriage, she had become a permanent fixture in his heart, one for which the loss of would be nothing short of devastating.

He longed to declare these feelings to her, to make known to her the depth of his love. But he had not the courage to declare it in the face of possible rejection. To hear her say aloud that she could never love him the way that he loved her, would be worse than to continue on in silent adoration, his love masked by a congenial arrangement of marriage between them, each living out their roles as master and mistress over his estate, but never more intimate than business partners and housemates.

※

Elizabeth was determined that Mr. Darcy, who had already been so valiant in coming forward to Mr. Bingley on her sister's behalf, should not suffer yet another night of uncomfortable sleep on the cot, which was far too short for his long frame to properly stretch out. Offering him the bed that night, she declared she would sleep on the cot.

"Absolutely not!" he argued. "What sort of gentleman would I be, to allow my lady to sleep on an uncomfortable cot, whilst I enjoyed the comfort of her bed?"

His turn of phrase, though meant innocently, caused a blush to rise to her cheeks. Disabusing the unladylike thoughts as soon as they arose, she countered, saying, "I could not see you suffer another night in such an uncomfortable bed either. You must choose, I think, between sleeping here in the bed, or returning to your own bed."

Darcy rubbed his lumbar region, which still ached from the previous night's restless slumber. "I will not deny that the prospect of stretching myself fully is far more agreeable than curling up on this small bed. But I cannot allow you to remain alone and unguarded. Will you not consent to a maid sleeping here, in lieu of Parker, as she is still ill?"

Elizabeth shook her head. "Impossible. As I mentioned previously, I wish for as few people as possible to know of my condition. You appear reluctant out of some delicacy towards me. Are we not husband and wife? And have we not shared a bed once before? Twice, if we are being precise. I am not so repulsed by you that I cannot contend with sharing a bed– under perfectly platonic terms, of course– when it is your very sense of chivalry which leads you to lend your protection to me, to safeguard me against my nocturnal wanderings."

Her speech seemed to have shocked him, but he consented. Elizabeth felt the heat rise to her cheeks once more. He retreated to his own quarters to dress for bed, and Polly entered to attend her.

"The woolen nightgown, if you please, Polly," Elizabeth requested.

"Are you certain, ma'am? The air this evening is quite warm. I fear such a warm gown will be too hot, and bring you discomfort in your sleep. Would you not rather wear your cotton nightgown?"

"I feel a sudden chill, Polly, and therefore I think the woolen one shall suit better."

"Very well, ma'am." Polly nodded.

Though she had been emboldened to invite Mr. Darcy to sleep in the same bed with her, Elizabeth recalled the vulnerability she felt on their wedding night, sleeping in such a thin shift, and treated the additional modesty the woolen gown provided as a sort of armor.

The woolen gown was uncomfortably warm for April, just as Polly said it would be. Nevertheless, Elizabeth felt a shiver as she climbed into her bed. Mr. Darcy knocked at the door before entering. He nodded to her before joining on the other side of the bed.

"I am tired and overwrought from the day's events, so I shall sleep now," she declared. "I wish you a good night's rest, Mr. Darcy." She quickly blew out the candle on her nightstand.

"Likewise, Mrs. Darcy," he bid her before blowing out his own candle.

Elizabeth shifted under the covers, her body facing away from him. She willed herself to try to sleep, but she was too keenly aware of his presence.

She felt the bed move as he adjusted his own position to a more comfortable one. "Mr. Darcy?" She whispered.

"Yes?" came his soft answer.

"Do you suppose Jane and Mr. Bingley will be happy together, once they are married?"

There was a moment of silence before he said, "I do not know. I have not yet had sufficient time to observe Bingley and your sister together since we parted from them last autumn. When I asked him of his feelings for her, his answer was almost glib; though he owned to loving her and having always intended marriage, he confessed a selfishness of enjoyment in a bachelor's life. Are you certain of Jane's feelings towards him?"

"I am not," she said. "When we were at Longbourn, I would have said differently, so convinced I was of Jane's being enamored, but now…"

"You begin to fear Miss Bingley's assertions may be true, that Jane's motives are purely mercenary," Darcy finished.

"Yes," Elizabeth said softly. "And I know what you must think of my family, of, of…me…" she trailed off again.

"Elizabeth," Darcy murmured, turning his body towards hers. "Regardless of how your family may appear, and whatever truth there may be to their motivation, I have never applied such to you. I know you did not intend to entrap me into marriage for my fortune, as others have insinuated."

"Thank you, for your faith in me." Elizabeth squeezed her eyes shut against the tears forming in them, letting a few drops leak onto her pillowcase. "It pains me to think that my own sister would stoop to such levels."

"Then there is something you should know."

Hearing the seriousness in his voice, Elizabeth turned to face him. The curves of his jaw were barely visible in the dim lighting. The warmth of his breath upon her sent another shiver up her spine.

"At the Netherfield ball," he began, "there was an incident. I stumbled upon Jane and Bingley in the study. It appeared she had lured him there under false pretense, claiming to have lost a necklace during her stay, when she was ill."

"What are you saying? That Jane attempted to compromise Mr. Bingley?"

"Yes, that is what I suspected, when I found them there. By all appearances…well, let us just say that had your father been the one to find them, I think the wedding the following morning might have been a double one."

"But they would not have had a license!" Elizabeth said, her voice raising slightly.

"It is a figure of speech. In short, I am of the belief that your sister intended to entrap him, and might have succeeded, had I not interrupted when I did. Bingley denied it entirely, being too much a believer in Miss Bennet's innocence, holding fast to the veracity of her story, but it was enough to induce me to persuade him that he would be better served by removing himself to London. His sisters were in agreement with me, and as they meant to go to Hurst Place, with or without him, and Bingley had no wish to remain at Netherfield alone, he agreed to the move. I think his inclination for Jane was slight enough that, had she not proceeded to follow him to Town and reinsert herself into his life, he might have forgotten about her for the next "angel" that came along, whomever she might be."

Elizabeth was silent for the present, her heart grieved at this piece of news. At length, she whispered, "Thank you for divulging this to me. However painful, I deserved to know the truth of my sister's conduct."

"I would have told you sooner, but I feared for how you might react."

"That I can well believe. I do not think I would have accepted it, had I not heard the reports of others and seen Jane's behavior for myself." Elizabeth felt her eyes beginning to close.

SUDDEN AWAKENINGS

"You must sleep now," Darcy said. "The hour grows late." This time, Elizabeth did not turn from him, nor did Darcy turn from her. They both closed their eyes, and the last thing Elizabeth remembered was the gentle sound of Darcy's snores.

※

Elizabeth wandered through a dark corridor. The light from her candle made eerie shapes on the wall, ghostly shadows that seemed to reach out to grab her. She turned down a side corridor, looking for the door to her bedroom, but each door she tried was locked. Reaching a dead-end, she turned around. Nothing about the house appeared familiar.

She returned to the central passageway, but now, she could not tell which way she had come from. There were several corridors, all leading off of this one, and she was unsure which one led to her bedroom. She chose the one she thought she had come from, but the paintings on the wall seemed strange to her. After a few steps, she turned back– only to find a wall blocking her path. She took a right down another corridor, but this, too, appeared to be the wrong one. Lost in this endless labyrinth of twists and turns, she became frightened.

Finally, she came across a large door that seemed somehow to be the correct one. She turned the handle with ease. In the room, Mr. Darcy was before her, standing by the fireplace as though he had been waiting for her there.

"Elizabeth." The sound of her name on his lips, coupled with the intense desire in his eyes, caused her to tremble. He was dressed in a loose-fitting white shirt, remarkably like the one she had given him at Christmas, with the neck unbuttoned, exposing his bare chest. "At last, you have come." He drew a few steps towards her as she came to him, unbidden. The door shut of its own accord behind her.

"What am I doing here, in your room?" She asked as he took her into his arms. She felt herself powerless to resist.

"Exactly what you meant to do," he murmured into her ear in a husky voice.

"I do not understand. I never meant to be here. I do not wish to trap you."

"You are not here to entrap me, but to offer yourself to me, willingly, as you have longed to do."

Heat rose to her cheeks as he said this. He leaned towards her and began planting kisses along her cheeks and her chin. "But I...but I do not want your money, Mr. Darcy," she stammered.

"What *do* you want, then, Elizabeth?" He continued to plant kisses downward along her neck.

"I want...you..." she whispered. This permission was all he needed before covering her lips with his. Elizabeth felt the intensity of her desire burst into flames as she returned his kiss, a passion like she had never before felt enveloping her as they kissed, again and again. She pulled him down onto the bed, the fervor of their kisses increasing all the more as she felt the weight of him atop her. Then suddenly, someone was shaking her, and she heard him saying her name repeatedly: "Elizabeth, Elizabeth– ELIZABETH!"

SUDDEN AWAKENINGS

Chapter 34

At first, waking to the sensation of Elizabeth cuddled up in his arms was welcome, and Darcy selfishly allowed her to remain there. The pleasure of holding her, of knowing she had not rejected him, that she *allowed* him to be in her bed, stirred more than the feelings in his heart.

Then, when she began kissing him, it was almost like a dream. A fire lit within Darcy's belly, and he began kissing her back without even meaning to. He could not believe this woman, who had taken so firm a hold on his heart, would willingly kiss him with such passion. He wished it would never stop.

He became aware, however, almost as soon as she began, that she remained in a deep sleep and was not in possession of her full faculties. Though he could continue on– in fact, he had every right to as her husband– he could not, in good conscience as a gentleman, allow her to continue. He broke their kiss and gently pushed her from him, shaking her.

"Elizabeth, Elizabeth." When this failed, he shook her a little harder, saying louder, "ELIZABETH!"

She woke with a start. "W-what? Mr. Darcy, what is the matter? Is the house on fire?" She leapt from the bed.

"No, my love, nothing of the sort." The term slipped from his lips without a thought. "You were, well, how to say this...you embraced me in your sleep and you began…your lips…" Darcy found himself at a loss for words.

"Oh, dear. Do you mean to say that I kissed you?" Even in the darkness, Darcy could discern the embarrassment in her voice and posture as she put her hands to her lips. "I–I beg your pardon, I did not mean to…I had no idea! Forgive me for so forwardly accosting you in your sleep."

"There is no fault. I am not offended by your actions. I am aware it was unconsciously done." He could not admit to her how much he enjoyed it. Not when she was so obviously mortified, even horrified, over what she had done.

Elizabeth seemed cold, or perhaps simply overwhelmed by her sense of modesty, for despite the heavy woolen nightgown she wore, she grabbed her wrapper from where she had laid it on the bureau and wrapped it around herself.

"You are too generous, sir, for this is not the first time I have overstepped the bounds of propriety in my sleep where you are concerned."

"If anyone is to blame, it is myself, for requiring you to remain chaperoned through the night."

"No, it is mine, for insisting we share a bed, and for refusing to allow a maid to attend me." She began pacing the floor. "You must think me wanton."

"Not at all." He shifted, grateful the darkness hid how pleased he was. *Too pleased. Had my sense of honor not demanded that I wake her…*

Elizabeth cleared her throat. "I shall wake Polly or one of the other housemaids and have them come up to me. You may retire to your own chambers, Mr. Darcy."

"Are you…are you angry with me?" he asked.

"No! Goodness, no. I am angry with myself, to be sure, but not with you. You have done nothing wrong. In fact, I must thank you for being a gentleman. A lesser man than you might have taken advantage of me, in my state."

"I shall wait until your maid comes to relieve me," he said.

"That will not be necessary," she said. "I am capable of remaining awake until someone arrives. You may leave now."

Not knowing quite how to respond, he bowed to her. "I bid you goodnight."

"Yes, goodnight to you as well."

The informality of their farewell struck him as odd. Then again, this was between a husband and wife who had just been kissing in her bed! Darcy hurried to his own bedchamber. The memory of her lips against his and the feel of her small body within his arms kept him awake long after.

Elizabeth closed the door behind him and leaned her back against it. *Of all the absurd things— for me to behave so wantonly towards Mr. Darcy in my sleep!* She knew from experience that a person could do all sorts of things in their sleep, whether it be feeding the pig or eating up all the treats in the larder, but she did not know it was possible for acts of this nature! Her cheeks flushed harder. A strange sensation filled her belly, causing her knees to weaken.

What must Mr. Darcy think of me now?

She loathed that she must keep her promise to summon a servant, for it would surely raise questions she would rather not answer. She pulled the bell cord by her bedside, and soon a sleepy Polly arrived, confused, but ready to do her mistress' bidding. The poor girl was tired enough that she asked no questions, but fell asleep on the cot straight away as directed. Her snores were as loud as she had warned they would be, and Elizabeth found no sleep the rest of the night. Even had

Polly been a silent sleeper, Elizabeth doubted she would have slept a wink. She saw the dream in her mind again and again, especially the parts where she kissed Mr. Darcy.

The kisses had been real! She recognized with a start, her heart suddenly torn between shame and enjoyment.

'Tis no more than lust! she chided herself. *A fantasy awakened by the presence of a man sleeping in my bedchamber.*

And a handsome one, too. She could not deny she found herself immensely attracted to him; every feature of his person exactly suited her tastes of what a man should look like. But was there more than that?

Certainly, an examination of his character proved that he was not so coldhearted nor arrogant as she had once supposed. He had shown himself, time and again, to be an absolute gentleman, kind, and generous, willing to endure discomfort and risk to protect her. Did that mean she loved him? What's more, did that mean he loved her?

Elizabeth was too much a stranger to love to be certain. Her parents' marriage lacked any sort of outward expressions of affection. They slept in the same bed, much for the same reasons Mr. Darcy had offered to sleep in hers, but other than that, Elizabeth had seen no clear signs that her parents loved each other any more than they loved George the pig.

Jane claimed to love Mr. Bingley, but it was becoming more and more clear that her love of him extended no further than his fortune, and Mr. Bingley's love appeared equally shallow. To whom could she look for an example of matrimonial love?

Her aunt and uncle Gardiner came to mind. Yes, they were a couple who clearly loved each other, and whose outward affection reflected it. As soon as she was able, Elizabeth would pay another call to Mrs. Gardiner, to ask for her advice on the subject.

Elizabeth took her breakfast in her bed the following morning, and remained in her quarters until the afternoon meal. She avoided Darcy's eye contact when they met, murmuring a small greeting before joining him at the table. Darcy wondered if she felt embarrassed after their encounter the previous night, and chose not to bring it up.

They were still dining when Mr. Bingley called. He burst into the room in apparent agitation.

"Bingley, good heavens! What is the matter?" Darcy rose from his seat.

"She has refused me!" Bingley answered, crushing his felt hat tightly with his fists as he paced the room.

"Jane refused you?" Elizabeth asked, incredulous.

"I cannot account for it! I did as you asked, Darcy, and went to Berkeley Street to request a private audience with Jane. Mrs. Jennings was presently entertaining Mr. Rushworth, which I thought odd, but she was happy to acquiesce. Jane accompanied me to another room, where I declared my intentions to her.

"However, she told me she could not countenance being wed to one so dear a friend as I, and though she held me in the highest regard, she could never view me with more than the deepest friendship. After flirting with me so openly, allowing me to court her all this time, I am outraged that she should treat me thusly!"

Angry tears were falling from his eyes now as he stormed about the room. Mr. Darcy urged him to calm himself, and soon entreated him to sit beside them on the sofa and contemplate what reasons Jane might have given for her refusal.

"Perhaps she feels you have toyed with her too long," Darcy suggested. "Perhaps she fears you were not serious in your proposal, or that you only made your declaration after speculation was raised."

"She should not have refused you!" Elizabeth said bitterly. "Not with her own reputation at stake. I, of all people, ought to know how quickly a woman's reputation can be ruined. If she does not wed, she will be branded as a strumpet!"

Bingley shook his head. "I pleaded with her not to throw away the happiness we could share. My home, my life, my fortune, all would be hers. I thought she reciprocated my feelings. But her refusal of me was so cold, one would think the past months we have shared together meant nothing to her!"

"I shall bring her to reason," Elizabeth said. "I shall enlist the help of my aunt and uncle. Together, we shall call upon her and make her see reason."

"I would rather you did not," Bingley said. "I would not have her compelled to marry me against her will. I have already witnessed the pain inflicted by such a union." He glanced at Darcy and Elizabeth. "Forgive me," he added. "I do not wish to remind you further. But as for me, I will never enter into such a union against the lady's wishes. If she will not have me, then I shall do my part to make restitution for my actions towards her. I shall supply her with whatever is needed, and remove myself to another part of the country."

Elizabeth did not know what all he meant by this, but she could speak no further. Her heart was too choked by Jane's refusal to know what to say or how to act. She feared for Jane's reputation, and that of their sisters.

"I have told you what I came to tell, and now have nothing further to say," Bingley said. "I suspect after my treatment of your sister, you shall not wish to associate with me further, so I shall bid you farewell."

Darcy protested such nonsense, declaring their friendship would endure, but Bingley would not hear him and departed.

SUDDEN AWAKENINGS

Despite Bingley's protests that he would not wish Jane persuaded to marry him, Elizabeth could not sit by and do nothing. She went to Berkeley Street, but was told that Jane and Mrs. Jennings were dining out at the home of Mr. Rushworth and his mother. Elizabeth declared she would wait for them to return. However, after some hours had passed, she developed a headache, which she attributed to her lack of sleep and nourishment. Discontent, but unable to wait any longer, she returned home, where a pot of warm broth enabled her to fall into a dreamless sleep that night.

The following morning, still desirous to see Jane and ascertain what could have caused her sudden change of heart, Elizabeth was preparing to go out, when the butler announced visitors.

"Mr. and Mrs. Rushworth to see you, ma'am."

"Oh, Bixby, tell them I am not at home, please," Elizabeth hastily replied.

"Mrs. Rushworth, being the former Miss Bennet, she desired me to tell you," Bixby added.

Elizabeth halted tying her bonnet and turned to him with a startled look. "Show them in, please, Bixby." The words fell from her lips in a dead tone of voice.

Removing her bonnet altogether, she left it on the side table and went to the drawing room, where presently, Jane and Mr. Rushworth made their appearance.

"Jane!" Elizabeth exclaimed.

Jane rushed to her sister's arms. "Oh Lizzy! I know this must seem sudden to you. I have come to tell you that Mr. Rushworth and I are married."

The grin on the happy fellow's face told her it was no jest. He bobbed his head. "We obtained the license yesterday and were married this morning, at St. George's, Mrs. Darcy. I can scarcely believe this lovely lady consented to be my wife, but here we are!"

Elizabeth blinked, unable to keep her mouth from hanging ajar.

"You are surprised, to be sure," Jane continued, "but will you not congratulate us, sister?"

Elizabeth recollected herself. "Yes, of course, my heartfelt congratulations, but do tell me, how did this all come about?"

Inside, she felt sickened. After all the attention Mr. Bingley had paid her, and Jane's public display of affection towards him, it was he whom Jane ought to have married! When she thought about the heartbreak he had borne after her refusal– she could not countenance such behavior from Jane. Yet she could not scold her in the presence of Mr. Rushworth. She forced herself to smile.

"It was all quite sudden. Mr. Rushworth and I spent much time together these past few weeks, but it was not until the opera the other night that we realized we could not live without each other. Mr. Rushworth came the very next morning to propose to me, and I accepted."

"But, but Mr. Bingley–" Elizabeth burst.

"Is a dear friend to me, but I realized that is all he ever would be," Jane interrupted. "When he proposed, less than an hour after Mr. Rushworth did– it is all right Lizzy, he knows about it, for we have no secrets from each other– well, you can hardly blame me for refusing him."

Mr. Rushworth, suspecting the two sisters wished to discuss matters between themselves, rose from his seat and busied himself by helping himself to the pastries and coffee set out on the breakfast sideboard in the adjoining room, which had yet to be cleared away after the interruption to the morning meal.

"You could have told him there was another, that you had already given Mr. Rushworth your hand," Elizabeth chastised.

"I did try, Lizzy, only he was in too great a despair to listen to me. The shock of my refusal to him was great. However, I do not think he shall mourn the loss of me for long. We have enjoyed each other's company these past months, but without a hint of marriage from him, so I do not think his request was in too great an earnest."

"Nevertheless, do you not think you owed him an explanation, at least, after your behavior at the opera?"

Jane lowered her voice. "I do not know why you are so shocked. I did little more than flirt for a moment with my arm around Mr. Bingley, and give him a peck on the cheek, to tease him, and to make Mr. Rushworth jealous enough that he might act."

"For shame, Jane!" Elizabeth hissed.

"It worked, did it not? As Mamma has told me, 'some men need a little motivation to inspire them to make the necessary declaration to the lady.' Did you not employ even further measures in order to entreat Mr. Darcy to marry you?"

"My 'measures' as you call them, were not adopted, but entirely unconscious," Elizabeth retorted.

Jane merely shrugged.

"What's more," Elizabeth went on, casting a glance to ensure that Mr. Rushworth was still occupied in the next room, "Mr. Darcy told me of your behavior at Netherfield, the night of our ball. I would not have believed it, had I not just witnessed you at the opera. Jane, Jane, this is so unlike you!" She shook her head in disapproval.

Jane stiffened. "How would you know what I am like? You have barely paid any attention to me these past few months. I am not like you, Lizzy. I am not clever. Nor am I accomplished, like Mary, and I have no fortune. I have only my looks to rely upon, and as Mamma constantly reminds me, these shall fade away in time. If I do not secure a match now, while I am in the prime of my beauty, I shall become destitute."

"But Mr. Bingley!" Elizabeth protested. "I thought you were in love with him. Did you not follow him to London for that very reason?"

"I did follow him, according to my mother's advice. I did all that I could to entrance him. And for what? For months, he strung me along, without a whisper of a proposal, until I began to despair of his ever offering for me. Then I had the occasion to meet Mr. Rushworth, whose worth, I must say, is as much greater than Mr. Bingley's as his fortune is more than twice his. It was a small matter to transfer my affections over from Mr. Bingley to Mr. Rushworth, whose ardor for me was increasing daily. Mr. Bingley was too late in his declaration, and not merely by an hour, Lizzy."

"But at the opera! You clearly looked to be enamored with Mr. Bingley. Do you not think it wrong to toy with him so? To play these games with him, all to make the other man jealous?"

"I can feel no guilt or remorse over a man who, for months, has toyed with me, and only proposed thanks to his friend's urging. And I do wish you would come off your high horse, Lizzy. For all your claims to innocence, you made precious few squawks when forced to marry Mr. Darcy. You could have retired to another county until any gossip died down, rather than go through with your wedding to him."

"That is enough!" Elizabeth said, accidentally raising her voice. Lowering it again, she said, "I will brook no further insults from you, Jane. I confess, I do not know you any longer. You are a stranger to me." She rose from her seat, just as Mr. Rushworth reentered the room.

"I thank you kindly for calling on us, Mr. Rushworth," Elizabeth said to him. "I wish you and Mrs. Rushworth well in your new life."

"Thank you kindly! We depart this afternoon to break the news at Longbourn, then journey on to Sotherton, so I may introduce my bride to my mother and acquaint her with her new home."

Elizabeth nodded, then bid them both farewell.

Mr. Darcy had been out that morning, tending to some business matters. When he returned, Elizabeth communicated with him about her sister's marriage.

"I cannot believe it! Of all the things!" He exclaimed.

"I was as incredulous as you are," Elizabeth said. "But Jane appears to have made her choice. Poor Mr. Bingley! Will you call on him to tell him, or shall you write?"

"I will call on him. It will not do for him to learn of this through the papers or someone else. I hope this incident shall teach him not to delay, where matters of the heart are concerned."

Elizabeth felt a grip on her own heart. The night time incident, coupled with the brewing sensation she felt within her, made her yearn to speak, but she did not know whether she should. *Suppose I am wrong about my feelings? Suppose I have merely awakened my carnal desires? Suppose I declare myself, only for him to reject me?*

These fears were enough to silence her for the present.

For now, she had business to conduct. Letters must be written, to her family, and to the Gardiners. A visit to them would also be in order, but she had not the emotional wherewithal for such a call that day. Not after all she had heard and endured that morning.

Chapter 35

As soon as he was able, Darcy called again at Berkeley Square. Bingley took the news of Jane's marriage better than Darcy thought he would. "At least this offers some explanation for her refusal of me. Had I only known her heart was already engaged to another! It is a bitter draught, to be sure, but I shall endure it. I would rather she marry another if her heart does not lie with me. I am determined not to think on it further. I shall retire to the country again soon. No, not to Netherfield. I do not think I shall ever return there. I have a mind to take up a place near Scarborough, where my sister Louisa's family is. Hurst tells me the waters are wonderful for the body and soul and the weather there is fair this time of year."

Bingley and his sisters soon called to take their leave. Bingley did not mention Mr. and Mrs. Rushworth once, but Miss Bingley, who inquired after the new Mrs. Rushworth's health, appeared disappointed to learn that they were reportedly happy in their new home together in Northamptonshire. Elizabeth wondered if perhaps Miss Bingley had once held hopes of her own for Mr. Rushworth, as Jane had suggested. Perhaps fate had been cruel to her, in sparing her from having Jane as a sister in law at the cost of losing yet another wealthy suitor to a Bennet sister.

SUDDEN AWAKENINGS

"I was quite shocked to receive your letter concerning Jane's marriage," Mrs. Gardiner told Elizabeth, when Elizabeth called the following week.

"I am more surprised that she did not call upon you herself to convey the news. I suppose I should be grateful she had the decency to tell me in person, rather than allow me to learn of it from the papers. Then again, these days, I suppose I have no right to be shocked by anything Jane does." Elizabeth shook her head.

"True enough," Mrs. Gardiner concurred. "But we must allow that Jane has only acted according to the principles given to her by her mother. Her entire life, she has been told her value lies in her beauty, and that her primary goal is to marry a wealthy man.

"Since you lived with us shortly before entering society, you were spared much of the pressure put on Jane and your sisters at that time, and were more immune to it once you returned to your family home. Your uncle and I have always impressed on you that your intrinsic value lies in your character, your heart, your mind, rather than your outward appearances or your fortune."

"Or lack thereof," Elizabeth laughed.

"Precisely!"

"But why did you not do the same for Jane, and for Mary, Lydia, and Kitty?"

"Oh, we wanted to, believe me! We asked that each of you might remain with us, in turn, for a year or so, but your mother refused. You were the only one she allowed, and I believe that is entirely due to your father. He saw, as I did, that there was a brightness to your spirit and an intelligence which your sisters lacked.

"He urged us to take you in, so we might make something of you that he could not, and persuaded your mother to allow it. I think perhaps she did not understand your wit, your sharp sense of humor, which she was largely without, and as such, she felt her influence over you was already lost; therefore it could do no harm to your chance of securing an eligible match to allow you to be influenced by us.

"She once hinted to me her belief that she thought you the most likely of your sisters to remain a spinster, and she hoped you might be the one to give her comfort in her old age, after your father has gone, for you remind her so much of him."

Tears welled in Elizabeth's eyes to hear such touching words. "She never said as much to me. I always felt I was the least favorite of her daughters, and that she never much cared for me nor was proud of me until I married Mr. Darcy."

"Your mother loves each of you in her own way, and misguided though she is, has always wanted the best in life for her children."

"I find it difficult to believe that Jane will be content having married for money over love."

"Perhaps. But people have differing values when it comes to marriage. Also, we do not know the depth of love that Jane and Mr. Rushworth may have for each other. It may be more than we credit. And feelings can grow over time," Mrs. Gardiner reminded her. "What of you, Lizzy? Are you happy in your marriage to Mr. Darcy?"

Elizabeth felt her throat constrict. "I hardly know. At first, I was entirely opposed to the idea. Mr. Darcy was, to me, arrogant, condescending, and viewed our family as beneath him. The last thing I wanted was to be married to such a person."

"And now?" Mrs. Gardiner prompted.

"Now I have come to realize that I misjudged him. Beneath his stoic exterior lies a man who is kind and considerate, who thinks of others before himself, and looks out for the welfare of those who are in his care. And as for my family...well, we both know he was entirely right about them." She blushed. "Mamma, Jane, even Kitty and Lydia, are as mercenary as he believed them to be, only I was unable to see it."

Mrs. Gardiner pressed a finger to her lip thoughtfully. "I think hope remains for Kitty and Lydia, having been in your care. I shall ask again if they might come to live with us, that I might continue the work you have begun with them. But back to you, my dear. You have said that you now view Mr. Darcy differently from how you once did. Have you come to care for him?"

"I, I, do not know," she stammered. Memories of kissing him flooded her mind, causing her complexion to color further still. "I feel something. But I cannot judge whether it is love or…something else. Aunt Gardiner, how did you know that you loved Uncle Gardiner?"

"I knew it early on, I believe. There was a moment in our courtship when he told me all he needed to succeed in life was the love of a good woman by his side; if he had her, then he could weather any storm, achieve any dream, and if he didn't have that, then it would all be for naught. I knew then, I wanted to be that woman, to be by his side through our whole lives."

Elizabeth remained pensive, absorbing her aunt's words.

At length, her aunt spoke again. "You need not decide upon your own feelings today, love. Everyone comes to realizations in their own way, some softly and slowly, and some like a sudden awakening. But let me tell you, once you do know your own heart, do not hesitate to make your feelings known to the person you love. There are few things worse than going through life without knowing the heart of the person you share it with."

Elizabeth thanked her for the advice and returned home.

Darcy let out an audible groan when Bixby announced the arrival of Lady Catherine de Bourgh. His aunt's visits were never pleasant, and were sure to contain a repetition of demands to which he had already refused.

"Well, Darcy, I hope you are satisfied," she launched, almost the second she entered the room. "That girl has utterly ruined the family! Her recent marriage to that Rushworth fellow is all anyone speaks of. I went to a luncheon party at Lady Linningtons, and no less than three ladies remarked upon it!"

Darcy was nonplussed. "Mr. Rushworth is a respectable man, with a substantial fortune. I suspect their remarks stemmed more from envy than shock."

"Far from it! No, everyone spoke of how utterly disgraceful it was for Miss Bennet to have married a divorced man. As her brother-in-law, I cannot believe you could countenance her marriage to him—especially when it appeared, by all accounts, she was in pursuit of your friend, Mr. Bingham...Bangley...whatever his name was."

"Bingley," Darcy corrected. "And the matter was entirely out of my hands. By the time Elizabeth or I knew of the marriage, it had already taken place."

"There is always annulment," Lady Catherine's eyes flashed.

"Aunt Catherine, you and I both know, annulments are not easy to come by, and are only granted under special circumstances. Besides, by that point, the dissolution of their union would have caused far greater scandal than the formation of it. It may not have been the outcome I had hoped for, but it was better than the alternative."

"It simply goes to show how determined those Bennet girls are to ruin our family's reputation, Darcy. If you had simply married Anne, as I had instructed you to, then you would have no connection to any of them. First your own hastily patched up marriage, and now this! The scandal—"

"Is nothing compared to other scandals this family has faced," he interrupted. "My cousin's indiscretions with Signorina Valentino, for instance. Perhaps your efforts would be better served by directing them towards the repair of his marriage. Mine is already in good order."

Lady Catherine's face grew purple. "How can you be so insensible to the damage this girl has caused? How do you have no regrets over bringing her into your home, your family? How could you choose *her* over your sweet cousin, Anne, who for years has believed you would make good on your mother's and my wishes to marry her?"

"Your wishes, yes, but not my mother's," Darcy pointed out.

"You dare contradict me! I heard it from your own mother's lips, when you were babies, that she desired nothing more than for you to marry Anne, that our two households would be forever united."

"She may have once spoken such sentiments, but I have every reason to believe that she changed her mind. On her deathbed, she instructed me to find true love, and made me swear not to marry anyone whom I did not love."

"And how well you have fulfilled your promise! Marrying a strumpet who wormed her way into your bedroom for the sake of your fortune, forcing you to take her as your wife out of your extreme sense of honor and duty!"

"How dare you, madam!" Darcy snarled.

"You are confusing lust for love, Darcy, and this woman has you bewitched. It is Anne who you have always loved, ever since you were children."

"Make no mistake about this!" he shouted. "I do not love her, nor have I ever loved her, and I never will!"

Darcy clamped his mouth shut, forcing himself to calm his temper. He placed the floor while his aunt glared at him from across the room.

"You will regret this!" Lady Catherine cried. "One day you will realize the mistake you have made, in choosing that girl over Anne.

"I do not regret my choice for one moment," Darcy spat. "Elizabeth has proven herself to be a woman that any husband ought to be proud of, and no one, least of all you, shall ever persuade me to discard her or part with her for any reason except death itself!"

Hearing his tone becoming incensed once more, Lady Catherine took a step back from him. "You're a fool, Darcy!" She spat. "Your reason left you the moment that creature walked into your life."

"Yes, it did. And I shall be forever grateful for it. Now, dear aunt, if you have nothing further to say on the subject, I shall be grateful if you would let me get on with other matters."

Lady Catherine growled, before turning on her heels and leaving.

Darcy slammed his hand on the table.

Elizabeth was still ruminating on all Mrs. Gardiner had spoken of when she entered the hall. Her heart beat quickly as she formulated the words she hoped to say to Darcy, to tell him of the growing feelings within her. Bixby informed her that Mr. Darcy was home, but he was entertaining a caller. From the drawing room upstairs, Lady Catherine and Mr. Darcy's voices were heard, and it appeared they were having a heated discussion. Elizabeth could only make out bits and pieces as she came up the flight of steps, but she discerned the phrases "strumpet", "honor and duty", "confusing lust for love", and "bewitched." She pressed her ear to the door in time to hear Darcy shout to his aunt.

"Make no mistake about this–I do not love her, nor have I ever loved her, and I never will!"

Her heart dropped, believing his words were about her. In the space of the silence that followed, Elizabeth could listen no more. She raced up the next flight of stairs to her bedchamber and shut the door before bursting into tears.

He does not love me. He never did, and he never will.

"Parker is well again, and shall resume her place in my chamber tonight," Elizabeth told Darcy at their evening meal. She had been unusually quiet, almost cold towards him, all day. He could not account for the sudden alteration. Darcy nodded. "I am glad to hear she is well again. I know Polly's snores have been trying for you."

Elizabeth changed the subject. "Have you heard any news from Georgiana?"

Darcy set his soup spoon down again. "She writes, but there is something about her letters which disturbs me, although I cannot put my finger on it."

"Oh? What does she say?"

"Nothing out of the ordinary," he replied. "She extols her friends' kindness and generosity towards her and speaks of picnics under the orchard, musical parties, and a visit to the local fair. But something about the style of her writing is amiss, as if she were excluding something."

"Could something have transpired which she is intentionally omitting?" Elizabeth asked.

Darcy shook his head. "I have never known her to be untruthful to me, not even by halves."

"Perhaps she is unwell, but does not wish to alarm you. I am certain if there was anything serious, the Culpeppers would write to us."

He nodded. "Yes, you are correct. It is only the fears of an overprotective brother. What news from Kenshire?" He gestured to the letter Elizabeth had been reading.

"Mrs. Wilson writes amusing anecdotes about her boys. Apparently, Henry has grown fond of insects and taken to studying them. Nanny tolerated them so long as he kept his specimens in the garden shed. But you can imagine the horror she expressed when the boy decided to bring some of his favorite insects– still living– into the nursery!"

Darcy chuckled. "Boys will be boys. I recall a similar horror on my nurse's face when George and I decided to bring our pet frogs into the nursery once."

Elizabeth laughed as well, the tension between them broken for the moment. "Speaking of Mr. Wickham, Mrs. Wilson says he has left the county again."

"Is that so? He did not mention to me his intention to do so."

"Perhaps he does not feel the need to ask permission of his patron in the same way that my cousin Collins does every time he sets foot outside the borders of his parish."

"I am surprised your cousin Collins does not ask my aunt's permission to eat, sleep, and visit the necessary room!"

His comment made Elizabeth laugh even harder. "I am sure it would satisfy her greatly if he did!"

"When does Mr. Wickham return to his duties? Did Mrs. Wilson make mention of how long he planned to be away, or where he had gone?"

"She did not know, but she suspected he had gone to West Riding. He had told Mr. Kirby that he planned to 'win over his lady love'. They supposed he meant Miss Silverman."

"How odd. I had heard that Miss Silverman is lately engaged to be married."

"Perhaps he hopes to implore her one last time, before all is lost. It would be a romantic notion if he did!" Elizabeth suggested.

"A rather desperate one, in my opinion," Darcy concluded. "Though I suppose it is no business of mine if he wishes to make a fool of himself to Miss Silverman."

Chapter 36

Elizabeth took a deep breath before knocking on the door of Lady Catherine's home on St. James' Square. She had been surprised to receive a missive requesting her presence for tea, but felt it would not do to offend the great lady any further than she already had. The butler showed her into the drawing room, where Lady Catherine sat with her pug on her lap.

"Good afternoon, Mrs. Darcy," Lady Catherine greeted." How kind of you to join me. I was not certain whether you would come."

"I could hardly refuse Your Ladyship's summons," Elizabeth said stiffly. She glanced at the furnishings surrounding her. Lady Catherine's taste in decor was ostentatious. The sofa and chairs were upholstered in hideous shades of green and pink stripe, clashing with the orange curtains. Gaudy paintings, mirrors, knick knacks and porcelain figurines cluttered every available surface, and several large potted plants claimed the floor areas near the seating arrangement. Elizabeth settled uneasily onto one of the chairs.

Lady Catherine stroked her dog's fur while saying, "I feel we have gotten off on the wrong foot, you and I."

Elizabeth pursed her lips. "I feel I cannot take my share of the blame, Your Ladyship. I do not feel I have done anything deserving of your censure. Let us not forget it was you who accosted me in my own home just after my engagement to your nephew."

"Yes, well, I have invited you here to 'bury the hatchet', so to speak. We are family now, after all, and there is no use in recalling any past grievances. If you can overlook my past transgressions, I shall endeavor to overlook your shortcomings."

"Then let us think on the past only as it gives us pleasure," Elizabeth offered cordially, though she doubted the sincerity of this proffered olive branch from Lady Catherine.

"Won't you take some tea, Mrs. Darcy?" Lady Catherine offered.

"Thank you, I will," Elizabeth answered.

"It is my own special blend," Lady Catherine went on, as she began to prepare the tea on the small table before her. "It uses flowers and herbs from my rector's garden."

Elizabeth nodded. Cousin Collins had bragged before of his famous garden, and how he supplied Her Ladyship's tea from it.

Lady Catherine poured the blend into a china cup with garish purple flowers painted on it, and handed it to Elizabeth. "I hope you will find it pleasing. It has worked wonders for my ulcers."

Elizabeth tasted a sip. The tea was sweet, with floral and fruity notes, but a bitter aftertaste that made her stomach turn.

"Do you like it?"

Elizabeth nodded weakly. "Oh yes, it is delicious."

"Excellent." Lady Catherine's eyes gleamed. "Have a scone as well. They are my cook's special recipe."

Elizabeth accepted the offered treat. The scone contained some sort of dark colored berries, perhaps blueberries or currants. She took a nibble off the corner. Lady Catherine smiled widely, taking a sip of her own tea.

Lady Catherine's dog spotted a squirrel out the window. Leaping off her lap, he ran towards the window, yipping and wagging his tail. He leaped up on the windowsill and began rapidly pawing the glass, trying to reach the squirrel, his yips growing louder.

"Otis, no! Stop that racket at once," Lady Catherine commanded. She rose from her seat.

"Allow me, my lady," the butler said, walking over and closing the curtains, so the dog would stop.

Elizabeth used the distraction to dump the remainder of her tea into a nearby potted ficus. Otis gave one last "arf" to signal his displeasure at being shut out from the squirrel. He wandered around in circles a few times before settling near Elizabeth's feet. Lady Catherine returned to her seat.

"Ah, I see you have finished your tea. Would you care for some more?"

"No, thank you, Your Ladyship."

"And how do you like the scone?"

"It is delicious, thank you."

"Have another," Lady Catherine pressed, holding out the platter.

"Oh, no, I couldn't."

"Please, I insist."

Elizabeth added another scone to her plate, despite barely having touched the first one. "I notice you are not eating any, Your Ladyship."

"My doctor tells me I must reduce my figure," she replied.

The dog began sniffing around Elizabeth's leg. She reached down and patted him on the head.

Lady Catherine began speaking of her daughter, telling Elizabeth how much she wished Anne were well enough to join her in London. "Her health has always been poor, since childhood. It is such a pity, for she misses all the entertainment the Season has to offer."

Conjuring up a compliment she was sure Cousin Collins would be proud of, Elizabeth remarked, "The *ton* has been deprived of its brightest jewel, it would seem."

This pleased Lady Catherine greatly, and she went on for several minutes about her daughter's skills at needlework and cards, lamenting that society in Kent was so limited, she had few opportunities to show off her talents.

While Lady Catherine was self-occupied, Elizabeth slipped one of the scones to the dog beside her, who happily gobbled it up. He then went to an empty chair on the opposite side and promptly went to sleep.

When a quarter's hour had elapsed, Elizabeth rose and thanked Lady Catherine for her invitation and the tea, and added that she hoped they might become better friends in due time.

"Certainly," Lady Catherine replied. "I am sure I shall have no cause to disagree with you in the future."

Elizabeth staggered as she came up the front steps of Darcy House. She pressed her hand to her head, attempting to clear the dizziness.

"Parker, ring for some tea, if you would, please," she requested as Parker took her bonnet and Spencer from her. "I must have a headache coming on."

"Certainly, madam," Parker answered.

Elizabeth made for the stairs, intent on heading to her room, but a sudden wave of blurred vision made the room spin. She thought better of it, and went to the library at the front of the house instead. Darcy was in the room, reading a book. He looked up when he saw Elizabeth enter.

"What is wrong? Are you ill?" he asked, as she slumped onto the sofa.

"I do not know. I believe it is the beginning of a headache. The light– it feels so bright."

Darcy turned to the butler, who had come to bring Elizabeth's tea. "Bixby, would you please draw the drapes?"

Bixby set the tea down before her and closed all the drapes, making the room feel dark, almost like a cave. He lit a few candles so they could see.

Elizabeth sat up and attempted to drink the tea, but her hand was shaking so badly, she could not raise it to her lips. Her fingers lost their grip. The cup fell to the floor and shattered.

"Oh, how clumsy of me!" She bent to pick up the pieces, but Bixby stopped her.

"Never mind, madam, I shall take care of it." He promptly rang for a maid and instructed her to bring a broom and dustpan.

Darcy left his chair and sat beside Elizabeth on the sofa. He placed the back of his hand on her forehead. "Elizabeth, you appear quite ill. Shall I summon the doctor?" Her brown orbs were fully dilated, making her look especially beautiful, despite her languid condition.

"No, thank you, I shall be all right, I am certain."

"At least allow me to assist you up the stairs and to your bed."

Elizabeth nodded drowsily. With Darcy's help, she rose, and gingerly stepped over the broken pieces of china. They had not reached the door, however, before Elizabeth fainted. Darcy caught her, breaking her fall before she reached the floor. She hung limply in his arms, like a child's rag doll.

"Elizabeth!" he cried.

Chapter 37

Fear gripped Darcy's heart at seeing his wife lying on the bed, unconscious. With a footman's help, he had carried her up the two flights of stairs to her bedroom. Bixby sent for the doctor who arrived shortly.

The doctor examined Elizabeth thoroughly. "I am not certain what is wrong with her. But her symptoms appear consistent with poisoning."

Darcy felt his mouth run dry. "Poisoning?" he repeated.

"Could something have been wrong with the tea?" Bixby suggested.

Darcy shook his head. "She did not drink any of it."

Parker, who was also hovering nearby, asked, "Perhaps something she ate during breakfast?"

"I do not believe so. If she had, she would have fallen ill much sooner," the doctor replied. "Was Mrs. Darcy home all day?"

"She went out earlier, sir, to call on Mr. Darcy's aunt," Parker told him.

"She called on Lady Matlock?" Darcy asked.

"No, sir. It was Lady Catherine whom she visited. Her Ladyship sent a message this morning, requesting her presence, while you were out."

Darcy clenched his fist. What had Lady Catherine given her?

"We must discover if Mrs. Darcy consumed anything while she was calling there," the doctor declared. "If she was, indeed, poisoned, then perhaps we might learn by what means, in order that I might properly treat her."

Parker wrung her hands. "I should have accompanied her! I would have, but Mrs. Darcy insisted she had no need of my services, and since I was behind on my work at home, I allowed her to leave unchaperoned."

"It is not your fault, Parker," Darcy sought to reassure her. "It is possible, had you accompanied her, you might now be in the same predicament.

Bixby left to order Darcy's carriage, while Parker was sent to fetch cool compresses for Elizabeth's head. Once they were out of the room, Darcy addressed the doctor in a low voice.

"Will she live?" His throat tightened.

The doctor pressed his lips together. "It is uncertain. Until I know what poisoned her, I can do little to treat her other than attempt to keep her comfortable. I cannot administer any medications or seek an antidote."

Darcy nodded slowly. His insides felt as though they had been reduced to ashes. How could he bear it if he lost Elizabeth?

Darcy did not wait for Lady Catherine's butler to announce him before bursting into her drawing room.

"What have you given to Elizabeth?" he demanded.

Lady Catherine was on her sofa, cradling a small dog that appeared to be dead.

"How dare you enter here, unannounced and unbidden!" She said through her tears. "Can you not see I am mourning the loss of my poor Otis!"

"Elizabeth lies at home right now, unconscious and weak. What did you do to her?" He put his hands on Lady Catherine's shoulders and shook her, roughly.

"I told you things would not end well if you married her. I warned you that you would come to see the mistake you have made, in not choosing Anne."

"What. Did. You. Do." He spat out each word.

"What makes you think *I* did anything at all?" Lady Catherine answered him. "I merely invited her to tea, to extend an olive branch to her. Surely, you can see nothing wrong with that."

Darcy's servants who had accompanied him returned from searching the kitchens.

"Sir," one of the footmen said. "We found these in her kitchen." He held up a platter of scones. "They must have been poisoned. The kitchen maid lies on the floor. Dead."

"We also found these." Another servant held up a basket of deep, luscious berries resembling blueberries, a jar of tea, and a receipt.

Darcy took the receipt and read it. It contained a list of ingredients for a custom tea blend. One of the ingredients listed was flowers from the belladonna plant.

"You gave her belladonna?" He picked up one of the hideous porcelain figurines off of her side table and smashed it against the wall.

"Darcy, be reasonable! Belladonna flowers are perfectly safe to drink. I have taken them in my tea for years, as a remedy for my ulcers. Mr. Collins grows them for me in his garden. Do you think I would be alive today if my tea blend contained a deadly quantity of them?"

She had a point. Although Darcy had not known that it contained belladonna, he knew she drank her special blend daily.

Lady Catherine glared at him. "Now, if you would, kindly leave me in peace to grieve my poor puppy."

Darcy crossed his arms. "How did your dog die, exactly?"

"It must have been something he ate," Lady Catherine insisted. "Perhaps your Elizabeth slipped him something, for he died not an hour after she left this house. I bet she had chocolate in her pocket and gave it to him!"

"Or perhaps whatever poison you intended for her made its way to your dog instead," Darcy said. Not waiting for her permission, he scooped up the dead animal from her arms and turned to leave.

"Stop!" Lady Catherine cried. "Give me back my Otis!" She ordered her butler to bar the way to the door, but Darcy and his servants pushed past him. Lady Catherine chased them all the way to the street, where Darcy's carriage waited. But Lady Catherine, with her large figure, was not as agile as Darcy and his footmen were. She could not reach the bottom step before they were off.

***

Elizabeth dreamed of Darcy, but it was not a pleasant dream. She kept running towards him, but he continued to remain out of reach. She called out to him to wait for her. He stopped and turned towards her, but instead of a smile, he wore a frown.

"I told you, Elizabeth, I do not love you. I never have, and I never will."

"But, why?" she cried.

"Because you forced me to marry you. You tricked your way into my bedroom, pretending to be sleepwalking, so that you would be compromised, and could lay your hands on my fortune."

"That isn't true! You know it isn't!"

He turned away from her and continued walking. She reached out to grab his arm. When he turned his head again, his face had become grotesque, like some devil or gargoyle. She screamed. She felt a jolt of pain, followed by a bright light. She appeared to be in her bedchamber, but there was a strange person hovering over her, whose face, to her mind, looked like a skull.

"Elizabeth, Elizabeth!" came Darcy's voice, only his face remained like that of a devil to her.

"Get away from me!" she shouted, thrashing about on the bed.

"Calm yourself," the strange person with the skull-face said. "It is only Mr. Darcy."

"No, no, get away from me, devil!" She screamed more, continuing to toss. Her head felt hot, but her body felt chilled, her stomach nauseous as if she were about to lose its contents. The bright light from the window seared her mind, causing a throbbing pain to her head. She felt someone holding her down, and forcing a bitter liquid down her throat, before everything fell back to darkness.

"I am sorry to have to do that," the doctor said, putting aside the spoon. "She appeared to be having violent hallucinations."

"What did you give her?" Darcy asked.

"Merely a tincture of valerian root, to calm her. It should not harm her."

Darcy had raced upstairs as soon as he returned home from Lady Catherine's. The shock of seeing his wife screaming and convulsing upon his entering the room, as well as the way she seemed not to know him, calling him a "devil" impressed heavily upon him.

Elizabeth was still now, having succumbed again to unconsciousness.

Darcy knelt beside her bed and desperately prayed she would recover.

⁂

The doctor examined the berries, the tea, and the contents of the dog's stomach and returned to Darcy House with his findings.

"There is no doubt about it," he said. "Mrs. Darcy was poisoned with belladonna. Both the tea and these scones are laden, although the tea contains only trace amounts of dried petals. However, these scones contain the full berries of belladonna. I am uncertain how many of them it would take to kill someone, but consuming one would certainly cause confusion, blurred vision, dilated pupils, and sensitivity to light. It could also cause delirium and hallucinations, such as what Mrs. Darcy appeared to be experiencing."

"Then the dog died of belladonna poisoning as well? And the kitchen maid?"

"I have not examined the kitchen maid. The dog ingested an entire scone, which is what killed it. The berries might appear to be blueberries at first glance, but they are most definitely belladonna. If the kitchen maid ate some, it is likely that which killed her as well."

"Then belladonna poisoning is fatal." Darcy's heart felt as though it had fallen through the floor into a giant pit of despair.

"Quite often, yes," the doctor said. "However, we do not know how much of it Mrs. Darcy consumed. If she only drank the tea, it is possible she may survive, unless Lady Catherine added the juice of the berries to the tea as well."

There was a knock on the door, precipitating Parker's entrance. "Forgive me, sir," she began. "I took the liberty of summoning Mrs. Darcy's relatives."

"Thank you, Parker."

He took Mr. and Mrs. Gardiner into the room where Elizabeth lay in feverish sleep.

"The poor dear!" Mrs. Gardiner gasped. She knelt by her niece's bedside and stroked her hair lovingly.

"I hope whomever did this to her is locked away!" Mr. Gardiner shook his head angrily.

As soon as Darcy had left his aunt's house, he had sent a messenger to Bow Street, and they had arrested Lady Catherine on suspicion of murder and attempted murder.

"The authorities are investigating all this right now," Darcy told the Gardiners, "but they have Lady Catherine de Bourgh in holding until it is resolved."

"Can anything be done for her?" Mrs. Gardiner asked the doctor.

"There is not much, no," he answered. "I have made her as comfortable as I can. If she awakens and experiences more hallucinations, you may administer another dose of valerian root. I must go to consult my library to see if I can determine any antidote or treatment. Send word if her condition worsens."

Darcy showed the doctor to the door. Before he turned to go upstairs, Bixby interrupted him. "I am sorry to bring you news at a time like this, but an express has arrived from Hertfordshire."

"From Hertfordshire?" He had only sent an express to Longbourn hours before, informing Elizabeth's parents about her condition. It was far too soon to expect a reply from them.

"Although it is addressed to Mrs. Darcy, I thought, perhaps, you might wish to read it. It may contain news from her family."

"Yes, thank you, Bixby."

Darcy broke the seal. It was from Elizabeth's sister, Kitty.

Dear Lizzy,
I wish I had time for more lengthy correspondence, but the urgency of the news which I have received compels me to be brief. Since our departure from Pemberley, Lydia has maintained a correspondence with Georgiana. In Georgiana's last letter to her, she communicated a surprising piece of news– Mr. Wickham has followed her to Gloucestershire these past three weeks, and she believes herself to be in love with him.

This alone would not give too much cause for alarm, but something which she said near the end of the letter hinted at her belief that we would be surprised the next time we meet her, for she should have a new name to call her own. In Lydia's ecstasy, she told me she feels certain Georgiana must mean to marry Mr. Wickham, for there could be no other reasonable explanation for such a statement. Lydia thinks it terribly romantic.

I argued that Georgiana could not possibly go through with such a thing, as her brother surely has not given his consent to such a scheme, but Lydia believes that Georgiana must have obtained Mr. Darcy's permission already, or else she would be taking off for Scotland with Mr. Wickham. Perhaps that is her plan, I do not know, but I felt this intelligence must be communicated to you straight away, for you will surely know Mr. Darcy's intentions and how to act.

I have seen Jane and her new husband, and will write more later concerning my thoughts about their newfound happiness.

For now, I remain, your beloved sister,
Kitty Bennet

Darcy gripped the page so tightly, the edge began to crush. *Wickham!* So the lady-love he had spoken of wooing was Georgiana, not Miss Silverman. He had long suspected Wickham might have some designs towards his sister, but thought that as long as she was under his protection, Georgiana would be safe. Now, he could see it was a mistake to allow her to travel to Gloucestershire.

With his wife still upstairs at death's door, Kitty's intelligence could not have come at a worse time. What was he to do?

He briefly pondered writing to Colonel Fitzwilliam, but the colonel was currently stationed at the training grounds in Kent. Too far away to reach Georgiana in time, even if the news was sent by express.

Mr. and Mrs. Gardiner came down the stairs.

"Your servant mentioned there was an express from Longbourn," Mr. Gardiner said, noting the worried expression on Darcy's face. "Is there some news from my sister and brother?"

Darcy shook his head. "No, the letter contains intelligence about my sister, who has been writing regularly to Lydia. I am afraid she may be in danger." He dared not say more, for the sake of Georgiana's reputation.

"You must go to her," Mrs. Gardiner said.

"But, Elizabeth–"

"There is nothing you can do for her here. Her fate is in God's hands. If there is a chance you may rescue your sister from whatever peril she is in, then godspeed to you."

Mrs. Gardiner was right. He could not save Elizabeth, but if he set off at once, he might arrive in time to prevent Georgiana from making a foolish mistake. As much as he hated to leave Elizabeth in her present condition, Georgiana needed him more.

Darcy rang for Perkins to pack a saddlebag and ready his horse. He would leave within the hour. In the meantime, Darcy went to his safe and retrieved some important letters he kept there. They might be needed, if he arrived too late to prevent the wedding.

Chapter 38

Dear God, have mercy on them both, Darcy prayed as his horses hooves pounded the pavement. *Let Elizabeth live, and help me to rescue Georgiana from Wickham's clutches.*

Darcy rode all night, only stopping to change horses. It was morning by the time he reached Gloucestershire, and not a moment too soon. The servants at Culpepper Manor told him that the family– and Georgiana– were all at the church.

"If you hurry, sir, you might make it in time for the wedding," they told him. They gave him direction to the village church.

They expected him to be pleased, but instead, he ordered them to send for the local magistrate and have him come to the church.

Please, God, do not let it be too late.

Though the horse was tired, there was no time to exchange it for one of the Culpepper's. Darcy kicked his heels against the animal's side, urging him on towards the village.

The church yard was empty, save for a single carriage, with a groom standing nearby to mind it. Giving the horse over to the care of the servant, he pressed a few coins into the lad's hand and promised to return.

Ascending the steps of the church, Darcy pushed open the heavy oak doors.

Georgiana and Wickham stood before the minister at the altar, both dressed in fine clothing. In the pews sat Mrs. Younge, along with the Culpepper family, whom Darcy recognized from the time he had met them at Georgiana's former school.

The minister was in the middle of his address. "If anyone has reason that this man and woman should not be united in holy matrimony, let him speak now, or forever hold his peace."

"I do." Darcy's voice echoed off the high ceilings of the church. Georgiana's head whipped around, as did everyone else's.

"Brother! You have come."

Darcy strode forward and addressed the vicar. "I oppose this union. This child is my ward, and does not have my permission to marry. In fact, by law, this marriage cannot take place."

Georgiana's smile fell. "What do you mean, Fitzwilliam? We have a letter of permission in your hand, approving of the match."

"Perhaps we had better take this to my office, so we can discuss," the vicar suggested. Leaving the Culpeppers and Mrs. Younge behind, they followed him to a small room adjacent to the sanctuary. Georgiana took the seat facing the minister's desk, while Wickham and Darcy remained standing.

"Reverend," Darcy addressed. "Are you aware this lady is underage?"

"I am, sir," he replied.

"And you are aware, I am certain, that under Hardwicke's Law, she is unable to marry in England without the express permission of her guardians?"

"Good sir," the vicar said to Darcy, "I can see by the lady's reaction that you are who you say you are. However, she and her intended presented me with a letter, stating your intention to allow her to be married to this gentleman."

"Yes, that is right, Fitzwilliam," Georgiana nodded. "I wrote to you, asking for your permission, and received a response granting it."

Darcy's brow furrowed. "I never received such a letter from you, nor do I remember writing one in response. May I see the letter?"

The vicar retrieved a letter from his desk and handed it to Darcy to read. Wickham shifted his feet noticeably, and his expression appeared nervous.

Darcy scanned the letter, which did appear to contain a signed statement indicating his approval of the match between Georgiana and Wickham, however he did not recognize it.

"I never wrote this," he declared. "This letter is, in fact, a forgery. The hand, though resembling mine, does not match. If you like, I shall prove it. Hand me that pen and paper, if you will."

The minister complied. Darcy penned his signature, then showed it to the vicar to compare. The pen strokes spelling out "FITZWILLIAM DARCY" in Darcy's bold hand appeared similar to that of the signature on the letter, but Darcy's "F" appeared larger, more confident, and there was a flourish to the "Y" which was missing altogether.

"Heavens! I have almost been hoodwinked." The minister exclaimed. "The pair of you had better explain yourselves," he eyed Georgiana and Wickham.

"Oh, I think it is obvious who the guilty party is." Darcy glared at Wickham, who turned pale.

Wickham gulped. "All right, I admit, it was me. I did it because I knew you would never grant your permission for one as lowborn as I to marry your sister."

"Fiend! I will have you locked up for trying to evade the law and deceive a clergyman," the vicar cried.

Georgiana stood up. "Oh please, sir! Do not do that. Brother," she urged, turning to Darcy, "I did not know George had forged the letter, but I know that if he did so, it was only because of his great love for me. I know that I am still young, but if you grant us your permission, we can still be married. I love George exceedingly, and he loves me. Please do not deny us your happiness out of disgust for George's origins."

"Georgiana, if it were merely that, I would not stand in your way. Do you truly believe I would withhold my blessing and my permission simply because you wished to marry beneath your station? But unfortunately, there is another obstacle, which prevents you from marrying George Wickham, even if you were of age to do so without my blessing."

Darcy withdrew the packet of letters from his breast pocket and gave them to the rector. "These letters prove that George Wickham is, in fact, the natural half-brother of Georgiana Darcy and myself."

"Our brother?" Georgiana's mouth hung slack. She looked at Wickham, but there was no surprise on his face. "You knew? You knew you were my brother, and you still attempted to marry me– how could you?"

"My plan would have worked if you had not shown up, Darcy," Wickham spat.

The vicar adjusted his spectacles as he looked up from scanning one of the letters. "Well, I must say, this is most unusual. First time I have ever come across this in all my years." He glared at Mr. Wickham. "You will most certainly face charges for this, young man! Attempting to deceive an ordained minister of the Church of England is no small matter, especially given your relationship to the intended bride."

Georgiana burst into tears before throwing herself into Darcy's arms.

Wickham used Darcy's momentary distraction to push past him and dash out the door.

Darcy released Georgiana and pursued him. Wickham tore through the sanctuary, past the Culpeppers, who were clustered together, likely whispering about the whole ordeal, and into the church yard, where the magistrate and the local constabulary had just arrived on horseback. Wickham saw them and made for a nearby field.

"Apprehend that man!" Darcy shouted to them. The magistrate gave his signal, and the men surrounded Wickham before he had gone far. They escorted him back to where the magistrate waited. The magistrate listened to the testimonies of Darcy and the vicar in regards to the fraud Wickham attempted to perpetrate before taking him away in shackles.

Mrs. Younge, they discovered, had been in on the plot with Wickham from the start. As soon as Darcy arrived and declared that the marriage could not take place, she had slipped away and stolen the horse that Darcy had left with the Culpeppers' groom. A search of her belongings revealed two tickets for passage on a ship to India.

Wickham confessed that he knew the marriage would not likely hold up once it was made public. Their plan had been for him to marry Georgiana and travel directly to London, where Georgiana's dowry was being kept. He and Mrs. Younge hoped that by undertaking swift action, the fraud would not be discovered until after he had withdrawn all of Georgiana's money from the bank. Afterwards, he and Mrs. Younge would flee to India. Darcy was grateful such a plan had not succeeded. Georgiana would have been left utterly ruined; her fortune gone and her reputation in tatters.

"I still cannot believe the lengths he would go to do this to me," Georgiana cried. Darcy had returned with her to Culpepper Manor, where Georgiana immediately took to her room. Darcy remained with her while Mrs. Culpepper and her daughter hovered nearby.

"Why did you not tell me that he was our brother?" Georgiana asked him. "I deserved to know such a thing, Fitzwilliam."

Darcy sighed. "You are correct, Georgie. I should have told you. I hoped to spare you from the knowledge that our father was not everything you believed him to be."

"But George is older than I am, that would mean..."

"Yes. Our father was unfaithful to our mother before you were even born. I was small at the time, but I will tell you what I later learned."

Darcy shifted his position on the bed so as to be more comfortable, then began his story. "Shortly after I was born, our mother entered a deep despair, and was not herself.

"During that time, our father turned to her maid for comfort, and the maid fell with child. Wishing to provide for her and the child, he sent them both away to some forgotten village in the north, where he regularly sent funds for their care. The maid fell in love with a man by the name of Wickham, and married him, but then she became ill and died.

"It was about this time that scarlet fever was spreading through the country, and I myself was gravely ill. Not knowing whether I would survive, and having learned that his other son was at that time bereaved of his mother, our father sent for George and his father to come to Pemberley. Mr. Wickham senior became the estate's steward, and he and George lived in a cottage nearby.

"I, of course, recovered, and shortly after, Father introduced me to George, as a playmate. I had no idea of his real connection to us. It was not until I was a young man, and I observed Father's indulgence towards George and the lack of concern for any foolhardy behavior he displayed, that I challenged him about the true nature of their relationship. He presented me with the letters, the same ones I showed to the vicar, between him and George's mother, which proved the relationship between them and confirmed George's parentage. George later learned the truth as well, which is why I believed, despite his deep desire to lay his hands on a fortune, he would stop short at you. I was wrong."

Mrs. Culpepper spoke up. "You must believe, we never would have allowed that man to enter our house and to court Miss Darcy if we had known what he was capable of, or that you would disapprove of the match. We had assurances from Miss Darcy that you both knew of his coming to Gloucestershire, and that you approved of his desire to marry her."

"There were many letters exchanged," Georgiana said. "I wrote to you almost daily, and George featured regularly in the tales of my adventures. In your replies, you seemed not only to condone, but to encourage his presence and courtship of me. So much so, that when he proposed marriage, I felt certain all that was wanting was your permission, and that you would readily grant it. I should have known the letters I received were not in your hand."

"Wickham has known me long," Darcy said. "He must have practiced my hand until he could copy it with near precision. Enough, at least, to fool you, my darling. But in all this time, I only received two letters from you; the first, stating your arrival, and another, which, I confess, did not sound like your usual style."

Georgiana nodded. "Mrs. Younge must have kept all the letters I sent to you which would have given away anything indicating George's presence. I suppose the last letter you received, she either rewrote herself, copying my hand, or she took out some of the pages which mentioned his name."

"It was a clever plan, and it nearly worked. Had you not hinted at your marriage to Wickham in your last letter to Lydia, which she shared with Kitty, it might have come to pass. It was Kitty who saw the danger, and sent an express to Darcy House, although she believed you were planning to elope, which would have ruined your reputation even further."

SUDDEN AWAKENINGS

Georgiana's tears began to flow again. "I feel such a fool! I believed myself to be in love with him!"

Julia Culpepper, who had been watching silently, trying to contain her own surprise over the whole affair, drew near to Georgiana and embraced her. "We were all fooled by Mr. Wickham. I myself thought he must be in love with you. I thought it was especially romantic that he should follow you all the way from Derbyshire. I should never have encouraged you, my friend."

"I do not blame you, dear Julia. I have no one to blame, except myself."

"No, the person to be blamed is Wickham, and his cohort, Mrs. Younge. Heaven knows I wish I had never let either of them darken my doorstep!" Darcy exclaimed.

"I hope it is the last time we are so betrayed by anyone close to us," Georgiana said.

"Unfortunately, my dear, there is another betrayal I must tell you about." He explained Elizabeth's present state, and Lady Catherine's devilry in poisoning her.

"No, not Elizabeth!" Georgiana cried. "Fitzwilliam, why did you not tell me sooner? We must go to her at once. Why did you leave her and come to me?"

"Because, my dear, her fate is out of our hands, and I knew I had only a prayer in heaven's chance of reaching you in time to prevent your being ruined by Wickham. Now that you are safe, yes, we must return to London."

Not once had Elizabeth left his mind, even for a moment, not even during the confrontation with Wickham. The image of her lying there in her bed, delirious from fever as the poison wracked her body, could not be extricated. Would she even be alive by the time they returned? No, he could not succumb to such thoughts. She would be alive. She had to be. His happiness, his very heart, depended on it.

Elizabeth drifted in and out of consciousness. The horrifying nightmares gave way to strange dreams, bewildering, but also beautiful. She saw herself once again in the labyrinth of corridors, trying every door, seeking to find something...someone?...but never finding what she sought. Then, she opened a door, and suddenly, she was in a meadow of flowers, pinks and blues and yellows, all mixed together. She heard water flowing nearby, and the rustle of trees in the distance.

Someone was walking beside her, and she instinctively knew it was *him*, the person she had been searching for. She reached out her hand, and he took it, held her fingers tightly in his, and whispered her name. A warmth invaded her senses, coming from his hand. A name. What was his name? She struggled to form the name with her lips, that of this person beside her who seemed so familiar, yet her consciousness fought against her, denying her what her heart told her she must know. A light appeared, even brighter than the sunlight around them, drawing her towards it. It was so beautiful, so warm. Much warmer than the hand of this person who held hers. She let go of him and began to walk towards the light, its pull growing ever stronger with each step. She heard the man call her name once more, urging her to come back to him. She turned towards him. As she did, his face came into view, and she recognized him. Darcy. The words fell from her lips, followed by another name. Fitzwilliam. The light faded away into total darkness, and she felt herself falling backwards, until her body shook and her eyes snapped open.

Chapter 39

The return to London took longer than his journey to Gloucestershire did. Darcy hired a postchaise to convey him and Georgiana. Even if Mrs. Younge had not stolen the animal he had rented on the last leg of his journey, he would have had to hire a carriage for them, as a single horse could not carry them both so far.

Georgiana's friends apologized many times for the events which transpired under their care, despite Darcy's assurances that it was not their fault.

"I hope we may meet again," Julia Culpepper told Georgiana as she bid her farewell, "and under better circumstances."

"I hope so too," she replied. "Perhaps next time, you might visit Pemberley. I do not think my brother will be inclined to allow me to travel without him anytime soon."

As they traveled along the country roads towards London, Georgiana noticed her brother's pensive mood.

"She will survive," Georgiana said. "Elizabeth is strong. Whatever she was given, she can fight this and overcome it."

"I hope you are correct," Darcy said softly. "I cannot bear to lose her."

Georgiana closed her eyes and prayed for Elizabeth's safe recovery.

Lady Matlock met them in the hall as soon as they arrived at Darcy House.

"We came to help as soon as we heard what happened," she explained.

"Is she…" The words stuck in Darcy's throat.

Lady Matlock nodded. "She is still alive, but you should go to her."

Darcy fairly flew up the stairs. Elizabeth lay still, her color wan. Mrs. Gardiner gently wiped Elizabeth's forehead with a cool cloth.

Darcy knelt beside his wife and took her hand. It felt cold and limp. He looked at her face. She was still breathing, but in short, shallow breaths.

The doctor approached them. "I have done all I can for her."

"Is there no antidote for what she has been given?" Darcy asked, his eyes shining.

The doctor shook his head. "None I have found. She is entirely in God's hands now."

Darcy felt his chest tighten. He could not lose her. He just couldn't! He did not know how he could bear it if he did.

Georgiana entered the room, accompanied by Lady Matlock. As soon as she saw Elizabeth lying there, she burst into tears. Lady Matlock cradled her in her embrace, and soon took her from the room.

"Let us give him some time with her," Mrs. Gardiner suggested, and the rest of them followed, leaving Darcy alone with Elizabeth.

Darcy pressed his lips to Elizabeth's hand. "You must fight, Elizabeth. You mustn't give up. Your family needs you. I– need you." He exhaled. Sorrow welled in him until it rose to the surface in sobbing. Darcy laid his head upon the bed beside her hand, unable to quench his tears.

Elizabeth's breathing grew slower. He felt her slipping away. He squeezed her hand tighter, willing her not to go.

"Please, Elizabeth. Do not go yet. Do not leave me. Come back to me, Elizabeth." Darcy grabbed her shoulders and shook her.

"Elizabeth, come back," he repeated, louder, his throat going hoarse.

Suddenly, she gave a huge gasp, and her eyes snapped open.

Darcy gave a shout of joy.

Hearing him cry out, the doctor and Mrs. Gardiner rushed in.

"She is alive!" Darcy exclaimed.

"Oh, praise God!" Mrs. Gardiner lifted her eyes upwards in thankfulness before coming towards her niece.

"W–where am I? What has happened?" Elizabeth asked weakly.

"Shh," Mrs. Gardiner hushed her, "Just rest. You have been extremely ill."

Elizabeth looked around the room. "I am at home."

"Yes, yes you are." Darcy's eyes still shone, his cheeks still damp.

"I remember…something…a field…you were there." Elizabeth tried to sit up, but her head immediately plopped back onto the pillow.

The doctor stepped forward. "Do not exert yourself, madam. You have been through quite an ordeal. Your body is weak." He explained the poison and the circumstances surrounding it.

"Yes, I remember," Elizabeth nodded. "Lady Catherine asked me to come for tea. The taste of her tea and scones was strange. I only drank one sip and ate a nibble off the corner of the scone, before I gave the rest to the dog."

"Then the dog suffered the fate intended for you," the doctor said.

"Poor Otis," Elizabeth lamented.

Darcy waited outside while the doctor completed his examination of Elizabeth.

Lord Matlock leaned against the wall and folded his arms across his chest. Shaking his head, he said, "I never would have believed it of my own sister that she would go to such lengths to try to harm Mrs. Darcy."

"She operated on the misguided belief that if I were widowed, I would miraculously turn my attention to Anne instead. I did tell her that nothing but death itself would induce me to part from Elizabeth. I did not expect her to take me literally, however." Darcy gave a snort.

"I suppose you would be interested to know how matters have progressed in your absence," Lord Matlock said. "Lady Catherine was taken to Bow Street, where, as you might expect, she refused to cooperate, and continued to insist she had done nothing wrong.

"However, they tracked down her cook, who fled after the death of the kitchen maid. In return for clemency, she divulged she had unwittingly been Lady Catherine's accomplice. Apparently, Catherine had given her the berries, claiming they were a rare and exotic berry, and asked her to bake the scones with them. She was instructed to use gloves, so as to avoid staining her hands. The cook, who had grown up in the city her whole life, had never seen belladonna, except for the flowers which are used in Lady Catherine's tea blend, so she did not recognize the berries as poisonous or suspect anything was amiss, until the kitchen maid ate one of the scones and promptly fell over dead.

"The cook mentioned that Lady Catherine had also requested some of the berry juice to be strained into a small vial, but she did not know what it was for. The Bow Street investigators found the vial near Catherine's tea set and deduced she must have slipped it into

Elizabeth's tea, to increase the potency of the belladonna within it. Elizabeth must have poured the remaining tea out; there was a dead potted plant next to where Elizabeth was believed to have sat."

"And of course, we know what happened to the dog, after Elizabeth gave the rest of her scone to it," Darcy added.

"Indeed." Lord Matlock shook his head. "Such a tragedy. Three victims of Catherine's crime."

At least Elizabeth will survive this ordeal. He had to hope the worst was past, that she would recover. "Will Lady Catherine hang?"

"No. I could not bear to see my own sister sent to the gallows, no matter what she has done. I begged for her to be committed to Bedlam hospital instead, though I do not know but that it may prove a worse fate for her, in the end."

"What will become of Anne, with her mother gone?"

"She will survive. She has her companion to care for her, and she has already come into her majority; Rosings and her fortune are hers to dispose of as she wills. She is an independent woman now. Although I do not know that she will remain so for long." Lord Matlock gave a small smile.

"Oh?" Darcy asked.

"Richard wrote to me recently, informing me of his desire to seek Anne's hand in marriage. He had some days' leave from his posting in Kent. He is at Rosings now, to offer himself to her."

It was a relief to know Anne would be cared for. He need never feel guilty about not marrying her himself. It was evident Colonel Fitzwilliam loved her and would always be devoted to her happiness.

The doctor summoned Darcy shortly and gave his prognosis.

"It is an absolute miracle!" he declared. "I could not believe it if I had not seen it with my own eyes."

Darcy's heart was hopeful. "Then she will make a full recovery?"

"I cannot say. Her lungs and heart are weakened, and her cough might never fully disappear. It is difficult to predict the extent of the damage done to her body by the poison. But as far as her survival goes, I would say she is out of the woods, so to speak. It is fortunate she consumed so little of the poison; had she drunk more of the tea or eaten more of the scone, her outcome might have gone the way of the poor kitchen maid."

"Or Lady Catherine's little dog," Elizabeth added.

The doctor ordered Elizabeth to remain in bed for some weeks, and to gradually restore her strength within the house before they attempted to move her. He promised to continue to supervise her care and to advise them when they should remove her to the countryside, where she might benefit from the fresh air and sunshine, or perhaps to Bath or the seaside, for the waters.

As soon as the doctor had left, Georgiana was permitted to visit Elizabeth.

She cooed and fussed over Elizabeth, and spoke many times of her regret at having gone to Gloucestershire rather than come with them to London, although Elizabeth could not fully understand it. Darcy decided he would wait until Elizabeth had recovered more before sharing the details of Georgiana's stay with the Culpeppers.

※

The next day, the Bennet family arrived. They had set off for London as soon as Darcy's express reached them, but were waylaid en route by a broken carriage. Mrs. Bennet fretted and fussed over

Elizabeth so much that eventually, Mrs. Gardiner suggested her efforts to help Elizabeth improve might be put to good use by sharing the receipts for her herbal remedies with the Darcy cook. Mrs. Gardiner knew they carried little effect, but Mrs. Bennet was convinced they did wonders for her nerves and helped her sleep more soundly, so they could not have any ill effects on Elizabeth.

Kitty and Lydia were better behaved than before. Georgiana confided in them about her misadventures in Gloucestershire, which made Lydia realize the dangers of fortune hunting and what it could drive a desperate person to do. She resolved not to marry unless it was for love, and to wait until a suitable man entered her sphere and chose to court her.

Kitty became a steadfast nurse to Elizabeth in the following days, taking such good care of her sister that Mrs. Gardiner was able to return to her own children on Gracechurch Street. Lydia took charge of reading to Elizabeth; her practice with the soldiers at the convalescent home had given her a taste for reading aloud, much to her surprise.

Mrs. Gardiner finally persuaded Mrs. Bennet to allow Kitty and Lydia to stay with them, and it was decided that after Elizabeth's recovery, they would live at Gracechurch Street for a year, before coming out again into society.

Chapter 40

As Elizabeth grew stronger with each passing day, Darcy continually thanked God for sparing her. The doctor was immensely pleased with her recovery.

"It is unlike anything I have seen before," he said. "For a woman so close to death's door to recover, with almost no trace that she was ever ill, it is utterly astounding!"

Within a few weeks, Elizabeth was up and walking, and by the time a month was complete, the doctor decided she was well enough to travel. She still coughed from time to time, and fatigued sooner than usual after physical exertion, which suggested she might have some lasting effects in her heart or lungs, but it was clear she was out of danger.

As soon as she was well enough, Darcy told Elizabeth about Georgiana's narrow escape from Wickham.

"The poor dear! If I had known his ulterior motives, I never would have entertained him at Pemberley or allowed Georgiana to be in his company."

"Nor would I have," Darcy agreed. "As much as I knew of his character, I wanted to believe he had changed; that he had truly turned over a new leaf."

"The knowledge that she is his sister should have kept him from attempting what he did," Elizabeth added. "Why did you not tell me?"

"I was ashamed of what my father had done. If this incident had not occurred, I likely would have taken the secret to my grave."

Elizabeth nodded her understanding.

Once Elizabeth was out of danger, Darcy wrote to the bishop over Kympton's diocese. With the vicar's testimony added to his own, it was an easy thing to have Wickham removed from his position as the rector of Kympton. The magistrate in the Culpepper's village issued Wickham a hefty fine for his crimes, and since he could not pay it, he was transported to Australia to serve out his sentence.

Darcy could think of no better person to replace him than Mr. Kirby, who was happy to accept the position, and promised to do far better serving the parish than his predecessor.

Authorities searched for Mrs. Younge, but she was never found nor heard from again. They pursued her as far as Wales, where the horse she had stolen was recovered near the river, leading them to speculate that she might have drowned trying to cross it, or that she disguised herself and changed identities once she reached a village on the other side. They searched far and wide for a woman of her description, or any stranger to those parts. The only report they came across was of an old beggar woman whom nobody had seen before, going by the name of Mrs. Olde, who bought passage on a ship to America and sailed from Bristol.

Elizabeth's body had recovered, but her spirit remained dampened. Darcy's words repeated over and over in her mind. *I do not love her, nor have I ever loved her, and I never will!*

She wondered whether he would try to seek an annulment. She had heard they were difficult to obtain, and usually came with a great deal of scandal.

Likely too much scandal for him to attempt it.

Still, the thought plagued her heart that perhaps he would be better off without her. She had, after all, forced him into this marriage.

Suppose I were to simply leave him and return to my parents, as Viscount Fitzwiliam's wife has done? Darcy could simply tell everyone I was visiting them.

But it would raise questions if she did not return, she realized.

No, I would not subject him to further scandal by my actions. We shall continue as we are, strangers living in the same household.

Even with Parker sharing her room again, it felt empty, not having Darcy there. She had become accustomed to his presence, of seeing his face when she awoke. When they returned home, she would ask Georgiana to share her room, she decided. It was not the same, but at least she was family.

Family.

Yes, they were a family now, regardless of the state between her and Darcy.

I would lose that if I returned to Longbourn.

I would not give up having Georgiana as one of my sisters, even if it means enduring the pain of continuing on as we are now.

❦

Darcy was not oblivious to Elizabeth's mood. She remained listless, somber, often lost in her own thoughts. When he asked if something was the matter, she dismissed it, but he could tell she was troubled.

It was the third day of their journey to Pemberley, and they were nearing Matlock Bath.

SUDDEN AWAKENINGS

"Let us take a visit to the Saint Elizabeth's Well," he suggested. "Georgiana did not accompany us the last time, and we can see how our souvenirs have progressed."

Georgiana was in agreement, as she had not seen the well since she was young.

Leaving the carriage and servants at the livery, they hiked the short distance down to the well. Elizabeth leaned on Georgiana's arm for support. Darcy wished she had chosen to lean on him; she increasingly kept her distance from him, ever since her recovery.

"It is as beautiful as I remember!" Georgiana exclaimed as they entered the shallow cavern where the water dripped down. The sound of droplets echoed off the walls of the cavern, dripping down onto the items left behind.

Elizabeth looked for her glove but she could not find it.

Darcy noticed her search. "Ah, here are our gloves," he pointed out the pair of gloves where he had laid them with the fingers intertwined.

The leather was completely covered over with minerals, permanently encasing the gloves and giving them the appearance of stone. Carefully, so as not to break off the minerals, Elizabeth lifted the souvenir to examine it. It was a work of art, a combination of nature and design. She handed it to Georgiana, who wished to gain a closer look as well.

"Now our hands will forever be entwined, just as our lives are," Darcy said. He took one of Elizabeth's hands in his own, and gave her a warm smile, wishing she might glimpse the love in his heart, searching her face for some indication that she shared his feelings.

God has spared her life. It is enough to have her with me. I must be content.

But such thoughts could not quell the desperate ache within him.

AMANDA KAI

⁂

A strange sensation filled Elizabeth's heart as she looked into Darcy's eyes and saw the warmth there. She pulled her hand away from his, confused by her own response to his tenderness.

"Thank you for this," she said, indicating the sculpture he had fashioned with their gloves. "It will be a treasured reminder of our visits to this well."

She recalled that the well was said to have healing properties. She yearned for healing, both in body and soul. Near one end of the mouth of the cave, there was a shallow pool where some of the water that dripped down collected. A statue of Saint Elizabeth, the mother of John the Baptist, was erected next to it. Visitors to the well knelt here to pray to God for healing, and to ask Saint Elizabeth to intercede on their behalf. Elizabeth knelt too, and dipped her fingers in the water briefly, before saying her own prayer to her Heavenly Father, thanking him for sparing her from death, and asking him to heal her. Then she returned to the others.

The way back to the carriage was more difficult, climbing uphill. She accepted Darcy's offer of his arm to assist her, which seemed to please him, although she could not fathom why. Surely he was used to offering a lady his arm for support by now.

"Do you think your prayer will be answered?" Georgiana asked after they were settled into the coach once more.

"I hope so," Elizabeth said. "The doctor told me that he felt the country air would be good for my lungs. Perhaps my cough may even disappear."

"There is something I still do not understand. Why did Aunt Catherine want to poison you? Her motive seems entirely unclear. I cannot see why she would hate you so much as to wish you dead."

"I do not understand it either." Elizabeth shook her head.

SUDDEN AWAKENINGS

Darcy spoke up. "She wanted to clear the way for me to marry her daughter. She believed that if I were widowed, she could convince me to let Anne take your place. A divorce would be too messy, cause too much scandal for the family. So she tried to let death part us."

"And nearly succeeded." Elizabeth shuddered.

"Losing you would not have made me turn to Anne, however. I told her, quite clearly, that I did not love Anne, and that I never would."

A shock of realization coursed through Elizabeth's heart. The words were not about her– they were about Anne! Of course, it all made sense. She had been a fool not to realize it before.

Just as suddenly, she recognized that she had been entirely mistaken. Darcy did not hold her in apathy; he never had. The idea that she had somehow forced him into this marriage was a lie. He had entered it with eyes wide open, for her sake, and not merely to save her reputation. He wanted to be joined to her, to build a life with her, and to walk hand in hand throughout all their days. That was the meaning of the souvenir he had fashioned from their intertwined gloves.

And then it was as if her heart was suddenly awakened and she saw him, all of him, not the man who she had thought him to be, but the one who had walked with her throughout everything, and she realized it was not merely lust that she felt for him.

It was love. Pure, unadulterated love.

As she looked to him across the carriage and saw the smile there, tears formed in her eyes, and feelings threatened to burst from her chest. With Georgiana sitting right there beside her, it was all she could do to keep her thoughts and emotions to herself.

It was afternoon when they drove across the bridge leading into Pemberley's grounds.

Home. We are home.

Elizabeth now truly felt that this was her home, and not merely the place where she was living. She had stopped thinking of Longbourn as her home some time ago. More than that, home was wherever Darcy was, whether they were at Pemberley, or in London, or any corner of the world.

The meadow nestled between the lake and the woods was in full bloom for summer, with brilliant wildflowers in shades of pink, blue and yellow. When she first arrived at Pemberley, this meadow had been dormant, the grasses dying out as the season shifted towards winter, and when she last saw it, it had just taken on the green grasses of spring. This was the first time she had seen it covered in flowers, and yet, somehow, the scene felt familiar to her. Perhaps she had seen it in a dream.

Mrs. Reynolds had a dinner of cold meats and sandwiches ready for them when they arrived. After they ate, Georgiana announced her wish to retire, as she was exhausted from their travels. Elizabeth knew she ought to be tired as well, but her heart was too full.

"I wish to walk through the meadow before it grows dark. Will you accompany me?" she asked Darcy. He nodded.

She fetched her bonnet and they set off. This time, he did not have to offer his arm to her before she linked hers with his. They passed through the rose gardens, which now displayed brilliant blooms in every shade of red, yellow and pink, and down the gravel pathway leading to the bridge across the lake. And then they entered the meadow, and Elizabeth found herself surrounded by the beautiful wildflowers, aglow with color as the sun gradually set behind the trees of the woods beyond them.

"I never paid much attention to this field before," she said. "It was outfitted for winter when I arrived, so I did not realize how beautifully it would be arrayed at this time of year."

"It is quite splendid. My mother loved to come to this meadow also, while she was alive," Darcy said.

Elizabeth felt a lump form in her throat. She knew it was time to speak what was in her heart. Her aunt had warned her not to delay telling her feelings to the one she loved, lest she miss her opportunity.

She drew a deep breath. "Now that my recovery is nearly complete, I no longer wish for Parker to remain in my chambers."

Darcy looked at her with alarm. "I know we are home once more, but I should hate to think that you might have an episode and end up wandering the woods again."

"Will you stay with me, then?"

His eyes searched her face, trying to discern her thoughts. She smiled at him reassuringly.

"If that is your wish," he murmured softly.

"The gloves," Elizabeth said. "I know now, why you intertwined them. I thought, for so long, that you only married me out of obligation, for the sake of honor."

"My honor did demand it, yes, but that was not my only reason," he said. "I knew you did not want to marry me, but I hoped, in time, you might come to respect me, even if you could never care for me."

"I do respect you," she said quickly. "I did not, at first, I admit it, but I have come to see that you are good and honorable, and kind, and…I do care for you, Fitzwilliam," Elizabeth answered, her eyes shining once more. "In fact I, I…I love you," she said almost breathlessly.

Darcy's voice grew hoarse. "Can it be? Do you truly love me?" He took her hands in his, his eyes full of wonder.

Elizabeth nodded, a smile forming on her lips.

Without hesitation, Darcy's lips met Elizabeth's in a kiss that was at once tender and passionate. She wrapped her arms around him, feeling a surge of emotion. The world seemed to stand still as they lost themselves in the moment.

His lips felt warm and soft against hers, his scent giving off the fragrant notes of his orange and sandalwood cologne and blended with the perfume of the wildflowers surrounding them. His arms clasped tightly around her waist, as if he wished never to let her go from that moment on.

They kissed again and again, drinking deeply in the love that they had found. These kisses far outpaced those of her dreams, and were more real even than those she had given him in her unconscious frenzy. A true expression of the love they shared.

When finally, they came up for air, Darcy said, "I have longed to tell you, from the very beginning, how much I ardently love and admire you."

"From the very beginning?" she teased. "I seem to recall you would not deign to dance with me at the Meryton Assembly."

Darcy laughed. "Very well, I admit to being a proud fool that evening! But it was not long after that I began to see the sparkle in your eyes and the humor in your wit. I cannot fix on the hour or the moment that I fell in love with you. I was in the middle before I knew I had begun."

Elizabeth leaned her head against his arm as they turned to walk back towards the house. "So then you were already in love with me, when I wandered into your room at Netherfield?" she asked.

"Admittedly, yes. A lesser man than I would have taken advantage of you. Here you were, looking so beautiful with your hair down, and in your nightgown." His words caused her to blush deeper. "And then you came into my chamber and laid down on my bed. It was all I could do to keep my wits about me. I know it is wrong, but I am not sorry that you came to my room that night. I do not think you would have accepted my addresses otherwise."

Now it was Elizabeth's turn to laugh. "No, I do not think I would have! I was utterly convinced you were the proudest, most disagreeable man of my acquaintance!"

"I *was* proud! I judged you before meeting you properly, all because Caroline Bingley warned me that your family were a greedy, grasping bunch."

"And so they are! But we had met before, do you remember? On the Longbourn Road? When you were lost and looking for the way to Netherfield?"

"Ah, yes, how could I have forgotten! You, an impertinent miss, refused to give me your name. And yet, you knew mine! How infuriated I was, and at the same time, curious to know more of you. Had Miss Bingley not warned me off, I might have asked you to dance at the assembly." There was a gleam in his eye.

"I tried hard to catch your notice. I even employed Mr. Bingley to entreat you," she reminded him.

"I recall. It was that action which spurred me to reject his petition in your hearing. How I regretted it afterwards!"

As the laughter between them died down, the look in their eyes turned once more to passion, and they fell again into each other's embrace, their kisses deeper and more full of desire even than before.

"Fitzwilliam," she murmured into his ear, "I was a fool not to realize your love for me before now."

"If anyone is the fool, it is I," he began, but she silenced him with a finger to his lips.

"We are both fools, perhaps," she said. "But I, more than you. I feel as though I was lost in a dream all these months, unable to see the reality before me. But now, I have fully awakened. I hope you can forgive me for not loving you sooner."

"Dearest, loveliest, Elizabeth! There is nothing to forgive. Let us think of the past only as it gives us pleasure, and look to the future with all of the promise it holds."

Elizabeth nodded, before returning to his embrace. The sun had fully set before the lovers returned to the house, with smiles on their faces, and not one servant dared ask where they had been for so long a time.

The sunlight filtering through the curtains woke Elizabeth the next morning. Rolling over, she saw the man beside her, and her heart flooded with love and happiness.

For some time, she simply watched his breathing. Then she drew closer and pressed her lips to his. His eyes popped open and he responded to her kisses, wrapping his arms around her waist as he did so.

"You are awake this time, are you not?" He asked teasingly. "This is not one of your dream-induced frenzies?"

Elizabeth giggled. "I am wide awake, I assure you." Her stomach growled loudly. "And hungry too, it would seem." She turned to exit the bed, but his arm caught hers.

"Stay," he murmured. Elizabeth complied, nestling herself in the crook of his arm, her head leaning upon his chest. He pressed a kiss to her hair. "Would that we were always this happy!"

"We shall be as happy or as miserable as we choose to be, so from now on, let us choose to be happy."

"You are right," he said, stroking her back gently with the arm that was wrapped around her. "No matter what circumstances may come our way, we shall always have each other."

"And Georgiana," she added.

"Yes, and Georgiana."

"And, Lord willing, our little ones."

"Little ones? Is there something you wish to tell me?" He teased her.

She giggled again. "No, it is far too early for that. It was only last night–" another snort burst from her lips.

"Yes, I am aware," he chuckled. "However, is it too soon to hope that you might be willing to try for a child?"

She shook her head, rising up and leaning over him once more. "Not too soon at all," she whispered, before bringing her lips to his in another passionate kiss.

Epilogue

One year later

A child's cry pierced through the night, suddenly waking Darcy from his slumber. He felt the space on the bed beside him, but it was empty. Had Elizabeth sleepwalked? He had not heard her nor noticed the movement as she rose. As the fog in his brain lifted, he recognized the child's cries as that of his own. Still sleepy, he slid his feet into his slippers and padded down the corridor to the nursery, which Elizabeth insisted be near to their chamber.

He found his wife, sitting in the chair, rocking their infant and trying to calm him.

"I fed him, but he still refuses to settle. Every time I attempt to lay him down, he cries for me to hold him."

Darcy smiled. "Already taking after his father." He leaned in to kiss her on the cheek and whisper in her ear, "He cannot get enough of you."

Elizabeth returned his grin with one of her own. "How demanding you both are, to need me at all hours of the night!"

"You ought to let the nurse take care of him, so you can rest. It is what I hired her for."

Elizabeth shook her head. "I did not carry this child in my own womb for nine months to hand him off to another once he is born. As much as I am able to, I shall nurse him myself and soothe him back to sleep in my own arms." She looked down at their son, who had quieted into a half slumber, his tiny fist clutching the ribbons on her nightgown.

"Let me take him then, so you can return to bed," he offered. "Tomorrow will be a busy day."

He referred to Kitty's wedding to Mr. Kirby. After several months under Mrs. Gardiner's tutelage, Kitty had completed her transformation from an impetuous schoolgirl into a refined young lady. The changes founded at Pemberley were further exemplified under the care of her wise and gracious aunt.

Lydia, too, had matured into a kind and generous person who no longer regarded marriage as her first object in life, although she was presently being courted by a gentleman in trade who was friends with Mr. Gardiner.

Mr. Kirby, who had already begun to develop feelings for Kitty when they met the previous year, found that his love flourished into full bloom when the Bennet family came again to spend Christmas at Pemberley. With his position as rector of Kympton firmly established, he now had an income that could support a wife, supplemented by a role as the convalescent home's chaplain– a position they could afford to pay thanks to a generous donation from the Darcy family.

Kitty and Mr. Kirby were to be married at the church in Kympton– officiated by the new curate there, and the wedding breakfast at Pemberley would follow. All the Bennet family and their relations had arrived to celebrate the nuptials, except for the Rushworths, who were due in the morning.

"Are you nervous about seeing your sister again?" Darcy asked Elizabeth. After hearing what Jane had said to Elizabeth during their last meeting at Darcy House, he could not forgive so easily. However, Elizabeth had a kind and forbearing heart towards Jane and could not hold a grudge against her for long. When Jane wrote to her some months after their bitter parting, acting as if nothing was wrong,

Elizabeth decided she would rather resume her friendship with her sister than wait for an apology which might never come.

"I will take the high road," Elizabeth said. "I will not bring up our last conversation, but will treat her with love, as I always have. She may not even recall the cruel words she said to me."

Darcy patted her shoulder. He knew how much it pained her that she and Jane had grown apart, and how altered Jane had become since leaving Longbourn.

"'It is one's Christian duty to forgive all manner of faults,'" Darcy said. "Is that not what Cousin Collins said during dinner?"

"Yes, right before Mary quoted from the book of Matthew."

Given the distance to Pemberley from Hunsford, it would have been perfectly understandable if the Collinses had declined the invitation to come. However, both were eager to come for the wedding. Darcy suspected it was because Mr. Collins wished to meet Mr. Rushworth; his new brother-in-law had a living which had just become vacant.

Mr. Collins had written to Darcy about the Kympton living after Mr. Wickham's removal, asking to be considered for the position. However, Darcy wrote back and kindly reminded Collins that he owed it to the residents of his present parish not to abandon them to the hands of a curate, and that he could not in good conscience present Mr. Collins with the living while there was a curate and friend of his in need of a rectory. However, Darcy did not think this would prevent Mr. Collins from applying to receive as many livings as he could hope to hold in his lifetime.

Elizabeth said wryly, "It is ironic, is it not, how easily they were able to forgive Jane's hasty marriage, yet not my own?"

"Let us not give way to bitterness my dear," Darcy cautioned.

"I am not bitter. I merely find humor in their hypocrisy, pandering to the Rushworths while disdaining us for the very selfsame sins they claim to abhor."

"Not all of us can be as rich as Mr. Rushworth."

"Indeed, some of us merely come close." She smiled.

The Collinses brought news with them from Rosings. The former colonel and his lovely wife sent their regards, and their regrets that Anne was unable to travel for the time being.

At first, Darcy thought it was due to her ill health, but Mr. Collins explained that the mistress of Rosings was presently in the family way. In fact, it seemed that Anne's health had altogether improved since her mother's departure from her life. Darcy wondered if perhaps years of drinking her mother's special tea blend was responsible for her ill health, for the weakness and cough disappeared gradually in the time since then.

The tea may also have been what addled Lady Catherine's mind to such a degree that she would resort to murder to achieve her own ends.

Darcy glanced down at the child in Elizabeth's arms. "He appears to be sleeping deeply now."

Elizabeth rose and gently placed the baby into his cradle. The child did not stir. They watched him for a few moments before quietly slipping out of the nursery.

"Let us return to bed," Darcy said. "There are still some hours left before morning."

"Must we? Only, I do not feel tired anymore." A grin appeared on Elizabeth's face.

"Is that so?" Darcy returned with a lilt in his voice. "I believe I can find some occupation to tax your energy, in that case."

"Is it mending your shirts?" She teased. "I believe I saw a hole in that lovely one I made for you the Christmas before last."

"No, I have a far better use for your skills than that." He winked.

"Then by all means, lead the way, Fitzwilliam."

With that, he scooped her up into his arms and raced down the corridor towards their chambers, to enjoy all the blissful delight that belongs to happily married couples.

Free book

Do you enjoy free stories? Sign up for my newsletter list and get a free copy of *Elizabeth's Secret Admirer- a Pride and Prejudice Novella* in your welcome email.

More books by Amanda Kai

<u>The Other Paths Collection</u>

Elizabeth's Secret Admirer- a Pride and Prejudice Novella

Not In Want of a Wife- a Pride and Prejudice Variation

A Favorable Impression- a Pride and Prejudice Variation

Sudden Awakenings- a Pride and Prejudice Variation

Miss Bingley and the Baron- A Companion to Not In Want of a Wife

What Happened at Vauxhall- A Companion to A Favorable Impression

<u>Regency Pride and Prejudice stories</u>

Marriage and Ministry- a Pride and Prejudice Novel

Christmas at Hunsford Parsonage- a Pride and Prejudice short-story, sequel to Marriage and Ministry

Unconventional- an Austentatious Comedy that Defies Expectations!

A Little Bit Foolish- a collection of Pride and Prejudice April Fool's stories

Contemporary romance

Love at the Library

Swipe Right for Mr. Darcy- a Modern Pride and Prejudice Retelling

Historical romance

Keys- a Marie Antoinette story

GET YOUR NEXT AMANDA KAI BOOK HERE

Acknowledgements

Although writing may appear to be a singular person's job, it takes a team to take my rough-hewn story and turn it into a polished, glittering gem for the reader to enjoy.

For this, I would particularly like to thank Jennifer Wilson, without whom this story might never have seen the light of the day. You were willing to wade through the first seven chapters of drivel and convinced me that there was a story worth finishing in there. I hope you enjoyed the immortalization of your family as characters in this story– it was the least I could do to repay the magnitude of help you have offered me.

To Anna Spencer, I thank you for reading the first draft, even before I had completed the ending, and pointing out some major inaccuracies that needed correcting. Thank you for praying for me and spurring me on.

I would also like to mention my thanks to Britaini Armitage and Jennifer Guthrie.

Britaini, thank you for making time in your crazy schedule to take on the role of editor for my books. Your feedback is invaluable, and your continual encouragement has kept me going many times when I wanted to quit.

Jennifer, your keen eyes have helped to spot more than one plot hole and inconsistency and to round out the story as it ought to be. Thank you for catching so many of my silly mistakes.

To my proofreaders, Tara Finlay and Kim Tiller, thank you for going over my manuscript with a fine-toothed comb to ensure that no punctuation is missing and to catch all those little errors that only a human reader can find.

Lastly, I would like to thank my family, for their continued support of my creative endeavors, and their celebration of my success.

Above all, I give glory to God for blessing me with the talents and drive to pursue my passion, and allowing me to bless others with my stories.

About the Author

Amanda Kai's love of period dramas and classic literature influences her historical and contemporary romances. She has written several stories inspired by Jane Austen, including The Other Paths Collection and Swipe Right for Mr. Darcy. Prior to becoming an author, Amanda enjoyed a career as a professional harpist, and danced ballet for twenty years. When she's not diving into the realm of her imagination, Amanda lives out her own happily ever after in Texas with her husband and three children.

Made in United States
North Haven, CT
19 February 2025